Sauria Monstra

SAURIA MONSTRA

Dinosaurs, Pterosaurs, and Other Fossil Saurians in Classic Science Fiction and Fantasy

Chad Arment, Editor

Coachwhip Publications
Landisville, Pennsylvania

Sauria Monstra
Copyright © 2009 Coachwhip Publications

ISBN 1-930585-77-2
ISBN-13 978-1-930585-77-5

Cover/Title Page: Dinosaur © Ismael Montero

Copyright permission for *The Beast of the Yungas* by Willis Knapp Jones
    courtesy Weird Tales, Ltd.

Coachwhipbooks.com

CONTENTS

SHORT STORIES

NOVEL

The Last of the Vampires
Phil Robinson

Do you remember the discovery of the "man-lizard" bones in a cave on the Amazon some time in the forties? Perhaps not.

But it created a great stir at the time in the scientific world and in a lazy sort of way, interested men and women of fashion. For a day or two it was quite the correct thing for Belgravia to talk of "connecting links," of "the evolution of man from the reptile," or "the reasonableness of the ancient myths" that spoke of Centaurs and Mermaids as actual existences.

The fact was that a German Jew, an india-rubber merchant, wending his way with the usual mob of natives through a *cahucho* forest along the Marañon, came upon some bones on the river-bank where he had pitched his camp. Idle curiosity made him try to put them together, when he found, to his surprise, that he had before him the skeleton of a creature with human legs and feet, a dog-like skull, and immense bat-like wings. Being a shrewd man, he saw the possibility of money being made out of such a curiosity; so he put all the bones he could find into a sack and, on the back of a llama they were in due course conveyed to Chachapoyas, and thence to Germany. Unfortunately, his name happened to be the same as that of another German Jew who had just then been trying to hoax the scientific world with some papyrus rolls of a date anterior to the Flood, and who had been found out and put to shame. So when his namesake appeared with the bones of a winged man, he was treated with very scant ceremony.

However, he sold his india-rubber very satisfactorily, and as for the bones, he left them with a young medical student of the ancient University of Bierundwurst, and went back to his *cahucho* trees, his natives and the banks of the Amazon. And there was an end of them.

The young student one day put his fragments together, and, do what he would, could only make one thing of them—a winged man with a dog's head.

There were a few ribs too many, and some odds and ends of backbone which were superfluous; but what else could be expected of the anatomy of so extraordinary a creature? From one student to another the facts got about, and at last the professors came to hear of it, and, to cut a long story short, the student's skeleton was taken to pieces by the learned heads of the college, and put together again by their own learned hands.

But do what they would, they would only make one thing of it— a winged man with a dog's head.

The matter now became serious: the professors were at first puzzled, and then got quarrelsome; and the result of their squabbling was that pamphlets and counterblasts were published; and so all the world got to hear of the bitter controversy about the "man-lizard of the Amazon."

One side declared, of course, that such a creature was an impossibility, and that the bones were a remarkably clever hoax. The other side retorted by challenging the sceptics to manufacture a duplicate, and publishing the promise of such large rewards to any one who would succeed in doing so, that the museum was beset for months by competitors. But no one could manufacture another man-lizard. The man part was simple enough, provided they could get a human skeleton. But at the angles of the wings were set huge claws, black, polished, and curved, and nothing that ingenuity could suggest would imitate them. And then the "Genuinists," as those who believed in the monster called themselves, set the "Imposturists" another poser; for they publicly challenged them to say what animal either the head or the wings had belonged to, if not to the man-lizard? And the answer was never given.

So victory remained with them, but not, alas! the bones of contention. For the Imposturists, by bribery and burglary, got access the precious skeleton, and lo! one morning the glory of the museum had disappeared. The man half of it was left, but the head and wings were gone, and from that day to this no one has ever seen them again.

And which of the two factions was right? As a matter of fact, neither; as the following fragments of narrative will go to prove.

Once upon a time, so say the Zaporo Indians, who inhabit the district between the Amazon and the Marañon, there came across to Pampas de Sacramendo a company of gold-seekers, white men, who drove the natives from their workings and took possession of them.

They were the first white men who had ever been seen there, and the Indians were afraid of their guns; but eventually treachery did the work of courage, for, pretending to be friendly, the natives sent their women among the strangers, and they taught them how to make *tucupi* out of the bread-root, but did not tell them how to distinguish between the ripe and the unripe. So the wretched white men made *tucupi* out of the unripe fruit (which brings on fits like epilepsy) and when they were lying about the camp, helpless, the Indians attacked them and killed them all.

All except three. These three they gave to the Vampire.

But what was the Vampire? The Zaporos did not know. "Very long ago," said they, "there were many vampires in Peru, but they were all swallowed up in the year of the Great Earthquake when the Andes were lifted up, and there was left behind only one 'Arinchi,' who lived where the Amazon joins the Marañon, and he would not eat dead bodies—only live ones, from which the blood would flow."

So far the legend; and that it had some foundation in fact is proved by the records of the district, which tell of more than one massacre of white gold-seekers on the Marañon by Indians whom they had attempted to oust from the washings; but of the Arinchi, the Vampire, there is no official mention. Here, however, other local superstitions help us to the reading of the riddle of the man-lizard of the University at Bierundwurst.

When sacrifice was made to "the Vampire," the victim was bound in a canoe, and taken down the river to a point where there was a kind of winding back-water, which had shelving banks of slimy mud, and at the end there was a rock with a cave in it. And here the canoe was left. A very slow current flowed through the tortuous creek, and anything thrown into the water ultimately reached the cave. Some of the Indians had watched the canoes drifting along, a few yards only in an hour, and turning round and round as they drifted, and had seen them reach the cave and disappear within. And it had been a wonder to them, generation after generation that the cave was never filled up, for all day long the current was flowing into it, carrying with it the sluggish flotsam of the river. So they said that the cave was the entrance to Hell, and bottomless.

And one day a white man, a professor of that same University of Bierundwurst, and a mighty hunter of beetles before the Lord, lived with the Indians in friendship, went up the backwater, right up to the entrance, and set afloat inside the cave a little raft, heaped up with touch-wood and knots of the oil-tree, which he set fire to and he saw the raft go creeping along, all ablaze, for an hour and more, lighting up the wet walls of the cave as it went on either side; and then *it was put out.*

It did not "go" out suddenly, as if it had upset, or had floated over the edge of a waterfall, but just as if it had been beaten out.

For the burning fragments were flung to one side and the other, and the pieces, still alight, glowed for a long time on the ledges and flints of rock where they fell, and the cave was filled with the sound of a sudden wind and the echoes of the noise of great wings flapping.

And at last, one day, this professor went into the cave himself. "I took," he wrote, "a large canoe, and from the bows I built up a brazier of stout cask-hoops, and behind it set a gold-washing tin tub for a reflector, and loaded the canoe with roots of the resin-tree, and oil-wood, and yams, and dried meat; and I took spears with me, one tipped with the *woorali* poison, that numbs but does not kill. And so I drifted inside the cave; and I lit my fire, and with my pole I guided the canoe very cautiously through the tunnel, and before long it widened out, and creeping along one wall I suddenly became aware of a moving of something on the opposite side.

"So I turned the light fair upon it, and there, upon a kind of ledge, sat a beast with a head like a large grey dog. Its eyes were as large as a cow's.

"What its shape was I could not see. But as I looked I began gradually to make out two huge bat-like wings, and these were spread out to their utmost as if the beast were on tiptoe and ready to fly. And so it was. For just as I had realised that I beheld before me some great bat-reptile of a kind unknown to science, except as prediluvian, and the shock had thrilled through me at the thought that I was actually in the presence of a living specimen of the so-called extinct flying lizards of the Flood, the thing launched itself upon the air, and the next instant it was upon me.

"Clutching on to the canoe, it beat with its wings at the flame so furiously that it was all I could do to keep the canoe from capsizing, and, taken by surprise, I was nearly stunned by the strength and rapidity of its blows before I attempted to defend myself.

"By that time—scarcely half a minute had elapsed—the brazier had been nearly emptied by the powerful brute; and the vampire, mistaking me no doubt for a victim of sacrifice, had already taken hold of me. The next instant I had driven a spear clean through its body, and with a prodigious tumult of wings, the thing loosed its claws from my clothes and dropped off into the stream. As quickly as possible I rekindled my light, and now saw the Arinchi, with wings outstretched upon the water, drifting down on the current. I followed it.

"Hour after hour, with my reflector turned full upon that grey dog's head with cow-like eyes, I passed along down the dark and silent waterway. I ate and drank as I went along, but did not dare fall sleep. A day must have passed, and two nights; and then, as of course I had all along expected, I saw right ahead a pale eye-shaped glimmer, and knew that I was coming out into daylight again.

"The opening came nearer and nearer, and it was with intense eagerness that I gazed upon my trophy, the floating Arinchi, the last of the Winged Reptiles.

"Already in imagination I saw myself the foremost of travellers in European fame—the hero of my day. What were Bank's kangaroos or Du Chaillu's gorilla to my discovery of the last survivor of the pterodactyles, of the creatures of Flood—the flying Saurian of the pre-Noachian epoch of catastrophe and mud?

"Full of these thoughts, I had not noticed that the vampire was no longer moving, and suddenly the bow of the canoe bumped

against it. In an instant it had climbed up on to the boat. Its great
bat-like wings once more beat me and scattered the flaming brands,
and the thing made a desperate effort to get past me back into the
gloom. It had seen the daylight approaching and rather than face
the sun, preferred to fight.

"Its ferocity was that of a maddened dog, but I kept it off with
my pole, and seeing my opportunity as it clung, flapping its wings,
upon the bow, gave it such a thrust as made it drop off. It began to
swim (I then for the first time noticed its long neck), but with my
pole I struck it on the head and stunned it, and once more saw it
go drifting on the current into daylight.

"What a relief it was to be out in the open air! It was noon, and
as we passed out from under the entrance of the cave, the river
blazed so in the sunlight that after the two days of almost total
darkness I was blinded for a time. I turned my canoe to the shore,
to the shade of trees, and throwing a noose over the floating body,
let it tow behind.

"Once more on firm land—and in possession of the Vampire!

"I dragged it out of the water. What a hideous beast it looked,
this winged kangaroo with a python's neck! It was not dead; so I
made a muzzle with a strip of skin, and then I firmly bound its
wings together round its body. I lay down and slept. When I awoke,
the next day was breaking; so, having breakfasted, I dragged my
captive into the canoe and went on down the river. Where I was I
had no idea; but I knew that I was going to the sea: going to Germany: and that was enough.

· · · · ·

"For two months I have been drifting with the current down
this never-ending river. Of my adventures, of hostile natives, of
rapids, of alligators, and jaguars, I need say nothing. They are the
common property of all travellers. But my vampire! It is alive. And
now I am devoured by only one ambition—to keep it alive, to let
Europe actually gaze upon the living, breathing, survivor of the
great Reptiles known to the human race before the days of Noah—
a missing link between the reptile and the bird. To this end I denied myself food; denied myself even precious medicine. In spite
of myself I gave it all my quinine, and when the miasma crept up

the river at night, I covered it with my rug and lay exposed myself. If the black fever should seize me!

• • • • •

"Three months, and still upon this hateful river! Will it never end? I have been ill—so ill, that for two days I could not feed it. I had not the strength to go ashore to find food, and I fear that it will die—die before I can get it home.

• • • • •

"Been ill again—the black fever! But *it* is alive. I caught a vicuna swimming in the river, and it sucked it dry—gallons of blood. It had been unfed three days. In its hungry haste it broke its muzzle. I was almost too feeble to put it on again. A horrible thought possesses me. Suppose it breaks its muzzle again when I am lying ill, delirious, and it is ravenous? Oh! the horror of it! To see it eating is terrible. It links the claws of its wings together, and cowers over the body; its head is under the wings, out of sight. But the victim never moves. As soon as the vampire touches it there seems to be a paralysis. Once those wings are linked there is absolute quiet. Only the grating of teeth upon bone. Horrible! Terrible! But in Germany I shall be famous. *In Germany with my Vampire?*

• • • • •

"Am very feeble. It broke its muzzle again. But it was in the daylight—when it is blind. Its great eyes are blind in sunlight. It was a long struggle. This black fever! and the horror of this thing! I am too weak now to kill it, if I would. I *must* get it home alive. Soon—surely soon—the river will end. Oh God! does it never reach the sea, reach white men, reach home? But if it attacks me I will throttle it. If I am dying I will throttle it. If we cannot go back to Germany alive, we will go together dead. I will throttle it with my two hands, and fix my teeth in its horrible neck, and our bones may lie together on the bank of this accursed river."

This is nearly all that was recovered of the professor's diary. But it is enough to tell us of the final tragedy.

The two skeletons *were* found together on the very edge of the river-bank. Half of each, in the lapse of years, had been washed way at successive flood-tides. The rest, when put together, made up the man-reptile that, to use a Rabelaisian phrase, "metagro-bolised all to nothing" the University of Bierundwurst.

The Lizard
Charles John Cutcliffe Hyne

It is not in the least expected that the general public will believe the statements which will be made in this paper. They are written to catch the eye of Mr. Wilfred Cecil Cording (or Cordy) if he still lives, or in the event of his death to carry some news of his last movements to any of his still existing friends and relations. Further details may be had from me (by any of these interested people) at Poste Restante, Kettlewell, Wharfedale, Yorkshire. My name is M'Cray, and I am sufficiently well known there for letters to be forwarded to wherever I may be at the moment.

The matters in question happened two years ago on the last day of August. I had a small high-ground shoot near Kettlewell, but that morning all the upper parts of the hill were thick with dense mist, and shooting was out of the question. However, I had been going it pretty hard since the twelfth, and was not sorry for an off day, the more so as there was a newly-found cave in the neighbourhood which I was anxious to explore thoroughly. Incidentally I may mention that cave-hunting and shooting were then my chief two amusements. It was my keeper who brought me news to the inn about the impossibility of shooting, and I suggested to him that he should come with me to inspect the cave. He made some sort of excuse—I forget what—and I did not press the matter further. He was a Kettlewell native, and the dalesmen up there look upon the local caves with more awe than respect. They will not own up to believing in bogies, but I fancy their creed runs that way. I used to have a contempt for their qualms, but latterly I have somehow or other learned to respect them.

I had taken unwilling helpers cave-hunting with me before, and found them such a nuisance that I had made up my mind not to be bothered with them again; so, as I say, I did not press for the keeper's society; but took candles, matches in a bottle, some magnesium wire, a small coil of rope, and a large flask of whisky, and set off alone.

The clouds above were wet, and a fine rain fell persistently. I tramped off along one of the three main roads that lead from the village; but which road it was, had better remain hidden for the present. And in time I got off this road and cut over the moor.

What I was looking for was a fresh scar on the hill side, caused by a roof-fall in one of the countless caves which honeycomb this limestone district; and although I had got my bearings pretty accurately, the fog was so thick up there that I had to take a good dozen casts before I hit upon the place.

I had not seen it since the 8th of August, when I first stumbled across it by accident whilst I was going over the hill to see how the birds promised for the following twelfth; and I was a good deal annoyed to find by the boot marks that quite a lot of people had visited it in the interval. However, I hoped that the larger part of these were made by shepherds, and perhaps by my own keepers, and remembering their qualms, trusted that I might find the interior still untampered with.

The cave was easy enough to enter. There was a funnel-shaped slide of peat-earth and mud and clay to start with, well pitted with boot marks; and then there was a tumbled wall of boulders, slanting inwards, down which I crawled face uppermost till the light behind me dwindled. The way was getting pretty murky, so I lit up a candle to avoid accidents, stepped knee-deep into a lively stream of water, and went briskly ahead. It was an ordinary enough limestone cave so far, with inferior stalactites, and a good deal of wet everywhere. It did not appear to have been disturbed, and I stepped along cheerfully.

Presently I got a bit of a shock. The roof above began to droop downwards, slowly but relentlessly. It seemed as though my way was soon going to be blocked. However, the water beneath deepened, and so I waded along to inspect as far on as possible. It was

a cold job, for the water was icy, but then I am a bit of an enthusi-
ast about cave-hunting, and it takes more than a trifle of discom-
fort to stop me.

The roof came down and down till I was forced into the water
up to my chin, and the air too was none of the best. I was beginning to get disappointed: it looked as if I had got wet through to
the bone with freezing cold cave water for no adequate result.

However, there is no accounting for the freaks of caves. Just
when I fancied I was at the end of my tether, up went the roof again;
I was able to stand erect once more; and a dozen yards further on
I came out on to dry rock, and was able to have a rest and a drop of
whisky. The roof had quite disappeared to candle-light overhead,
so I burned a foot of magnesium wire for a better inspection. It
was really a magnificent cave.

But I did not stop to make any accurate measurements or drawings then, and for reasons which will appear, I have not been near
to do so since. I was too cold to care for prolonged admiration,
and I wanted to (so to speak) annex the whole of the cave's main
contours before I took my departure. I was first man in, and wished
to be able to describe the whole of my find. There is a certain keen
emulation about these matters amongst cave-hunters.

So I walked on over the flat floor of rock, stepping over and
through pools, and round boulders, and dodging round stalactites
which hung from the unseen roof above, and slipping between slimy
palings of stalagmite which sprouted from the floor. And then I
came to a regular big subterranean tarn which stretched right
across the cavern.

Spaces were big here and the candle did little to show them. It
burned brightly enough and that pleased me: one has to be very
careful in cave-hunting about foul air, because once overcome by
that, it means certain death if one is alone The air in this cave,
however, did not altogether pass muster; there was something new
about it, and anything new in cave smells is always suspicious. It
wasn't the smell of peat, or iron, or sandstone, or limestone, or
fungus, though all these are common enough in caves; it was a sort of
faint musky smell; and I had got an idea that it was in flavour rather
sickly. It is hard to define these things, but that smell, although it

might very possibly lead to a new discovery, somehow did not cheer me. In fact at times, when I inhaled-a deeper breath of it than usual, it came very near to making my flesh creep.

However, hesitations of this kind are not business. I nipped off another foot of magnesium wire, lit it at the candle, and held the flaming end high above my head. Before me the water of the tarn lay motionless as a mirror of black glass; the sides vignetted away into alleys and bays; the roof was a groined and fretted dome, far overhead; and at the further side was a beach of white tumbled limestone.

I pitched a stone into the black water, and the mirror woke (I was pleased to think) for the first time during a million years into ripples. Yes, it's worth even a year of hard cave-hunting to do a thing like that.

The stone sank with a luscious *plop*. The water was very deep. But I was wet to the neck already, and didn't mind a swim. So with a lump of clay I stuck one candle in my cap; set up a couple more on the dry rock as a lighthouse to guide my return; lowered myself into the black water, and struck out. The smell of musk oppressed me, and I fancied it was growing more pronounced. So I didn't dawdle. Roughly, I guessed the pool to be some five-and-thirty yards across.

I landed amongst the white, broken limestone on the further side, with a shiver and a scramble, and there was no doubt about the smell of musk now; it was strong enough to make me cough. But when I had stood up, got the candle in my hand again, and peered about through the dark, a thrill came through me as I thought I guessed at the cause. A dozen yards further on amongst the tumbled stone was a broken "cast," where some monstrous uncouth animal had been entombed in the forgotten ages of the past, and mouldered away and left only the outer shell of its form and shape. For ages this too had endured; indeed it had only been violated by the eroding touch of the water and some earth tremor within the last few days: perhaps at the same time that the "slip" was made in the moor far above, which made an entrance to the caves.

The "cast" was half full of splintered rubbish, but even as it was I could see the contour of its sides in many places, and with care the debris could be scooped out, and a workman could with plaster of Paris make an exact model of this beast which had been lost to the world's knowledge for so many weary millions of years. It had been some sort of a lizard or a crocodile, and in fancy I was beginning to picture its restored shape posed in the National Museum with my name underneath as discoverer, when my eye fell on something amongst the rubble which brought me to earth with a jar. I stooped and picked it up. It was a common white-handled penknife, of the variety sold by stationers for a shilling. On one side of it was the name of Wilfred Cecil Cording (or Cordy), scratched apparently with a nail. The work was neat enough to start with, but the engraver had wearied with his job; and the "Cecil" was slip-shod, and the surname too scratchy to be certain about.

On the hot impulse of the moment, I threw the knife far from me into the black water, and swore. It is more than a bit unpleasant for an explorer who has made a big discovery to find that he has been forestalled. But since then I have more than once regretted the hard things I said against Cording (if that is his name) in the heat of my first passion. If the man is alive, I apologise to him. If, as I strongly suspect, he came to a horrible end there in the cave, I tender my regrets to his relatives.

I looked upon the cast of the saurian now, with the warmth of discovery quite gone. I was conscious of cold, and moreover the musky smell of the place was vastly unpleasant. And I think I should straightway have gone back to daylight and a change of clothes down in Kettlewell, but for one thing. I seemed somehow or other to trace on the rock beneath me the outline of another cast. It was hazy, as a thing of the kind would be if seen through the medium of sparsely transparent limestone, and by the light of a solitary paraffin-wax candle. I kicked at it petulantly.

Some flakes of stone shelled off, and I distinctly heard a more extensive crack.

I kicked again, harder; with all my might in fact. More flakes shelled away, and there was a little volley of cracks this time. It did not feel like kicking against stone. It was like kicking against something that gave. And I could have sworn that the musky smell increased. I felt a curious glow coming over me that was part fright, part excitement, part (I fancy) nausea; but plucked up my courage, and held my breath, and kicked again, and again, and again. The lamina, of limestone flew up in tinkling showers. There was no doubt about there being something springy underneath now, and that it was the dead carcass of another lizard, I hadn't a doubt. Here was luck; here was a find. Here was I, the discoverer of the body of a prehistoric beast preserved in the limestone down through all the ages, just as mammoths have been preserved in Siberian ice.

The quarrying of my boot-heel was too slow for me. I stuck my candle by its clay socket to a rock, and picked up a handy boulder and beat away the sheets of the stone with that; and all the time I toiled, the springiness of the carcass beneath distinctly helped me. The smell of musk nearly made me sick, but I stuck to the work. There was no doubt about it now. More than once I barked my knuckles against the harsh, scaly skin of the beast itself—against the skin of this anachronism which ought to have perished body and bones ten million years ago I remember wondering whether they would make me a baronet for the discovery. They do make scientific baronets nowadays for the bigger finds.

Then of a sudden I got a-start: I could have sworn the dead flesh moved beneath me.

But I shouted aloud at myself in contempt.

"Pah!" I said, "ten million years; the ghost is rather stale by this!" And I set to work afresh, beating away the stone which covered the beast from my sight.

But again I got a start, and this time it was a more solid one. After I had delivered my blow and whilst I was raising my weapon for another, a splinter of stone broke away as if pressed up from below, flipped up in the air, and tinkled back to a standstill. My blood chilled, and for a moment the loneliness of that unknown cave oppressed me. But I told myself that I was an old hand; that this was childishness; and, in fact, pulled myself together. I refused to accept the hint. I deliberately put the candle so as to throw a better light, swallowed back my tremors, and battered afresh at the laminated rock.

Twice more I was given warnings and disregarded them in the name of what I was pleased to call cold common reason; but the third time I dropped the battering stone as though it burnt me, and darted back with the most horrible shock of terror which (I make bold to say) any man could endure and still retain his senses.

There was no doubt about it, the beast was actually moving.

Yes, moving and alive. It was writhing, and straining, and struggling to leave its rocky bed, where it had lain quiet through all those countless cycles of time, and I watched it in a very petrifaction of terror. Its efforts threw up whole baskets full of splintered stone at a time. I could see the muscles of its back ripple at each effort. I could see the exposed part of its body grow in size every time it wrenched at the walls of that semi-eternal prison.

Then, as I looked, it doubled up its back like a bucking horse, and drew out its stumpy head and long feelers, giving out the while a thin, small scream like a hurt child; and then with another effort it pulled out its long tail and stood upon the débris of the limestone, panting with a new-found life.

I gazed upon it with a sickly fascination. Its body was about the bigness of two horses. Its head was curiously short, but the mouth opened back almost to the forearm; and sprouting from the nose were two enormous feelers, or antennae, each at least six feet long, and tipped with fleshy tendrils like fingers, which opened and shut tremulously. Its four legs were jointless, and ended in mere club feet, or callosities; its tail was long, supple, and fringed on the top with a saw-like row of scales. In colour it was a bright grass-green, all except the feelers, which were of a livid blue. But mere words go poorly for a description, and the beast was outside the vocabulary of to-day. It conveyed somehow or other a horrible sense of deformity, which made one physically ill to look upon it.

But worst of all was the musky smell. That increased till it became well-nigh unendurable, and though I half-strangled myself to suppress a sound, I had to yield at last and give my feelings vent.

The beast heard me. I could not see that it had any ears, but anyway it distinctly heard me. Worse, it hobbled round clumsily with its jointless legs, and waved its feelers in my direction. I could not make out that it had any eyes; anyway they did not show distinct from the rough skin of its head; its sensitiveness seemed to lie in those fathom-long feelers and in the fleshy fingers which twitched and grappled at the end of them.

Then it opened its great jaws, which hinged, as I said, down by the forearm, and yawned cavernously, and came towards me. It seemed to have no trace of fear or hesitation. It hobbled clumsily on, exhibiting its monstrous deformity in every movement, and preceded always by those hateful feelers, which seemed to be endued with an impish activity.

For a while I stayed in my place, too paralysed by horror by this awful thing I had dragged up from the forgotten dead to move or breathe. But then one of its livid blue feelers—a hard armoured thing like a lobster's—touched me, and the fleshy fingers at the end of it pawed my face and burned me like nettles. I leaped into movement again. The beast was hungry after its fast of ten million years; it was trying to make me its prey; those fearful jaws—

I turned and ran.

It followed me. In the feeble light of the one solitary candle I could see it following accurately in my track, with the waving feelers and their twitching fingers preceding it. It had pace, too. Its gait, with those clumsy, jointless legs, reminded one of a barrel-bellied sofa suddenly endowed with life, and careering over rough ground. But it distinctly had pace. And what was worse, the pace increased. At first it had the rust of those eternal ages to work out of its cankered joints; but this stiffness passed away; and presently it was following me with a speed equal to my own.

If this huge green beast had shown anger, or eagerness, or any of those things, it would have been less horrible; but it was absolutely unemotional in its hunt, and this helped to paralyse me; and in the end when it drove me into a *cul de sac* amongst the rocks, I was very near surrendering myself through sheer terror to what seemed the inevitable.

I wondered dully whether there had been another beast entombed beside it, and whether that had eaten the man who owned the penknife—Cordy, or Cording, his name was.

But the idea warmed me up. I had a stout knife in my own pocket, and after some fumbling got it out and opened the blade. The feelers with their fringe of fumbling fingers were close to me. I slashed at them viciously, and felt my knife grate against their armour. I might as well have hacked at an iron rail.

Still the attempt did me good. There is an animal love for fighting stowed away in the bottom of all of us somewhere, and mine woke then. I don't know that I expected to win; but I did intend to do the largest possible amount of damage before I was caught. I made a rush, stepped with one foot on the beast's creeping back, and leaped astern of him; and the beast gave its thin, small scream, and turned quickly in chase after me.

The pace was getting terrific. We doubled, and turned, and sprawled, and leapt amongst the slimy boulders, and every time we came to close quarters I stabbed at the beast with my knife, but without ever finding a joint in its armour. The tough skin gave to the weight of the blows, it is true, but it was like stabbing with a stick upon leather.

It was clear, though, that this could not go on. The beast grew in strength and activity, and probably in dumb anger, though actually it was unemotional as ever; but I was every moment growing more blown, and more bruised, and more exhausted.

At last I tripped and fell. The beast with its clumsy waddle shot past me before it could pull up, and in desperation I threw one arm and my knees around its grass-green tail, and with my spare hand drove the knife with the full of my force into the underneath of its body.

That woke it at last. It writhed, and it plunged, and it bucked with a frenzy that I had never seen before, and its scream grew in piercingness till it was strong as the whistle of a steam engine. But still I hung doggedly on to my place, and planted my vicious blows. The great beast doubled and tried to reach me; it dung its livid blue feelers backwards in vain efforts: I was beyond its clutch. And then, with my weight still on its back, it gave over dancing about the floor of the cavern, and set off at its hobbling gait directly for the water.

Not till it reached the brink did I slip off; but I saw it plunge in; I saw it swim strongly with its tail; and then I saw it dive and disappear for good.

And what next? I took to the water too, and swam as I had never swam before—swam for dear life, to the opposite side. I knew that if I waited to cool my thoughts, I should never pluck up courage for the attempt. It was then or not at all. It was risk the horrors of that passage, or stay where I was and starve—and be eaten.

How I got across I do not know. How I landed I cannot tell. How I got down the windings of the cave and through that water alley is more than I can say. And whether the beast followed me I do not know either. I got to daylight again somehow, staggering like a drunken man. I struggled down off the moor, and on to the village, and noted how the people ran from me. At the inn the landlord cried out as though I had been the plague. It seemed that the musky smell that I brought with me was unendurable, though by this time the mere detail of a smell was far beneath my notice. But I was stripped from my stinking clothes and washed and put to bed, and a doctor came and gave me an opiate; and when twelve hours later wakefulness came to me again, I had the sense to hold my tongue. All the village wanted to know from whence came that hateful odour of musk, but I said stupidly I did not know. I said "I must have fallen into something."

And there the matter ends for the present. I go no more cave-hunting, and I offer no help to those who do. But if the man who owned that white-handled penknife is alive, I should like to compare experiences with him; and if, as I strongly suspect, he is dead, these pages may be of interest to his relatives. He was not known in Kettlewell or any of the other villages where I inquired, but he could very well have come over the hills from Pateley Bridge way. Cording was the name scratched on the knife, or Cordy: I could not be sure which; and, as I have said, mine is M'Cray, and I can be heard of at the Kettlewell Post Office, though I have given up the shooting on the moor near there. Somehow the air of the district sickens me. There seems to be a taint in it.

The Monster of Lake LaMetrie
Wardon Allan Curtis

Being the narration of James McLennegan, M.D., Ph.D.

Lake LaMetrie, Wyoming
April 1st, 1899
Prof. William G. Breyfogle,
University of Taychobera.

Dear Friend—Inclosed you will find some portions of the diary it has been my life-long custom to keep, arranged in such a manner as to narrate connectedly the history of some remarkable occurrences that have taken place here during the last three years. Years and years ago, I heard vague accounts of a strange lake high up in an almost inaccessible part of the mountains of Wyoming. Various incredible tales were related of it, such as that it was inhabited by creatures which elsewhere on the globe are found only as fossils of a long vanished time.

The lake and its surroundings are of volcanic origin, and not the least strange thing about the lake is that it is subject to periodic disturbances, which take the form of a mighty boiling in the centre, as if a tremendous artesian well were rushing up there from the bowels of the earth. The lake rises for a time, almost filling the basin of black rocks in which it rests, and then recedes, leaving on the shores mollusks and trunks of strange trees and bits of strange ferns which no longer grow—on the earth, at least—and are to be seen elsewhere only in coal measures and beds of stone. And he who casts hook and line into the dusky waters, may haul forth ganoid fishes completely covered with bony plates.

All of this is described in the account written by Father LaMetrie years ago, and he there advances the theory that the earth is hollow, and that its interior is inhabited by the forms of plant and animal life which disappeared from its surface ages ago, and that the lake connects with this interior region. Symmes' theory of polar orifices is well known to you. It is amply corroborated. I know that it is true now. Through the great holes at the poles, the sun sends light and heat into the interior.

Three years ago this month, I found my way through the mountains here to Lake LaMetrie accompanied by a single companion, our friend, young Edward Framingham. He was led to go with me not so much by scientific fervor, as by a faint hope that his health might be improved by a sojourn in the mountains, for he suffered from an acute form of dyspepsia that at times drove him frantic.

Beneath an overhanging scarp of the wall of rock surrounding the lake, we found a rudely-built stone-house left by the old cliff dwellers. Though somewhat draughty, it would keep out the infrequent rains of the region, and serve well enough as a shelter for the short time which we intended to stay.

The extracts from my diary follow:

April 29th, 1896.

I have been occupied during the past few days in gathering specimens of the various plants which are cast upon the shore by the waves of this remarkable lake. Framingham does nothing but fish, and claims that he has discovered the place where the lake communicates with the interior of the earth, if, indeed, it does, and there seems to be little doubt of that. While fishing at a point near the centre of the lake, he let down three pickerel lines tied together, in all nearly three hundred feet, without finding bottom. Coming ashore, he collected every bit of line, string, strap, and rope in our possession, and made a line five hundred feet long, and still he was unable to find the bottom.

May 2nd, Evening.

The past three days have been profitably spent in securing specimens, and mounting and pickling them for preservation.

Framingham has had a bad attack of dyspepsia this morning and is not very well. Change of climate had a brief effect for the better upon his malady, but seems to have exhausted its force much sooner than one would have expected, and he lies on his couch of dry water-weeds, moaning piteously. I shall take him back to civilization as soon as he is able to be moved.

It is very annoying to have to leave when I have scarcely begun to probe the mysteries of the place. I wish Framingham had not come with me. The lake is roaring wildly without, which is strange, as it has been perfectly calm hitherto, and still more strange because I can neither feel nor hear the rushing of the wind, though perhaps that is because it is blowing from the south, and we are protected from it by the cliff. But in that case there ought to be no waves on this shore. The roaring seems to grow louder momentarily. Framingham—

MAY 3rd, MORNING.

Such a night of terror we have been through. Last evening, as I sat writing in my diary, I heard a sudden hiss, and, looking down, saw wriggling across the earthen floor what I at first took to be a serpent of some kind, and then discovered was a stream of water which, coming in contact with the fire, had caused the startling hiss. In a moment, other streams had darted in, and before I had collected my senses enough to move, the water was two inches deep everywhere and steadily rising.

Now I knew the cause of the roaring, and, rousing Framingham, I half dragged him, half carried him to the door, and digging our feet into the chinks of the wall of the house, we climbed up to its top. There was nothing else to do, for above us and behind us was the unscalable cliff, and on each side the ground sloped away rapidly, and it would have been impossible to reach the high ground at the entrance to the basin.

After a time we lighted matches, for with all this commotion there was little air stirring, and we could see the water, now halfway up the side of the house, rushing to the west with the force and velocity of the current of a mighty river, and every little while it hurled tree-trunks against the house-walls with a terrific shock that threatened to batter them down. After an hour or so, the roaring began to decrease, and finally there was an absolute silence. The water, which reached to within a foot of where we sat, was at rest, neither rising nor falling.

Presently a faint whispering began and became a stertorous breathing, and then a rushing like that of the wind and a roaring rapidly increasing in volume, and the lake was in motion again, but this time the water and its swirling freight of tree-trunks flowed by the house toward the east, and was constantly falling, and out in the centre of the lake the beams of the moon were darkly reflected by the sides of a huge whirlpool, streaking the surface of polished blackness down, down, down the vortex into the beginning of whose terrible depths we looked from our high perch.

This morning the lake is back at its usual level. Our mules are drowned, our boat destroyed, our food damaged, my specimens and some of my instruments injured, and Framingham is very ill. We shall have to depart soon, although I dislike exceedingly to do so, as the disturbance of last night, which is clearly like the one described by Father LaMetrie, has undoubtedly brought up from the bowels of the earth some strange and interesting things. Indeed, out in the middle of the lake where the whirlpool subsided, I can see a large quantity of floating things; logs and branches, most of them probably, but who knows what else?

Through my glass I can see a tree-trunk, or rather stump, of enormous dimensions. From its width I judge that the whole tree must have been as large as some of the California big trees. The main part of it appears to be about ten feet wide and thirty feet long. Projecting from it and lying prone on the water is a limb, or root, some fifteen feet long, and perhaps two or three feet thick. Before we leave, which will be as soon as Framingham is able to go, I shall make a raft and visit the mass of driftwood, unless the wind providentially sends it ashore.

MAY 4th, EVENING.

A day of most remarkable and wonderful occurrences, When I arose this morning and looked through my glass, I saw that the mass of driftwood still lay in the middle of the lake, motionless on the glassy surface, but the great black stump had disappeared. I was sure it was not hidden by the rest of the driftwood, for yesterday it lay some distance from the other logs, and there had been no disturbance of wind or water to change its position. I therefore concluded that it was some heavy wood that needed to become but slightly waterlogged to cause it to sink.

Framingham having fallen asleep at about ten, I sallied forth to look along the shores for specimens, carrying with me a botanical can, and a South American machete, which I have possessed since a visit to Brazil three years ago, where I learned the usefulness of this sabre-like thing. The shore was strewn with bits of strange plants and shells, and I was stooping to pick one up, when suddenly I felt my clothes plucked, and heard a snap behind me, and turning about I saw—but I won't describe it until I tell what I did, for I did not fairly see the terrible creature until I had swung my machete round and sliced off the top of its head, and then tumbled down into the shallow water where I lay almost fainting.

Here was the black log I had seen in the middle of the lake, a monstrous elasmosaurus, and high above me on the heap of rocks lay the thing's head with its long jaws crowded with sabre-like teeth, and its enormous eyes as big as saucers. I wondered that it did not move, for I expected a series of convulsions, but no sound of a commotion was heard from the creature's body, which lay out of my sight on the other side of the rocks. I decided that my sudden cut had acted like a stunning blow and produced a sort of coma, and fearing lest the beast should recover the use of its muscles before death fully took place, and in its agony roll away into the deep water where I could not secure it, I hastily removed the brain entirely, performing the operation neatly, though with some trepidation, and restoring to the head the detached segment cut off by my machete, I proceeded to examine my prize.

In length of body, it is exactly twenty-eight feet. In the widest part it is eight feet through laterally, and is some six feet through from back to belly. Four great flippers, rudimentary arms and feet, and an immensely long, sinuous, swan-like neck, complete the creature's body. Its head is very small for the size of the body and is very round and a pair of long jaws project in front much like a duck's bill. Its skin is a leathery integument of a lustrous black, and its eyes are enormous hazel optics with a soft, melancholy stare in their liquid depths. It is an elasmosaurus, one of the largest of antediluvian animals. Whether of the same species as those whose bones have been discovered, I cannot say.

My examination finished, I hastened after Framingham, for I was certain that this waif from a long past age would arouse almost any invalid. I found him somewhat recovered from his attack of the morning, and he eagerly accompanied me to the elasmosaurus.

In examining the animal afresh, I was astonished to find that its heart was still beating and that all the functions of the body except thought were being performed one hour after the thing had received its death blow, but I knew that the hearts of sharks have been known to beat hours after being removed from the body, and that decapitated frogs live, and have all the powers of motion, for weeks after their heads have been cut off.

I removed the top of the head to look into it and here another surprise awaited me, for the edges of the wound were granulating and preparing to heal. The colour of the interior of the skull was perfectly healthy and natural, there was no undue flow of blood, and there was every evidence that the animal intended to get well and live without a brain. Looking at the interior of the skull, I was struck by its resemblance to a human skull; in fact, it is, as nearly as I can judge, the size and shape of the brain-pan of an ordinary man who wears a seven-and-an-eighth hat. Examining the brain itself, I found it to be the size of an ordinary human brain, and singularly like it in general contour, though it is very inferior in fibre and has few convolutions.

MAY 5th, MORNING.

Framingham is exceedingly ill and talks of dying, declaring that if a natural death does not put an end to his sufferings, he will commit suicide. I do not know what to do. All my attempts to encourage him are of no avail, and the few medicines I have no longer fit his case at all.

MAY 5th, EVENING.

I have just buried Framingham's body in the sand of the lake shore. I performed no ceremonies over the grave, for perhaps the real Framingham is not dead, though such a speculation seems utterly wild. To-morrow I shall erect a cairn upon the mound, unless indeed there are signs that my experiment is successful, though it is foolish to hope that it will be.

At ten this morning, Framingham's qualms left him, and he set forth with me to see the elasmosaurus. The creature lay in the place where we left it yesterday, its position unaltered, still breathing, all the bodily functions performing themselves. The wound in its head had healed a great deal during the night, and I daresay will be completely healed within a week or so, such is the rapidity with which these reptilian organisms repair damages to themselves. Collecting three or four bushels of mussels, I shelled them and poured them down the elasmosaurus's throat. With a convulsive gasp, they passed down and the great mouth slowly closed.

"How long do you expect to keep the reptile alive?" asked Framingham.

"Until I have gotten word to a number of scientific friends, and they have come here to examine it. I shall take you to the nearest settlement and write letters from there. Returning, I shall feed the elasmosaurus regularly until my friends come, and we decide what final disposition to make of it. We shall probably stuff it."

"But you will have trouble in killing it, unless you hack it to pieces, and that won't do. Oh, if I only had the vitality of that animal. There is a monster whose vitality is so splendid that the removal of its brain does not disturb it. I should feel very happy if someone would remove my body. If I only had some of that beast's useless strength."

"In your case, the possession of a too active brain has injured the body," said I. "Too much brain exercise and too little bodily exercise are the causes of your trouble. It would be a pleasant thing if you had the robust health of the elasmosaurus, but what a wonderful thing it would be if that mighty engine had your intelligence."

I turned away to examine the reptile's wounds, for I had brought my surgical instruments with me, and intended to dress them. I was interrupted by a burst of groans from Framingham and turning, beheld him rolling on the sand in an agony. I hastened to him, but before I could reach him, he seized my case of instruments, and taking the largest and sharpest knife, cut his throat from ear to ear.

"Framingham, Framingham," I shouted and, to my astonishment, he looked at me intelligently. I recalled the case of the French doctor who, for some minutes after being guillotined, answered his friends by winking.

"If you hear me, wink," I cried. The right eye closed and opened with a snap. Ah, here the body was dead and the brain lived. I glanced at the elasmosaurus. Its mouth, half closed over its gleaming teeth, seemed to smile an invitation. The intelligence of the man and the strength of the beasts. The living body and the living brain. The curious resemblance of the reptile's brain-pan to that of a man flashed across my mind.

"Are you still alive, Framingham?"

The right eye winked. I seized my machete, for there was no time for delicate instruments. I might destroy all by haste and roughness, I was sure to destroy all by delay. I opened the skull and disclosed the brain. I had not injured it, and breaking the wound of the elasmosaurus's head, placed the brain within, I dressed the wound and, hurrying to the house, brought all my store of stimulants and administered them.

For years the medical fraternity has been predicting that brain-grafting will some time be successfully accomplished. Why has it never been successfully accomplished? Because it has not been tried. Obviously, a brain from a dead body cannot be used and what living man would submit to the horrible process of having his head opened, and portions of his brain taken for the use of others?

The brains of men are frequently examined when injured and parts of the brain removed, but parts of the brains of other men have never been substituted for the parts removed. No injured man has even been found who would give any portion of his brain for the use of another.

Until criminals under sentence of death are handed over to science for experimentation, we shall not know what can be done in the way of brain-grafting. But the public opinion would never allow it.

Conditions are favorable for a fair and thorough trial of my experiment. The weather is cool and even, and the wound in the head of the elasmosaurus has every chance for healing. The animal possesses a vitality superior to any of our later-day animals, and if any organism can successfully become the host of a foreign brain, nourishing and cherishing it, the elasmosaurus with its abundant vital forces can do it. It may be that a new era in the history of the world will begin here.

MAY 6th, NOON.
I think I will allow my experiment a little more time.

MAY 7th, NOON.
It cannot be imagination. I am sure that as I looked into the elasmosaurus's eyes this morning there was expression in them. Dim, it is true, a sort of mistiness that floats over them like the reflection of passing clouds.

MAY 8th, NOON.
I am more sure than yesterday that there is expression in the eyes, a look of troubled fear, such as is seen in the eyes of those who dream nightmares with unclosed lids.

MAY 11th, EVENING.
I have been ill, and have not seen the elasmosaurus for three days, but I shall be better able to judge the progress of the experiment by remaining away a period of some duration.

MAY 12th, NOON.
I am overcome with awe as I realise the success that has so far crowned my experiment. As I approached the elasmosaurus this morning, I noticed a faint disturbance in the water near its flippers.

I cautiously investigated expecting to discover some fishes nibbling at the helpless monster, and saw that the commotion was

not due to fishes, but to the flippers themselves, which were feebly moving.

"Framingham, Framingham," I bawled at the top of my voice.
The vast bulk stirred a little, a very little, but enough to notice. Is
the brain, or Framingham, it would perhaps be better to say, asleep,
or has he failed to establish connection with the body? Undoubtedly he has not yet established connection with the body, and this
of itself would be equivalent to sleep, to unconsciousness. As a man
born with none of the senses would be unconscious of himself, so
Framingham, just beginning to establish connections with his new
body, is only dimly conscious of himself and sleeps. I fed him, or
it—which is the proper designation will be decided in a few days—
with the usual allowance.

MAY 17th, EVENING.

I have been ill for the past three days, and have not been out of
doors until this morning. The elasmosaurus was still motionless
when I arrived at the cove this morning. Dead, I thought; but I
soon detected signs of breathing, and I began to prepare some
mussels for it, and was intent upon my task, when I heard a slight,
gasping sound, and looked up. A feeling of terror seized me. It was
as if in response to some doubting incantations there had appeared
the half-desired, yet wholly-feared and unexpected apparition of a
fiend. I shrieked, I screamed, and the amphitheatre of rocks echoed and re-echoed my cries, and all the time the head of the
elasmosaurus raised aloft to the full height of its neck, swayed
about unsteadily, and its mouth silently struggled and twisted, as
if in an attempt to form words, while its eyes looked at me now
with wild fear and now with piteous intreaty.

"Framingham," I said.

The monster's mouth closed instantly, and it looked at me attentively, pathetically so, as a dog might look.

"Do you understand me?"

The mouth began struggling again, and little gasps and moans
issued forth. "If you understand me, lay your head on the rock."

Down came the head. He understood me. My experiment was a
success. I sat for a moment in silence, meditating upon the wonderful

affair, striving to realise that I was awake and sane, and then began in a calm manner to relate to my friend what had taken place since his attempted suicide.

"You are at present something in the condition of a partial paralytic, I should judge," said I, as I concluded my account. "Your mind has not yet learned to command your new body. I see you can move your head and neck, though with difficulty. Move your body if you can. Ah, you cannot, as I thought. But it will all come in time. Whether you will ever be able to talk or not, I cannot say, but I think so, however. And now if you cannot, we will arrange some means of communication. Anyhow, you are rid of your human body and possessed of the powerful vital apparatus you so much envied its former owner. When you gain control of yourself, I wish you to find the communication between this lake and the under-world, and conduct some explorations. Just think of the additions to geological knowledge you can make. I will write an account of your discovery, and the names of Framingham and McLennegan will be among those of the greatest geologists."

I waved my hands in my enthusiasm, and the great eyes of my friend glowed with a kindred fire.

JUNE 2nd, NIGHT.

The process by which Framingham has passed from his first powerlessness to his present ability to speak, and command the use of his corporeal frame, has been so gradual that there has been nothing to note down from day to day. He seems to have all the command over his vast bulk that its former owner had, and in addition speaks and sings. He is singing now. The north wind has risen with the fall of night, and out there in the darkness I hear the mighty organ pipetones of his tremendous, magnificent voice, chanting the solemn notes of the Gregorian, the full-throated Latin words mingling with the roaring of the wind in a wild and weird harmony.

To-day he attempted to find the connection between the lake and the interior of the earth, but the great well that sinks down in the centre of the lake is choked with rocks and he has discovered nothing. He is tormented by the fear that I will leave him, and that he will perish of loneliness. But I shall not leave him. I feel too much pity for the loneliness he would endure, and besides, I wish to be on the spot should another of those mysterious convulsions open the connection between the lake and the lower world.

He is beset with the idea that should other men discover him, he may be captured and exhibited in a circus or museum, and declares that he will fight for his liberty even to the extent of taking the lives of those attempting to capture him. As a wild animal, he is the property of whomsoever captures him, though perhaps I can set up title to him on the ground of having tamed him.

JULY 6th.

One of Framingham's fears has been realised. I was at the pass leading into the basin, watching the clouds grow heavy and pendulous with their load of rain, when I saw a butterfly net appear over a knoll in the pass, followed by its bearer, a small man, unmistakably a scientist, but I did not note him well, for as he looked down into the valley, suddenly there burst forth with all the power and volume of a steam calliope, the tremendous voice of Framingham, singing a Greek song of Anacreon to the tune of "Where did you get that hat?" and the singer appeared in a little cove, the black column of his great neck raised aloft, his jagged jaws wide open.

That poor little scientist. He stood transfixed, his butterfly net dropped from his hand, and as Framingham ceased his singing, curvetted and leaped from the water and came down with a splash that set the whole cove swashing, and laughed a guffaw that echoed among the cliffs like the laughing of a dozen demons, he turned and sped through the pass at all speed.

I skip all entries for nearly a year. They are unimportant.

JUNE 30th, 1897.

A change is certainly coming over my friend. I began to see it some time ago, but refused to believe it and set it down to imagination. A catastrophe threatens, the absorption of the human intellect by the brute body. There are precedents for believing it possible. The human body has more influence over the mind than the mind has over the body. The invalid, delicate Framingham with refined mind, is no more. In his stead is a roistering monster, whose boisterous and commonplace conversation betrays a constantly growing coarseness of mind.

No longer is he interested in my scientific investigations, but pronounces them all bosh. No longer is his conversation such as an educated man can enjoy, but slangy and diffuse iterations concerning the trivial happenings of our uneventful life. Where will it end? In the absorption of the human mind by the brute body? In the final triumph of matter over mind and the degradation of the most mundane force and the extinction of the celestial spark? Then, indeed, will Edward Framingham be dead, and over the grave of his human body can I fittingly erect a headstone, and then will my vigil in this valley be over.

Fort D. A. Russell, Wyoming,
April 15th, 1899.
Prof. William G. Breyfogle.
Dear Sir—The inclosed intact manuscript and the fragments which accompany it, came into my possession in the manner I am about to relate and I inclose them to you, for whom they were intended by their late author. Two weeks ago, I was dispatched into the mountains after some Indians who had left their reservation, having under my command a company of infantry and two squads of cavalrymen with mountain howitzers. On the seventh day of our pursuit, which led us into a wild and unknown part of the mountains, we were startled at hearing from somewhere in front of us a succession of bellowings of a very unusual nature, mingled with the cries of a human being apparently in the last extremity, and rushing over a rise before us, we looked down upon a lake and saw a colossal, indescribable thing engaged in rending the body of a man.

Observing us, it stretched its jaws and laughed, and in saying this, I wish to be taken literally. Part of my command cried out that it was the devil, and turned and ran. But I rallied them, and thoroughly enraged at what we had witnessed, we marched down to the shore, and I ordered the howitzers to be trained upon the murderous creature. While we were doing this, the thing kept up a constant blabbing that bore a distinct resemblance to human speech, sounding very much like the jabbering of an imbecile, or a drunken man trying to talk. I gave the command to fire and to fire again, and the beast tore out into the lake in its death-agony, and sank.

With the remains of Dr. McLennegan, I found the foregoing manuscript intact, and the torn fragments of the diary from which it was compiled, together with other papers on scientific subjects, all of which I forward. I think some attempts should be made to secure the body of the elasmosaurus. It would be a priceless addition to any museum.

Arthur W. Fairchild
Captain, U.S.A.

The Slaying of the Plesiosaurus
Edwin J. Webster

Captain Charles Jackson stood before his tent and looked anxiously to the north, where far in the distance loomed up the forbidding slopes of the great Central African mountain range. It was now four days since Lasca, his head scout, had left camp for an exploring tour of the mountains and the region at their base. Captain Jackson was in charge of one of the surveying parties sent north from the Transvaal to take an inspection of the possible routes for the great Cape-to-Cairo railway, which would bring together the northern and southern portions of England's African empire. Lasca was faithful, intelligent, and had hunted over southern and central Africa for years. There were no hostile tribes in that region and the captain was at a loss to explain the absence of his trusted scout.

A man, weary, footsore, his clothes torn to rags, broke through the underbrush at the foot of the little hill on which the camp was located. Slowly, like a person who had run until exhausted, he climbed towards the camp. It was Lasca. His rifle was gone, so was his revolver and cartridge belt, and even as he drew near the camp, he looked around like a man who has escaped some peril, the memory of which still haunts him. His face was drawn and haggard, and in the eyes of the bronzed old Arab was a timid, frightened look no one had ever seen there. "Dead, all dead," replied Lasca, not sullenly, but in the tone of a man who has passed beyond caring, when Captain Jackson asked him what had become of the rest of this party. "A devil arose from the waters and seized them. It was kismet that I should not die then, so I live. Though after what I have seen I do not greatly care for life."

"Were they seized by some animal?" inquired the English captain in perplexed tones. He had known Lasca for years and did not
doubt his faithfulness. And he had seen the grim old Arab fighter
face death unmoved many times and could not understand what
had so fearfully shaken his iron nerves.

"It was no animal, my captain," replied Lasca earnestly. "I, who
have fought and hunted over Africa for years, know all the animals
and there is none that can stand before the bullets of a Lee-Metford.
It was in very truth a devil that seized them. I am not a man to be
frightened at old wives' tales. And I saw him with my own eyes and
felt his burning breath. But I will tell you the tale from the beginning, that you may not think Lasca, who has faced danger with you
many times, was terrified by a vision in the night.

"With the four men you gave me I traveled north until we came
to the foot of the mountains. We were well armed, the natives were
friendly, and we had no thought of peril. As we went up the mountains I noticed we met few natives, but I gave the matter little
thought. The peak to the north is said to have once been a volcano,
though that was so long ago that scarcely the tradition of it is left.
Where once it poured out fire, there is now a lake.

"Now the thought in my mind was that we should explore this
lake, for perhaps the water might be of use when the steel road is
laid. But when I tried to get a guide every native was unwilling to
go with me. They all said the lake had no bottom, but connected
with hell, and that the devil came up through the water and seized
all, man or beast, who ventured near it. At last, by offering a high
price, I persuaded a native to lead me in sight of the lake. When I
saw it I laughed at his fears, for the lake is like a jewel, set in the
top of the mountain. All around it are high cliffs with palm trees,
and it is beautiful to look upon. At one point there is an opening
through the cliffs and a steep roadway down to the lake itself. The
native, though in fear, brought us to the top of the roadway. Then
he refused to go any farther, even when I offered him more pay. I
was angry, and drawing my revolver told him that if he did not
guide us down to the lake I would shoot him. But even then, though
clearly in terror of my revolver, he refused to lead us down the
roadway.

"'Better to die by the little gun,' he answered me, 'than to be seized by the devil, and living dragged down through the waters to hell.'

"When I saw that neither threats nor bribes would persuade, I let him stay, and, accompanied by the men you sent out with me, I started down the roadway toward the lake. For I thought the natives had been frightened by a hippopotamus, or very big crocodile, or some other animal living in the lake; and having our rifles I felt little fear. The pathway was smooth, as if it had often been traveled over by some big snake. This I wondered at, but being a fool I thought myself wise, and that I knew of all the animals in Africa and feared none. The water of the lake is not blue, but green like the ocean. After I had explored the sides, I thought it might be useful to know the depth. So we built a raft and paddled out on the water. The captain remembers that he gave me three sounding lines before I started. I tied a heavy stone to one of the lines and let it down, but it did not touch the bottom. I tied the second line to the first, but that did not touch. Then I fastened on the third line, but still the stone sank down the length of the three lines, nearly two miles. So I gave the order to haul up the line. My men were busy drawing it up and I was idly watching the lake, when I saw something dark coming up through the deep water.

"'It is the big crocodile the natives think is the devil,' I said to my men. 'I will show him what a rifle can do.'

"But as I prepared my gun the thing drew nearer, and through the clear water of the lake I could see that it was no crocodile. I called to my men to drop the line and get their rifles ready. Even then I thought it was only a water serpent that had grown to an unusual size. But before I could get a clear view of the creature, so swiftly was it swimming toward the top, there was a little uprising of the water at the side of the raft and the thing broke through to the surface. And then I knew that the natives had not lied, and that there was a devil in the lake.

"First came up a head, larger by far than that of any elephant, with grinning jaws and big teeth. Then came the neck, like that of a snake, but rising fully forty feet from the body. The body resembled a huge turtle, but larger than six hippopotami together.

It had fins and a long, heavy tail that lashed the water to foam. From the grinning jaws to the tail must have been nearly a hundred feet, though it seemed much farther.

"The Lake Devil lifted his head far in the air above us and opened his jaws. A tall man could have stood upright in them and his head would scarcely have reached the upper jaw. As we saw the head above us all thought we were dead. My men fired wildly and leaped into the lake. But I thought, devil or not, I would hit him with at least one bullet. Taking aim at the waving neck, I fired. The bullet was from a Lee-Metford and struck him fairly in the neck, but made no more impression than a pebble thrown by a child. The Lake Devil struck downward with his head and the heavy logs of the raft were splintered as if they had been rotten twigs. Each man swam towards the shore as quickly as possible. I had dived deep and swam under water when I left the raft. When I rose to the surface I heard a scream and saw one of my men snatched up in the Lake Devil's jaws and hurled into the air. Then I swam faster, not looking back. And three times more I heard a scream, and I knew that all my men were dead. But I did not look around until my feet touched the bottom. Then I saw that the Lake Devil was swimming after me. His swimming was as the rush of one of the steamers that travel over the Great Water.

"I ran through the shallow water and up the steep bank. But the Lake Devil swam faster, and reached the shore and chased after me. I heard the hissing of his breath and felt the wind of it on my cheek. And as I ran I drew my revolver and fired backwards as swiftly as I could pull the trigger, but without looking around or ceasing to run. Perhaps one of my shots hit him in the eye, or he may have wished to return to the lake and devour the bodies of my comrades. Whatever the reason, he stopped his pursuit. But I ran on and on, without stopping, up the steep bank and through the forest and down the side of the mountain. For I had seen the Lake Devil and I, Lasca, who have faced death many times, was afraid so that I trembled like a scared child and my bones seemed to melt within me. And I ran on until darkness came and then I fell to the ground and slept. For I had no fear of wild animals, since I had seen the Devil and still lived." Lasca drew a long breath and seated himself wearily on the ground. Captain Jackson was greatly puzzled over the matter. Had it been any other of the men in the camp he would have been inclined to laugh at the tale. But Lasca, the fierce old Arab, who all his life had seen battle and sudden death in all the various forms they are to be met with in Central Africa,—it must have been some real and terrible danger so utterly to unman him. Captain Jackson's sporting blood was aroused and he determined to follow up the adventure.

"Well, Lasca," he replied, "there's only one thing to do, and that is to find out more about this creature you call a lake devil. Though what kind of an animal he may be I can't imagine from your description."

"I know every kind of animal in Africa," said Lasca decidedly. "He is no animal, but a devil that came up from the center of the earth. Bullets will not pierce his skin, and it is death to go on the lake. Even a devil cannot fight against fate, and it was not kismet that I should die. But to go on the lake a second time would be to laugh at fate, which none can do and live."

"Devil or not," answered Captain Jackson, "we'll organize a hunting party and find out about your monster. His skin may be too thick for bullets, but if he's flesh and blood dynamite will get him."

The next day the hunting party started out, despite the protest of Lasca, who had no wish for a second interview with the "devil." Through the tangled jungle they made their way until they reached the foot of the mountains. Night overtook them before they had gone more than half way up the side. The tents were pitched and the following day the start was made a dawn. It was nearly noon when they reached the top. High cliffs fringed the little lake, which lay spread out before them deep, placid, and without a suggestion of danger. The party halted to view the lake and decided which was the best way to make the descent to its level.

"There is the path which we descended," said Lasca, pointing to the east where a smooth roadway seemed to run down to the lake. "But there is still time to turn back and not tempt fate by hunting Lake Devils."

The forest for miles around was deserted, for the natives shunned the top of the mountain as an accursed place. Even wild animals seemed less common than in other parts of that region. The only living thing in sight was a big bull elephant that could be seen making his way down the road towards the lake.

"That elephant must be a rogue who has wandered here from some far-away place," observed Lasca. "The natives told me that none of the animals living near here would water at the devil's lake."

The big elephant marched down to the lake, waded out until the water was up to his body, and began drinking. When he had drunk his fill he commenced to wash, spraying himself all over with big streams from his trunk.

"That old fellow seems to be enjoying himself without any thought of danger from lake devils," said Captain Jackson.

Out in the middle of the lake appeared a little eddy. Lasca saw it first and silently pointed it out to the English captain. Nearer and nearer to the shore came the eddy, but still the big bull elephant stood spraying himself, unconscious of all danger. Then dimly through the clear lake Captain Jackson could make out some huge creature rushing toward the shore. A flurry of waves, and with a splash and road a gigantic head broke through the water. It was followed by a snaky, twisting neck, nearly forty feet long. Then came the body, like that of a turtle, but far larger than that of any turtle since the ages when geological monsters, beside whom the largest animals of to-day are small, ruled land and sea. Too late the big elephant saw his terrible peril and turned to rush toward the shore. The snaky head shot out, the big jaws opened and then closed with a snap, grasping the elephant about his body as a cat snatches a mouse.

Over and over in the water, kicking with his feet, striking with his trunk, and trying in vain to thrust with his tusks, the elephant rolled. No creature in the African jungle could have matched him in strength, but against the survival of a past age even the elephant was helpless. Nearer and nearer in shore came the Lake Devil, clutching the big elephant in his unbreakable grip. The water was churned to foam by the desperate efforts of the elephant to free himself. But still the Lake Devil pushed forward until all his body was resting on the bottom. The elephant had also succeeded in getting all four feet firmly planted on solid ground and threw all his strength into one supreme effort to get away. Failing in this, he twisted his body around and began striking fierce, lashing blows with his trunk at the head of the monster. Then the Lake Devil exerted all his tremendous strength. The snaky neck and huge head swung around, the elephant being lifted clear off his feet. For a second the air vibrated with the shrill, agonized trumpetings of the elephant. Then the Lake Devil gave a little push with his fins and his body moved toward the deeper water. The big head sank under, carrying the shrieking elephant with it. Another instant and, with a rush like the launching of a battleship, the Lake Devil shot out toward the middle of the lake and sank down into its unfathomable depths.

"It is death to go out on the lake," said Lasca sullenly. "Our bullets will not hurt him. Why throw our lives away? When even the big rogue elephant was helpless, what can men do against the Lake Devil?"

"It would be suicide to go on the lake," answered Captain Jackson decidedly. "That fellow could sink anything smaller than an ocean liner. Our only hope will be to get him to attack us on land. Then we can try our bullets on him. If they don't work, we can use the dynamite. But we won't try that unless it is a case of life or death, for it would blow him to pieces and destroy the skeleton."

The little party moved slowly around the side of the lake to the pathway between the cliffs. Even Captain Jackson felt nervous as they approached the lake, the lair of the great plesiosaurus, the prehistoric monster before whose might the strongest and fiercest of modern animals would be helpless.

Lasca glanced apprehensively at the smooth sides of the roadway.

"They have been worn smooth by the journeyings of the Lake Devil," he murmured. "The guide said that although he is clumsy on land, he can outstrip the swiftest runner."

Captain Jackson halted his men about a hundred yards from the shore of the lake.

"There is no use in going any nearer. I wish he was hungry, so that we could decoy him to the shore."

"The Lake Devil is always hungry and always angry," said Lasca decidedly. "We have only to disturb the water in some manner and he will show himself.

"Then may Allah protect us!"

The captain ordered his men to get their rifles in readiness for instant use. Then he unstrapped a little bag, and drew out three dynamite cartridges. One of them he handed to Lasca, another he slipped into his own pocket.

"These two will explode if we throw them," he said. "But we don't want to do that until it is absolutely necessary. I'll fix a fuse on the third one and throw it out into the lake. The explosion will probably disturb his majesty and he will come to the surface to see what is the matter. Then we can use our rifles. If he makes a rush at us on land we will have a good target, and finally, if the bullets don't seem to have any effect, we can try the dynamite. That probably will be too much even for a plesiosaurus."

He adjusted a fuse to the dynamite cartridge, and walking to the shore, lighted it and threw the cartridge far out into the lake. The explosion came just as the cartridge reached the surface and sent up a big column of water. Then he ran back to where his men were standing. All seized their rifles and stood anxiously watching the lake for indications of the appearance of the plesiosaurus.

For a moment there was nothing but the waves tossed up by the dynamite to show that anything unusual had taken place. Suddenly a big head and huge, snaky neck broke through the water. The plesiosaurus had risen to see who had dared disturb his domain. The head waved back and forth uncertainly. Then he saw the intruders and began to swim at terrific speed toward the shore.

"Here he comes," said Captain Jackson grimly. "Cool is the word now. Try and hit him in the eyes."

The Lee-Metfords began to talk and the bullets splashed the water all around the swiftly advancing head. Some of them may have struck, but the monster only came at greater speed. In a seemingly incalculably short time he had reached the shallow water. The long, snaky neck appeared in plain sight, then the huge, turtle-like body, black, slimy and threatening. Over the shallows the monster scrambled, his fins carrying him forward swifter than a man could run. Inured to danger as all the party were, they could feel their hearts throbbing at the sight of the antediluvian monster, ninety feet long, and with jaws that could crush a dozen men. The plesiosaurus was plainly enraged by the bullets which kept pattering harmlessly against his thick hide. His red, bloodshot eyes glared, the slime was dropping from his lips, and he seemed rather some monster that had come up from the depths of hell, than any creature of flesh and blood.

Now he had gained the land and was still hurrying on.

"Steady, steady," said Captain Jackson. "Aim at his eyes."

A bullet smashed into one of the glaring eyes, making a splash as if it had struck a pool of blood. The plesiosaurus only seemed to increase his speed. He was now near enough so they could see the dark blood oozing from bullet wounds in neck and body. They appeared in pin pricks and only angered him the more. Now he was eighty, now sixty yards from the little group. Lasca stooped and picked up his dynamite cartridge.

"Wait a second longer," gasped Captain Jackson. "I don't want to destroy the body."

As the plesiosaurus still rushed forward Lasca could not restrain himself.

"Throw now!" he exclaimed. "Throw now or we are dead!"

Captain Jackson drew out his cartridge. It was time, for the waving, snaky head, forty feet from the ground, would in an instant more be lowered for a deadly sweeping clutch.

"Drop on your faces when I throw!" shouted the English captain. And he hurled the dynamite cartridge straight towards the plesiosaurus. Lasca had already thrown his, and both Captain Jackson and Lasca dropped on the ground.

Two terrible explosions, so near together that they seemed one, and the air was full of pieces of flesh and bone and blood. Lasca's cartridge had fallen a little short, but even as it touched the ground the plesiosaurus had dropped his head, as if to grasp the deadly missile. Captain Jackson's cartridge had struck directly in front of the big, turtle-like body. Except for the blood-bespattered ground and the fragments of flesh and bones, it was hard to believe that the strongest and most terrible monster on earth had a second before been advancing in deadly charge. Against dynamite even the champion of antediluvian ages had been helpless.

"It was dynamite or death," said Captain Jackson, mournfully. "But it was too bad we had to use it. His body would have been worth a fortune."

Lasca shook his head decidedly.

"Twice have I looked the Lake Devil in the face, and Allah has preserved me," said the old Arab. "And I am glad it is no longer possible to see him. For the sight is not a nice one, nor the memory of it pleasant to a man who has lived long, and committed many sins, and knows that the time is not far distant when Azrael, the Angel of Death, will call him to account."

The Pterodactyl
Thomas Charles Sloane

Sheldon, my associate in the strange adventure I am about to relate, was an ex-Army officer, who, in some Indian campaign, had been shot through the knee, the injury producing a permanent lameness. By reason of this disability he had retired with honour from the service some years before our acquaintance began.

He was a large, powerful man, with a vigour of speech and manner which conveyed the impression of strong virility. His forehead was seamed with an ugly scar which, I understood, had been inflicted by some scalp-taking savage. I presently discovered that his mind, direct and soldierly, possessed a marked vein of poetry and that the rough camp-life on the frontier had not obliterated a delicacy of feeling and an exquisite taste for the beautiful and marvellous which, in hours of repose, lent flavour and entertaining variety to his conversation.

It was this circumstance, coupled with his military experience, which soon led us in the Gun Club to follow his lead in many matters, and when he suggested an autumn excursion into the mountains of Virginia for turkey and other game, we readily took up the idea. It thus happened that late in October, 1900, we found ourselves at the little station of Brownhills, where we were met by Hank Bowls, who was to act as guide and chief huntsman for the party.

It had been arranged that we should take up quarters in an old Log house some twenty miles distant, in the very heart of a mountainous, wooded region.

At nightfall of the following day we reached our destination. Though the old house had been put in some repair for our reception, the collapse of the chimney rendered a fire impossible, so we were obliged to establish our kitchen in the open air. While reconnoitring with this object in view my attention was specially attracted by a tall hickory at the side of the house, the limbs of which partly overhung the roof.

Some hours after we had turned in we were all wakened by a shout from Cummings who, I discovered on sitting up in my bunk, was standing in the middle of the room, gazing intently at the rafters.

What in Heaven's name is the matter with you, doctor?" I called, leaping to the floor.

Before Cummings could reply, a low, ominous growl, accompanied by a sniffing sound, came down from the roof.

"A panther!" cried Hank. "I reckon it's the same that carried off Dobbin's calf last week—and he's a big one! Hold up!" he shouted, grasping Cummings by the shoulder, as the doctor was making for the door. "Don't go out, or the brute will be upon you, teeth and claws!"

The panther, if panther it was, which had remained silent during this monologue, sniffed and growled again in the same low, menacing manner, as if resenting Hank's untimely interference; and I noticed by the sound that he had shifted his position to a point almost over the door.

Sheldon, who had seized a lantern, now began to grope about the room in quest of a gun, and then I suddenly remembered that all the guns stood without at the corner of the house near the tall hickory I have mentioned.

"It's certain death to go out there!" declared Hank, positively. "The infernal brute will be on you like a thunderbolt in a fit!"

The brute without, irritated, no doubt, by the sound of our voices, now uttered a louder and more threatening growl, and we could hear his claws tearing at different parts of the roof, as though seeking the best means of ingress to his prey.

Without having noticed Sheldon in particular, I afterwards remembered that he had been the last to quit his bunk on Cummings' alarm, and had stood with blanched face as though petrified with terror—incommensurate, or so it seemed to me, with his character and the extent of the danger. Having mastered himself, he now seemed for the first time, to think clearly. Seizing a pillow of straw, he stepped swiftly to the door and stood with his hand on the latch listening, as though to locate the exact position of the panther, now tearing and clawing savagely at the roof. My blood curdled as I realized that the savage animal was exactly over my head; but before any of us thought of fathoming Sheldon's purpose he had cautiously opened the door. I saw the flicker of a match, and the next instant the blazing pillow held above his head, Sheldon leaped towards the guns.

The panther immediately ceased tearing at the roof above me. I could hear the scraping of its claws as it bounded towards the farther eave, where, with a scream of dismay it paused.

I dare say fifteen seconds elapsed—to us it seemed a quarter of an hour—before Sheldon reappeared, still bearing his shield of flame, but with two guns and a quantity of cartridges. Scarcely had he closed the door when I heard the panther drop to the ground, the next instant it threw itself with a yell of baffled fury against the stout timbers.

"Open on him!" cried Cummings, excitedly.

"The shot will never cut through the door!" retorted Hank. "But the rest of us can hold it against him while the Major fires through the crack."

While he was speaking we had placed ourselves in position, holding the door very slightly ajar. At the next attack of the furious animal Sheldon discharged his gun, as it appeared to us, into the panther's very throat.

There was a moment's silence. Then a long-drawn, rising wail, which pierced our ears like a knife. It was repeated across the clearing, again and again, at successively greater intervals, till it seemed to die away in the heart of the woods.

"He's gone!" said Hank.

"But not dead," rejoined Sheldon.

Cummings then told us how he had heard the panther alight on the roof, probably from some overhanging limb of the hickory.

A few splinters of wood below the eaves, the deeply-scored claw-marks in the rough door, and a slender trail of blood across the

clearing and into the woods were the visible traces which the morning revealed of our savage nocturnal visitor. Hank, who followed
the trail some distance into the woods, discovered nothing further.
And so the incident closed—but for the consequence to which it
led.

It had fallen to my lot to remain on guard during this first day,
and with my nerves still somewhat shaken I was by no means dis-
pleased when Sheldon, excusing himself to the others, expressed
his intention of bearing me company.

After sitting for an hour in almost unbroken silence, gazing list-
lessly into the woods, he abruptly asked:—

"Do you ever imagine you have lived before?"

I parried the question.

"It is probable, Hossman, that you will think me unreasonably
superstitious if I tell you that, like some doting old woman, I have
been unnerved by a dream. A dream, too, which, like the wild
imaginings of a drunken man, centres about a strange, unnamable,
impossible monster, which by me and those with me seems to have
been regarded with fantastic terror and reverence."

I waited, silent, knowing not what to say.

Presently he continued:—

"In one shape and an other this dream has occurred three times.
First, when I was at Tucson; that night my brother and his entire
command were massacred on the Gila by the mountain Apaches!
The second occasion was five years later, at Yuma: next day a despatch announced my wife's death in hospital in Philadelphia! Last
night it came again, for the third time, and Cummings' cry of alarm
seemed so confused with the cries of others from the world of shadows that I was scarcely able to shake off the horrible illusion that I
was in the temple at Dion, struggling for my life before the God of
the Caves."

He regarded me with a smile—rather forced, I thought—and
paled visibly as he continued:—

"One is seldom conscious in dreams of any circumstance ante-
dating the situation in which one finds oneself, so that who I was
and whence I came were things of no moment. I found myself traversing a path over rugged hills, scrambling amid blackened rocks,

and diving into gloomy canyons, from one of which I presently emerged upon a broad highway and mingled with a throng of gaily-attired travellers, who seemed bent upon some festival, the import of which beneath the stratum of consciousness I fully understood. The way was strewn with fragments of red cloth and dyed quills—the confetti of the carnival. A kind of screechy, querulous music was produced by those around me upon some reed-like instrument held to the lips, and here and there I noticed the coppery gleam of a weapon which some disarranged garment had exposed— a circumstance that I marked with a feeling of interest. In and out through the throng ran groups of girls intent upon the pranks and merriments of youth, accosting with perfect freedom and entire absence of bashfulness any whom they chose. One of these young women, in passing, favoured me with a coquettish fillip upon the cheek, and as I caught the bright smile in her dancing eyes my heart warmed toward her, though I felt that some about me regarded the freedom with disfavour. A little later, on passing me again, she purposely slipped. As I aided her to rise I ventured to impart a salute upon her cheek, which was immediately suffused with a deep blush, though this, I fancied, was in no way due to resentment. Instantly, however, a tall, black-robed man near me turned, and, without warning, levelled a blow at me with a short axe of bronze. It narrowly missed my head, but caught my feathered head-dress, which fell to the ground; and I noticed that, whereas the heads of all were decorated with many-coloured plumes, none were red save mine.

"'Son of a priest!' muttered my assailant, in tones vibrant with hate, 'will not the fruits of the land suffice you that you must needs ravish the blossom?'

"Then another interposed:—

"'By the fire of the Bird, 'tis Torqua and the daughter of Narbin! Put up your weapon! See you not that he flies with the red eagles of Dion?'

"With the easy grace of a courtier the speaker stooped and restored to me my fallen helmet, but as he turned away he spat upon the ground, and I knew that his hate envenomed the dust. Before I could acknowledge either the affront of the one or the mock courtesy

of the other we were forced apart by those attracted by the incident, and I heard on all sides low-spoken words of reproof:

"The armed men of Narbin—armed in spite of the priestly
edict—were on the road to Dion to offer sacrifice to the God of the
Caves. If this offering were accepted, I knew that the blood of our
order must flow around the altars and that a new priesthood would
arise to minister among the people. If only they could be apprised
before the hour of sacrifice, the crafty men of Narbin might be
undone. I pressed forward, thinking to enter Dion in advance of
the plotters, but soon found this hope vain; at every step some fresh
incident revealed their numbers and their insolence. After having
been pricked in the arm by the dagger of a stranger, without other
provocation than the mere movement to pass him, I realized that I
was walking under the menace of death, and that I was a prisoner,
not, perhaps, in chains, but held far more securely by a thousand
unspoken threats lurking in every glance and gesture of my companions.

"We were now approaching the city, its spiked and embattled
walls already casting their shadows across our way.

"Before passing through the great gate I glanced toward the
field of mounds, and observed with foreboding that workmen were
busy upon the great mound of Chalma, which contained the tumuli
of the priests. I wondered if the spirit of revolt had infected the
officers of the city, for I knew that this mound was only opened for
the reception of the most exalted dignitaries. My companions had
by this time gathered about me in such a manner as to guard me
on all sides, and thus intercept any communication, either by look
or sign, which I might attempt to hold with others.

"Thus we reached the many-terraced slope at the base of which
stood the temple. Through the gloomy portals we swept, and then,
in utter silence and darkness, passing along its sinuous passages,
we emerged at last into the great hall of sacrifice, said to be in the
heart of the mountain. Here we prostrated ourselves, and in the
hush, broken only by the half-audible voices of the distant priests,
I ventured a stealthy glance about me.

"To the right, and far in front, sputtered and smoked the altar
of invocation, near which stood a grey-bearded old man, of whose

flesh and blood I was the sole surviving remnant. His voice alone must summon the God of the Caves. I hoped that by some miracle dumbness might fall upon his tongue, that it might fail to do its familiar office, and thus that the sacrifice might be for that day at least postponed. At no great distance yawned the cavernous way through which the monster god must come, and I strained my gaze to pierce the solid blackness, while my ears seemed splitting in the effort to hear the first soft beat of a muffled wing. To the left of this opening, in many loops and folds, hung the great scarlet curtain, behind which was solemnized the last mysterious rite, the translation of the favourite of Heaven, without pain or death, into the realms of everlasting felicity. Then the murmur of the priestly ritual suddenly ceased, and a clear, strong note from a shell trumpet pealed through the vast hall. In the train of its echo a thin voice rose:—

"'O God of the Caves, we await thee!'

"Like the pattering sound of many raindrops, or the rustle of a million leaves, swelling into the deep, full tone of some mighty cataract, rose the murmur of the multitude:—

"'O God of the Caves, we await thee!'

"Again that thin voice:—

"'Out of the profound darkness wert thou born, O Winged Flame of Heaven!'

"And again the soft thunder of the response:—

"'And thou comest to us as a light for ever.'

"At intervals, from some far-off chamber deep in the foundations, I could hear the distant beat of the drums with which the priests sought to persuade the reluctant deity, whose wont it was in time of displeasure to feign a deep slumber from which only the most vehement supplication might arouse him.

"At length out of the inky gulf there stole a faint phosphorescence, suffusing, very gradually, the satiny blackness with the hue of moonshine. Then a mighty, unearthly voice, as through a tunnel rolling, cried:—

"'Let none look up!'

"The glimmer grew into a flood of pale, tremulous radiance, which streamed forth into the hall, illuminating the intervening space and touching hundreds of forms in the prostrate multitude. Then a rhythmic, stealthy sound, like the very footfall of Silence, crept around me, and in the awe of Eternity I pressed my hands to my eyes.

"When at last I ventured one swift glance, I beheld, suspended from the lofty wall, above and beyond the Veil of the Transmutation, a huge, bird-like shape, with great, extended wings, which shed a shower of mild sparkles as if bejewelled with myriads of fireflies. There it hung, slowly swaying, pendulum-like, to and fro, so that the lustre of its presence came and went in great, deliberate throbs of light, while its green eyes scanned with indifferent glance the levelled ranks of its mute, motionless worshippers. Whoever came beneath the spell of those mesmeric eyes, for him earth was at an end, for he was the favourite of Heaven, the groves of singing birds, in the pleasant valleys which are under the world, beckoned him to bask for ever in the shade of their immortal verdure. Thither would he be borne through the dark and bewildering mazes of the subterranean ways by the benignant but awful God of the Caves. For many minutes this silent, terrific contemplation continued, until my very flesh seemed to be quivering and tense. I wondered where was the elector of the sacrifice, for I knew such matters were all prepared beforehand, and that the favour and preference of the hierarchy were sure credentials to the favour of Heaven. Suddenly that thin voice rasped through the stillness:—

"'O Seneschal of the Elect! has the blood of the youth of Dion turned to water that none dare claim thy approving glance?'

"A contagious sigh, like the stirring of some vagrant wind, rustled through the multitude. I felt my nerves relax, and with the return of ordinary perception I became aware of a slight struggle to my right, as though someone were being forcibly withheld. Then in hoarse, suppressed tones came the words:—

"'Die, then, accursed fool!'

"This was followed by a gurgling, smothered cry, and, raising my head, I saw a form half rise on its hands and pitch forward, while an arm was suddenly withdrawn; before the form fell I saw the haft of a dagger in its back. At the same moment a slight murmur swept through the hall, and now, to my left, a slender figure had arisen and stood swaying in unison with the motion of the great bird.

"I became so absorbed in this singular pantomime as to forget momentarily the horrible incident I had just witnessed. Not for some minutes did I recollect and realize its significance. Meantime the slender figure continued its rhythmical movements, until from the green eyes shot scintillating gleams like the atoms of a dissolving emerald. Then, as the figure began to walk slowly like one in a trance, I perceived that it was a maiden, and it needed not the low comment of those about me to tell me it was the daughter of Narbin. Moving among the prostrate people whom she saw not, and who, in profound awe, made way for her, her charmed eyes riveted on that supernal form which now had ceased to sway, she reached the open space and passed beneath the Veil of the Transmutation. Then, guided by unseen hands, the great scarlet curtain fluttered between. There was a heavy swooping sound, a shimmering palpitation of sparkles as of the incandescent dust of meteors, then a long, loud, shrill, heart-shattering cry—the God of the Caves had disappeared into the screened sanctuary!

"Not until that moment, when the men of Narbin were already on their feet and the vaulted dome seemed rocking with the acclamation of the multitude, did I comprehend the crafty manipulation by which, in the very presence of the pontiff, the daughter of Narbin had been substituted for the elector of the sacrifice, and the acceptance of the God of the Caves secured, as it were, with the sanction of the very priesthood it must annihilate, since their offering had not been deemed worthy. Once, in the days of Chalma, a youth, the pawn of some malcontent faction, had been wrested from behind the great curtain, and another, a priest of the reigning order, proffered and accepted in his stead. Might I not venture to re-enact this miracle of history? I saw the bewildered, uncertain movement of the priests, the consternation of my venerable kinsman. Already the black plume of Narbin was nodding near the altar of the invocation. I knew that the opportunity had come— nay, was passing—and rising with a new, fierce valour in my veins, I seized a spear, sprang forward, and rushed under the Veil. There I paused. The God of the Caves had descended, and now at my feet stretched one mighty wing, like a many-wrinkled gauze of gold, through whose translucent folds ran a complex network of red veins as in some gorgeous patterned fabric. The body, insignificantly small in comparison, lay huddled in the midst. By the rapid palpitation of its radiance and the eager, convulsive shuddering of its outline I knew that the daughter of Narbin was beneath. As I stood the creature raised its head, its beak dripping with the blood of a horrible repast and transfixed me with a long, steady gaze.

"Many moments must have passed thus. Then my blood, congealed at first with terror, resumed its natural flow and warmed in my veins till fear forsook me, and I would have approached nearer the magnetic loadstar of my being had I not shrunk from profaning with my foot the golden livery it seemed to wear.

"Suddenly a jeering voice broke in upon the spell:—

"'Thinks Torqua to become the beloved of the God? Not you, aspiring youth, but at some future day, perhaps. For the God of the Caves has looked upon you, and none may cheat him!''

"At the same instant I was violently withdrawn by a powerful hand, and found myself without the sanctuary. What carnage was here! Around me lay the mangled corpses of a hundred priests, seized, weaponless as they were, and butchered at their own altars. The aged pontiff had fallen where he stood, and his bleeding head—the starting eyeballs glazed with horror and the mouth fallen open, with the silly tongue protruding—had been thrust upon the brazen staff of his office and fixed to the altar of the invocation. The air still rang with the shouts of contending men and reeked with the odour of death; I knew that for the time anarchy was abroad in the city. Above me swung the copper axe of Narbin. I threw up my arms, for I possessed not even a dagger, and strove to flee. But 'twas a vain effort. Down hissed the cruel blade, ripping through my shoulder like the tusk of a mastodon, so that I stepped upon my own arm as I ran. Falling thus, I rolled under the stone chair of the pontiff, and ere the last blow fell, bringing the awful blackness of oblivion, I seemed again to gaze into two great green eyes, ringed with red circles and scintillating like portentous stars entangled in a palpitating cloud of moonlight."

As Sheldon finished this recital I found myself spellbound. His look, as of one who spoke from some inner prompting; the fervid flow of unaccustomed eloquence; the solemn mimicry of priestly incantation, and the swift expression of fear, reverence, and horror which impressed his features, were the words and actions of another age, through which I saw, as through a crevice in a wall, the violent political upheavals and barbarous pageantry of some prehistoric race.

As he finished, he half turned, looking behind him. And I, too, found my eyes involuntarily seek the ground as if to behold the severed arm of Torqua, with its quivering fingers clutching at the tainted air of those ancient shambles.

When at last Sheldon recalled me from my reverie his ordinary manner had returned; but his words then I have since pondered long and often:—

"We called it a dream, Hossman. Let us say, rather, it is a memory."

Not until the return of the others compelled my mind to move in other channels was I able to fully shake off the nightmare of antediluvian horror which the tale of Torqua's fate had provoked.

Hank, it seemed, had, at a point some two miles distant, unexpectedly come upon the trail which he had lost in the morning, leading through the bottom of a ravine into some rocky lair, into which, he believed, the panther had crept either to die or recuperate its energies. I was pleased to observe that Sheldon manifested a sportsmanlike interest in the narration. It was agreed by all that the courage and ingenuity he had displayed on the preceding night entitled him to the pelt, for those of our party best versed in woodcraft were convinced that the panther might be traced to its present hiding-place, and, if not already dead, easily dispatched.

Guided by Hank, we proceeded in company along the creek bottom, arriving without incident at the mouth of the ravine, where we easily picked up the trail. It was arranged to divide into three parties, Sheldon and I beating up the ravine, while the others skirted along the high ground at either side. By this means we thought that the panther might soon be started, while, if it endeavoured to quit the ravine it was certain to find a vigilant enemy on either hand.

A tiny fleck of crimson, visible from time to time upon some fragment of stone or fallen log, guided us for a considerable distance along the brink of a slender rivulet which had possessed itself of the bed of the ravine.

Near this point we began to climb among the bushes and rocks which concealed the course of the rivulet. A little way up the slope we found that the stream emerged abruptly from a slanting fissure in the face of the rock, and here a final bloodstain seemed to indicate the panther's last retreat.

We determined to explore the fissure, but before plunging into it Sheldon lighted the lantern he had brought in anticipation of just such a contingency.

Within, we found ourselves at once entangled in a mass of dead bushes which so choked the path that we were forced to wade in the shallow bed of the stream. The steep slant of the walls soon rendered an upright position impossible, and we were obliged at last to fall upon all fours.

Moving in this manner, we presently entered a sort of flume or sloping tunnel, so narrow that I began to fear we might become hopelessly wedged in. I was on the point of suggesting a retreat, when Sheldon, who was in front, with a laboured grunt and exclamation of relief suddenly moved freely forward. Following him with an effort, for I was by no means so active as he, I found myself able to stand, though still nearly knee-deep in icy water. When he had relighted his lantern, which for some time he had been carrying in his teeth, and which had been extinguished by the suddenness of his release from the granite prison, we found ourselves in a sort of grotto through which ran the stream we were following.

Though loath to oppose Sheldon, I yet shrank from prosecuting farther what now seemed to me a foolhardy quest: I remembered that night was at hand, that a heavy storm of rain was threatening, and that our companions were quite ignorant of our whereabouts. Another objection I was at the time ashamed to formulate: on the farther side of the grotto my eyes lit upon a tumbled heap of earth and rock accidentally fashioned into the shape of the head and open jaws of a toad, from which issued the stream like a greedy tongue ready to lick up a hapless insect. This excited in me a sensation of the most intense repugnance and fear.

Through the throat of this gigantic fossil-like structure we would be obliged to pass, and I felt it an omen of evil that Nature had provided the mysteries beyond with so forbidding a threshold.

Undeterred by such reflections, Sheldon had already preceded me, and I presently heard him calling from the inner cave.

Thither with reluctance I followed, and soon entered a large chamber, the silence of which was intensified rather than broken by the tinkle of a slender waterfall, a leap in the course of the stream which, after all, had an exterior source, and entered the cave in this manner from some point above.

Finding nothing here, we continued our search for some distance, until we came to a splintered and jagged parapet overlooking what appeared to be a vast gulf of impenetrable gloom, into which the original wall might at some remote period have fallen. Leaning over this, we discovered, by the aid of the lantern, a wide-spreading declivity thickly strewn with loose stones, but owing to our feeble light we were unable to guess to what depths it might reach. Sheldon wished to descend, but, yielding to my counsel, we determined upon a more careful inspection of the chamber in which we were, and in the course of this made a most singular discovery. Traced as if by a pencil of fire upon the grey surface of the rock was the blackened outline of a colossal bat, with wings widely extended as though clinging to the wall. After some scrutiny I fancied it bore an exaggerated resemblance to pictures and descriptions I had seen of an ancient monster, the pterodactyl. It was almost as though one of those creatures had reposed upon the spot.

To my conjecture Sheldon replied with many eager questions, though he forebore to allude to an idea which I now believe was in his mind as well as my own—namely, the resemblance of the tracing to the monster of his dream.

Although this Satanic portrait was probably nothing more than a fantastic accident, it seemed to hold our attention with so gruesome an interest that I quite lost count of time, until, suddenly, my ear was impressed by an unusual sound. The tinkling waterfall had changed its tone: the tiny rivulet was now a brawling stream. It needed little reflection to explain this. The storm without had at last broken, and now, from the heights above, a thousand rivulets were all streaming together into their wonted channel.

Filled with alarm, I hurried to the outer grotto, where I found what I dreaded. The tunnel through which we had squeezed our way had become the flume of a copious torrent, and all thought of egress in that direction was now out of the question: we would, without doubt, be prisoners for some hours!

This dilemma apparently rather pleased Sheldon than otherwise, though he professed much regret. His words however had a ring of insincerity about them, and were, or so I imagined applied rather to me than to himself. Almost immediately he returned to the contemplation of the outlines so strangely burned upon the wall, and his growing abstraction and the look of concentration in his eyes filled me with vague apprehension so that I felt an inexplicable sensation of relief when he suddenly broke silence.

"Well, Hossman, I like the poster; suppose we wait for the play?"

Knowing that we must have several hours before us, and not being over-fond of the mood which Sheldon's sinister raillery betokened, I was not loath to join him in a further exploration of the cavern.

Returning, therefore, to the parapet, we began to pick our way among the loose fragments of rock which covered the declivity. One of these, slipping from beneath my foot, after rolling for several seconds struck at the bottom with a bound and plunged with a hollow splash into some invisible water. Other pieces dislodged by its descent began to grind and slide threateningly, and, fearing a granite avalanche, we bore off in haste to the left, and soon reached a wide platform freer from débris, from which a short, steep slope reached to the edge of a dark pool.

So murky was the water that it received the ray of the lantern with scarce a glint, and, but for the plunging stones, we might have supposed ourselves on the brink of a bottomless volcanic shaft. This pool I afterwards discovered to be of great extent; but, although my feet circumscribed the whole circuit of its infernal shores, I am to this day unable to guess its exact size.

Before continuing our course I made a careful survey of our position trying to fix any prominent peculiarities well in mind. Moving a large stone into a conspicuous position, I leaned my gun against it for a landmark, it being apparent this maw of darkness might conceal some immeasurable labyrinth.

As usual Sheldon preceded me, bearing the lantern above his head. In this manner we proceeded for more than an hour. I began to think that the circuit of the lake must be nearly completed, and now scanned the reaches ahead in momentary expectation that the next cape in the irregular shore must bring into view some mark of our starting-place.

While thus engaged my eye was arrested by what seemed to be a reflection of the lantern from the surface of the lake at a considerable distance. After a little, observing this with greater intentness, I felt my limbs suddenly stiffen with weird fear—for these eccentric movements were not those of Sheldon's lantern. Who then, or what was it, moving off there through the thick gloom above the black water—here and there, to and fro—in quick lines and slowly-executed circles, like some erratic star bewildered in a universal night and wandering through pathless space? Then I noticed its pulsating glimmer as of a firefly, and the Horror that has no name clutched at my throat. Was the creature of Sheldon's dream cruising upon this inky sea? Was this the infernal bird of the caves that glutted its craw with the flesh and blood of human sacrifice? Were we in the presence of the winged reptile, fit accomplice of canting hypocrisy and priestly oppression, in whose name unknown millions had sunk degraded to the mud and expired in despair?

On slid the accursed thing through many moments of wavering and objectless flight, and when at length it neared the shore it was far behind us, so that I was unable to distinguish more than its luminous outline.

"Do you know whom it is seeking?" asked Sheldon.

Poor wretch! I had almost forgotten his existence. Now I realized in an instant what an evil moment had befallen us.

Turning, I grasped his arm. Even as I did so, his gun, slipping from his nerveless hand, splashed into the water. I reached after it, and thrust in my arm to the shoulder; then, clutching by the brink, lowered myself, feet foremost, and felt for the bottom. If only it had caught on some projection of the side!

How vain was my hope! In that black hole there was neither side nor bottom!

Fortunately, we still had the lantern. Seizing Sheldon, who now lagged limply behind, I pressed forward. If we but could find the other gun, this devilish divinity which had outlived the youth of the world and the evil age of its own sway might be shorn of its terror for all time.

That we were in the haunt of a living pterodactyl I was certain; and equally certain was it that the creature was able amid the darkness to light its own path. Then, I reflected, after all, Nature abounded with creatures similarly able to emit a luminous phosphorescence. Though this was not a known property of the pterodactyl, yet there was little very startling in the discovery, nor was it strange that this attribute, linked to its forbidding aspect, should have powerfully impressed the hearts and minds of primitive men.

Suddenly all trace of the phosphorescence vanished—hidden, no doubt, by some intervening spur. The creature had disappeared on the shore between us and the cave.

That cave! I shuddered with uncontrollable terror as the shadow seared upon its wall recurred to my imagination.

As my excitement gradually abated I felt more and more the encumbrance of Sheldon's fainting steps. I had half borne him, as it seemed, an interminable mile, and still there was no sign of the stony slope or the gun at its foot. The character of the shore, too, had changed; the comparatively smooth ledge which overlapped the lake had given way to great broken steps, over which we climbed with great labour, and I was now continually obliged to assist my companion, who seemed to lack all energy for any effort. Against my judgment, I was forced to admit that he needed repose, and while in this mind I came upon a deep sort of recess in the rock well suited to the purpose.

Entering this I obliged him to lie down, and, having extinguished the lantern, I placed myself at the portal. After some time Sheldon fell asleep, and I heard him muttering broken words and phrases of a strange tongue. Then I, too, overcome by weariness, nodded into that calm which resembles death in all but the awakening.

I am convinced that I had not slept for more than ten minutes at the outside when I started up. My first thought was of Sheldon.

He was not there! I felt for the lantern. It, too, was gone! About me the darkness lay dense as a velvet pall, and a terrible thought burned into my brain. In this fearsome place Sheldon had deserted me! Once, only, I called:—

"Sheldon!"

Though I stifled my very heartbeats to listen, no responsive sound came to my listening sense.

The situation was fraught with the most dreaded perplexities. Yet I must live—and to live I must go on.

Creeping upon my hands and knees along the edge of the rocks, I groped my way for endless minutes, rising many feet above the lake, until the bones of my knees cut through the flesh and my palms were raw from the rough stones.

Suddenly this miserable progress was stopped. A great rock rose before me, lying full to the verge. I stood up to lean against it, but immediately recoiled. At my pressure it had yielded!

Filled with a new dread, I began to creep around it, and had moved but a few yards when, with my right hand advanced like the hoof of an animal, my left suddenly slipped from beneath me. Clutching desperately at the edge, with a superhuman effort I brought myself back to an erect position. I had all but fallen over the brink. How was this? I had followed the brink on my right; here was another on my left!

A little reflection dispelled the mystery. The great table along which for the last hour I had hobbled and crept here ended in a slender point. What was beneath—the shore or the lake?

I lit a precious match and held it till the flame burned to the finger, peering intently downwards into the gloom.

I could discover nothing. The abyss into which I had all but fallen was bottomless! I felt well-nigh paralyzed with the peril of my position. My brain grew giddy; the whirling darkness was streaked with fire. I flattened myself upon the ground and shrank against the unstable rock. The poise of its enormous mass was disturbed. It lurched heavily, grinding on the edge, then tumbled headlong.

Seconds of awful suspense ensued. Then up from the depths came a far-off, hollow boom. Tremors shook the ground again and again. Then, what sickening sensation was this? The earth moved;

it slid, grinding and rasping, into the thundering depths; jarred, as though from the heaving shoulder of a struggling giant, I was hurled many yards into the water.

Dazed and astounded though I was, terror gave me strength and despair courage. I swam for my life, though the lake was rocked with great billows; but when I had reached the shore I feared to climb upon it. I believed that the abyss which separated the lake from the rocky table along which I had journeyed had closed. What effect would this settling of the foundations have upon the walls around? After long waiting through minutes devoid of incident I clambered up and sank in utter exhaustion upon the ledge.

Listening to the restless lapping of the still unquiet water, the torpor of fatigue enchained my senses, and, in a horrible waking dream, Torqua, with the epaulettes of a soldier, and Sheldon, with the cunning face of a priest, peered down upon me out of the hooded darkness, until at last they seemed to lean together above my body and blend in one. Then a thin voice cried:—

"Out of the darkness wert thou born, O Winged Flame of Heaven!"

Immediately many murmurs, that seemed to be rolling and reverberating through vast aisles, made answer:—

"And thou comest to us as a light for ever!"'

Again that horrible thin voice:—

"Is the blood of the youth of Dion turned to water—"

But—Hark! Another!

"Halloa!"

And again—this time louder:—

"Halloa!".

Surely that was not the voice of a dream, nor the cry of a wraith in the caves of the ghosts? I sat up and listened. A far-off sound, like the dull crack of a whip, came to my ears.

Sheldon! Surely that was Sheldon, and he had found the gun!

In a voice so shaken that the sound went wavering on like a succession of broken echoes, I gave an answering "Halloa!"

The silence was dumb.

"Sheldon!" I shrieked, mustering all my strength into one great cry.

Then came an answer, distant and indistinct—but it was no echo.

Forgetful of the darkness, of the abyss, of the insidious monster whose reptile presence had chilled and tainted the air about me, I hurried forward, careless alike of path or obstacle. Suddenly, turning an angle of the shore, I stopped in astonishment. Scarce a hundred yards away, dazzling the air with brandished lanterns were two figures. As I paused, they shouted.

I could hardly believe my eyes. Neither of the figures was that of Sheldon. Instead, Cummings and Hank stood before me. Me they had not discovered in the darkness, and I saw that they both faced in another direction. Shouting out as I advanced, I hurried forward.

Cummings and Hank barely turned to recognise me. Then the former, in a voice hoarse with excitement. exclaimed:—

"In Heaven's name, Hossman, what is that?"

Moving from beneath a projection, of which in the gloom I had been unaware, I gazed upward. At about two hundred yards distance, to the left poised in space and sowing the air with rills of pale radiance, hung the pterodactyl; it was so near that the low humming of the wings was quite audible. In such wise did it maintain itself that it seemed scarce to move, being intent upon some object beneath which was beyond our vision.

Hanging thus in mid-air, the mighty sweep of its lambent wings, over the edge of which protruded its gleaming claws—the cruel set of its crocodile mouth tense with the strain of a devilish concentration—the ominous poise of its enormous head, and the curve of its snake-like neck—all were such as might well inspire terror in mere mortals.

As I stared with fascinated gaze I presently became conscious that it was very gradually moving towards us as though pulling on some invisible cord.

Then, O horror! above the rocky shoulder of a cape we had passed some hours before now made visible by this infernal light, appeared the face of a man!

"Sheldon!" gasped Cummings.

Climbing, with uplifted eyes, Sheldon, for it was indeed he, mounted to the crest. Then extending his arms as if in supplication, we distinctly heard the invocation of the priests of Dion—

"O God of the Caves, we await thee!'"

"What is he saying?" muttered Hank.

The pterodactyl, with a sudden movement drew back in such a manner as to fully expose its body and blunt tail, spotted and ringed with phosphorescent dots as though clad in a cuticle of fire.

"It's going to drop. *Shel*—don! *Shel*—don!! *Shel*—don!!!" shrieked Cummings.

At his shoulder Cummings held a gun, and almost with the cry came the report. But the bullet sped far below its mark, and found another for which it was never intended. I saw Sheldon start—half turn, sway where he stood, then—pitch forward into the lake. At the same instant, like a meteor, down darted the pterodactyl, clapping the water with its wings. Then rising, with a discordant screech of fury, it spun round and round in a rage of disappointment, until, perceiving us, it suddenly turned full on us, its green eyes aflame with vengeance, snapping its ponderous jaws with incredible speed the while, and hissing like an enraged goose as it sped towards us.

"It's the Vulture of Hell!" screamed Cummings, throwing aside his gun. Bounding up the stony slope with the agility of a hare, he disappeared.

Through all this I had stood without the power of motion, beads of agonized sweat bursting from my very brain it seemed.

Now, with no time for retreat, I dropped to the ground and concealed myself beside the very rock against which some hours before I had leant the gun which had just dealt death to poor, infatuated Sheldon. Here, unnoticed, I lay as the monster passed me in its pursuit of Cummings. In a short time it returned and began circling about above the spot where Sheldon's body had disappeared. As it passed over me a second time there dropped upon my hand a fleck of red froth, which I hastily wiped away. It must have contained a virulent poison, for from that momentary contact it has continued to affect me to this day.

To attempt to recover Sheldon's body was clearly as dangerous as it was futile. Therefore, with a low call summoning Hank from his place of concealment, we made our way by stealth up the slope, through the cave where was the portrait, and so out through the toad's mouth to the grotto.

Here Hank and I found Cummings lying unconscious. Between us we dragged and bore him through the flume, now comparatively clear of water, to the outer air; and there, with some difficulty, we revived him. But there was madness in his eyes, and I hailed the return of insensibility, when it speedily came, with a sigh of relief.

A little later, pausing to rest by a pool, I was startled to find that my hair was absolutely white.

That night Cummings raved incessantly, and we were obliged to guard him by turns. The next day, through a drizzling rain, we tramped to Brownhills and took train for our homes.

It was many weeks before health of either mind or body was securely mine again. Often, in the stillness of night, I would leap from my bed with cries of terror, living over again in dreams the awful experience which had brought to Sheldon death, to Cummings madness, to myself blanched locks.

Two years later Dr. Cummings died in a sanatorium. His attendant told me that at the last moment he fancied himself still fleeing from a great, winged monster of fire, which in his ravings he called the Vulture of Hell.

It has been conjectured that some creatures of the reptile world may hibernate for ages. If so, perchance in some dark, silent abyss the pterodactyl sleeps still.

Of that remarkable infatuation which Sheldon had termed a memory little may be said. As for the weird fatality of his career, which has made the dream of one life and the climax of another so closely coincide, it has never ceased to excite the marvel of my mind. Fancy has wrought in me his epitaph, and much musing has made the thought less strange:—

TORQUA. PRIEST OF DION.
TWICE TO HUMAN KNOWLEDGE,
HE ESCAPED A TERRIBLE IMMOLATION.
REST TO HIS SOUL,
THOUGH SUCH REPRIEVES BE TRANSITORY,
FOR WHAT DESTINY HAS ORDAINED
SURELY FATE WILL FULFIL.

The Monster of "Partridge Creek"
Georges Dupuy

[M. Georges Dupuy, the well-known French writer and
traveller, who has made many explorations in the Polar regions, here relates a most extraordinary experience which
befell him in the frozen steppes of Alaska. M. Dupuy, whose
good faith is beyond question, takes full responsibility for
his narrative, which is, it may be noted, however remarkable, in no way contradicted by known scientific facts. The
drawings which accompany this article have been made
from sketches and descriptions supplied by M. Dupuy.]

The story which follows is in no sense a romance. I wish, in the
first place, to ask the readers of the following narrative to believe
that I am in no way attempting to impose upon their credulity.
Concerning the amazing spectacle I am about to describe, I report
nothing but plain facts, however astounding and apparently incredible they may seem at first glance, precisely as they appeared to
my own eyes—and I am possessed of excellent sight—and to those
of my three companions—all three white men—without counting
five Indians of the Klayakuk tribe, who have their camps on the
shores of the River Stewart.

The following are the names of the three ocular witnesses who
are ready to testify to the truth of my assertions: the first is my hunting companion for many years, Mr. James Lewis Buttler, banker,
of San Francisco; the second is Mr. Tom Leemore, miner, from
McQuesten River, in the Yukon Territory; and lastly, the Reverend
Father Pierre Lavagneux, a Canadian Frenchman and missionary

at the Indian village of Armstrong Creek, not far from McQuesten. In the course of ten years' rambling in the four quarters of the world it has been my lot to witness a great number of amazing spectacles, and the strange experience of which I speak had become no more than a vivid recollection when, a few days ago—on January 24th, 1908—the following letter reached me at Paris. It came from Father Lavagneux, who passes his life with his savage flock six hundred miles northwest of the Klondike. I give it here word for word:—

"Armstrong Creek,
"January 1st, 1908.
"My Dear Son,—The 'trader' of McQuesten has just stopped here with his train of dogs and sledges. He has had a hard journey from Dawson, by Barlow, Flat Creek, and Dominion. I expect to receive by him in another fortnight fresh provisions and news of the outside world. To-day is the first day of the New Year, and I want this letter to express my affectionate wishes for your health and happiness. I hope it will give me the pleasure of receiving you under my humble roof, here, at the other end of the earth. I will not believe that you will let your old friend in the Great North leave his old carcass to the Indians (who will some day or other make his coffin out of branches) without seeing him once more.

"I have received your book, the reading of which has given me the greatest pleasure. By the way, you are wrong in regard to that poor fellow, John Spitz. Alas! he is no longer mail carrier of the Duncan district. He died, poor fellow, at Eagle Camp, soon after you departed, not having survived the wound he received from the 'bald-face,'* which you will remember.

"Talking of ferocious animals, will you believe me when I tell you that ten of my Indians and myself saw again, on Christmas Eve, that horrible beast of Partridge Creek passing

* The bald or cinnamon bear—the brown bear of the Arctic regions.

like a whirlwind over the frozen surface of the river, breaking off with his hind feet enormous blocks of ice from the
rough surface? His fur was covered with hoar-frost, and his
little eyes gleamed like fire in the twilight. The beast held
in his jaws something which seemed to me to be a caribou.
It was moving at the rate of more than ten miles an hour.
The temperature that day was forty-five degrees below zero.
At the corner of the 'cut-off' it disappeared. It is undoubtedly the same animal that we saw before. Accompanied by
Chief Stineshane and two of his sons I followed the traces,
which were exactly like those which we all saw—Leemore,
Buttler, you, and I—in the mud of the 'moose-lick.' Six
times, on the snow, we were able to measure the impression of its enormous body, the same size as we found it before, almost to the twentieth of an inch. We followed them

to Stewart, fully two miles, when the snow began to fall slightly and blotted out the traces."

It was on receipt of this letter that I decided to write the story of my own experience, which it recalled so vividly to mind, and of which it afforded a striking confirmation.

The Story of My Friend Buttler.

The station of McQuesten, that far-off corner of the strange country of the Yukon, where the eight months of winter are so terrible but the short summer so marvellously beautiful, was on four occasions my chosen retreat during the eight years that I have known the North. A friend of mine in San Francisco, Mr. Buttler, who had come to Dawson City in order to purchase gold-mining concessions, had promised to join me in order that we should go hunting together. I was taking my coffee one afternoon in the veranda of Father Lavagneux's cabin when all at once I heard someone whistle from the farther bank of the river. A bark canoe, paddled by two Indians, was coming up the river in the shadow of the trees. Buttler was with them.

"My dear fellow," he said, smiling as I met him, and endeavouring to hide his visible agitation, "I have something very strange to tell you. Do you know that prehistoric monsters still exist?"

I broke out laughing, and together we returned by the little path which led to the Father's house. When Buttler had taken off his muddy boots and was ensconced in a comfortable seat he began to recount his story as follows:—

"Leaving Gravel Lake, where I arrived on Tuesday evening, my last stage was the mouth of Clear Creek, where I knew that you would send someone to meet me. Travelling was frightfully bad— forty miles of marshy country. At last, at nightfall, I descended a hill, and had the pleasure of seeing Grant's cabin, which was lighted up. Grant was at home, and a good supper was waiting for me. Early the next morning (yesterday) he came to tell me, in his reserved and silent manner, that three fine moose were feeding quietly behind the plateau of Partridge Creek. After swallowing a hasty mouthful all four of us—Grant, your two men, and I—started out from the hut. We made a wide *détour*. At the top of a hill, where we had hidden ourselves, all of us stretched full length on the ground, we perceived, a short distance off in the valley, near a 'moose-lick,'* three enormous moose moving slowly forward and quietly browsing on the moss and lichens. All at once they gave three simultaneous bounds, and, one of the males giving vent to the striking bellow which these animals utter only when they are hunted or mortally wounded, the three went off at a mad gallop towards the south.

"What had happened?

"We decided to approach the spot where the animals had taken fright so suddenly. Arriving at the 'moose-lick,' a spot about sixty feet long and fifteen wide, we saw in he mud, and almost on a level with the water of the 'lick,' the fresh imprint of the body of a monstrous animal. Its belly had an impression in the slime more than two feet deep, thirty feet long, and twelve feet wide. Four gigantic paws, also deeply impressed, had left at each end of the main imprint, and a little to the side, footprints five feet long by two and a half feet wide, the claws being more than a foot long, the sharp points of which had buried themselves deeply in the mud. There was also the print, apparently, of a heavy tail, ten feet long and sixteen inches wide at the point.

"We followed the tracks of the monster in the valley for five or six miles, and then, at the ravine of Partridge Creek—a place which the miners call a gulch—they ceased suddenly as if by enchantment."

How the Monster Appeared to Us.

The next day, at five o'clock in the morning, Father Lavagneux, Buttler, Leemore, a neighbouring miner hastily summoned, myself, and five men of the tribe, crossed the River Stewart in two canoes. Neither of the first two guides, who were overcome with terror, nor the sergeant of the Mounted Police, who received our

* A sulphur spring, rarely freezing in the winter, where animals come to drink at all seasons.

story with scepticism, nor the letter-carrier, would consent to accompany us.

All day long we searched, without result, the valley of the little River McQuesten, the flats of Partridge Creek, and the country between Barlow and the lofty, snow-covered mountains.

At last, towards evening, tired out, after having toiled for a long time through the great marsh, we lighted a fire at the top of a rocky ravine. The sun was setting. Lying by the fire we let our eyes wander over the glittering expanse of marsh which we had just traversed.

The tea was boiling and everyone was preparing to dip his tin cup into the pot, when suddenly a noise of rolling stones and a strange, harsh, and frightful roar made us all spring to our feet.

The beast for which we had been looking—a black, gigantic form, the corners of his mouth filled with blood-stained slime, his jaws munching something, I know not what—was slowly and heavily climbing the opposite side of the ravine, making the large boulders roll into the valley as he went!

Struck with terror, Father Lavagneux, Leemore, and myself tried to utter a cry of fright, but no sound issued from our parched throats. Unconsciously we had seized each other's arms. The five Indians were crouching down with their faces against the ground, trembling like leaves shaken by the wind. Buttler was already rushing down the hill.

"The dinosaurus!—it is the dinosaurus of the Arctic Circle!" muttered Father Lavagneux, with chattering teeth.

The monster had stopped scarcely twenty paces from us, and, resting upon his huge belly, was staring, motionless, at the red sun, which was bathing all the landscape in a weird light.

For a full ten minutes, riveted to the spot by some strange force which we could not overcome, did we contemplate this terrible apparition.

We were, however, in full possession of all our senses. There was not, and never will be, in our minds the least doubt as to the reality of what we saw. It was indeed a living creature, and not an illusion, which we had before us.

The dinosaurus then turned his immense neck, but did not seem to see us. His withers were at least eighteen feet above the ground.

His entire body from the extremity of his yawning jaws—which were surmounted by a horn like that of a rhinoceros—to the end of the tail must have measured at least fifty feet. His hide was like that of a wild boar, garnished with thick bristles, in colour a greyish-black. His belly was plastered with thick mud.

At this moment Buttler returned to us. He told us that he thought the animal weighed about thirty tons.

Suddenly the dinosaurus moved his jaws, visibly chewing some thick viscid kind of food, and we heard a sound like that of the crunching of small bones. Then, with a sudden movement, he raised himself on his hind legs, and giving utterance to a roar—a hollow, indescribable, frightful sound—and wheeling round with surprising agility, with movements resembling those of a kangaroo, he sprang with a prodigious bound into the ravine.

On the 24th, Buttler and myself, having taken two days' rest, started for Dawson City, for the purpose of demanding from the Governor fifty armed men and mules.

Here my story ends. For a month we were the laughingstock of the Golden City, and the *Dawson Daily Nugget* published an article about me, which was at the same time flattering and satirical, entitled "A Rival of Poe."

The Diplodocus
Porter Emerson Brown

He looked up from his paper.

"This Burbank guy," he said, "is sure a wonder, ain't he?"

I nodded.

"I suppose before long he'll be grafting corn onto beans and getting succotash," he continued speculatively. "And then he'll fix his apple trees so's they'll bear pertaters, thereby saving all the trouble of digging 'em.

"I shouldn't be at all surprised," I assented. "The wonders that science each day unfolds are almost unbelievable."

He nodded profoundly at my very trite remark.

"Yes," he agreed. "And that same science is folding up a few wonders, too, that we don't never hear nothing about. Take my friend Vertigo Smith, for instance."

"Who was he?" I queried interestedly.

"You never heard of him?" responded my vis-a-vis; as one who asks a question, knowing beforehand the answer.

"No," I replied.

"And you ain't lonesome," he observed. "Lots o' people never heard of him; and never will. But in his way, he has this Burbank party skinned a league. I'll tell yer about him if yer got time," he volunteered.

I had the time, plenty of it: and I so said. Whereat, taking a long draught from the glass at his elbow, and wiping his trailing mustache on the back of his hand, he began:

"Back in ninety-nine I was prospecting around through Californy, looking for gold but finding nothing but sore feet and a thirst. Fate was sure handing me out a deal from the bottom of the deck, and I was reduced at length to one burrer, loaded with a shovel and the habliments I was standing in. I retained said shovel and raiments only because I couldn't sell 'em and said burrer only because I couldn't give him away.

"Well, one afternoon I'm tramping along with despair in my heart and even less in my stomach, wondering weakly whether there's enough meat on the burrer to pay for mending the teeth I'm liable to break picking it off, when suddenly I comes to a turn in the trail and there before me spreads a vegetationous valley full of the most fullsome verdure that ever you see.

"In the middle of this valley three stands a 'dobe mansion and all around it the most amazing collection of sheds and shacks that ever you laid your lamps on. There were some high ones and some low ones and some long ones and some short ones. And what with the house, they all looks like a big Buff Cochin hen surrounded by a bunch of the most ill-assorted chickens that ever was.

"However, I ain't hypercritical, 'Where ther's life, there's beans,' says I to myself. And if a party desire to efface the beauteous visage of Nature by sticking around on it a lot of five and ten-cent stone edifices, it ain't none of my funeral as long as I can get a hand-out myself. 'Git up, there, Gehenna,' says I to the burrer; and we prepare to teeter down into the aforesaid verdant valley.

"Halfway down the hill there's another bend in the trail. And as we comes around this I stops short while the burrer does even better—for he turns a back somersault; and then sets there on the shovel too frightened to bat an eye.

"The one glimpse I has is plenty sufficient. I stands back to trying to make my convolutions convolute.

"Before me, meandering saloobriously across the plain, is the worst looking collection of fauna that ever made merry to an inebriate's Home. It was sure a psychopathic ward assemblage, and then some. Four-footed things with wings, and two-footed ones without, and birds with hair on 'em and fishes with laigs—great suffering Jemima! It was sure enough to make a party pin blue ribbons on himself until he couldn't see out, and take up his residence permanent in the cellar of the headquarters of the W. C. T. U.

"With my eyes bugged out so's you could 'a' knocked 'em off with a stick, I watched the procession out of sight and then turned to the burrer. He was setting there with a faraway look in his eyes talking to himself.

"'Come on, Gehenna,' says I, nudging him gently with my short spikes. 'Le's get a move on ourselves toward yon villa and put an end to this debauch of starvation that we've been on; for if we're seeing things like that to-day, to-morrow will behold us making suicide pacts and picking mud turtles out of each other's hair."

"Poor Gehenna has all he can do to get up on his pins and we're a very shaky pair as we wend our way onward to the Edison concrete villa which looked as though it had been made in an ice cream mold and pourd out before it had time to set properly.

"As we nears the colony of juvenile houses that I have before aloodod to, I sees that they're all coops and cages of different kinds. Some of 'em has barred winders, some of 'em hasn't. Some of 'ems empty. Some of 'ems full. But I keeps my eyes resolutely to the fore; for I ain't takin' no chances. When a party has set on the edge of his bed for weeks at a time, throwing his boots at a blue jellyfish with pink wings and a plug hat, he learns that curiosity is a curse and he don't pay no attention to no zoological exotic until it trips him up. But the burrer being denied the valyooble data that is mine immediately begins to rubber like an up Stater in a sightseeing truck with the result that he becomes so obsessed with terrifying fears that his legs won't work, and I has to carry him the rest of the way. And as we comes around the career, we sees setting before the door, an old man teaching a large hornpout to set upon its hind laigs and beg.

"After focusing my already bugged eyes on this new spectacle, I begins to wonder if Gehenna himself is trooly reel. So I kicks him; and when he kick's me back and I find it hurts, I am delighted beyond words.

"So I smiles on the old party with deep sympathy and fellerfeeling.

"That's right," I says encouragingly. "Humor yerself. When you get 'em as bad as that, it ain't a particle of use to try to kill 'em. So just set down and have a good time with 'em and byme-bye they'll go away."

"'What's the matter with you?' asks the old man, sort o' peevish like.

"'I don't know,' I says to the old party, 'whether it's stomachache or backache that's ailing me. All I can tell yer is that I ain't tasted food for so long that I've forgot even the smell of onions.'

"'Lie down, Lucy,' says the old man to the hornpout; and the last named settles down comfortably with its head between its fore paws, the old party climbs up onto his feet. 'Come on in the house,' he says, 'and I'll see if I can get a snack for yer.'

"Taking Gehenna under my arm for company, I follers him into the house.

"The old man watches me thoughtfully as I loads into my shrunken frame four dollars' worth of pork and beans and biscuits.

"'I hopes my pets ain't frightened you,' he says, at length, apologetically, combing his whiskers with his fingers.

"'Oh, not at all,' I rejoins, p'litely. 'I've had 'em myself, several times. They're unpleasant, but not necessarily dangerous. And if you'll swear off gradually, say cutting down half a pint a day at first, and then slowly increasing the strigency, it's surprising how quick you'll get rid of 'em.'

"He brushes my well-meant suggestions aside with an impatient wave of the hand and, stooping over, takes from the floor a long, bloo snake with green wings and three sets of laigs.

"'Do you see this?' he says.

"'Yes,' I replies. 'And I may as well confess it's the first time I ever knowed delirium trimmings was contagious!'

"'Feel of it,' he says. 'It won't hurt you.'

"I grins.

"'I know it," I says, 'and good reason why, hain't there. I wore out three pairs of shoes and put my shoulder out of joint on two separate occasions finding out that simple fact.'

"'Try,' he says, shoving the snake at me.

"'Why sure,' I says, 'If it'll please yer any.'

"I put my hand out confidently expecting it to go right through the snake and flat on the table. But it don't. And I gives a yell that sends Gehenna scuttling under the stove and falls plumb over backward in my chair.

"'Easy,' says the old party. 'They ain't no danger.'

"'Ain't, eh!' I says, a trifle peevishly, I fear, 'I know that well enough. But it's the strain on your credulousness that I objects to,' and I goes back three steps to get a flying start.

"'Well, set down and have a piece of prune pie,' he says.

"Jest at this juncshure, for a piece o' pie, prune or otherwise, I'd have set down in the middle of a school of gryphons and gargoyles and been glad or the chance. So I done it. And the old party, after slicing me out a wedge of the succulent provender aforesaid, sets down opposite me again.

"'I,' he says at length, impressively, puttin' down the snake and taking out of his vest pocket a creature that looked like a smallpox microbe magnified one million times, 'am Vertigo Smith.'

"'I don't wonder,' I says. 'Was the name bestowed or acquired?"

"'It was given me by my payrents,' he rejoins, 'who was well-intentioned parties, but sadly illiterate. They seen it in a almanac and, thinkin' it sounded good, they gives it to me.'

"He continues:

"'I,' he says, 'am a second Burbank. Or rather, I should say, Burbank is a second me. For he deals with senseless and inanimate things like flowers and trees and froot and cord wood and such futile and contemptible inyootilities, while I devote my tireless energiees and unlimitless genius to the animile kingdom. Them,' and he waves his hand blithely at the snake and the smallpox germ, 'are some of my eggsperiments. This,' he goes on, patting the microbe gently, 'is the result of mixing the life blood of the scorpion with that or the cock-roach, and again crossing the combination with the tarantula. I eggspect to time to be able to instill into this lovely little creature the instincts and flesh of the sloothhound, and finally of my cultivated rhinoceros, passing on my way through the lion, the tiger, the leopard, the grizzly bear, the rattlesnake, the Gila monster, and the panther.'

"'That'll make a fine pet when you get it finished, won't it?' I queries. 'It'll be a nice thing to replace lapdogs with.'

"He ignores my untimely facetiousness.

"'It will add greatly to zoology," he asserts.

"'And subtract greatly from anthropology,' I suggests.

"'And it'll make a fine watch dog,' he says.

"'You're right,' I agrees. 'The burglar will immediately begin to bump the dodo for first place, and that's no lie.'

"'Among my other interesting eggsperiments,' he goes on, 'was crossing a cat with a mouse. But this wasn't entirely successful, being as when the resultant animile grew old enough to find out what it was, it chased itself to death.

"'I have also,' he goes on, intermingled the blood of a horse and the ostrich, thereby securing a maximum speed with minimum of weight; and I found that the feathers you could get off a horse would pay for his keep; whereby I got Edison's newly discovered storage battery which has been coming out sence I was a boy, beaten eighty ways for Christmas.

"'Also by weaving my way around through the species of Gorden setter, cow, and giraffe, I have obtained a animile meek, intelligent, that gives milk, that will do simple little errands like fetching you yer gloves and shutting the door, and that as well can be used to double advantage in the cherry picking season.'

"'If you could get a hen and a egg beater in that combination somewhere,' I ventured helpfully, for I am getting a heap imbued with his ideas by this time, 'and hang a bottle of good Four X around its neck, all you'd have to do would be to whistle and it would bring you a neggnog any time you was thirsty!"

"He ignores me. 'At present,' he says, 'I am much interested in parasites. A parasite is a zoological antidote. Cats is parasites for mice, dogs is parasites for cats.'

"'I see!' I eggsclaims. 'Jest like drunkards is parasites for whiskey, and panic is parasite for money.'

"'That's the idea,' he approves, 'except that you must stick to the fauna. Now,' he goes on, 'take mosquitoes for eggsample. You live, say, in Noo Jersey, or Pelham Manor, or some other badly infested State. Every time you go out on the plazza after four o'clock, you're kep' so busy slapping your laigs and neck that you can't converse in anything eggcept profanity. Now just imagine what a wonderful, priceless relief it would be if you could have, say, half a dozen mosquito parasites to set around on the back of your chair, or along the welts of your shoes, and nail the mosquitoes as fast as they come! And then, when bedtime had arrived, they'd set on your piller beside your head and pop every dad-blamed stygomia that tried to tap a blood vessel"

"'Fine!' I agreed. 'Immense?'

"'I think so,' he acquiesced, complacently. 'We can afford to sell 'em for a quarter apiece. They'll be self-supporting in summer and will hibernate all winter among your summer clo'es, keepin' the moths out of 'em and living on a small quantity of camphor.'

"'It sounds fine,' I says. 'It sure does!'

"'It is fine,' he says. 'But there's more money in big things. And the biggest thing of all is the diplodocus.'

"'The what?' says I.

"'The diplodocus,' he says. 'It's a reptile,' he says, 'or a mammal or a fish, or a bird, or something like that. I don't know what it is. But I'm going to find out or bust a suspender trying. Andrew Carnegie bought the skeleton of one the other day for twenty thousand or fifty thousand dollars, 'r something like that. And if the skeleton is worth that much the finished product ought to be worth a million. So,' he announced, impressively, 'I'm going to raise a herd of 'em for the home and eggsport trade. I figure that when I get 'em to multiplying right, I'll have an income of twenty or thirty millions per annually. I'll work slow and secret at first, selling stuffed ones to the natural hist'ry mooseums. Then I'll branch out, taking zoological gardens and circus menageries. And after they all get supplied I can sell 'em for domestic animals. They'd be fine for moving houses or towing canal boats.'

"Well, to stretch a short story, the old gent took a great fancy to me; and I did to him. So when he offered me a job helping him with the specimens, I took it and settled down with him in the poured-out villa.

"And though I was nervous at first it wasn't long before I got use' to it and didn't mind it no more'n if I'd always lived in a psychopathic ward. And Gehenna he used to have good times, too, playing with horsetriches and the kangaroosters.

"There was a lot of animiles there that I hadn't seen. He kep' 'em in an immense corral around the corner of the mountain. There was some elephants he was makin' over into mastodone and mammoths

and behemoths and things, and a two' laigged rhinoceros that was
as big as from here to yonder and back.

"We used some of the fancy stock to start our diplodocus with.
We had one biped that was worked up through a penguin to a
hippotamos that was a peach. And another creation that was composed of kangaroos, whales and emus. And soon, by arduous, un-
remitting. effort we began to get results, and after several years
there came one day something that looked a whole lot liked the
desired fauna.

"When it got big enough to balance itself with having its head
and tail resting on the ground, we stood around one day looking at
it.

"'There's something wrong,' remarked old Smith, loogoo-
briously. 'It looks more like a cuspido than a diplodocus. What's
ailin', dyer 'spose?'

"'You can search me, I says. 'It looks as though it had lost its
last friend, and that friend owin' it money. I don't believe it's got
enough initiative to bite if you was to click your finger in its mouth
and make faces at it.'

"Old Smith brought his hand down on his knee so hard he liked
to split the cap.

"'You've hit it,' he eggsclaimed. 'It's too mushy and meek and
lowly and humble looking. All them things we bred it through were
soft and lumpy animiles like cows and hippotamuses and things.
It wants a little bit o' fervor injected into it—some stamina and
gumption, by heck. We should have mixed in the rhinoceros and
the rogue elephant. That would straighten it up and stiffen it out
and make it a diplodocus and a diplodocus right.'

"'That's so,' I agrees. 'We'll insert the requisite blood and sperit.
This present disappointing specimen, though, will help to increase
the stature.'

"Well, that was what we done. We got the old rogue elephant
that was that cantankerous that he had to be handled with a der-
rick and dynamite, and the rhinoceros who was a natural born
misanthrope and a fighter from the word go, and 'way behind that,
and proceeded to go back along the family tree of our diplodocus
and grafted them on at what we deemed suitable intervals.

"You can imagine we were some eggcited as we waited. Our first diplodocus wasn't no slouch. We'd had to build a special barn for it that was as big as the main tent of a three-ringed circus; it would take you ten minutes to walk around it and the longest ladder in the place wasn't long enough to reach to its ridgepole. So you can imagine that our second was going to be some pumpkins. Old Smith had it all framed up that he wouldn't let him go for a cent under half a million; and then only after he had a large family of descendants strewed over the valley.

"Well, he was right. That second diplodocus equated, and even eggsceeded our fondest hopes. He was so big that his skeleton would make the one Carnegie bought look like an X-ray photograph of a dress form. It sure towered above its maternal ancester like the Singer building above the subway.

"To say that Vertigo and me was delighted is expressing it feebly. We was in transports of joy. Ecstatic happiness oozed out of us at every pore, and between, and all that morning, we just took hold of hands and danced around our new diplodocus. It was like playing Ring-Around-a-Rosy in a department store.

"Day by day we watched our creation grow and expand, bush physically and mentally. Them big animiles, as a rule, are slow in machuring. But this one was right up to the speed limit. In less'n a week he could stand alone. He was weaned at three months. And after that it kep' me and Vertigo busy fourteen hours a day rustling enough provender to keep them two diplodocuses from starving to death.

"Le' me tell yer, it was some kind of a parious job, was feeding them exotics. They had some dog is them somewhere, and from that the new one had a habit of wagging his tail; the old one was too puny. And Rover (we'd named the new one that) smashed the end of the house off one afternoon, in showing his gratitude for a couple of bales of hay we'd give him. Another day he knocked down three of them giant redwoods and an orange tree. We found some of the oranges four miles down the valley.

"Well, everything went along all right for about sis months. Me and Vertigo was as happy as kittens under a stove and Rover was thriving to beat three of a kind. Not a cloud was upon our horizons.

We dwelt to the soft sunshine of sweet content and wouldn't have swapped place's with the Czar of all the Rooshias and some of the Rooshions.

"That's always the way, I've noticed. It's always serene just before something's doo to be handed to you in the place where it will hurt the worst. Whenever things is going along on castors and your liking yourself particularly well, and feeling particularly good, and beginning to believe that the Golden Rule might possibly not be a fake after all, you're doo for a bump.

"We got ours. It come in the night. It usually does.

"I had just rolled over on the other side and was getting nicely started on the second lap of the Morpheus handicap, when I heard a noise that sounded like the end of the world.

"I come out of it, and fetched Vertigo a kick.

"'You're on your back,' I hollered in his ear.

"But then the noise come again; and I knowed I was wrong. And additional proof came in another minute; for the house was yanked right off from over me and I was gazing up into the starry heavens and wondering what had happened.

"And then it burst forth in all its fury. The air was filled with wild, discordant yowls. The redwood trees was falling like grain before the patent reaper; and our D. T. menagerie could be heard in a little concerted specialty that sounded, however, feeble and unimpressive to comparison to the main noise.

"It came to me in a flash. It was Rover! We had injected too much elephant and rhinoceros! Our impetuousness had made us incautious. Alas! How true it is that careless work carries its own penalties.

"I lay there in the Californy midnight, and my union suit thinking over these things when, all of a sudden, the diplodocus, who had just finished setting the middle distance with our coop of jackassowaries, got his lumps on me.

"Giving a wild shake of his head, and emitting a horrid snort, he threw the last jackassowary straight up at Cassyopeer's chair and charged at me.

"It took me less than a fraction of a split second to leave the woven wire. Vertigo was already standing in the middle of what once had been the room, combing his whiskers with a shoe and staring helplessly about.

"'The horsetriches!' I yelled at him, as I flew past.

"A word in the wise, you know; and he was wise, all right, and getting wiser every minute.

"The barnyard was a sight. Rover had done a clean job. There was just one horsetrich left out of all the strange creations of Vertigo's great genius. Even the diplodocus' old lady was a contribution to the festival.

"I grabbed the horsetrich by one wing and Vertigo he grabbed the other. We swung ourselves on his back, me in front, and stuck our heels into its sides. It responded nobly to our encouragement and slid off down the valley at rate of speed that would have had the Empire State Express looking like a traction engine.

"But did we lose the diplodocus? Never on your immortal life! He hadn't missed our steed's tail feathers by a foot when we started forth from the barn yard. As we passed what had once been our happy home, he was spreading himself for further orders, emitting the most blood-chilling yelps every leap; and every third jump his kangaroo blood would assert itself and he'd slam his tail down on the ground and give himself a push, and hurtle through the air for a good ninety foot.

"The memory of that ride is with me yet, particularly after a bedtime snack of pigs' feet and ice cream, or mince pie and Welch rarebit. Often in the still watches, I awakes the house with weird yells and the frightened boarders come running to my room to find me astride the radiator, urging it on to frantic endeavor, while the cold sweat runs down my pallid, somnambulistic visage in streams, by heck!

"As we flossed by the end of the valley I could hear those frightful yowls coming nearer and nearer. I dared not look around. We were covering the ground at the rate of at least three miles per minute, and it required all my skill to keep my place.

"I clutched our faithful horsetrich around the neck. On we raced, and on, and on—I heard a shrill yell in my ear. Vertigo's hand suddenly slipped from the waistband of my union suit. Our steed (ours no longer, alas, but now mine alone), pressed on more swiftly and I knew Vertigo was gone. Poor Vertigo! ... Poor, poor Vertigo! He come down three days later in San Antonio, Texas, and broke up one of the most successful revival services they'd ever had there...

"Another fifty or seventy-five miles, and I felt, rather than heard, the diplodocus again at our heels. I stole a harried glares over my shoulder. Yes, there he was, his bared, glistening teeth not a yard away, his little eyes flashing venomously. He made a swipe for me—and missed. Another—and suddenly my poor horse-strich was yanked out from under me and I was going on alone through the air.

"I lit in a small but well ventilated, hole in the ground that turned out to be the other end of the Mammoth Cave. It was too small for the diplodocus to enter. That is the only thing that saved my life.

"For three weeks I subsisted on fish. They were blind and a cinch to catch; though much harder to eat. And at length I was found by a guide who was taking a party of school-teachers from Beebe, Indiana, through the simplest ramfications of the wonderful burrow. I was delirious, they told me, and sadly emanciated; and when they discovers me, I'm setting on a stalagmite with a blind tadpole in each hand, singing in feeble accents. However, I know nothing of all that myself for I was out of my head for several weeks."

He ceased
"But did you ever go back?" I queried.
He eyed me with squelching scorn.
"Did I ever go back!" he repeated. "Did I ever go back!" And then, "Say, what do you take me for, anyhow, hay?"
I didn't answer his question. It would not have been polite. And, besides, he was much bigger than I.

The Last Haunt of the Dinosaur
Henry Francis

The May sun was shining into the largest of a set of rooms at one of the colleges in Oxford, as a man of about fifty years of age was walking up and down it, occasionally looking at a drawing hung against the wall, which depicted the outline of some antediluvian creature, half-reptile, half-animal, the name and identity of which certainly could not be found in any work on natural history of the present day.

The sketch had been built up from every available source, to represent the form which the draughtsman had imagined in his mind a Dinosaur to have looked like when alive.

Owen Griffith, the occupier of the room and the draughtsman, was a medical professor of the University, a good shot and a rider to the hounds in his time, and a hearty sportsman, but also an enthusiastic seeker from the depths of the earth of information as to what birds, beasts, and fishes inhabited this world in those times, when, more than probably, man was not existent.

The door of the room was opened and a young man named Lyall Somers came into the apartment. He had just got his degree, and had passed through the Science Schools with honours. He had come to have a talk with the Professor about a proposed excursion to South Africa, to hunt up the fossils of animals long since extinct, and to obtain, if possible, the skins and skeletons of a very rare kind of antelope, which far-shooting guns and European shooters would soon, it was thought, exterminate.

The two men were fast friends; both in their way athletes, and both full of eager enquiry into everything scientific.

They made arrangements to leave England by a Cape steamer in June, and to be away for six months, taking with them good guns and supplies, and all the requisite necessaries for an extended expedition into the centre of Africa, in pursuit of their two hobbies, geological lore and sport.

Their voyage to the Cape of Good Hope passed without remarkable incident, and they reached the Karroo, in Cape Colony, early in July, where, after examining the strata of rocks and finding many fossils of extinct creatures, their delight was great to learn from reports of Zulus and others, that in a country north of Khama's land, there was a place where "stone-bones," as the Hottentots called them, abounded in every cave, and where as yet game, and especially antelopes, could be shot in numbers.

The travellers were not long in setting out for this favoured spot of geology and sport. They both looked fit for the undertaking. Each strong and hearty for his years, and eager for fresh discoveries. Owen Griffith had let his beard grow untouched after leaving Oxford, but Somers still clung to his razor, only allowing a moustache above his lip. The men were dressed in true sportsman's style, each carrying his own rifle with the requisite ammunition about his person, but the Professor kept to his soft felt hat.

After passing through Mafeking and Khama's territory, they arrived at a place which they supposed, from its hilly and precipitous character, to be not far from the sources of the Vaal river. Here they reached the kraal of an old African chief, who manifested a most friendly disposition towards the Englishmen. He promised to assist them in getting to the place where the fossils were said to be found, and where game was abundant, but he was most urgent in warning them not to take a direct course to this promised land of geological treasure, as the straight road thither passed through a valley infested by demons and spirits of uncommon shape and form, from whom no human being could escape, and who destroyed all life within their reach.

The friendly old man procured negro carriers for the expedition, and with a parting injunction to the two travellers to avoid the "Valley of Death," and the hideous monsters said to inhabit it, started them on their journey.

July is the winter time of South Africa, and the sportsmen enjoyed themselves as they marched along, for the country swarmed with game, and during the day they managed to procure a specimen of the rare antelope they so much wished to obtain, and the trophies of which were one of the objects of the expedition.

In the evening the camp was formed near a running stream of water, and a survey was taken of their following. The Englishmen had brought two Zulus from the Karroo, and the old chief had supplied them with a headman and twelve carriers, so that their force consisted of seventeen men, all told. Several head of game, eland and hartebeest, springbok and other deer, had been shot as they came along, and the camp was redolent with frizzling venison to a late hour of the night.

After their supper Griffith and Somers were stretched out, lying at full length to leeward of the large fire, the smoke of which somewhat saved them from mosquitoes, when the young man asked his companion:

"What do you think, Professor, of the old chief's story about uncommon and dangerous beasts on our way?"

"I cannot make up my mind," replied the elder. "I have been thinking about it all day. He said this beast, or spirit, or devil, for he called it many names, when it moved about quickly, did so by a succession of spring-like jumps as a kangaroo does, only that it could leap over trees—that, of course, was a natural exaggeration. Now, the Dinosaurs, of prehistoric history, are supposed to have jumped about in this same manner, as may be gathered from the deep imprints of their hind feet, which were left in the sandy mud that has now become sandstone, but these Saurians belonged to quite another period. They have been extinct for centuries."

"Why should they be?" said Somers. "From what I can see, and you say, they must have had a shape just like the dragon St. George is said to have slain, and that not so many centuries ago."

"Do you think there ever was a St. George?" asked the Professor, with a fine expression of incredulity on his scornful lips.

"The tradition about St. George is as likely to be true as the figures and casts of extinct beasts which are set up in half the museums of the world," exclaimed his young companion.

"Show me the fossils of St. George, and I will tell you," replied Griffith, with an air of superiority, between the puffs of smoke from his lips.

"Ah, well! Some people are fossil mad. Not that I say you are, but you have got these Dinosaurs on the brain. With some men, I believe, they are creatures of the brain, but supposing that there were such beasts, I cannot see why some should not be alive still, in unknown places. People say the dodo may still be found in Madagascar."

"I don't believe it," broke in the Professor, sententiously.

"I heard you once say," rejoined Somers, "that there was nothing improbable in the appearance of a sea serpent."

"That is different—wholly different!" cried out the elder man, roused to animation by the discussion of his pet subjects. "There were monstrous beasts on earth once, enormous creatures, carnivorous and otherwise. This can be proved from their bones found all over the world; so, too, there may have been enormous sea monsters, and there may be now; we cannot get to the bottom of the sea to find out. The conditions of life in the two elements, land and water, are distinct. The earth mammals were buried in some way, under sand or mud from glaciers or earthquakes, whilst their bones remained, but the water is different. The sea would not bury its denizens. The sea serpent and monsters would remain in the water. In my opinion, the evidence is in favour of their existence now."

"I am going to sleep," muttered Somers, and he was soon unconscious of monsters and everything else, and his companion followed his example, after making up the fire.

The next morning preparations were made to resume the journey. The travellers suggested that as they went along they should keep near the stream of water beside which they had bivouacked, but a difficulty at once arose. The greater part of the old chief's carriers refused to take this road, saying it led down to the "Valley of Death," from which no man ever came out, and again, almost using the identical words of the friendly chief, a description was given of some hideous, wild, and ravenous creature as large, it was said, as a house, whose lair was somewhere in this valley, towards which the water ran.

The Englishmen argued the case, pointing to their splendid rifles, one of which, a two-ounce muzzle-loader that had killed an eland at 800 yards, the day before, and had excited the admiration of the carriers, was particularly shown to them by Somers—but it was of no use. Four men only consented to accompany the sportsmen through the valley, so that it was arranged that the others should carry the baggage round the hills that surrounded this place, and meet the Englishmen at a point beyond, where the water made its exit from the dwelling-place of dread and frightful beasts.

At the last moment one of the four negroes struck, and the large cavalcade that came thus far with the two travellers was reduced to five persons, who started in single file; a man who acted as guide in front, then the two Oxford men, and after them two carriers, carrying their blankets and cooking utensils. These continued their journey along the banks of the stream for a few miles through a country barren of trees, and sparsely covered with grass, until the party arrived at a very narrow gorge between two hills; after traversing this for some distance, the ravine suddenly opened, and the road ceased; the stream, by which they had journeyed, no longer meandered gently in its course, but dashed over rocks in a sparkling cascade, into a large valley, which was to be seen spread out before their feet. The pathway hitherto trod became merely a difficult and very steep track, down a cliff, into this valley.

But the view in front of the men was truly magnificent. Before them, looking north, was a vale clothed in verdure of tropical splendour. Here and there could be seen green savannahs of grass, leading down to the stream that ran through the middle of it, and around these natural meadows, up to the cliffs of rock, which enclosed the valley, masses of forest were growing primeval, and so thick and dense with foliage, that no sunshine penetrated their depths. In the blue distance, the eye viewed a very large lake, which simmered in the noonday heat, and appeared on the horizon of their view, showing that the exit of the water from the valley was there or somewhere near.

The men descended the face of the cliff slowly. The barefooted natives having not much difficulty, but the boot-shod Europeans were obliged to be extremely careful, or they would have slipped

and fallen on the face of a rock, where there was nothing to hold
on by.

At length they reached the bottom, and wearied by their down-
climb, and the walk of the day, pitched their small tent on a piece
of open ground near the foot of the cliff. Somers set to and boiled
the kettle, and prepared the evening meal, and Griffith took a stroll
with his rifle. He brought back a report that there must be some
large animal in the valley; the tracks looked like those of an elephant,
as large pathways had been made in the bed of the stream and
alongside the banks, parallel to and close to the water.

"It was getting dusk," continued the Professor, "and I could not
make out the footprints in the running water, but if there is a rogue
male elephant about, he would cunningly lie in wait for anything
coming to the water and would kill it. This may account for the
tales of monsters."

The camp fire that night was made up of large logs of wood,
and the men went to sleep around it with their feet towards the
blaze. The night passed quietly.

All was hushed save the distant cry of some animal in the forest, and the murmur of the small waterfall.

Towards the morning one of the negroes was sitting up, preparatory to rising to feed the fire with fresh fuel, when he was suddenly seized by some wild animal, and his despairing shrieks for
help as he was carried off roused the entire party.

"What is it? What can it be?" cried Griffith, springing up in the
tent and seizing his rifle. Somers was already outside. The other
two negroes had run behind the white men.

It was plain that one of the blacks had disappeared, and a large
black form was seen diminishing into the gloom of the forest towards the water. No further sounds were heard after the shrieks
and screams of the unfortunate victim, and the crunching made by
the mysterious monster. The travellers waited for broad daylight
for further explanation.

As the light increased, they followed the tracks, when emerg-
ing into the open a terrible sight was revealed. On a rock, about
two hundred yards distant, in a glade of the forest and overhanging the stream, a horrible looking monster, with a body like an

enormous rat, a tail like an alligator, with a long neck and head like a python, was tearing to pieces and devouring their late comrade. Somers took a deliberate aim and fired at the creature, which merely looked up, and, as if not liking the noise of the gun's report, carried the remainder of the unhappy negro's body in its mouth, and sliding off the rock into a pool of water formed by the stream, disappeared from sight.

"What a dreadful beast!" exclaimed Somers, white with excitement and alarm. "It's body is larger than an elephant's."

"It is a Dinosaur, a carnivorous Dinosaur," burst out the Professor, breathless with eager curiosity. "There is no doubt about that. The appearance corresponds in every particular with the description and drawings of a Dinosaur, both in America and Europe"; and he would have gone on with his excited talk, so full was he of the discovery, but the young mail cut him short.

"What we have to do is to kill this beast! Never mind what it is like. Let us see how to destroy it."

And after some deliberation they determined to seek the creature, and try what shooting at it at very close quarters would achieve.

"I should think a two-ounce ball just behind the shoulder would settle the matter," said Somers, carefully reloading his rifle. "There is no demon about it, or anything supernatural—only flesh and blood; we can kill it if we try."

They started off in their quest of the Dinosaur, but although they searched the stream most carefully, they could not find the brute, and suspected that, having had its meal for the day, it was hiding, either in some hole in the water, or in the dark recesses of the forest.

After a fruitless search the men returned to their camp. A larger fire than usual was made, and after a night of fitful sleep, and a hasty meal in the morning, the two sportsmen shouldered their rifles, determining to follow the water all the way to the lake they had seen in the distance, and to find this dire beast of prey.

More by habit than from choice, a negro led the way by a few yards, the whole party proceeding cautiously down the valley. The beauty of the country was enchanting. Everywhere on each side of the stream, birds and butterflies of gorgeous appearance, showed themselves and fluttered from bush to bush, and feathery bamboos and the broad leaves of wild bananas mingled their foliage, but the watercourse itself bore testimony to the murderous nature of the semi-reptile that had made this fair scene its home. It was plain, that where any animals came to drink, this terrible creature sprang upon them and devoured them, and many places by the water had the appearance of the floor of a slaughterhouse.

The party had gone down the stream for a long distance, when finding the track of the Dinosaur looked old, they resolved to return, and as the path by the water was free from jungle, and easiest to walk upon, they were wending their way slowly back, when as they passed through some scrub, mixed with rocks and grass, the Dinosaur, with neck curled like a snake, leaped from the incredible distance of at least twenty yards on the unfortunate negro in front, seizing the man's head in his mouth at the same moment, and crushing in the skull with its bite. The Professor instantly fired his rifle, loaded with an express bullet, at the creature's eyes and head, and the beast for the moment let go the negro and made a dart at Griffith, and he again fired at it. In the meanwhile Somers discharged both barrels at the animal's body, but the balls glanced off its hide as if from a steel plate.

The effects of the Professor's shots must have told on the Dinosaur, for it lowered its head; at the same time emitting a dreadfully foul and suffocating stench from its mouth, which nearly stupefied the two sportsmen, and made them beat a hasty retreat. The remaining negro ran off as fast as possible.

When the two Englishmen had run to a distance of some three or four hundred yards they stopped and gasped for fresh air, the poisonous breath of the reptile having quite overcome them, and then reloaded their rifles as quickly as possible.

"We must attack the creature again," said the Professor. "It is of no use firing at its body. I believe that my shot injured an eye, if it did not destroy the sight, but your bullets went off the beast's back, with a sing in the air, that I could hear above all the noise. I was always of the opinion that the hides of these creatures must have been very thick and—"

"Never mind about that now, Griffith," muttered Somers. "That will keep for the lecture room. Let us agree how we will shoot, and stick to that. What I advise is that we try to keep close to the Dinosaur's side, and I will fire both barrels into its body just behind its small forelegs, the skin of all animals is thin in that exact part. You fire your express straight into its mouth as it rears up. I could see the horrid brute's jaw gape, both when it was in the air and as it seized that poor black fellow."

They mutually agreed on this line of action, and retraced their steps. The Dinosaur had hardly moved, but with the front part of its body resting on the corpse of the negro, was swaying about its head, rubbing its right eye on the ground, the sight being plainly injured.

Somers, who was leading, took the cue from this, and approached the creature very slowly and cautiously on its right side. The stench and fetid odours emanating from it were horrible, but the two sportsmen held on, and crept up little by little. As soon as Somers was near enough to put the muzzle of his rifle almost touching the creature's skin, he fired both barrels at once. The recoil of the gun threw the young man back, but the Dinosaur, with a swift turn, drew itself up on its hind legs and arching its long neck brought its jaws down on Somer's head with a crash. The sun helmet that the sportsman wore was fortunately steel lined like a hunting cap, and although the beast's teeth went through it, inflicting severe wounds on the wearer's head, the cap came away in the reptile's mouth, and Griffith instantly shot at the creature's eyes, and the Dinosaur dropping the cap, renewed the attack. It was very severely wounded, but again raising itself up and curling its neck, with open mouth it seized the Professor by the right shoulder, and the bones of the man's upper arm crunched under the reptile's bite, as his rifle dropped from his hand. By this time, short as it was, Somers recognised the position, swiftly picking up his comrade's rifle, he put the mouth of the barrel close to the Dinosaur's left eye, and pulled the trigger. The beast at once let go the Professor's arm, and with a frightful hiss, leaped into the air, and was seen dragging itself slowly down the bed of the stream, towards the lake at the end of the valley.

Wounded as both the men were, Griffith's right arm being, of course, quite useless, they followed the trail of the Dinosaur. The water of the stream was crimsoned with the blood which was flowing from the animal's side.

"He has got four ounces of honest lead in his heart or lungs," said Somers, grimly, as they stopped an instant to look at a large pool of frothy blood which had run from the Dinosaur's wound as it had rested on its way for a while.

The Professor said little. The wounds from the reptile's teeth on his arm made him feel faint, and all the two Englishmen could do was to follow their quarry. At length they dragged themselves to the brink of the lake, which they had seen at a distance from the cliff, only to trace the Dinosaur to the water, into which it had gone and disappeared.

The sportsmen were completely done up with wounds and excitement, and they fell down sick and wearied, and utterly exhausted, and the remaining negro soon joined them, his eyeballs starting from his head with fear. The two Englishmen could go no further, and they sent the negro forward to try and find the baggage bearers, who were to meet them somewhere in that neighbourhood. He found them, and the kind old chief's headman appeared, and produced from the baggage a flask of brandy, a few spoonfuls of which revived the sufferers, and they signed to the man to lead them out of the valley.

After a time the travellers got back to Cape Town, satisfied for the present with their search for Saurian fossils, and when in due time they reached Oxford, they corrected the drawing of a Dinosaur which is hanging in the Professor's room.

The Great Beast Of Kafue
Richard Dehan

It happened at our homestead on the border of Southeastern Rhodesia, seventy miles from Tuli Concession, some three years after the War.

A September storm raged, the green, broad-leaved tobacco-plants tossed like the waves of the ocean I had crossed and re-crossed, journeying to and coming back from my dead mother's wet, sad country of Ireland to this land of my father and his father's father.

The acacias and kameel thorns and the huge cactus-like euphorbia that fringed the water-courses and the irrigation channels had wrung their hands all day without ceasing, like Makalaka women at a native funeral. Night closed in: the wooden shutters were barred, the small-paned windows fastened, yet they shook and rattled as though human beings without were trying to force a way in. Whitewash fell in scales from the big tie-beams and cross-rafters of the farm kitchen, and lay in little powdery drifts of whiteness on the solid table of brown locust-tree wood, and my father's Dutch Bible that lay open there. Upon my father's great black head that was bent over the Book, were many streaks and patches of white that might not be shaken or brushed away.

It had fallen at the beginning of the War, that snow of sorrow streaking the heavy curling locks of coarse black hair. My pretty young mother—an Irishwoman of the North, had been killed in the Women's Laager at Gueldersdorp during the Siege. My father served as Staats gunner during the Investment—and now you know the dreadful doubt that heaped upon those mighty shoulders a bending load, and sprinkled the black hair with white.

You are to see me in my blue drill roundabout and little home-spun breeches sitting on a cricket in the shadow of the table-ledge, over against the grim stark figure in the big, thong-seated armchair.

There would be no going to bed that night. The dam was over-full already, and the next spate from the hill sluits might crack the great wall of mud-cemented saw-squared boulders, or overflow it, and lick away the work of years. The farm-house roof had been rebuilt since the shell from the English naval gun had wrecked it, but the work of men to-day is not like that of the men of old. My father shook his head, contemplating the new masonry, and the whitewash fell as though in confirmation of his expressed doubts.

I had begged to stay up rather than lie alone in the big bed in my father's room. Nodding with sleepiness I should have denied, I carved with my two-bladed American knife at a little canoe I meant to swim in the shallower river-pools. And as I shaped the prow I dreamed of something I had heard on the previous night.

A traveller of the better middle-class, overseer of a coal-mine working "up Buluwayo" way, who had stayed with us the previous night and gone on to Tuli that morning, had told the story. What he had failed to tell I had haltingly spelled out of the three-weeks-old English newspaper he had left behind.

So I wrought, and remembered, and my little canoe swelled and grew in my hands. I was carrying it on my back through a forest of tall reeds and high grasses, forcing a painful way between the tough wrist-thick stems, with the salt sweat running down into my eyes... Then I was in the canoe, wielding the single paddle, working my frail crank craft through sluggish pools of black water, overgrown with broad spiny leaves of water-plants cradling dowers of mar-vellous hue. In the canoe bows leaned my grandfather's elephant-gun, the inlaid, browned-steel-barrelled weapon with the diamond-patterned stock and breech that had always seemed to my childish eyes the most utterly desirable, absolutely magnificent possession a grown-up man might call his own.

A *paauw* made a great commotion getting up amongst the reeds; but does a hunter go after *paauw* with his grandfather's elephant-gun? Duck were feeding in the open spaces of sluggish black water. I heard what seemed to be the plop! of a jumping fish, on the other side of a twenty-foot high barrier of reeds and grasses. I looked up then, and saw, glaring down upon me from inconceivable heights of sheer horror, the Thing of which I had heard and read.

At this juncture I dropped the little canoe and clutched my father round the leg.

"What is it, *mijn jongen?*"

He, too, seemed to rouse out of a waking dream. You are to see the wide, burnt-out-looking grey eyes that were staring sorrowfully out of their shadowy caves under the shaggy eyebrows, lighten out of their deep abstraction and drop to the level of my childish face.

"You were thinking of the great beast of Kafue Valley, and you want to ask me if I will lend you my father's elephant-rifle when you are big enough to carry it that you may go and hunt for the beast and kill it; is that so?"

My father grasped his great black beard in one huge knotted brown hand, and made a rope of it, as was his way. He looked from my chubby face to the old-fashioned black-powder 8-bore that hung upon the wall against a leopard kaross, and back again, and something like a smile curved the grim mouth under the shaggy black and white moustache.

"The gun you shall have, boy, when you are of age to use it, or a 450-Mannlicher or a 600-Mauser, the best that may be bought north of the Transvaal, to shoot explosive or conical bullets from cordite cartridges. But not unless you give me your promise never to kill that beast, shall money of mine go to the buying of such a gun for you. Come now, let me have your word!"

Even to my childish vanity the notion of my solemnly entering into a compact binding my hand against the slaying of the semi-fabulous beast-marvel of the Upper Rhodesian swamps, smacked of the fantastic if not of the absurd. But my father's eyes had no twinkle in them, and I faltered out the promise they commanded.

"Nooit—nooit will I kill that beast! It should kill me, rather!"

"Your mother's son will not be *valsch* to a vow. For so would you, son of my body, make of me, your father, a traitor to an oath that I have sworn!"

The great voice boomed in the rafters of the farm kitchen, vying with the baffled roaring of the wind that was trying to get in, as I had told myself, and lie down, folding wide quivering wings and panting still, upon the sheepskin that was spread before the hearth.

"But—but why did you swear?"

I faltered out the question, staring at the great bearded figure in homespun jacket and tan-cord breeches and *veldschoens*, and thought again that it had the hairy skin of Esau and the haunted face of Saul.

Said my father, grimly—

"Had I questioned my father so at twice your age, he would have skinned my back and I should have deserved it. But I cannot beat your mother's son, though the Lord punish me for my weakness... And you have the spirit of the *jager* in you, even as I. What I saw you may one day see. What I might have killed, that shall you spare, because of me and my oath. Why did I take it upon me, do you ask? Even though I told you, how should a child understand? What is it you are saying? Did I really, really see the beast? Ay, by the Lord!" said my father thoughtfully, "I saw him. And never can a man who has seen, forget that sight. What are you saying?"

The words tumbled over one another as I stammered in my hurry—

"But—but the English traveller said only one white man besides the Mashona hunter has seen the beast, and the newspaper says so too."

"*Natuurlijk*. And the white man is me," thundered the deep voice.

I hesitated.

"But since the planting of the tobacco you have not left the *plaats*. And the newspaper is of only three weeks back."

"*Dat spreekt*, but the story is older than that, *mijn jongen*. It is the third time it has been dished up in the Buluwayo Courant sauced up with lies to change the taste as belly-lovers have their meat. But I am the man who saw the beast of Kafue, and the story that is told is my story, nevertheless!"

I felt my cheeks beginning to burn. Wonderful as were the things I knew to be true of the man, my father, this promised to be the most wonderful of all.

"It was when I was hunting in the Zambezi Country," said my father, "three months after the Commandants of the Forces of the United Republics met at Klerksdorp to arrange conditions of peace—"

"With the English Generals," I put in.

"With the English, as I have said. You had been sent to your— to her people in Ireland. I had not then thought of rebuilding the farm. For more than a house of stones had been thrown down for me, and more than so many thousand acres of land laid waste...

"Where did I go? *Ik wiet niet.* I wandered *op en neer* like the evil spirit in the Scriptures," the great corded hand shut the Book and reached over and snuffed the tallow-dip that hung over at the top, smoking and smelling, and pitched the black wick-end angrily on the red hearth-embers. "I sought rest and found none, either for the sole of my foot or the soul in my body. There is bitterness in my mouth as though I have eaten the spotted lily-root of the swamps. I cannot taste the food I swallow, and when I lie down at night something lies down with me, and when I rise up, it rises too and goes by my side all day."

I clung to the leg of the table, not daring to clutch my father's. For his eyes did not seem to see me any more, and a blob of foam quivered on his beard that hung over his great breast in a shadowy cascade dappled with patches of white. He went on, I scarcely daring to breathe—

"For, after all, do I know it is not I who killed her? That accursed day, was I not on duty as ever since the beginning of the investment, and is it not a splinter from a Maxim Nordenfeld fired from an eastern gun-position, that—" Great drops stood on my father's forehead. His huge frame shook. The clenched hand resting on the solid table of locust-beam, shook that also, shaking me, clinging to the table-leg with my heart thumping violently, and a cold, crawling sensation among the roots of my curls.

"At first, I seem to remember there was a man hunting with me. He had many Kaffir servants and four Mashona hunters and wagons drawn by salted tailless spans, fine guns and costly tents, plenty of stores and medicine in little sugar-pills, in bottles with silver tops. But he sickened in spite of all his quinine, and the salted oxen died, just like beasts with tails; and besides, he was afraid of the Makwakwa and the Mashengwa with their slender poisoned spears of reeds. He turned back at last. I pushed on."

There was a pause. The strange, iron-grey, burnt-out eyes looked through me and beyond me, then the deep, trembling voice repeated, once more changing the past into the present tense—

"I push on west. My life is of value to none. The boy—is he not with her people? Shall I live to have him back under my roof and see in his face one day the knowledge that I have killed his mother? Nay, nay, I will push on!"

There was so long a silence after this that I ventured to move. Then my father looked at me, and spoke to me, not as though I were a child, but as if I had been another man.

"I pushed on, crossing the rivers on a blown-up goatskin and some calabashes, keeping my father's elephant-gun and my cartridges dry by holding them above my head. Food! For food there were thorny orange cucumbers with green pulp, and the native women at the kraals gave me cakes of maize and milk. I hunted and killed rhino and elephant and hippo and lion until the headmen of the Mashengwa said the beast was a god of theirs and the slaying of it would bring a pestilence upon their tribe, and so I killed no more. And one day I shot a cow hippo with her calf, and she stood to suckle the ugly little thing while her life was bleeding out of her, and after that I ceased to kill. I needed little, and there were yet the green-fleshed cucumbers, and ground-nuts, and things like those."

He made a rope his great beard, twisting it with a rasping sound.

"Thus I reached the Upper Kafue Valley where the great grass swamps are. No railway then, running like an iron snake up from Buluwayo to bring the ore down from the silver-mines that are there.

"Six days' trek from the mines—I went on foot always, you will understand!—six days' journey from the mines, above where L'uengwe River is wedded to Kafue, as the Badanga say is a big water.

"It is a lake, or rather, two lakes, not round, but shaped like the bowls of two wooden spoons. A shore of black, stone-like baked mud round them, and a bridge of the same stone is between them, so that they make the figure that is for 8."

The big, hairy forefinger of my father's right hand traced the numeral in the powdered whitewash that lay in drifts upon the table.

"That is the shape of the lakes, and the Badanga say that they have no bottom, and that fish taken from their waters remain raw and alive, even on the red-hot embers of their cooking stove. They are a lazy, dirty people who live on snakes and frogs and grubs—tortoise and fish. And they gave me to eat and told me, partly in words of my own *moder Taal* they had picked up somehow, partly in sign language, about the Great Beast that lives in the double lake that is haunted by the spirits of their dead."

I waited, my heart pumping at the bottom of my throat, my blood running horribly, delightfully chill, to hear the rest.

"The hunting spirit revives in a man, even at death's door, to hear of an animal the like of which no living hunter has ever brought down. The Badanga tell me of this one, tales, tales, tales! They draw it for me with a pointed stick on a broad green leaf, or in the ashes of their cooking-fires. And I have seen many a great beast, but, *voor den donder!* never a beast such as that!"

I held on to my stool with both hands.

"I ask the Badanga to guide me to the lair of the beast for all the money I have upon me. They care not for gold, but for the old silver hunting-watch I carry they will risk offending the spirits of their dead. The old man who has drawn the creature for me, he will take me. And it is January, the time of year in which he has been before known to rise and bellow—*Maar!*—bellow like twenty buffalo bulls in spring-time, for his mate to rise from those bottomless deeps below and drink the air and sun."

So there are two great beasts! Neither the traveller nor the newspaper nor my father, until this moment, had hinted at that!

"The she-beast is much the smaller and has no horns. This my old man makes clear to me, drawing her with the point of his fish-spear on smooth mud. She is very sick the last time my old man has seen her. Her great moon-eyes are dim, and the stinking spume dribbles from her jaws. She can only float in the trough of the wave that her mate makes with his wallowings, her long scaly neck lying like a dead python on the oily black water. My old man thinks she was then near death. I ask him how long ago that is? Twenty times have the blue lake-lilies blossomed, the lilies with the sweet seeds that the Badanga make bread of—since. And the great bull has twice been heard bellowing, but never has he been seen of man since then."

My father folded his great arms upon the black-and-white cascade of beard that swept down over his shirt of homespun and went on—

"Twenty years. Perhaps, think I, my old man has lied to me! But we are at the end of the last day's journey. The sun has set and night has come. My old man makes me signs we are near the lakes and I climb a high *mahogo*, holding by the limbs of the wild fig that is hugging the tree to death."

My father spat into the heart of the glowing wood ashes, and said—

"I see the twin lakes lying in the midst of the high grass-swamps, barely a mile away. The black, shining waters cradle the new moon of January in their bosom, and the blue star that hangs beneath her horn, and there is no ripple on the surface, or sign of a beast, big or little. And I despise myself, I, the son of honest Booren, who have been duped by the lies of a black man-ape. I am coming down the tree, when through the night comes a long, hollow, booming, bellowing roar that is not the cry of any beast I know. Thrice it comes, and my old man of the Badanga, squatting among the roots of the *mahogo*, nods his wrinkled bald skull, and says, squinting up at me, 'Now you have heard, Baas, will you go back or go on?'

"I answer, '*Al recht uit!*'

"For something of the hunting spirit has wakened in me. And I see to the cleaning of the elephant-gun and load it carefully before I sleep that night."

I would have liked to ask a question but the words stuck in my throat.

"By dawn of day we have reached the lakes," went on my father. "The high grass and the tall reeds march out into the black water as far as they may, then the black stone beach shelves off into depths unknown.

"He who has written up the story for the Buluwayo newspaper says that the lake was once a volcano and that the crumbly black stone is lava. It may be so. But volcanoes are holes in the tops of mountains, while the lakes lie in a valley-bottom, and he who wrote cannot have been there, or he would know there are two, and not one.

"All the next night we, camping on the belt of stony shore that divides lake from lake, heard nothing. We ate the parched grain and baked grubs that my old man carried in a little bag. We lighted no fire because of the spirits of the dead Badanga that would come crowding about it to warm themselves, and poison us with their breath. My old man said so, and I humoured him. My dead needed no fire to bring her to me. She was there always...

"All the day and the night through we heard and saw nothing. But at windstill dawn of the next day I saw a great curving ripple cross the upper lake that may be a mile and a half wide; and the reeds upon the nearer shore were wetted to the knees as by the wave that is left in the wake of a steamer, and oily patches of scum, each as big as a barn floor, befouled the calm water, and there was a cold, strange smell upon the breeze, but nothing more.

"Until at sunset of the next day, when I stood upon the midmost belt of shore between lake and lake, with my back to the blood-red wonder of the west and my eyes sheltered by my hand as I looked out to where I had seen the waters divided as a man furrows earth with the plough-share, and felt a shadow fall over me from behind, and turned... and saw... *Alamachtig!*"

I could not breathe. At last, at last, it was coming!

"I am no coward," said my father, in his deep resounding bass, "but that was a sight of terror. My old man of the Badanga had bolted like a rock-rabbit. I could hear the dry reeds crashing as he broke through. And the horned head of the beast, that was as big as a wagon-trunk shaking about on the top of a python-neck that topped the tallest of the teak-trees or *mahogos* that grow in the grass-swamps, seemed as if it were looking for the little human creature that was trying to run away.

"*Voor den donder!* how the water rises up in columns of smoke-spray as the great beast lashes it with his crocodile-tail! His head is crocodile also, with horns of rhino, his body has the bulk of six hippo bulls together. He is covered with armour of scales, yellow-white as the scales of leprosy, he has paddles like a tortoise. God of my fathers, what a beast to see! I forget the gun I hold against my hip—I can only stand and look, while the cold, thick puffs of stinking musk are brought to my nostrils and my ear-drums are well-nigh split with the bellowing of the beast. Ay! and the wave of his wallowings that wets one to the neck is foul with clammy ooze and oily scum.

"Why did the thing not see me? I did not try to hide from those scaly-lidded great eyes, yellow with half-moon-shaped pupils, I stood like an idol of stone. Perhaps that saved me, or I was too little a thing to vent a wrath so great upon. He Who in the beginning made herds of beasts like that to move upon the face of the waters, and let this one live to show the pigmy world of to-day what creatures were of old, knows. I do not. I was dazed with the noise of its roarings and the thundering blows of its huge tail upon the water; I was drenched with the spume of its snortings and sick-ened with the stench it gave forth. But I never took my eyes from it, as it spent its fury, and little by little I came to understand.

"*Het is jammer* to see anything suffer as that beast was suffer-ing. Another man in my place would have thought as much, and when it lay still at last on the frothing black water, a bullet from the elephant-rifle would have lodged in the little stupid brain be-hind the great moon-eye, and there would have been an end...

"But I did not shoot!"

It seemed an age before my father spoke again, though the cuckoo-clock had only ticked eight times.

"No! I would not shoot and spare the beast, dinosaurus or bron-tosaurus, or whatever the wiseacres who have not seen him may name him, the anguish that none had spared me. 'Let him go on!' said I. 'Let him go on seeking her in the abysses that no lead-line may ever fathom, without consolation, without hope! Let him rise to the sun and the breeze of spring through miles of the cold black water, and find her not, year after year until the ending of the world. Let him call her through the mateless nights until Day and Night rush together at the sound of the Trumpet of the Judgment, and Time shall be no more!'"

Crash!

The great hand came down upon the solid locust-wood table, breaking the spell that had bound my tongue.

"I—do not understand," I heard my own child-voice saying. "Why was the Great Beast so sorry? What was he looking for?"

"His mate who died. Ay, at the lower end of the second lake, where the water shallows, her bones were sticking up like the bleached timbers of a wrecked ship. And He and She being the last of their kind upon the earth, therefore he knows desolation... and shall know it till death brings forgetfulness and rest. Boy, the wind is fallen, the rain has spent itself, it is time that you go to bed."

The Lizard God
Charles J. Finger

It is not pleasant to have one's convictions disturbed, and that is why I wish I had never seen the man Rounds.

He seems to have crossed my path only to shake my self-confidence. The little conversation we had has left me dissatisfied. I look upon my collection with less interest than I did. I am not as pleased with the result of my investigations as they appear in my monograph on THE SAURIAN FAMILY OF EQUATORIAL AMERICA.

Doubtless the mood that now possesses me will pass away, and I shall recover my equanimity. His story would have upset most men. Worse still was his unpleasant habit of interjecting strange opinions. Judge for yourself.

It was when passing through the Reptile room on my way to the study that I first saw him. I supposed him to be a mere common working-man passing away an idle hour; one of the ordinary Museum visitors. Two hours later, I noticed that he was closely examining the lizard cases. Then, later, he seemed interested in my collection of prints illustrating the living world of the antediluvian period. It was then that I approached him, and, finding him apparently intelligent, with, as it seemed, a bent towards lizards, and, further, discovering that he had travelled in Peru and Colombia, took him to the study.

The man had some unusual habits. He was absolutely lacking in that sense of respect, as I may term it, usually accorded to one in my position. A professor and curator naturally becomes accustomed to a certain amount of, well, diffidence in laymen. It is a tribute paid to us. But Rounds was not that way. He was perfectly at ease. He had an air of quiet self-possession; refused the chair I indicated, the chair set for visitors and students, walked to the window, threw up the lower sash, and sat on the sill, with one foot resting on the floor and the other swinging. Thus, he looked as if he were prepared to leap, or to jump or run.

He gave me the impression of being on the alert. Without asking permission, he filled and lit his pipe, taking his tobacco from a queerly made pouch, and using but one long taloned hand in the process.

"What I was looking for," he said, "is a kind of lizard. Yet it is not a lizard. It is too hard and thin in the body to be that. It runs on its hind legs. It is white. Its bite is poisonous. It lives in the equatorial districts of Colombia."

"Have you seen one?" I asked.

"No," was the reply. Then after a moment there came a staccato: "Why?"

"Because there is no such living creature," I said.

"How do you know?" came from him swiftly, almost before I had finished.

"The lizard group is thoroughly classified," I said. "There is nothing answering to that description. In the first place."

"Does that make it non-existent? Your classification of what you know?" he interrupted.

"I have made a study of the Saurians," I said.

"No, you haven't," he contradicted. "You have read what other men have written and that is not the same thing."

"Really," I began, but he broke in.

"I mean to say that you have never been in any new equatorial country," he said. "Your manner shows that. You are too quiet. Too easy. Too sedentary. You would have been killed because of your lack of vigilance."

That is, as nearly as I can repeat and remember, the opening of the conversation. There was an air of challenge about the man that I found unpleasant. Of course I admitted the fact that I was not an explorer myself, and that mine was the humbler if more tedious task of collecting and arranging data. At that he said that, in his opinion, organized expeditions were little more than pleasure jaunts taken at the public expense. His viewpoint seemed to me most extraordinary.

"Such an expedition," he said, "must fail in its main purpose because its unwieldiness destroys or disperses the very things it was organized to study. It cannot penetrate the wilds; it cannot get into the dry lands. The needs of the men and horses and dogs prevent that. It must keep to beaten tracks and in touch with the edge of civilization. The members of such an expedition are mere killers on a large scale, and to kill or to hunt a thing is to not know it at all. Further, the men in such expeditions are not even hunters. They are destroyers who destroy while keeping themselves in, safety.

"They have their beaters. Their paid natives. Humbug! That's the only word to describe that kind of thing. Staged effects they have. Then they come back here to pose as heroes before a crowd of gaping city clerks."

I mentioned the remarkable results obtained by the Peary and Roosevelt expeditions and pointed to the fact that the specimens brought back and properly set up by efficient taxidermists did, in fact, give the common people some notion of the wonders of animal life.

"Nothing of the kind," he said. "On the contrary, the gaping fools are misled, if they think at all, when they look at your museum stuff. Look at that boa-constrictor you have out there. It is stuffed and in a glass case. Don't you know that in its natural surroundings you yourself would come mighty near stepping on one without seeing it? You would. If you had that thing set up as it should be, your museum visitors would pass the case believing it was a mere collection of foliage. They wouldn't see the snake itself. See what I mean? Set up as they are in real life they'd come near being non-visible."

The man walked up and down the study floor for half a minute or so, then paused at the desk and said:

"Don't let us get to entertaining one another, though. But remember this, you only get knowledge at a cost. I mean to say that the man who would know something really worth knowing can only get the knowledge at first hand. The people who wander around this junk shop that you call a museum go out as empty headed as they came in. Consider. Say a Fiji islander came here and took back with him from the United States an electric bulb, a stuffed possum, an old hat, a stalactite from the Mammoth cave, a sackful of pecan nuts, a pair of hand-cuffs, half a dozen packing cases full of things gathered from here and there, and then set the whole junk pile up under a roof in the Fiji islands, what would his fellow Fijians know from that of the social life of this country? Eh? Tell me that."

"You exaggerate," I protested. "You take an extreme point of view."

"I don't," he said.

His contradictions would have made me angry perhaps, were they not made in so quiet a tone.

"Take anything from its natural surroundings," he went on, "and it is meaningless. The dull-eyed men and women who wander through this Museum of yours are merely killing time. There's no education in that kind of thing. Besides, what they see are dead things anyway. You can't study human nature in a morgue."

He resumed his seat on the window sill, then took from an inner pocket a leather wallet, and drew from it a photograph which he tossed across so that it fell on the desk before me. I examined it carefully. It had been badly developed and badly printed, and, what was worse, roughly handled. But still, one could distinguish certain features.

It pictured the interior of a building which was roofless, and above the rear wall was what I recognized as tropical vegetation, mainly by its wild luxuriance. Against the rear wall there seemed to be something like a giant stone lizard standing on its hind legs. The one foreleg that showed was disproportionately short. The body, too, was more attenuated than that of any lizard. The thing was headless and the statue, idol, or whatever it was, stood on a pedestal, and before that again was a slab of stone. My attention was caught by the head of the thing, which was to be seen in a corner. It was shaped roughly triangularly. The jaws were broad at the base and it had, even in the photograph, something of the same repulsive appearance as the head of a vampire bat.

"It is the result of the imagination of some Indian," I said. "No postdiluvian saurian ever existed of that size."

"Good God, man, you jump to conclusions," he growled. "This is only a representation of the thing itself. Made in heroic size, so to say. But see here."

He leaned over my shoulder and pointed to a kind of border that ran along the base of the pedestal. Examining closely, I made out a series of lizards running on their hind legs. "They," he explained, "are cut into the stone. It is a sort of red sandstone. They are a little bigger than the living creature. But look at this."

The particular spot that he indicated was blurred and dirty, as though many fingers had pointed to it, and I took the magnifying glass for closer inspection. Even then I only saw dimly a something that bore resemblance to the carved figures.

"That," he said, "is as near as ever I came to seeing one of the little devils. I think it was one of them, but I am not sure. I caught sight of it flashing across like a swiftly blown leaf. We took the picture by flashlight, you see, so I'm not positive. Somerfield, of course, was too busy attending to his camera. He saw nothing."

"We might have another picture made," I said. "It would be interesting."

"D'ye think I'd be able to carry plunder around travelling as I was then?" he asked. "You see, I went down there for the Company I'm working for. I was looking gut for rubber and hard woods. I'd worked from Buenaventura. From Buenaventura down to the Rio Caqueta and then followed that stream up to the watershed, and then down the Codajaz. If you look at the map, you'll see it's no easy trip. No chance to pack much. All I wanted to carry was information. And there was only Somerfield along."

"But Somerfield—he, I suppose, was the photographer, was he not? Did he not take care of the negatives?"

"Well, you see, he did take care of his negatives. But circumstances were different at the time. He had laid them away somewhere. After I killed him, I just brought away the camera and that was all."

I gasped at the audacity of the man. He said the words, "I killed him," so quietly, in so matter of fact a way, that for the moment I was breathless. Like most other men, I had never sat face to face with one who had taken the life of another.

It was, therefore, a startling thing to hear Rounds confess to having killed a fellow-man. It was awesome. And yet, let me say that at once I was possessed of a great desire to learn all about it, and down in my heart I feared that he would decide he had said something that he should not have said, and would either deny his statement or modify it in some way. I wanted to hear all the details. I was hugely interested. Was it morbidity? Then I came to myself after what was a shock, and awoke to the fact that he was talking in his quiet, even way.

"But those Tlingas held the belief, and that was all there was to it," he was saying.

I came to attention and said, "Of course, it is natural," for I feared to have him know that I was inattentive even for that short space, and waited for elucidations.

"It seems," he went on, "that the tribe was dying out. Helm, who first told me something of it at Buenaventura, was one of those scientists who have to invent a new theory for every new thing they are told of. He said it was either because of eating too much meat, or not eating enough. I forget which. There had been a falling off in the birth rate. The Tocalinian who had lived with them, and who joined us at the headwaters of the Codajaz, maintained that there had been too much inbreeding. So there was some arrangement by means of which they invited immigrants, as it were. Men from other neighboring tribes were encouraged to join the Tlingas. And they did. The Tlingas had a fat land and welcomed the immigrants. The immigrants on their part expected to have an easy time."

As Round talked, he became even more passionless, if that were possible. He moved from his place on the window sill and sat on the corner of my desk. I had forgotten my uneasiness at being in the presence of one who had taken his fellow's life.

He went on:

"When there's a falling birth rate, things change. There are manners and customs evolved that would seem strange to you. There come laws and religions, all made to match current requirements. Celibacy and sterility become a crime. Virginity becomes a disgrace, a something to be ridiculed."

"It seems impossible," I said.

"No," he said, and smiled, ever so slightly. "You have that in part. You ridicule what you call old maids, don't you?"

Again I was too slow with my reply. If I ever meet him again, I shall show him the fallacy of many of his arguments.

"Men with most children had most power and wealth. The childless were penalized, were punished. The sterile were put to death. There grew up a religion and a priesthood, ceremonials, sacrifices and rituals. And they had their god, in the shape of this lizard thing. Of course, like most other gods, it was more of a malevolent creature than anything else. Gods generally are, if you will consider a little. I don't care what creed or religion gets the upper hand, it's Fear that becomes the power. Look around and see if I'm not right.

"Well, Somerfield and I walked into that kind of thing. Now, like me, he had worked for the Exploration Company a good few years and had been to all kinds of places prospecting—Torres Straits, the Gold Coast, Madagascar, Patagonia. We prospectors have to get around in queer corners and the life's a dull one. All monotony, and worry mixed up. A kind of piebald life. But Somerfield had queer notions. He worked at the job because he could make more money at it than at anything else, and that gave him a chance to keep his family in Ohio in comfort. He was mighty fond of his family. Besides, the job gave him more time with the wife and kids than the average man gets. When he was at home, he was at home three months on end at times. That's better than the ordinary man.

"Now, this being so, Somerfield was what he was. He had ideas about religion. He was full of the notion that things are arranged so that if you live up to a certain code, you'll get a reward. 'Do right, and you'll come out right,' was one of his sayings. 'The wages of sin is death' was another. Point out to him that virtue got paid in the same coin, and he'd argue. No use. In a way he was like a man who wouldn't walk under a ladder or spill salt. You know the sort.

"Naturally, for him things were awkward at the Tlinga village. We stayed there quite a while, I should tell you. He lived in his own shack, cooking for himself and all that. He was full of ideas of duty to his wife and so on. I fell in with the local customs and took up with a sweetheart, things falling out so well that there was one of their ceremonials pretty soon in which I was central figure. Ista, it seems, made a public announcement. That would be natural enough with a tribe so concerned about the family birth rate. But it made me sorter mad to hear the natives everlastingly accusing Somerfield of being an undesirable. But they never let up trying to educate him and make him a Tlinga citizen. They were patient and persistent enough. On the other hand, I was looked on as a model young man, and received into the best society.

"About the time we were ready to strike west, Ista, that was my girl, told me that there would have to be a new ceremonial. She took my going in good part, for there was nothing more I could do.

They were sensible enough to know that man was only an instrument in the great game, as they understood it. Ista had led me out to a quiet place to put me next. I remember that vividly because of a little thing that happened that doesn't mean anything. I often wonder why resultless things sometimes stick in the mind. We were sitting at the base of a tall tree and there was a certain bush close by with berries bright red when they were unripe. They look good to eat. But when they ripen, they grow fat and juicy, the size of a grape, and of a liverish color. I thought that one of them had fallen on my left forearm and went to flick it off. Instead of being that, the thing burst into a blood splotch as soon as I hit it. That was the first time I had been bitten by one of those bugs. They are about the size of a sheep tick when empty, but they get on you and suck and suck, till they are full of your blood and the size of a grape. Queer things, but ugly. Ista laughed as you would laugh if you saw a negro afraid of a harmless snake. It's queer that it should always be considered a joke when one person fears something that another does not.

"But that has nothing to do with the story. What has, is that Ista wanted to tell me about the ceremonial. She did not believe in it at all. Privately, she was a kind of atheist among her people, but kept her opinions private. She had thought out things for herself and had her own beliefs, but they were not the beliefs the Tlingas were supposed to hold. But after all she did not tell me much besides her own disbeliefs. When you think of it, no one can tell another much. What you know, you have to discover alone. All she told me was what was going to be done, and that was about as disappointing as the information you might get about what would take place in initiation in a secret society. Something was lost in transmission.

"Well, at last the ceremonial started up with a great banging of drums and all that. It was a fine scene, let me tell you, with the tumbled vegetation, glaringly colored as if a scene painter had gone crazy. There were the flashing birds—bloodcolored and orange, scarlet and yellow, gold and green. Butterflies too—great gaudy things that looked like moving flowers. And the noise and chatterings and whistlings in the trees of birds and insects. There were flowers and fruits, and eatings and speech makings. As far as I could gather, the chief speakers were congratulating the hearers upon their luck in belonging to the Tlingas, which was the greatest tribe on earth and the favorite of Naol, the lizard god. We capered round the tribal pole, I capering with the rest of them of course. Somerfield took a picture of it. Then there was a procession of prospective mothers, with Ista among them. Rotten I thought it. Don't imagine female beauty, by the way, as some of the writers on savage life would have you imagine it. Nothing of the kind. White, black or yellow, I never saw a stark woman that looked beautiful yet. That's all bunk. Muscular and strong, yes. That's a kind of beauty in its way. True as God, I believe that one of the causes of unhappy marriages among white folk is that the lads are fed upon false notions about womanly beauty and when they get the reality they think they've captured a lemon.

"Presently the crowd quieted down and the men sat around in a semicircle with me and Somerfield at the end.

"Then a red-eyed old hag tottered out and began cursing Somerfield. She spat in his face and called him all outrageous names that came to her vindictive tongue. Lucky it was that he had been put next, and so, forewarned, was able to grin and bear it. But, Lord, how she did tongue-lash him. Then she took a flat piece of wood shaped like a laurel leaf which was fastened to a thin strip of hide, and showed him that. It was a kind of charm, and on it was cut one of the running lizards. She wanted him to rub it on his forehead. Of course, with his notions of religion, he wouldn't do it. That's natural. When she passed it to me, I did what she wanted done. I never was particular that way. Symbols mean nothing anyway and if fools are in the majority it's no use stirring up trouble. It's playing a lie, of course, but then that's the part of wisdom, it seems to me, sometimes. It's in a line with protective coloring. You remember what I said about the proper mounting of your specimens, don't you? Well, it's like that. That's why persecutions have never stamped out opinions nor prohibitions appetites. The wisest keep their counsel and go on as usual. The martyrs are the weak fools. But let's see. Where was I? Oh, yes. The old woman and the piece of wood.

"She began running from this one to that, kind of working herself up into a frenzy. Then she started to chant some old nonsense. There was a rhythm to it. She sang:

"'Nao calls for the useless.'

"Then the rest of them would shout:

"'Nao calls. Nao calls.'

"There was a terrible lot of it. The main purport was that this Nao was the ruling devil or god of the place. It called for the sacrifice of the useless. Many men were needed so that the one should be born who would lead the Tlingas to victory. That was the tone of it, and at the end of every line the old woman crooned, the crowd joined in with the refrain:

"'Nao calls. Nao calls.'

"Of course they became worked up. She handled them pretty much the same as a skilful speaker does things at a political meeting or an evangelist at a revival. The same spirit was there. Instead of a flag, there was the tribal pole. There was the old gag of their nation or tribe being the chosen one. I don't care where you go, there is always the same thing. Every tribe and nation is cocksure that theirs is the best. They have the bravest and the wisest men and the best women. But I kept nudging Somerfield. It was hard on him. He was the Judas and the traitor and all that. 'Damn fool superstition,' he muttered to me time and again. But of course he was a bit nervous, and so was I. Being in the minority is awkward. The human brain simply isn't strong enough to encounter organized opposition. It wears. You spend too much energy being on the defensive.

"After a time, when the song was done, the old hag seemed pretty well played out. Then she passed the piece of wood I told you of to a big buck, and he started to whirling it round and round. He was a skilful chap at the trick, and in a little had it making a screaming sound. Then presently some of the birds fell to noise-making just as you will hear canaries sing when someone whistles, or women talk when a piano commences to play. I saw something of the same down in Torres Straits. They call it the Twanyirika there. In the Malay peninsula they use something of the kind to scare the elephants out of the plantations. They've got it on the Gold Coast as well. It's called the Oro there. Really it's all over the world. I've seen Scotch herd boys use something like it to scare the cattle, and Mexican sheep herders in Texas to make the sheep run together when they scatter too far. Of course there's really nothing to be scared of, but when it comes near you, you feel inclined to duck. To me, it was the feeling that the flat piece of wood would fly off and hit me. You always duck when you hear a whizzing. Still, the priests or medicine men trade on the head-ducking tendency. So, somehow, in the course of time, it gets so that those that listen have to bow down. Oh yes! You say it's ridiculous and fanciful and all that sort of thing. I know. I have heard others say the same. It's only a noise and nothing to be scared of. But then, when you come to think of it, most men are scared of noise. They're like animals in that respect. What is a curse but a noise? Yet most men are secretly afraid of curses. They're uneasy under them. Yet they know it's only noise. Then look at thunderings from the pulpit. Look at excommunications. Look at denunciations. All noises, to be sure. But there's the threat of force behind some of them. The blow may come and again it may not.

"As I said, everyone bowed down and of course so did I, on general principles. Somerfield didn't, and the old buck whirled that bull-roarer over him ever so long, and the red-eyed hag cursed and spat at him, but he never budged. That sort of conduct is damned foolishness according to my notion. But then you see, in a kind of a way he was backing his prejudices against theirs, and prejudices are pretty solid things when you consider. Still, he took a hell of a chance.

"On the trail next day, for we left the following morning, I argued with him about that, but he couldn't be budged. He said he stood for truth and all that kind of thing. I put it to him that he would expect any foreigner to conform to his national customs. He'd expect a Turk to give up his polygamy, I said, no matter what heartbreakings it cost some of the family. But he had a kink in his thinking, holding that his people had the whole, solid, unchanging truth. Of course, the argument came down with a crash then, for it worked around to a question of what is truth. There you are. There was the limit. So we quit. As I tell you, the human brain is not constituted to do much thinking. It's been crippled by lack of use. We are mentally stunted in growth. I remember that I began to say something about the possibility of there being several gods, meaning that some time or other men with imagination had deified some natural thing, but it came to me that I was talking nonsense, so I quit. Yet I know right well that many tribes have made gods of things of which they were afraid. But it's small profit to theorize.

"It was near sun-down when we came to the building shown in that photograph. The vegetation was so thick thereabouts that the temple, for I suppose it was that, appeared before us suddenly. One moment we were crawling like insects between the trunks of great jungle trees that shot upwards seventy feet or more without a branch, as if they were racing for dear life skyward, and then everything fell away and there was the old building. It startled both of us. We got the sensation that you get when you see a really good play. You forget your bodily presence and you are only a bundle of nerves. You walk or sit or stand, but without any effort or knowledge that you are doing it. We had been talking, and the sight of that building, so unexpected, startled us into silence. It would anyone. Believe me, your imperturbable man with perfect, cool self-possession does not exist. Man's a jumpy thing, given to nerves. You may deny it and talk about the unexcitability of the American citizen and all that bunk, but let me tell you that your journalists and moving picture producers and preachers and politicians have caught on to the fact that man is jumpy, and they trade on their discovery, believe me. They've got man on the hop every which way and keep him going.

"There had been a gateway there once, but for some reason or other it had become blocked with a rank vegetation. The old gap was chocked full with a thorny, flower-bearing bush so thick that a cat could not have passed through. Somerfield switched on one of his theories as soon as he got over his first surprise. Worshippers, he held, had brought flowers there and the seeds that had dropped had sprouted. It looked reasonable.

"Above the lintel was carved one of those running lizards. That we noticed early. You can't see it in the picture because we took that from the edge of a broken wall. You see, all the walls stood, except the one to the left of this doorway, and that had partly fallen and what was left was chin high. We saw at a glance that the people who had built that temple were handy with tools. The stones of the wall were quite big—two feet or more square—and fitted closely. There was no mortar to hold them, but the ends had been made with alternate grooves and projections that dovetailed well. The stone was a kind of red sandstone. But I told you that before.

"When we looked over the broken wall and saw that stone lizard, we had another shock. I don't care how you school yourself, there's a scare in every man. That's what annoys me, to see men posing and letting themselves be written up and speechified over as fearless. Fearless General this and Admiral that. Our fearless boys in the trenches. It sickens me. Why the whole race has been fed up on Fear for ages. Fearlessness is impossible. Hell-fire, bogey-men, devils, witches, the wrath of God—it's all been fear. Things that we know nothing of and have no proof of, have been added to things that we do know of which will hurt, and on top of that there has been the everlasting 'cuidado' lest you say a word that will run foul of current opinion—so what wonder that man is scary? It's a wonder that he's sane.

"After we took that picture we debated for the first time where we should camp that night. A new scare possessed us. In the end, we decided to camp inside the temple because of the greater security afforded by the walls. The truth is that some half fear of a giant lizard had gotten hold of us. So, as it was the lizard that scared us, we decided to stay in the lizard temple. Man's built that way. He likes to keep close to the thing that he fears. I heard a man who was a banker once say that he always mistrusted the man who would not take a vacation. As I take it, his idea was that the man who knew some danger was nigh, wanted to be around where he could catch the first intimation of a crash. But then, too, besides that, there is a sense of comfort in being within walls, especially with a floor paved as this one was. Besides, it was a change from the trees with their wild tangled vines and their snake-like lianas. So we decided on the temple.

"That night I was a long time getting to sleep. The memory of the old hag and the bull-roarer was in my mind. I kept thinking of Ista too. It was a warmer night than usual, and, after the moon dropped, pitchy dark. I slept stripped, as I generally do, with a light blanket across my legs so that I could find it if needed without waking up.

"I awoke presently, feeling something run lightly and swiftly across my face. I thought it was a spider. It seemed to run in a zig-zag. Then feeling nothing more, I set it down to fancy and dropped off to sleep again, my face turned towards that idol. Later, I felt the same kind of thing run across my neck. I knew it was no fancy then and my scare vanished because there was something to do. So I waited with my right hand poised to grab. I waited a long time, too, but I have lots of patience. Presently it ran down my body, starting at my left shoulder and I brought down my hand at a venture, claw fashion, and caught the thing on the blanket. I felt the blanket rise and then fall again, just a little of course, as I lifted my hand with the beast in it, and by that knew that it had claws. You bet I held tight. It seemed to be hard and smooth. It was a wiry, wriggling thing, somewhat like a lizard. But it was much more vigorous than any lizard. I tried to crush it but could not. As to thickness, it seemed to be about the diameter of one of those lead pencils. It was like this I had it."

Rounds picked up a couple of lead pencils from the desk and took my hand in his. He told me to close my fist and then placed one pencil lengthwise so that an end of it was between my first and second finger and the rubber-tipped end lay across my wrist. The other pencil he thrust crosswise so that the pointed end stuck out between the second and third finger and the blunt end between the index finger and thumb.

"There you have it," he said. "That's how I held the little devil. Now grip hard and try to crush the pencils and you'll have something of the same sensation I had. Holding it thus, I could feel its head jerking this way and that violently, and its tail, long and lithe, lashing at my wrist. The little claws were trying to tear, but they were evidently softish. I could hear, or thought I could, the snap of its little jaws. It was about the nastiest sensation that I ever experienced. I don't know why I thought that it was venomous, but I did. I tried to smash the thing in my hand—tried again and again, and I have a good grip—but I might just as well have tried to crush a piece of wire. There was no give to it. It tried to wriggle backwards, but I had it under its jaws, tight pinched with my knuckles. So there we were; it wriggling, writhing and lashing, and me lying there holding it at arm's length. I felt the sweat start on me and the hair at the nape of my neck rise up, and I did some quick and complicated thinking. Of course, I dared not throw it away, but I got to my feet and, as I did so, tried to bend its head backwards against the stone floor. But the head slipped sideways. I called on Somerfield for a light then and he struck one hurriedly and it went out immediately. All that I saw was that the thing was white and had a triangular-shaped head.

"Somehow I ran against Somerfield before he got another match struck and he swore at me, saying that I had cut him. I knew that I had touched him with my outstretched hand that held the beast. I drew back my hand a little and remembered afterwards that I then felt a slight elastic resistance as if the thing that I held had caught on to something, as it had before to my blanket. Afterwards I found that the thing had gotten Somerfield's neck. As he struck another match, I saw the low place in the wall and flung the beastly thing away with a quick jerk. You know the kind of a motion you'd make getting rid of some unseen noxious thing like that. That's how I never really saw the creature and can only conjecture what it was like from the feel of it.

"On Somerfield's neck, just below the angle of the jaw, was a clean-cut little oval place about half an inch in length. It did not bleed much but it seemed to pain him a lot. He maintained that the beast was some kind of rodent. Anyway we put a little chewed tobacco on the place and, after awhile, tried to sleep again. We didn't do much good at it, neither of us. He was tossing and grumbling like a man with the toothache.

"Next morning the bitten place had swollen up to the size of an apple and was a greenish yellow color. He was feeling sick and a bit feverish, so I made him comfortable after looking around to see whether there was anything to harm him in the courtyard, then went to hunt water. I remember that I gave the head of the idol a kick with the flat of my foot for spite, as I passed it. Like a kid, that was, wasn't it? Now I was running back and forth all the morning with the canteen, for he drank a terrible quantity. His eyes grew bright too and his skin flushed. Towards noon he began to talk wild, imagining that he was at home. Then I judged it best to let him stay there in the temple, where he was, so to speak, corralled. Coming back shortly after from one water-hunting trip, I heard singing, and, looking over the wall, saw him sitting on the slab in front of the idol. He must hare fancied that he was at home in Ohio and had his kids before him, for he was beating time with his hands and snapping his fingers and thumbs and singing:

"'London bridge is fallen down,
    Fallen down, fallen down.'

"It was rotten to hear that out there, but I was half way glad to see him that way, knowing that he wasn't miserable. After a little, he quit his babbling and took more water; emptied the canteen in fact, so back I had to start for more.

"Returning, I found things changed, He was going around crouched like a hunting Indian, peering here and there, behind the idol then across to the head, as if seeking someone. He had the facon in his hand. 'Rounds stabbed me,' he was saying. 'It was Rounds, damn him, that killed me.' Over and over again he said that. He was talking to invisible people, creatures of his mad brain. One would have thought, if one had not seen, that the temple court was crowded with spectators. Then he rose to his feet and, with the knife held close to his breast, began walking round and round as if seeking an outlet. He passed me once, he on one side of the wall and I on the other, and he looked me square in the eye, but never saw me. So round and round he went with long strides, knees bent and heels never touching the ground. His eyes were fixed and staring and his teeth clenched. Now and then he made long, slashing stabs in the air with the facon.

"Suddenly he saw me, and there was a change. The blood lust was in his eyes. He was standing on the slab in front of the idol, then made a great leap and started for the broken wall where I was. I saw then that the lump on his neck had swollen to the size of a big goitre. His whole body was a-quiver. There was an animal-like celerity in his movements that made me shudder. Then I knew that I dared not let him get on the same side of the wall with me. But he leaped at the gap from a distance that I would have thought no human could compass, and hung on to the wall with one arm over, snarling with teeth bared and slavering lips. I smashed him over the head with the canteen, gripping the strap with mg right hand. He fell back with the force of the blow but immediately came at the gap again, then changed his mind and went to tearing around the chamber with great leaps. He was a panther newly caged. He sprang on to the head of the idol and from that to the pedestal, and then to the slab in front of it. Then he went across and across the floor, sometimes screaming and yelling, and then again moaning and groaning. One side of his face was all bloody where I had smashed it with the canteen. Seeing him so, a thing not human, but with all the furtive quickness of an animal and its strength too, I felt sorry no more. I hated him with a wild hate. He was dangerous to me and I had to conquer him. That's fundamental. So I stood, gripping the strap of the canteen, watching, waiting. He came at me again striding and leaping. That time he got one leg over, with both hands gripping the top stones. The facon he dropped on my side of the wall, but I had no time to stoop for it just then. There were other things to do. He was getting over. It took some frantic beating with the canteen and he seemed to recover from the blows more quickly than I could get the swing to strike again. But I beat him down at last, though I saw that he had lots more life in him than I, with that devil of madness filling him. So, when I saw him stumble, then recover and begin that running again, I picked up the knife and leaped over the wall to settle the matter once and for all. It was an ugly thing that I had to do, but it had to be done and done quickly. At the root of things it's life against life."

Rounds ceased and fell to filling his pipe. I waited for him to say more, but he made as if to leave, though pausing a moment at my desk to pick up and examine a piece of malachite. I felt it incumbent upon me to say something to relieve the tension that I felt.

"I understand," said I. "It was a horrible necessity. It is a terrible thing to have to kill a fellow-creature."

"That wasn't a fellow-creature," he insisted. "What I killed was not the partner I knew. Don't you understand?"

"Yes, I understand," I replied. Then I asked, "Did you bury him?"

"Bury him? What for? How?" Rounds seemed indignant. "How could I bury him in a stone-paved court? How could I lift a dead man over a wall chin high?"

"Of course! Of course," I said. "I had forgotten that. But to us who lead quiet lives, it seems terrible to leave a dead man unburied."

"Do you feel that way about the mummy you have out there?" he asked, indicating the museum with his thumb. "If not, why not? But if you want the story to the bitter end, I dragged him to the only clean spot in the place, which was that slab in front of the idol. There I left him, or it. But things take odd turns. By the time I got back to the Tlinga village, they knew all about it and the priests used the affair to their own advantage. Mine was incidental. Yet I did reap some benefit. According to the priests, I had accepted the whole blessed lizard theory, or religion, or whatever it was, and had sacrificed the unbeliever to the lizard god. Ista helped things along, I suspect, for with me as a former mate, there was some fame for her. Anyway they met and hailed me as a hero and brought tribute to me. Gold dust they gave me. I wanted them to quit their damned foolishness and tried to explain, but it was no use. You can't teach a mob to have sense. Well, adios. But remember this. Don't be too cocksure."

The Beast of the Yungas
Willis Knapp Jones

"Fear?" the explorer repeated, pushing back his sherbet glass with a quick, nervous hand. "Oh, I suppose I've hung back as often as the next man, but in time one gets calloused to fear, I imagine."

Several of the dinner guests expressed polite interest, but Grace Demming, debutante daughter of the hostess, looked at the guest of honor with an expression in her wide-set gray eyes like one regarding a super-creature. "Haven't you ever been afraid, Mr. Winslow?" Her rich contralto voice was very lovely.

"If you mean fear as those fiction writers describe it, when a man's soul is turned to water, I can't say I've ever experienced it, nor come in contact with it except—perhaps—" He paused awkwardly, glanced at the ladies around the table, then finished hurriedly: "No, never."

Mrs. Mason, the dowager next to him, caught him up quickly as though scenting a choice bit of gossip. "Was it something terrible?" she' inquired. "You needn't be afraid to tell us. It couldn't be nearly so unprintable as many things we read every day in the papers."

"Well," the explorer began, "it isn't scandalous. I didn't mean to give that impression. In fact—to tell the truth, it's something I've been trying to drive out of my mind, but it persists in coming back without bringing an explanation with it."

Miss Demming's gray eyes seemed to plead with him, too. He had been especially conscious all evening of the way they held him, seeming to draw him out.

And now there was a strange aloofness in that girl as though she were curtained off from the world. His explorer instinct made him want to know more about her. He had gone into Afghanistan once just because he had read that a certain temple in Mangfu had a curtain screening off a mystery that not more than two people then alive had seen. He wanted to pierce the veil.

"I'm afraid you won't be satisfied," Winslow began. "I don't know what caused the fear. I can't tell you any of the details, but the thing that seared my soul was a look of fright in the eyes of another man." He made a gesture as though to repel the host of memories crowding in upon him. "It's not a pretty story. After all, I believe I'd better not tell it."

If that were meant for a refusal, its only effect was to make the guests more interested. All of them urged him to continue—all but Miss Demming; yet her half-parted lips and that inscrutable something in her eyes made him go on.

"It was in Bolivia that it happened—Bolivia, that unexplored country where anything might be true. I was in La Paz concluding some Inca investigation. Strange rumors had been filtering in about some queer beast that the Indians of the Beni region had seen. The scientists of the capital were trying to convince us that the description fitted a diplodocus, or some other prehistoric creature like it."

From the looks of interrogation, he knew that he was talking beyond most of them. "The diplodocus," he hastened to explain, "was a huge creature from ten to fifteen feet high and perhaps forty feet long that lived ages ago during the Pleistocene period before the tyrannosaurus came along and killed them off. You've probably seen reconstructions of them in museums, looking like a kangaroo with a long, tapering tail. At any rate, the jungle Indians were claiming to have seen a creature that has been extinct for at least 25,000 years.

"Frankly, I didn't believe a word of the story. I thought that some of those coca-crazed savages had gone on a spree; it was good newspaper stuff, however, like the creature that was reported in Argentina later. The upshot was that my committee at home read about it and cabled me to investigate. I didn't object. I love Bolivia. There's not a country I know of that is richer in interest for foreigners, and here was a chance to visit a part I'd never seen.

"I needed a few more pongos—those Indians that can carry anything up to a trunk on their shoulders—and while I was looking for them, I ran across Manion, or rather he ran across me. Nobody knew Manion. He was a silent chap who did nothing in the daytime but sun himself in front of the Congressional Building on the plaza, and when the cold evenings of the *alto plano* descended, he would disappear into the *pension* where he boarded. People said he was cracked. He had drifted into La Paz a few months before, no one knew from where. Where so many foreigners are fugitives, it doesn't do to make too many inquiries, but I half suspected he didn't know any too much about himself. He had a lot of uncomfortable habits. One was to tap incessantly at a silver plate embedded in his skull, when he was pondering. It reminded me of the old-fashioned wireless decoder where a hammer jars apart the filings. Perhaps he was trying to clarify his thoughts in the same way.

"But he would never tell us how he acquired the plate or the limp. Once, later when I had taken him with me, I saw scars on his body and he explained that he thought he had had an argument and after it they had given him some false ribs, which wasn't any explanation at all.

"Since he was a likable chap and could take the place of my secretary, who was down with dysentery, I gave him a job. He wrote a copperplate hand, could handle the porters, and was a big help.

"The day we left La Paz he appeared in a faded and worn flying suit with double wings on the breast. He apologized for it by saying he had no other roughing costume and had not wanted to bother me about an advance on his wages. Later he let drop that he had been in the Lafayette Escadrille, but that was a lie. I've looked over their records and no Manion or name like it appears in their roster.

"If I had been superstitious or gifted with prophecy we never should have left La Paz; but unfortunately, man can't see what lies ahead. I won't describe that trip, day after weary day. All the colors of an artist's palette could never reproduce its splendor, but all the tortures of the Inquisition are puny beside the sufferings it laid upon us. Sometimes we would toil for hours through knee-deep grasses with rain so heavy that it was like a curtain to push against. Then the torrid sun would trans form the jungle in a twinkling into a vapor bath where we could scarcely breathe. But through all the hardships, Manion was always ready with a song. He seemed to know only one, but when we were dog-tired and needed to push on farther, his singing helped.

"He had evidently never been in the jungle before, and everything was wonderful. When all I could see was the next three feet of the trail, he would want to stop to be told about a new bird he had seen in one of the snakewood trees.

"But where he excelled was as a revolver shot. I never saw anyone so quick on the draw and so sure in aim. Once"—Winslow shuddered— "a boa constrictor, twined about a branch above the trail, swung down it head like a battering ram and with a single blow dislocated the neck of one of our Indian bearers. I was next in line, but before I could get out my revolver or that battering head could swing back, Manion put three shots into it. Then with hands absolutely steady, he stopped to reload his revolver. Out of curiosity, I felt his pulse—as slow as a child's. When not a single tremor betrayed his excitement, I thought he must a man without nerves. That's what makes the rest of it so horrible."

Again the explorer stopped and took a sip of water. His own hand shook slightly as he set down the glass. After a moment he went on. "Manion had shot a twenty-eight-foot boa without disturbing his calm. You can see the skin in the museum, for I brought it back. He wanted to take the head, too, with the three bullet holes below the frontal bone so close together that a quarter would have covered them. We were rather short of carriers, however, so he had to give up the idea.

"It was a long journey to the place where the guides told us the animal had been seen, and far from any beaten path. No white people had penetrated that far before, so Manion, Jenkins (the botanist and geologist) and I—the only white people of the party— were a constant source of interest and fear to the few Indians we met. When we reached the tribe whose members had seen the animal, I found that neither my Aimara or Quechua, nor any of the Beni dialects Jenkins thought he knew were any use. Even the guide had difficulty making himself understood, but he did make out that they had recently seen that prehistoric animal. We were soon led to the place.

"If—mark I say 'if'—there's a place in this world where creatures of the Miocene and Pleistocene Ages might be expected to survive down to our own day, the valley we reached is the one. It was a sunken plain, about twenty or thirty miles square and full of that riot of vegetation which must have covered the earth when the diplodocus roamed it, for they ate only grass. You know how La Paz is situated—a sheer drop of one thousand feet below the surrounding plain. Well, this region was something like it, except that it had no exit, no river winding out of it, no path up the slope—only straight, sheer cliffs. Without elaborate tackle nothing down there could get out, and nothing outside, falling by accident over the edge, would live to want to get out. We went three-quarters of the way around before we found the place where the walls were lowest and least steep. There we made camp.

"We intended to make a permanent camp in the valley itself, but when we ordered the carriers to go down the three-hundred-foot vine ladder that they had constructed, there was a mutiny. Don't tell me sign language doesn't exist. Not one of our carriers had been told by us the reason for our coming, and yet all of them, without understanding a word of the jargon of that region, knew all about the beasts supposed to be hidden by the tangle of foliage below.

"They were afraid even of staying near the place, and I am sure that if we had carried out our plan and had us three white men make our camp below, they would have deserted, leaving us helpless in the jungle. It was Manion's idea to have two of us explore the lower valley by daylight, the other one staying with the carriers.

"Jenkins, who had been ill for a large part of the trip, suddenly took a turn for the worse. He was useless. He could do nothing but lie in the smaller of the lean-tos, leaving Manion and me to set in place the ladder the Indians had woven.

"It was almost dark before we completed the work, and we were so excited that we could not wait till morning. We descended to the lower level, not knowing what we should find, perhaps some footprints in the soft ground. But in our brief survey we found nothing, so, as it was growing dark, I suggested we had better return to camp.

"Manion wouldn't leave. He wanted to spend the night there in the valley, hoping to hear something. With Jenkins sick, I could not ye well accompany him, especially as the Indians had been nervous and jumpy all day. Yet I hesitated to leave Manion. He laughed at my fears He had two revolvers and was not at all afraid. Finally I gave in after he promised to sleep close to the ladder, to which he could retreat in case of danger.

"As I climbed the vine ladder, I looked back. I shall never forget the sight. Already the valley foliage was deepening in color where it lay closest to the western ledge. It would not have been difficult to imagine anything in that tangle of green. I called down a warning as I saw Manion brushing the ground where he was going to sleep. And as I went up the ladder, I heard him singing to himself that song that was so continually on his lips. It certainly had a haunting strain; I've never heard anybody else sing it. *Bonny Eloise* I think it is called. It goes—"

A cry like that of a stricken bird broke into his story. Grace Demming, her face suddenly dead white, leaned forward, clutching the tab for support. Her glass of water overturned and the water spread slowly across the tablecloth, but no one moved. "Jimmy!" she moaned. "Then he didn't die in France."

Instant confusion reigned. Several of the company protested that she must be mistaken, that he could not possibly have reached South America. In the babble of sound, Miss Beardsley told Winslow that Miss Demming had been engaged to an aviator who had been reported killed in battle. Could that wound in the head have played pranks with his memory? The whole thing sounded preposterous, but Miss Demming was convinced.

"It was Jimmy," she insisted. "Something you said made me begin to suspect. Then you mentioned his writing, and now the only song he ever sang. Wait!" She burst out of the room, her mother following. In an instant she had returned with a photograph of a man in a flying suit. There was no doubt about it, then. Manion and the Jimmy Kent to whom Miss Demming had been engaged were the same. The explorer recognized him at once.

"Where is he?' she cried. "Tell me, where is he?"

Winslow looked at her sadly. "I am sorry, Miss Demming," he said gently. "He's dead."

It seemed as though a whisper echoed his words. The girl clutched at her throat, pale as the lace that edged her collar. Her gray eyes appealed for more details.

"Yes, there's no doubt of it. Manion—I mean Kent—came back the next day convinced that we had been hoaxed and that no animal existed except in some Indian's delirious imagination. We started back toward La Paz, but somewhere in the lowlands, perhaps the night he roamed the sunken valley, he had contracted jungle fever. We did all we could to make him comfortable, but in spite of all, he died, conscious to the end and entirely without pain. I wish you could see the paradise where we buried him, under a beautiful chonta palm, and we scattered orchids over the place before we left."

There was a scattered volley of questions. "Didn't you see the animal?"

The explorer shook his head. "How could one see a beast that has been extinct for centuries?"

Then the bald old man beside Miss Demming spoke up. "But I don't see what your story proves, Mr. Winslow. Where was the fear you spoke of?"

"Didn't I say? It was—it was in the faces of the Indians when they talked about the valley. The superstitious terror in their countenances when we told them we were going to camp in the valley was enough to make strong men shiver. But I don't blame them, exactly. It was the fear of the unknown that gripped them, so that I was glad enough to leave them and return to civilization. But I wonder whether there aren't almost as many superstitious terrors among the civilized."

The conversation switched, and soon the guests left the table and went to the porch, where coffee was served.

The explorer, wishing to escape from the others, had slipped into the house and was standing alone, watching the light of an automobile on the mountain road above him, when he sensed a presence. He had withdrawn from the group but Mr. Demming had found him. "Perhaps the others believed your story, perhaps not. But Kent was engaged to my daughter. He fell behind the German lines and we never had definite proof of his death. Grace has never been herself since, always hoping that he would someday return. Now I want the truth."

The explorer nodded wearily. "It's your right," he acknowledged dully. "I should never have begun the story in the first place. Again and again I have tried to efface its horror from my mind, but it leaps out, as it did tonight."

"Then part of it is true? I beg of you, be careful."

"I know, Mr. Demming. Unfortunately, it is true—true to the point where the boy and I parted. The rest of it I have never told a soul. Sometimes at night it fairly screams for utterance.

"I said he came up in the morning. He didn't. Shortly after I reached the camp, I threw down a blanket for him and some food. Then he made a fire and I went into the lean-to. Suddenly I heard a scream—his voice. It was too dark to see or do anything. Again and again I called his name. Only the echoes and the scream of the vampire bats answered me. All night I shuddered, waiting, waiting. When the first streak of light came, I took a gun and went down after him. At first I found nothing. Then I picked up his footprints, far apart, slipping and dodging as though he had been running. The reason for his haste was not apparent until I saw in the muck the mark of a gigantic foot. About ten feet farther on was another, and in between the trail of a heavy tail.

"Farther on was a trodden space about a thick, bushy growth. The tracks were mute evidence of the story. A mad chase and flight, dodging about the bush, with the huge creature finally breaking down the vegetation. Then I noticed other footprints, smaller, coming from another direction, from where the ladder hung.

"And finally, under the trampled bushes, I found Manion, dead. His face! Deadly terror had graven unforgettable lines on it, such horror and loathing as I never saw before. Please God I'll never have to see it again! And his body—not a sign of bruise or hurt upon it, the only mark, a messy green slime on one hand, as though an animal had slobbered over it.

"As I caught the significance, the world began making dizzying circles about me, and when next I knew anything, it was almost evening. Manion was lying in the same place, his sightless eyes staring as though seeing into hell. Hastily I buried him, as I said, at the foot of a palm and dropped orchids over his grave.

"Jenkins, when I found him, was in a fever of excitement. The carriers had deserted with most of our provisions. It was imperative to start back at once to save the lives of both of us. My nerves were in terrible shape, and Jenkins was about helpless, but we eventually reached La Paz."

"And you left Manion's body for that horrible animal to dig up and eat?"

The explorer shook his head. "No, that's the thing that makes me believe an unbelievable fact. Manion, who, as I knew, was a cool, accurate shot, had died of fright, paralyzed by the sight of some monster, and the beast had the chance to eat him any time during the night. His hand bore evidence that the creature had sniffed him, but there was no sign of bite. Do you know any modern South American animal of any size that would not have eaten him? I don't. I know, however, that the diplodocus is herbivorous. Grass forms its diet. So I think he may have seen such a prehistoric animal as the Indians mentioned. I don't know. People would call me crazy if I told them I believed it. But some day I'm going back to Bolivia. The nights when I think about Manion, I can not sleep. I must go back to see what it was that shocked him lifeless with that horror that I saw painted indelibly on his features. Perhaps—who knows?"

The Paradise of the Ice Wilderness
Jul. Regis

We were half a dozen good friends, enjoying a glass of beer at the village inn, and we had just asked the sea captain for a story.

He put down his pipe and produced two small cuttings from his pocket-book. He cleared his throat and began:

Well, I should like to refute those strange hypotheses and statements which have been produced from many quarters regarding what occurred at the bay of Chantanga east of Cape Tscheljuskin in North Siberia during the winter of 1896-'97. It happened during the trip along the coast of North Asia, which I then made with the Swedish whaler, *The White Bear*, and the story which I am going to tell you will thus be the narrative of an eye witness to a queer occurrence in North Siberia on Christmas Eve in 1896.

For those among you who peradventure have not heard anything about the matter, I will read both these cuttings.

"December 29th, 1896. A Curious Discovery. On the morning of Christmas Day, a trapper of Russian nationality arrived at the little town of Popigaisk, near the mouth of the Chantanga in Chantanga Bay, telling the people in town and asking to be believed, that he had seen, some miles north of the town, fresh tracks of a large animal; and he was quite sure that this animal was a mastodon. If the man was right in his supposition, this means an astonishing bit of news. Our correspondent adds that a heavy snowfall has already blotted out the tracks of the animal."

"January 9th, 1897. A Christmas Guest from the Primitive Ages? A week ago we published a short article regarding a queer discovery in unknown Siberia. It seems now as if the discovery may be confirmed from another source. Many persons have certainly been looking for the tracks of the mastodon without result, but if we dared believe the Esquimau Amsalic, he has been close upon making a nearer acquaintance with the strange animal. He, too, had been searching for the tracks, until dusk began to fall and with it a fine, thick snow, which made it impossible for him to proceed any further. He was about to turn back, when, in the darkness, he heard a loud cracking—like that of ice breaking up in spring, he said. The next instant heavy clumsy feet resounded against the frozen ground and a clumsy, gigantic body of unusual shape rushed past by him so closely that he felt the rush of air. The animal had undoubtedly been frightened by something, perhaps by Amsalic himself. Since this narrative has been made public, several hunters have set out to hunt the mysterious animal."

When these articles were printed, I was frozen in with my ship and crew in the Polar Sea, but I have been told that they aroused considerable interest in certain quarters. Various ideas were debated; everyone had his own version of the matter. The most fantastic comments were published. Nevertheless, the truth seems more fantastic still.

On August 1st I sailed from Hammerfest, as captain, with my vessel, the old splendid *White Bear*, which, in spring, 1899, collided with an iceberg and sank off Archangel. The plan of the expedition was the usual one: to proceed along the north coast of Europe and Asia as long as possible, hunting for the whales and seals which are getting scarcer year by year. It was no new and untried enterprise. Already in the middle of 1800 an attempt had been made to create a regular whale traffic in those waters. Such an expedition usually stayed away a year, but proceeded in the summer as far as possible. In the winter it lay frozen in by the ice and returned the following spring with heavily-laden vessels.

We thus coasted along the shore of Kola and Kanin south of Koljugow and up towards Karuporten, a voyage which is a little longer in reality than in description. We were lucky. In three months we were able to discharge a full cargo at the company's station on Nova Semlja. Encouraged by our progress we continued eastwards, so that at the beginning of the winter we found ourselves at 114° eastern longitude in Nordenskiolds sea, after having followed about the same course as the Vega. Here, at the mouth of the Chantanga, we ultimately became icebound for the winter and had to prepare for an arctic winter sojourn.

The vast ice desert which surrounded us would have been irritating in its monotony if the eye had not found a fixed point in the expanse of white. Hardly fifty yards to our right was s little island, also covered with ice, from which one had a view of the narrow sound that separates the island from the mainland. The island was a mass of rock, in some pasts unusually high over the water's edge, while the mountain top in its center had a height of say three thousand feet. The island, which has no name on the chart, was christened by the crew "Hermit Island."

While the ship was being pushed out of the water by the ice, we built ourselves a winter hut on the island. Our new residence was very comfortable. The house was divided into one large and one small room. In the former resided a part of the crew and in the latter the mate, trapper Jenssen, the controller of the company, a young man, named Berg, who was much like on board the steamer on account of his friendly and pleasant manner, and lastly myself. The rooms were lighted and warmed by a dynamo which we had on board.

Under such circumstances it is not surprising that life is likely to be lonely and sad. And it was worst at Christmas time. We felt homesick, while we were sitting at a late breakfast on the 24th of December on Hermit Island. Everyone of us was taken up with his own thoughts, even the controller, Berg, showed a gloomy face, and we expected no pleasant Christmas.

But if we wanted a stimulating interruption, we got it. We had not quite finished our meal when the ship's cook threw open the door and rushed in, followed by a sailor. I asked in astonishment what was the matter, but the man was so bewildered that he could not reply, and the sailor explained, instead.

"Well, captain, we have made a discovery!" he said.

Their whole appearance was one of such helpless astonishment that I followed the two men without a word. My four comrades accompanied me, of course, and our two guides led us to the foot of a cliff, where the whole of the crew was standing staring at something. Not a little inquisitive, we made our way to them through the snow. At the side of the perpendicular stone wall a compact mass of ice had been gathering through the ages. Its size and color hinted a great age. The secret which it was hiding would, however, never have been revealed, if the cook, who was a very smart fellow, had not made a fire on exactly this spot in order to get some fresh water for the kitchen. The result was astonishing. When the cook returned for more water, the fire had melted a deep hollow in the ice at the side of the cliff, and when, by chance, he cast a glance through this ice window, what he saw was sufficient to make him sit down in the snow, dumb with astonishment.

The sparkling fire continued its work, and when we arrived, the hollow was over six feet deep, making a cavity in the ice wall outside of which the fire was burning. There was nothing unusual in all this but through the clear ice wall, the contours of a big animal could be seen. Embedded in the blue ice, we saw two curved tusks, each as long as a full-grown man.

"Ohoy," exclaimed Berg, his jovial mind soon mastering the astonishment. "More fuel! We are going to melt out the poor thing!"

Wood was fetched and the fire crackled and blazed.

The flames threw red reflections in among the ice rocks, and the shadows were deep violet and farther away blue. Above us the stars were sparkling and bright northern lights fluttered over half the sky. The intense heat caused the icy water to rush around our feet, but, while the undermost layers of wood hissed and sputtered and smoked in the snow-water, the uppermost flamed briskly, fed with dry bushes, which in more protected places had carried on a hopeless fight against the arctic cold. Round the fire all the crew of *The White Bear* were standing, gazing almost in stupor, at the scene and at each other. The contours of the big animal emerged more and more. The ice grew thinner and whiter. All at once a little black spot appeared. It grew bigger, and a brown-grey, hairy hide was bared.

"What the—is it not a mammoth?" cried Berg in his impulsive manner.

So it was. My men wished to cut out the animal with their axes, but I forbade it, fearing to injure the body. The ice melted slowly away, and finally the colossus stood free, under an arched roof of dripping ice. The shapeless beast measured about eleven feet in height and twelve feet in length—the trunk wag longer than the tallest man among the crew. The second mate, who always boasted of his knowledge, remarked that such discoveries had been made before in several places in Siberia and that the ice hermetically sealed and preserved the dead body and saved it from decay, as the cold hindered the activity of the decaying organism. The flesh of the animal before us was, therefore, as fresh as if it had lived yesterday and not several thousand years ago. In order to confirm his word, the man inserted his knife in the animal's side and behold—some drops of blood squirted out of the cut! At this sight, several of the fellows paled and I, too, grew more than astonished. This blood, that I saw dripping before my eyes, had been coursing through the veins of the animal during the primeval ages!

The crew, however, had brought more wood and the red flames from the fire threw a weird shining reflection on the thousand or more years old ice wall.

This scene in the darkness of the frozen expanses of the Polar Sea at Christmas time was so like a saga, that we hardly should have been astonished if the big animal body had awakened to life and stepped out among us. The hide was steaming, and the hairy trunk shook. Berg was polishing his nose loudly—would the mastodon lift its trunk in a thundering answer?

In eager curiosity the ship's mate was running about the animal, fingering it, measuring it and all the while holding a short scientific lecture to us others who were regarding the wonder in silence.

But this animal? Did not the legs shake under it? Did it not slowly alter its position? What would happen now?

Frozen and hungry, but not less interested, we waited breathlessly for the continuation of the adventure. And it came, though it took time.

When the fire had been fighting the thousand year old ice for some hours the colossus from antiquity began to stagger, and with a noise which shook the ground, the gigantic animal fell heavily on one side, extinguishing the flames as if he had blown out a candle. But simultaneously something else happened. Just where the colossus had been standing beside the wall of the cliff, we discovered a vault and within this we saw...

Several years have now passed since this event happened, but still I can hardly describe what we heard and saw when the thousand year old ice-field revealed its secret to us. During the whole of a long winter we had only seen ice, ice in every conceivable formation.

The monotony of the white and solitary ice-fields that stretched to the horizon had almost killed us. We had lost all hope of a change. I do not know whether you will understand me, but the mere prospect of an adventure of such unexpected proportions as this quite bewildered us.

Before our eyes there opened a rocky passage, covered with bleached skulls and skeletons, the bones of animals. These were creatures from hoary antiquity, which had guarded the secret! Above us loomed the heavy rock formations of the mountain, in their shadow hiding a world-startling mystery. For already from without we could see that the passage led into the depths of darkened caverns, into a system of passages and caves.

"Forward boys—follow your leader!" cried Berg and stormed into the darkness.

"Wait—a lantern!" I cried.

"Not necessary—it is already lighter here!" His answer sounded hollow, as if it had come from a mine.

We stood bewildered, not believing our eyes or ears. Finally four others and myself penetrated into the passage. From a distance, Berg called to us. The echoes changed each of his words to a rattling volley of musketry.

It was a low irregular vault, half dark for about a thousand yards ahead and filled by violently scattered rocks which in some places only gave space enough to creep through. The cleft finally widened into a high vaulted grotto, which lost itself in twilight in all directions—a silent and sinister place, whose inhabitants had been dumb for generations. Everywhere these bones! Eloquent, even if dumb evidences of races that perished long ago! A cold, dry air of decay and death filled our nostrils, yet the place was not uncanny or even sinister. The ground was covered with gorgeously shaped plants, many of which were luminous or strangely colored. There were ferns of a height that seemed enormous to us—unknown kinds of trees, flowers in subdued tints, mostly pale red, some with white stripes. It was a radiance of pale and clear colors that was delightful. While we were devouring the scene with our eyes, Berg joined us. Some yards farther on we were stopped by a murmuring sound. A watercourse slowly sought its way between the stones. And on its margins we found big bleached human bones. I took one of the grinning skulls in my hand. It stared at me with its empty eye cavities as if it were saying:

"Solve my secret, if you can!"

But where did this vegetation come from, this rich verdure in the midst of the ice wilderness? After having followed the watercourse for a while, we found the explanation. It stopped suddenly at the foot of a wall of rock, where a whirlpool was in action. I dipped my hand in the water. It was warm. A subterranean spring then—and further away—very, very high up—faint light was visible. There must be an opening.

The mate declared that we were standing on a volcanic crater bottom in what had been a fire-vomiting mountain, extinct long ago.

It was a paradise we had discovered, a paradise of twilight and solitude, it is true, but a pleasure garden compared with the cold expanse which outside stretched in all directions. We balanced ourselves on the stones and crossed over the watercourse and walked up the opposite shore, which sloped up from the water. Arrived at the top we found before us a large expanse, whose borders were lost in the darkness on all sides. Here and there phosphoric fungus growths spread a pale light over the bed rock. I sniffed the air.

"Queer," I remarked. "It seems to me as if..."

"It smelt of stables, yes," Berg interrupted me with a snort.

"And hundreds of them," added the mate emphatically.

Berg set up an hallooing. The echo replied with a hollow roar that startled us.

"What a mighty echo," remarked Berg, a trifle pale. After it had died away, a sinister silence fell over the cavern. We did not move.

"Down there, where the earth is softer…" the mate muttered in a perplexed voice.

"What?" I exclaimed.

He pointed along the shore.

"Do you not see the earth is full of footprints?"

"By Jove!" exclaimed Berg. "Footprints of the mammoth!"

"Or of a still bigger animal," the mate continued. "Some are old and dried up. Some were made later. Some were made today!"

He spoke the last sentence in such bewilderment, that we all drew nearer.

All at once it seemed darker and uncannier about us than ever before.

"Hm," said Berg with a voice which he tried to make steady. "For my part I am turning back."

"Yes, let us go back!" I repeated.

At the same instant the echo was heard before us again, though we had only spoken in whisperings. Out of the darkness came a roar, strong as the trump of doom, and uttered at short intervals. It was heard again and again, followed by a sound as if a sledge-hammer were regularly being thrown against the earth. My hair seemed to rise on my head and I lifted my arms, for I thought that the mountain was going to fall over me.

Something panted and stamped among the rocks, something roared and rumbled. Without a sound the mate held up his hand and pointed.

I followed his glance.

"Great Heaven!" I whispered.

There—between some gigantic ferns stood a comrade to the prehistoric animal we had just melted out of the ice, but living and, it seemed, of quite a different kind. The legs were those of an elephant, the body large and the throat thick and covered with long, strag-gling, red bristles. The head was enormous and finished almost abruptly with a large, broad mouth. The tail, which was furiously whipping the leaves of the giant ferns, was long, resembling that of a lizard.

The giant lizard, or whatever I am to call the thing, set up a hissing sound and approached us.

There was no mistake about it; its eyes were staring at us! It looked at us with a greediness which unrolled a perspective of horrible views for our inner sight.

For a moment we stared at each other, the animal from antiquity and the men from the Swedish whaler, *The White Bear*. Then the mate set off at top speed over stock and stone towards the entrance of the passage, followed closely by the rest of us. One of us cried out, but I do not think it was I.

We were running for life, and after us came a roll like thunder, when four heavy feet stamped against the bottom of the crater and the panting animal voice rose and fell. I sent up a silent prayer to the great Someone, that we might be permitted to get outside ere those feet...

The mate was running like a madman before me, to my left Berg, behind us the others and lastly the animal. In this order we entered the passage.

As it was very narrow and hardly would permit an animal of such dimensions to pass through it, we felt pretty safe here, but we didn't think of that. We imagined that the beast was close on our heels and on we ran. We used up the last remnant of air in our lungs to reach the entrance. But the cold had already begun to close it, and we had hard work to break it open again. Without a snowstorm raged, and it was a white death that confronted us. When we had worked halfway out to the ship, a man with a lighted but snowed-over lantern, met us. The North wind had raised its mighty voice, and the ice was already jamming *The White Bear*. For two weeks we worked day and night to save the ship. When we finally succeeded, we had drifted so far out that we dared not risk another attempt to reach the Hermit Island.

The ice wilderness up there still hides a sealed-up paradise. But by all top-lanterns and yard-arms, I am in no hurry to penetrate into that hidden region a second time.

The Ancient Horror
Hal Grant

"It will be interesting if they happen to find the lizard and it turns out to be the real thing."

"What thing?" I asked. Rutherford had been reading the paper to himself.

By way of reply, he handed me the paper, at the same time pointing to a head-line carrying the information that scientists were on their way to Africa to search for a PREHISTORIC MONSTER SEEN BY HUNTERS IN NORTHERN AFRICAN SWAMP."

From the writer's description, I gathered the idea that the creature was supposed to belong to one of the species of gigantic saurians that roamed the earth during the reptilian age, some five hundred millions of years ago.

I thought the story a hoax and said so. Rutherford didn't agree with me, calling my attention to the fact that the men—whose names were given—were all well known, which made it unlikely that any writer would use them in connection with anything that savoured of deceit.

"I believe they have evidence warranting such an expedition, or they would not go. Moreover, I shall not be surprised to read, at some future date, that they have discovered the thing, whatever it is, and that it furnishes them with some very interesting experiences."

Well, every one has a right to his opinion, even though he has no foundation upon which to base it, so I didn't argue with him, beyond saying that I presumed he had some very good reason for being so positive.

Perhaps he thought I was a trifle sarcastic. At any rate he looked at me through contracted eyes for a moment, as if trying to make up his mind about something; then, having filled his pipe, he reached for a match and, after lighting the tobacco, he said quietly, "Yes, I do believe there are living descendants of those saurians and that they are, in appearance, like the old fellows we read about. Also, I believe I have good reason for thinking there are some that resemble no known species, and, since you won't take any stock in my belief until you have some proof, I am going to give you some, provided, of course, that you will accept my unsupported word that what I tell you is true."

Rutherford is not one given to making statements that are not true. If he says he knows a thing to be so, from personal knowledge, that settles it. He always was that way, even in school. More than once I have known him to take a licking when, by simply misstating the facts, he would have saved himself. Knowing him as I did, I told him to go ahead and give me the proof, if he wanted to, but, that I'd take his word for the "reason" without any further evidence. I hadn't the slightest idea as to what his "proofs" were, or I should not have taken the chance of missing them. Aside from a tale of fiction, I've never heard, or read of anything that approached his story for horror.

And the setting was perfect. Rutherford and I, alone in the hunting lodge on the shore of a northern lake at night, with the November wind howling through the trees that surrounded the house on three sides, and driving torrents of rain and sleet against the windows and upon the shakes that covered the roof. An eerie night, for an eerie tale.

"I've never told this story before," he began, "because there is little chance of being thought anything but a liar. I've often wanted to tell it though, and this moment seems very opportune. Every word is gospel truth."

"In this case, as in all others, cause and effect are operative," he began. "If I hadn't caught the flu in the winter of nineteen hundred and five, I should never have known anything about it.

"I had a pretty bad case of it and, only by the skin of my teeth, did I manage to pull through. Even at that, I barely missed 'going west,' for I was left with a lung complication that my doctor thought was a touch of T.B.

"As soon as the weather permitted, he ordered me into the mountains for an indefinite time. 'Any place,' he said, 'where there are lots of pine trees and clean air.' It seems odd that, out of all the familiar places on earth, which I might have chosen, I should have selected a place I had never heard of before, just because the name, when I read it on the route marked out in a railway time table, reminded me of a little girl I used to like back in my school days.

"Maybe you will remember her, Elsie Hampton. She went to school with us, back there, in Stowe, Vermont. She lived back on the hill, beyond the big house that Butler, the hotel man, built. You remember, he never finished it? Got killed by being thrown out of his buggy, while driving a crazy horse. Drunk at the time, if I remember correctly."

I nodded and, refilling his obnoxious pipe, he went on.

"That's how I happened to go to Hampton and, as it turned out, I would have had some trouble finding a better place, every thing considered. It was two thousand feet above sea level, just at the edge of the foothills. There were plenty of pines, firs and balsams. Air as clear as crystal. Fishing and hunting 'till you couldn't rest and, to make it more attractive, it was off the tourist track. Nobody ever stopped there (it was before the days of 'Automobile Tramps' and there was no such thing as a 'Tourist Camp').

"But the town was modern and up-to-date, provided with gas, electricity and a plentiful supply of pure water, piped from a reservoir ten miles back in the hills. There had been a hot controversy over the construction of the reservoir, due to the heavy cost, but the 'Boosters' had won out, and in the end, every one was happy.

"I had been there but a short while when things began to happen that set the town by the ears, particularly that part of the town that had opposed the idea of putting in the reservoir. One beautiful afternoon, just at the time the women were getting supper started, every tap in town went dry. Inside of half an hour the water works department was being called up and 'called down' by indignant housewives, who wanted to know what had become of their water supply.

"Well, the department found it out almost as soon as the women did, and it wasn't long before the engineers were loping along the pipe-line leading to the reservoir, followed by a crowd of idlers; being one of that class, I was with them.

"There was no break in the pipe and no cause for the stoppage of the water ways found until the reservoir was reached. Here they found cause in plenty. The huge, artificial lake was dry and the creek that fed it was pouring into a great hole in the center of the basin, near the dam and, from the roar that issued forth, one could guess that the water was falling some distance.

"Ordinarily, a hole may be stopped up. This was more than a hole; a continuous stream of water of considerable size failed to fill it. Evidently there was a cavern, or a number of caverns, underneath the surface with outlets, possibly sufficiently large to carry away any overflow.

"There were two newspapers in Hampton. One backed up the 'Boosters,' while the other stood with the 'Conservatives,' and the reservoir incident furnished the rival papers with a plentiful supply of material for publication.

"As might be guessed, the conservative organ was mean and caustic. Of course, nobody could have foreseen such a catastrophe—for it amounted to that.

"The other paper tried to explain, and really did explain. The cause was entirely obvious. The creek, for at least that part of it that had passed over the spot where the hole now was, had flowed over this rock cover of an underground chamber, or chambers, of huge dimensions. In view of what occurred a year later, I believe there must have been at least two, or more. This thin plate, or cover, had been strong enough to support the weight of the stream, but it was constantly growing thinner and it was apparently not strong enough to bear the greater strain imposed upon it by the water in the reservoir.

"The conservative paper admitted this but tried to convince its readers that the engineers should have known, from the formation of the rocks, that such an accident was liable to occur.

"And so they went at it, hammer and tongs, until, like a bolt from the clear blue sky, came another phenomenal occurrence.

This, I suppose, might have been anticipated, although I don't see how.

"A man by the name of Wilson owned a large farm that abutted upon the creek. In fact, a part of the lake formed by the reservoir encroached upon Wilson's property, and would have covered a large part of it, were it not for a retaining wall that had been built to keep the water back. This wall ran from a point near the upstream end of the reservoir to within a hundred feet of the dam. The remaining space was filled by a sort of mound, rising some fifteen feet, or more, above the surface of the water at high level. This mound was very much like a turtle's shell in shape, a hundred feet in length, about fifty feet wide at its base. I mention the mound at this point in the story, because it played an important part in a later incident, and I want you to remember the details.

"One morning, while the principal topic of conversation was still the reservoir cave-in, Wilson came into town, all het up! Winding up in the Mayor's office, he sprung a sensation upon that official by declaring that his farm had 'sunk out of sight.' This was, to be sure, a mean and unusual trick for a farm to play upon its owner and the Mayor was both astonished and sympathetic. Wilson didn't want sympathy, he wanted damages, which put an entirely different light on the story. At first, the Mayor thought Wilson was crazy, but he soon changed his mind and, calling in the County Attorney, asked Wilson to tell the story in detail.

"Wilson said he had been aroused from sleep by a strange noise, a sort of tearing sound mixed with a great roar and, upon getting up and going to his window, which faced the reservoir, he had seen a great gush of water, spurting up through the hole in its bed, and that a few moments later there had been another tearing, crashing noise and all his best garden land had broken away from higher and less valuable land, and 'dropped plum out of sight.'

"He was still standing, open mouthed, at the window when there came another explosion, followed by a tearing noise and a great chasm appeared in the northern end of the depression into which his farm had sunk and through this came a rushing volume of water. By this time, Wilson said, he thought he'd 'better put on some clothes and investigate.'

"Continuing, he said that, when he reached the side of the cave-in, he saw that it was rapidly being filled with water that came pouring into it through the rent in the upper end. He had watched until morning when, the water, having reached a point a few inches below the firm edge of his remaining land, had ceased to rise, and he concluded it had gone as high as it ever would.

"At first he was mystified, but at last decided that his misfortune was due to the cave-in of the reservoir, the water having washed the underpinning from beneath his property. Well, both the Mayor and the County Attorney agreed with him—forgetting in the excitement induced by the fantastic story, that Wilson was there to secure damages.

"Of course the Mayor couldn't do anything for Wilson, and the County Attorney, seeing no better way out of the tangle, advised the man to get a lawyer and bring suit.

"The case didn't come to trial—not then—for the city figured a way out of the trouble into which the cave-in had drawn it.

"Analysis showed that the water in the newly formed lake was the same water the city had been getting from the reservoir and so an appraiser fixed a valuation upon the sunken property that satisfied Wilson, and, this settled, preparations were begun to connect up the lake with the pipe line.

"But, the chain of unusual happenings was not yet at an end. The day before Wilson was to receive the money for his land, water began to flow through the hundreds of taps that had been left open since they ran dry. An investigation revealed the fact that the reservoir had begun to fill up again and, as soon as the news reached the County Attorney's office, payment to Wilson was held up, pending such a time as might be needed to show whether or not the reservoir would fill and remain full.

"When it became apparent that there was to be no more trouble with the water supply, the City called the deal off. Wilson then took his case into court and lost.

"He carried it up on an appeal, and lost again, the higher court sustaining the lower and justifying itself in so doing by stating that what had occurred was 'an act of God,' for which the city was not liable.

"During the trial, I became acquainted with Wilson and, afterwards he invited me out to his place. I was glad to go with him for
his invitation carried with it the assurance of better conditions of
living for me, for I had been unable to secure suitable quarters in
any of the farm homes outside of Hampton. I conjectured that, if
Wilson's place suited my fancy, I could very likely make arrangements with him which would enable me to remain at his place in-
definitely. I did succeed in doing so and, who knows but that I
might have met with the same unpleasant experience he did, had
not Fate willed it otherwise.

"Adventure, like romance, lies just around the corner. One does
not need to go to Africa, as these scientists are doing, in order to
find adventure any more than it is necessary to go to Europe for
romance, and the adventure ahead of me that summer day, as I sat
in Wilson's rattling Flivver, en route to his place, was very real.
No other man ever lived through an experience more bizarre, more
horrible than the one that was waiting for me, at Wilson's place.

"It didn't take us long to cover the distance between Hampton
and the farm which, even with most of the tillable land under water,
was a beautiful place. That part of the property covered with the
water from the reservoir had been practically the only really flat
land in the whole estate; the rest was rolling and hilly, and for the
most part, covered with timber. The lake lay almost in the center
of the 'farm,' as Wilson called it and, while it completely ruined
the farm for agriculture, it added immensely to its charm and
beauty. Roughly oval and nearly a mile in diameter, it twinkled in
its bed like a great sapphire encircled with emeralds. Owing to its
depth, which, according to Wilson's estimate, was something about
five hundred feet, the water would remain cold always, which made
it an ideal place for any trout which entered from the creek, to live
and breed in.

"I said as much to Wilson that evening after supper. Evidently,
he had never thought of such a thing; his mind was centered upon
his loss. He mulled the thing over in his mind for a moment, and
as the possibilities of such a proposition grew upon him, he said,
'if that danged lake had fish in it, I wouldn't take any price you
could name for it. I could get more out of the water then than I

ever got out of the land and still own it.' And I knew he was right. Given fish, he had the world by the tail. It would make a wonderful summer resort, for cottages could be built along the lake which would bring high rent for the season. He surely needed fish.

"And the fish came, but not until we had about given up all hope that they would. I had become Wilson's star boarder, for he had invited me to stay there as long as I liked, as his guest. I spent the days helping Wilson keep house. He was a widower for some years, and wandered about the lake, looking for signs of fish.

"Then, one afternoon, just at sun-down, I saw one leap out of the water. I shouted to Wilson, who answered the call on the run and got there in time to see another one jump up out of the blue depths. He gripped my arm and said, 'Rutherford, I shall need some help, financially. If you want to go in with me, we'll split the profits. What do you say?' I thought the matter over for a moment, then told him I'd furnish the needed capital. We stayed there, at the side of the lake, until dark, talking the matter over and watching the 'dollars,' as Wilson was pleased to call the trout, jump out of the water. We then went back to the house to make further plans for the next season.

"Two weeks later we had a dozen summer cottages well on the road toward completion. We expected to build more, later, but we figured a dozen, to start with, would be sufficient, which shows how nearly a couple of greenhorns can come to making a correct guess. We could have rented a hundred, if we had them. Later I wished I had never thought of building a single cottage. But who could have dreamed of such consequence?

"The cottages, which were erected on a sufficiently large, cleared space, on the southeast shore of the lake, were completed before the cold weather set in, and after closing the board shutters over the windows to protect them from possible breakage, we devoted our time to planning a campaign for the Spring.

"Winter passed reluctantly it seemed to Wilson and me, but it gave way to Spring at last and shortly after I went to the city. There I had a series of talks with certain dealers in fish, which resulted, as soon as the fishing season opened, in a big window display of strings of trout that made the disciples of Isaac Walton almost wild to swing a fly over their habitat. A carefully worded legend that accompanied the display gave the necessary information. The season opened with all our cottages occupied and we were making money.

"Very shortly after, we began to hear strange noises, in the night. If we had been very near a seaport town I should have thought the sound, though rather sharp, was given by a ship's siren. However, since we were better than eighteen hundred miles from the ocean, and a thousand miles from any other body of water large enough to float a ship, we concluded that it was a particularly awful whistle on the railroad, that ran some three miles to the west of us. It bothered us for about a week, then, like all other noises that occur at frequent intervals, it ceased to bother us much. There was some speculation among the cottagers but, when we told them it probably came from some engine, they accepted the statement for fact, and forgot all about it. Besides, what does a little noise amount to when the fishing is good? And it was.

"There was only one fault to be found with our lake, or its environment. Owing to the altitude and the added fact that it lay so deep down among the hills, the nights were too chilly to permit of comfort on the lake after dark. However, there was plenty of warmth during the daytime, so it didn't matter so very much.

"Along about the first part of July, however, we had a stretch of very hot weather. The warmth continued well into the night, and the early evening hours found the lake pretty well dotted with boats and canoes, passing back and forth near the shore and pretty well out into the lake.

"The first break in the calm order of our lives came one evening, during this hot spell. Wilson and I were down at the lake, cleaning some trout we had caught. It was about eight, or a little later and it was getting dark rapidly. We had practically no twilight. We had just finished our job when a long, agonizing scream, as one in mortal anguish, came vibrating over the lake, from some point down in the southwestern corner. Dropping our fish, Wilson and I ran down the shore, in the direction of the cottages, only to find all the women, and a couple of men huddled in a frightened group, down by the shore. In reply to our queries, one of the men said that the scream came from young Barnaby who, with his father and mother, occupied one of the cottages.

"As it chanced, no one had been out on the lake, except the young man. All the other men, with the exception of the two who were on the shore when we got there, were in Hampton, laying in more supplies. When his mother called to young Barnaby to come in, he answered he would be 'back in a few moments,' but for some unearthly reason, had started toward the deepening darkness of the western shore. The boy's mother had remained on the cottage porch, following the lad with a mother's anxious eyes, as he paddled away into the shadows. The two men, also watching from the shore, commented upon the boy's 'whim.'

"Up to this point there was perfect agreement; then started differences of opinion, as to what followed. One man said he was certain the boy had started to change ends, in the canoe, and had capsized it in so doing. His neighbor was equally certain that he had dimly seen the young man stand up in the canoe and, with the paddle, strike at something and then suddenly pitch forward, out of the canoe, screaming as he fell.

"All this was told by the two men, while the four of us, in two boats, were racing toward the spot where the boy was last seen.

"Although the man who declared the accident had been due to the boy's attempt to 'change ends' still stuck to his opinion, I felt, somehow, that he was wrong.

"Barnaby was, I had been told, a crack swimmer and, considering that he must have been close to shore when be fell into the water, I was convinced that merely being capsized would hardly have elicited such a cry of agony. No! I felt, absolutely, that there had been some sort of an attack made upon him and that he had tried to fight off the attacker, whoever, or whatever it was, with his paddle, and that he had failed in the attempt. And, as I tried to guess what sort of danger the unfortunate boy had faced, chills of horror went down my spine.

"So thoroughly convinced was I that something terrible had happened to Barnaby, and that he was beyond help, that the sight of his overturned canoe, as we drew near it, acted only as a sickening confirmation. Yet, knowing that it was useless, I urged a careful search and, with the others, called his name, again and again. They may have hoped; I did not. I merely knew the boy was dead.

"I kept my thoughts to myself, however, since my suspicions would only make matters worse. It would be bad enough to believe her only son had been drowned, but, I doubted whether her reason would bear the shock of the awful thing I had in mind. Wilson followed my example.

"Having no grappling irons, we would not drag the lake that night, but I told Mrs. Barnaby, who bore up remarkably well, that I would get some from Hampton in the morning. Hampton had none, so we had to devise them from clumsily made heavy rods and hooks.

"Young Barnaby's father wanted to go with us, but I prevailed upon him to remain with his wife. I felt it was best, because, while I did not expect to recover the body, I realized the possibility of something very sinister, and I felt it would be better for him not to see what the irons might bring to the surface. Maybe he sensed something of my thought, for he consented at last to remain behind.

"We loaded the clumsy drag with the rope attached (I had bought eight hundred feet, in order to make sure we had enough) into the boat and, with Wilson at the oars, pulled over to the place where the accident occurred. We had some trouble getting the drag into the water, owing to its awkward shape and weight, but we finally succeeded in lowering it. It seemed as if the drag would never reach bottom. Five hundred feet is a long way down.

"When, finally, the drag came to rest, I sat down in the stern of the boat and told Wilson to row slowly. He did. He did even better than that; he hardly moved at all. I thought the drag might have caught on some snag, but Wilson assured me there was no such thing in the whole area of the lake. It required the combined efforts of eight men, two to a boat, to pull that thing.

"We worked all day, dragging every foot of the lake within a radius of several hundred yards from the spot where the boy went down. We found nothing that day nor the next day, nor any day within the week of heartbreaking labor.

"It was labor lost, but it was necessary. There was no use running the risk of, not only driving a mother and, perhaps, a father crazy, but of ruining our business. And, of course, I might have been mistaken.

"The Barnaby cottage was vacant the day after we ceased to drag the lake, and it looked, for a while, as though the others might be, too; but, after talking the matter over, the occupants decided that it was only an accident, sad, indeed, but only too common and, since going back home would not help these parents to recover their boy, they might just as well try to forget. So they stayed and the vacant cottage was soon rented again.

One thing, however, they didn't forget—that the 'accident' happened in the evening; so, although the warm spell continued, they kept off the lake after sundown.

"Nearly a month went by with no untoward happening. Even those night noises ceased and I began to think I had let my imagination run wild, and that young Barnaby's death had been due to a simple capsize of his canoe. Then, there was another accident and, this time, it was a particularly horrible one. To add to its sinister aspects, it took, for its victims, the young couple who occupied the cottage in which the Barnaby family had lived.

"The young man and his wife,—their name was Whipple,—had been married only a little over a year. Mrs. Whipple, a rather frail woman of the neurotic type, temperamental, crotchety and stubborn as the Devil, was soon to become a mother and her condition, of course, didn't make her any easier to get along with. She was a beauty, though, and Whipple adored her.

"But, unreasonable as she was, Mrs. Whipple realized that she was in no condition to risk being tipped into the water, even if she had been a good swimmer, so she kept off the lake, contenting herself with sitting in the bow of the boat, which was tied to a stake driven into the ground, a few feet from the edge. There was absolutely no shore, no beach, and the water, at the edge of the lake, grew suddenly deep.

"No one will ever know what prompted her to insist upon going out on the lake that night. Probably it was just an unaccountable whim, common to women. Had Whipple been a little more coaxingly diplomatic, he might have talked her out of the notion, but, unfortunately, he emphatically negatived her suggestion that he take her 'for a little boat ride' before they went to bed, and the fat was in the fire. What had been, when made, just a simple, wheedling request, became a demand, backed up by evidence of approaching hysterics.

"According to Holy Writ, which is accepted by many people as being true, Eve succeeded in getting Adam to eat the apple, even when he knew the consequences were going to be disastrous, so what could be expected of a man, so deeply in love with his wife, who only feared the possibility of an unpleasant result of his yielding? Whipple held out, for a little time but, in the end, she devilled him into taking her and, to make the matter worse, she insisted upon going, 'straight across to the opposite shore and back.'

"I was present at the time; that is I was within hearing distance, having been, engaged in conversation with the man next door to Whipple. When I heard him, grudgingly, consent to take his wife across, I had a feeling of dread, a premonition of something dreadful in connection with it. Using all the tact I possessed, I tried to dissuade her from going. But it was useless. She listened, politely enough, for she was well brought up, but she was unshaken and what more could I do? True, I might have taken hold of the painter and refused to allow Whipple to take the boat, as I had a 'hunch' to do. But that would have necessitated an explanation, which I could hardly give, so I contented myself with saying that I wouldn't do it under the circumstances. Which helped not at all.

"I've known people to laugh at 'a hunch.' They claim there is nothing to it, that the 'feeling' is due to some trifling nervous disorder, entirely physiological. Some attribute it to over-stimulation of the nerves by alcohol, or tobacco. Well, perhaps it is due to any one, or all of these causes, but I've never known it to fail in my own case, and I've had plenty of chance to test it out. The proof, of course, is entirely one-sided, for, if I 'feel' that I'll be sorry later if I do a certain thing, and I obey that 'hunch,' I never know that punishment would really have followed had I disregarded the feeling. It is like taking the Pasteur treatment for suspected rabies infection. If the treatment is taken before rabies develops in the person, it can never be known, for certain, that there was any need for the treatment. All that is known is, if there is an infection and the treatment is not taken, the person dies, most horribly. So with a 'hunch.' It may be all bunk, as the cold-blooded, matter-of-fact people claim, but it doesn't cost much to play the 'hunch' and, as a rule, I do.

"I stood there, on the shore, watching the outline of the boat grow dimmer and dimmer as it neared the middle of the lake. It was the second night of the new moon. The starless sky was like black velvet. And it seemed ominously still to me. At the first terrible ullulation of a woman in deadly peril, which came echoing across the black stretch of water, I felt, not so much of surprise, as confirmation of a previous certainty. None the less; my very soul sickened with dread and horror and when, an instant later, the hoarser cry of a man smote my ears, I knew the tragedy was complete—both Whipple and his wife were past help.

"I must have been very close to hysteria for, when Wilson, whose teeth were chattering, grasped my arm, I shook him off with an oath, and ran for the boat, closely followed by the other men.

"As a rule, I am not much bothered by 'nerves.' It is not due to any courage of an unusual sort, for I have known fear many times, but I certainly had them that night, when we pulled across the lake toward the spot from which had come those terrible cries. Although I have crawled out into the mud and filth of 'No Man's Land,' in the blackness of a rainy night, knowing that death would be my portion it I should betray my presence by a sound, my nerves were steady although fear was in my heart. I knew in what manner I should die and the knowledge helped. But the awful mystery that lay behind the need for going out on the lake shook me and, had any one touched me, suddenly, I am sure I should have screamed.

"A hundred yards distant from the farther shore we came upon the boat and drew alongside of it. It was empty. Suddenly my eye caught sight of something white at the bottom of the boat, near the stern. Pulling the craft along, I reached for the object. It was a bit of muslin, torn from a woman's dress, and remembering that Mrs. Whipple had been wearing a white dress that night, I turned sick.

"When I lifted my hand from the gunwale of the boat, preparatory to beginning a search that I knew would be fruitless, I noticed that it felt sticky. It struck me as strange, since the boat had not been lately painted. I was about to dip my hand into the lake, to wash it when a thought struck me. Lighting a match—for it was too dark to see anything clearly—I looked to see what had befouled my hand.

"It was blood.

"Wilson had been watching me and as I hastily dipped my hand into the lake, with a shudder I could not prevent, he asked in the tone of one who dreads the answer, 'Was that—' He didn't finish the question. I nodded and I felt the boat quiver as a spasm of shaking seized him.

"We knew, but we continued to search—we and the others, who had caught up with us. Although I was ignorant as to what it was that had brought about the death of three people, I was certain there was something sinister and terrible in that lake of ours, and I was afraid.

"When we dragged the lake, we found no bodies—and I knew there would be nothing left to find.

"This ended our enterprise. One week after the last accident found every cottage vacant. And no wonder. Not only were the women wrought up to the breaking point over the affair itself, but their nights were made hideous by their dreams and the infernal sound of that siren, whistle, or whatever it was which grew increasingly worse. It was a heart-shaking sound.

"After the last of our guests had packed up and gone, Wilson and I determined to solve the mystery, for we were convinced there was a mystery hidden somewhere in that lake.

"Fortunately for us, nothing had been said concerning the disappearance to arouse suspicion in Hampton. It was known that some people had been drowned, which was, of course, unfortunate, but not unusual. And we did not further enlighten them.

"I have no idea just what it was that suggested a connection between the sounds that disturbed our slumber and the happenings on the lake, but I found myself associating them in my mind. Wilson, when I mentioned it to him, scoffed at the notion. 'How,' he asked, 'could a noise tip a boat over?' and when I tried to explain that the thing that made the noise might be the cause, he wanted to know how a locomotive could leave its rails and accomplish such a thing. You see, he had accepted as fact, the idea that the sound we had been hearing emanated from a mechanical contrivance. I told him my idea of the situation and I'm inclined to believe that he thought I had gone crazy, for when I asked him to put in a night with me, trying to locate the noise, he refused.

"In deference to his opinion that the disturbance could be traced to some engine, I made it a point to investigate. The men were very courteous and obliging, and blew the whistles of engines that traveled over that stretch of the company's right of way, but none of them gave forth the sound, the origin of which I was trying to discover.

"I told Wilson about my findings, and when I told him I was convinced the noise came from the lake, he consented to stand watch with me, but I could see that he took no stock in my belief.

"For three nights we watched but heard nothing, and Wilson was ready to drop the matter. I had a hard time getting him to go out the fourth night, but grudgingly he came with me.

"Since the noises seemed always to have come from the southwestern shore and, because it was there the accidents had occurred, we had used that as our watching post. Unlike the eastern shore, which was open and fairly flat, the western side dropped sharply down to the water. Some of the trees, their footing broken away by the cave-in, lay flat in the water, attached to the shore only by their roots, their branches obscuring considerably the nearer reaches of the lake.

"We found one tree which had rooted a little farther back from the line of break, had therefore, partly escaped the fate of its fellows. Held by its roots, it reached out over the water, at an angle of some twenty degrees. It was a large conifer and its tough branches with broken limbs placed across them, afforded a safe and comfortable resting place, although being out over the lake and with nothing to break the wind, it was far from warm. As I have said already, the nights out there were cold.

"There were no dangerous land animals about, so we carried no arms and, I feel sure any arms we might have taken would have been useless against the creature we were hunting. So, with a

packet of lunch and a thermos bottle of hot coffee, Wilson and I
set out for our point of observation.

"The night was clear, when we started from the house, but, after
an hour or so, it began to thicken and a mean, cold drizzle set in. We
were warmly dressed, however, so, aside from the ordinary dis-
comfort of damp skin, wherever it was exposed, we suffered none.

"It was, as nearly as I could judge, (I didn't think of looking at
my watch) about half past ten o'clock when I was aroused from a
half doze by an odd noise that I could not for a moment classify. It
woke me up, however and now fully alert, I waited for a repetition
of the sound. I heard it again presently, and this time I recognized
the sound. It was a grunt, a regular hog's grunt. If it differed in
any respect from the familiar vocalizations one hears coming from
the pig-pens, I didn't realize it at the moment, although it did seem
to be an unusually healthy grunt.

"My only feelings, as I remember, were those of mild astonishment; not so much because I had heard the grunt of a hog, (which
might have escaped from its pen and wandered down to the lake),
but because the sound came from the lake, and not from the land.

"There is nothing in the sound of splashing water to scare one.
Yet, there by the lake, with the cold drizzle wetting my hands and
face, I shivered when I heard that noise.

"Wilson, his back against a crotched branch, was fairly asleep,
(though he swore he wasn't) and I was in the act of waking him
when, like a blast from the siren of an ocean liner, the most awful
roar I ever heard, tore through the night air, from out there in the
darkness, nearly shattering my ear-drums.

"It fairly brought me to my feet and, as for Wilson, if I had not
been lucky enough to grab his coat, as he was disappearing downward, through the branches of the conifer, what happened to him
later, might have happened to him that night.

"I had only just recovered from my mental balance and got
Wilson back to safety when it came again. And I knew it was the
same screaming noise we had been hearing all the time. And I knew
also that that noise was in some way responsible for the distress-
ing disappearances of our tenants, and I knew that the originator
of that sound was of enormous size.

"It would be difficult to adequately describe my feelings, as I sat crouched there upon our none too secure platform, peering out into the black darkness, trying to discover what manner of creature it was that had given voice to that soul-shaking scream. Fear I knew, but there was something else beside fear; something of unrecognized dread; perhaps a premonition of some dreadful occurrence. And when the splashing sound came nearer, I had to exercise great self-control to keep from backing out of those branches as quickly as possible and out of the neighborhood. And Wilson, I believe, was even worse off, for his teeth were chattering and he seemed dumb with fright.

"Then the splashing noise gave way to another sound, this time to a swishing, sucking sound, like that made by an oar, pulled forcibly through the water. Whatever that thing was, it was swimming, not like our ordinary animal swims,—by moving its legs—but, rather after the manner of a seal—by paddling with flippers. And it was heading toward the north end of the lake.

"As the sound of its movements through the water came from directly in front of us, I dimly perceived, like a vague, black shadow against a wall of blackness, a vast, undulating body. I could not make out its shape for there was not light enough, but I knew it was enormous and, as I thought of it in connection with the terrible screams of those unfortunate men and that helpless woman, the muscles of my throat tightened and—I am not ashamed to admit it—tears filled my eyes. Wilson apparently had been following the same line of thought. He was almost un-nerved. and sat there picking at his fingers and repeating, over and over, 'Poor little woman! Poor little woman!' When I could stand it no longer, I shook him and made him shut up.

"When the last of the monster's shadow had passed, we painfully rose from our cramped position and crawled back to shore and started for home, around the north end of the lake, hoping to get another and, perhaps clearer view of the monster. But we didn't catch sight of it again. Perhaps it changed its course or, more likely, had sought its hiding place.

"I am not a drinking man but when we reached the house and Wilson poured a stiff peg of liquor for himself, I asked him to give me one too. And we needed that drink if ever any drink was needed, for we were pretty badly shaken up.

"It was long past our usual bed hour, but we didn't feel very sleepy, although probably from force of habit, I suggested turning in. Wilson, however, much to my secret delight, refused to take any chances of dreaming about that thing. 'No, sir!' he said, 'I'm going to keep my clothes on and stay awake.' So, after another drink, we filled our pipes and prepared to wait for daylight.

"'What kind of a fish was that?' Wilson's question aroused me from the train of thought into which I had wandered and, my mind engaged, I replied, an aquatic antique. This did not, of course, make things any clearer for him so I asked if he knew anything about the history of the earth, and the strange creatures that had lived upon it, in ages long past. His knowledge was very limited so, drawing on my memory of lessons learned years before, I tried to answer his query in such a manner as to enable him to understand the probable meaning of what we had seen.

"So far as repeating what I had read was concerned, my task was simple. But any proper answer, that is, one that would cover what we had dimly glimpsed out there on the lake, required something more and I was obliged to resort to deductive reasoning in order to supply it.

"Briefly I told him that the age of the earth was estimated to be between 860,000,000 and 1,000,000,000 years and that, according to the age of the rocks, this great span of years was divided into ages, such as the Azoic, followed by the Palæozoic, Mesozoic and Cenozoic. I told him that, accepting the idea that roughly 1,000,000,000 years represented the earth's age, the Mesozoic era lay back of us some 500,000,000 of years. Then I told him, as well as I could, what sort of monsters and giant reptiles inhabited the earth and its water at the time; then, in an effort to account for the monster in the lake, I drew upon my imagination. Perhaps I guessed wrongly, but I know of no other way. For there is no record, so far as I know, of any creature, except some of the land species possibly, that could equal, in size, the thing whose shadow we had seen.

"I am inclined to believe I was not far wrong because it is common geological knowledge that vast continental changes were taking place at that remote time, and basing my conjecture upon that fact, I told him that during some of those tremendous upheavals, certain ones of the reptile family had probably been caught in some of the great caverns that were formed and, unable to escape, had adapted themselves to their changed environment.

"True it was, that this thing was different from any species known, but is it certain that all the reptiles that lived away back in those ages had been classified? I wasn't at all certain that they had been, so this creature might be a direct descendant of some distinct and unknown class. Or, I thought it might be possible that reptile might be some sort of hybrid, bearing a composite resemblance to its ancient forebears. Why not? If you can crossbreed asses and horses and get offspring which, though unmistakably different from either of its parents, in all essential features, resembles both, why could not some similar sort of crossbreeding have occurred with members of the reptile family?

"All sorts of fossil remains of pre-historic reptiles have been discovered in North America, and those creatures, when alive, lived here. Moreover, America, it is known, is fairly honeycombed with caverns, some of enormous extent. Many have water in them; although not sufficient, perhaps, to accommodate a lizard as large as this particular one. Is it certain that all the caverns have been discovered?

"Take this particular case for an example. When the bed of the reservoir caved in, where did the water go if not into some vast cavern, or caverns? And, had there not been such a cavern or caverns under the bed of the creek, would there have been any cave-in? Of course not.

"Following this line of deduction, I came to the conclusion that, in the subterranean depths, this reptile, with perhaps many others, had been born and, since even a lizard cannot live in water that is entirely stagnant, inlets and outlets must have existed, to keep the water, at least comparatively fresh.

"Space alone, is limitless, so there must have been a limit to this cavern or caverns and, when the water broke through from above, it was filled to the point where the rock walls were burst and the earth, having lost its support, fell, forcing the water upward and forming the lake. When the water reached a certain level, or was on a plane with the bed of the creek, the reservoir filled up again, underground, the outlet having been too small to carry away the flow of the stream. If my premise was correct, then the presence of the lizard in our lake was easily accounted for. It simply came up through the same hole through which the water came.

"That was the explanation I gave Wilson and I thought, and still think, that it was correct.

"After breakfast I went to the north end of the lake. I believed I had hit upon the real solution of the reptile's presence in the lake and wanted to verify it if possible. I had an idea that the lizard might take it into its head to come up from below, and give me a chance to see it. I wanted Wilson to accompany me but he said he had too much work to do about the place.

"I waited near the hole until about noon, but seeing no sign of it, I concluded that it had either come up early or, what was more likely, was hiding down there in the darkness, until nightfall. Instead of turning homeward, however, I decided to settle another question. For some time now, we had seen no trout jumping and I thought they might have been frightened out of the lake and returned to the reservoir. Wilson and I, although we did not know until the night before, just what had caused the accidents, thought it better to go without fish than to take any risks out on the lake. But if they were in the reservoir again I meant to catch a few.

"The knoll, or mound, about which I told you in the beginning, lay directly between me and the reservoir and, since it was easy to climb I started up its side. It was covered with low brush and weeds that hid the surface of the ground from view, but did not greatly impede my progress. I plowed my way to the top and started across the rounded back, toward the reservoir. I had gone only a few paces when, without warning, the ground gave way beneath my feet and I soon found myself, in a heap, in the gravel, at the bottom of what seemed to me to be an over-sized cistern.

"I was not injured but I was considerably shaken up, for I had fallen about ten feet. For a moment I was inclined to laugh at myself, for I cut a funny figure sitting there, hunched up. But there was nothing to laugh at. I found myself in a serious position, for I was imprisoned at the bottom of a hole, surrounded by unscalable walls of loose gravel. Moreover, no one had seen me at or near this isolated place, so unless a miracle happened, no one ever would come in time to find me alive. Well, sitting there, staring at the opening through which I had fallen would do no good, so I began to take my surroundings into serious consideration.

"It soon became evident that the hole had been dug by some one for a definite purpose; what that purpose was I had no idea. The opening at the top, I discovered, had been covered with planks which, in the course of a short time had become covered with earth and vegetable matter; in turn this furnished soil in which had grown the weeds that hid the spot. None of the boards had fallen into the hole, nor was there anything I could use to enable me to reach the opening. As there was nothing else I could do, I decided to kick gravel from the walls and heap it up until the pile was high enough to enable me to reach beyond the broken boards, grasp some bush, or other thing, and get out.

"I knew I had a tedious job ahead, for I had only my hands to use as a shovel. At one side of the hole, quite a pile of gravel had fallen of its own weight, which gave me a good start, I thought. Throwing double handfuls into the center of the floor soon proved to be a bad job. My hat also proved too slow a method, so I spread my coat, filled it, then carried it over to the slowly growing mound, on which I dumped these accumulations.

"I had a heap about three feet high when, in scooping up another double handful, my fingers came in contact with the surface of a box. I soon had it uncovered fully and found it to be about a foot deep, fifteen inches wide, and about two feet long. I was about to kick the cover off, in order to find out what, if anything, it contained, when I was moved to examine it a little more closely first. It was a good thing I obeyed the impulse, because, after carefully prying off the cover, which had begun to show signs of dry rot, I discovered a two gallon canister of nitro-glycerine.

"The reason for the hole became apparent at once, it had been used as a chamber for explosives while the reservoir was in process of construction, and this box very likely had been overlooked when the work was finished.

"Very carefully I carried it over and laid it on its side, on top of the little heap of gravel. Digging further I found another box, and another, until I had found fifteen. I piled these, pyramid fashion, under the hole through which I had fallen; then holding my breath and taking care not to make a false step, I climbed to the top and soon found myself in the sunshine once more where I could breathe freely.

"When I reached the reservoir, I found the trout jumping. The fish problem settled, I started back toward the house for my tackle. I was about half the way to the fence when I saw Wilson, a long stick in his hand, trying to head off a cow that had broken from the corral, and was now headed for the lake.

"Mules are supposed to be, and are, stubborn, but when it comes to downright 'orneryness,' I think a cow is pretty much of a fool. Added to this, cows are nervous things, ready to stampede at a moment's notice and when they get a notion into their heads, you can't club it out.

"Now, this cow was a Holstein, and valuable so, when Wilson saw her heading for the lake he very naturally objected, considering the sort of tenant that lake harbored.

"I was too far away to be of assistance and the beast was too much for him alone. Dodging past his swinging club, she drove, head on, for the water, her tail, so it seemed, flapping, in derision. She was still on the gallop when she reached the water, so she went entirely under. I saw her come up, a few yards from the bank and, cow-wise, start for the farther shore. I don't know why a cow will always, under similar circumstances, make for the farthest point, unless it is because as I said, they are just plain fools.

"In his anxiety over his cow, Wilson forgot something he should have remembered: if the lake was a dangerous place for the Holstein, it was even more dangerous for him. But he may never have thought about the lizard at all. At any rate he ran to the little dock that projected out into the water, and, getting into the boat that was tied there, began to row frantically after old bossy.

"I was too far away to warn him of his danger, although it didn't actually seem great then; the lake, like a great blue gem bathed in the golden rays of the afternoon sun, suggested nothing further than dimpled beauty, made somewhat sinister by the knowledge that, deep down in its sapphire depth there had been, and might at the moment be, a nameless and monstrous horror. I guess I have become a bit of a fatalist; it seems to me, things are pretty much laid out for us from the beginning. We are supposed to be 'free moral agents,' according to the clergy, yet I wonder if we really are. Of course, Wilson did not have to go out on the lake. Nor would he have gone if he had stopped to think. But blame can hardly be attached to him for not stopping to think. He never did.

"By the time I reached the spot where the cow went into the water, the animal was about a hundred yards from shore, headed back, for Wilson had overtaken her and made her turn back. There wasn't a thing to be nervous about, so far as appearances went, but I was worried, and I urged him to hurry. He waved his hand and nodded and that was the last thing he ever did. His hand had barely grasped the oar again when, silently, from the blue depths, there came into view, just behind Wilson, the awful head and neck of the creature, whose shadow we had dimly seen that night, when we sat crouched on a shaky platform spread over the branches of the fallen conifer.

"Up it rose, to a height of seven or eight feet, while I, gazing upon its utter frightfulness, stood paralyzed and dumb. I saw its cavernous mouth, fully three feet from snout to the angle of the jaw; saw it open and reveal its gleaming, needle sharp teeth over the head of the unfortunate man; and I was utterly helpless. If my own life had been at stake, I could not have uttered a cry of warning.

"I think Wilson must have sensed something, somehow, for I noticed (I can see that look even now) a look of fear spread over his rugged features. But it was too late for, just as he was m the act of turning his head to see what was behind him, the end came. There was a slight working of the terrible jaws, perhaps due to some sort of gustatory suggestion of the thing's instinctive machinery, then, like a flash, down came the obscene head, the jaws closed, with a snap and Wilson, only his legs protruding beyond the lizard's snout, was snatched from his seat with the speed and ease with which a hen picks up a kernel of corn.

"Horror unspeakable overpowered my mind, and I think I lost consciousness for a moment. Maybe I went mad for a time, for I have no remembrance of having gone to the house, nor, until awakened by a terrific crash of thunder, did I have a realization that anything had taken place.

"When I regained my senses, I sat slumped over in one of the kitchen chairs. I felt dazed, like one who has been on a long drunk. Shadows of strange memories passed through my mind, suggesting nothing definite. Then another frightful crash swept the cobwebs from my brain and I felt memory coming back with a rush.

"Other things came quickly, and perhaps fortunately, to occupy my mind, and demand my attention, for one of the worst storms I had ever witnessed, was brewing fast and furiously. The house, stout though it was, trembled and creaked beneath the onslaught of the elements gone wild.

"Getting up from the chair I staggered to the window. The sky was overcast with heavy clouds, those immediately overhead being a grayish black, while, down in the southwest an unearthly, greenish mass of whirling cumuli, writhed and twisted, high up in the heavens. That there were several currents of air, coming from as many different directions was evident, from the manner in which the tops of the trees behaved. They fairly threshed about. Presently the temperature began to drop and great clouds from the northwest drove past, beneath the blackness far overhead, and then the flashes of lightning became appalling, as the fire forks darted from cloud to cloud, while deafening peals of thunder sent every loose thing a-rattle.

"Then the rain came; came in torrents that were veritable cascades of driven water, beating in at every crack and crevice. There was a blinding flash a hundred yards from the house and a tall tree, splintered into kindling, flew in all directions; this the gale whirled and tossed about, finally driving it into the lake, the surface of which was beaten into froth.

"I heard a crash overhead and knew the chimney had gone by the board. This was followed by a ripping sound, and the roof of the chicken house, looking like the flapping wings of some enormous bird, went sailing away across the lake; and when the house itself began to slide upon its foundation I expected it to follow. It did not, however; neither did it lose its roof, although, as I discovered later, there wasn't a whole shingle left on it.

"Suddenly the hideous racket was augmented by a sound that over-rode all other noises. Every window pane was shattered; every door was driven from its hinges, while through the openings, a deluge of water rushed, flooded the house and knocked me into a corner.

"I have heard about the 'Crack of Doom' many times, and, if it is going to be any worse than that crack, I don't want to hear it. However, it seemed to serve one useful purpose, for after it came, the awful racket began to subside and, within the hour, only an occasional rumble bore evidence of energy still at work. The rain continued, however, until it seemed the oceans were being drained to furnish the water.

"Wet, cold and weary, I waded through the water that swashed back and forth through the lower rooms, to the stair leading to the second floor. I dragged my aching body up the stairs, down which little streams trickled, for the windows, upstairs, also were shattered, I went from room to room, seeking some place of shelter out of the wind, where I might perhaps find some dry clothing and lie down. The second floor was pretty well soaked but I found shelter at last, in a large closet in the rear. This part of the house was toward the east and since the storm had come from the southwest and north, it was comparatively dry there. In this closet I found Wilson's Sunday suit, some shirts and a pair of shoes, together with a few pairs of socks. The suit was too small, and the shoes too large, but I was in no position to be particular, so I put them on. Unless you have been in a similar predicament, you cannot know the comfort of dry clothing of any kind or make.

"After wringing out my own clothes and hanging them over the backs of chairs to dry if the rain ever let up I piled some things on the floor and, upon these, for a bed, I soon forgot all about the storm and what had gone before it.

"A ray of sunlight on my eyes, reflected from a mirror, awoke me. My watch had stopped, so I didn't know just what time it was, although I judge it must have been about nine o'clock. I was a bit stiff and hungry, but otherwise, in pretty good shape. After drawing the chairs, over which my clothes hung, into the sunshine, I went down stairs, dug the wet ashes out of the stove, made a fire and cooked some ham and eggs and coffee for myself. Then I started out to learn the extent of the damage.

"There was plenty. The roof of the barn had fallen in, driving the walls outward. Luckily the weather had been warm, so the cattle were still kept outside. I found them at last, in a small apple orchard, apparently no worse for having been out in the storm, contentedly eating grass. I say had been, because practically every one of the trees had been ruined, the branches having been torn off.

"Then, for no particular reason, I strolled down to the lake. Except for a lot of floating shingles, branches and boards, it was the same, smiling, beautiful blue body of water—the last place in the world, I thought, where such terrible tragedies could take place, and the most unlikely hiding place for the horror that had caused the events. Soon I became aware of a muffled sound like a rushing of water over a fall, and wondered what caused it. A little later, I noticed that the flotsam was drifting toward the north end of the lake. This was odd, since there was no current and, curious to learn why, I started in the same direction. Soon the muffled sound became louder. It was coming from the lake! Puzzled for a moment, like a flash the explanation came to me and I started north on the run.

"I soon reached the place where the noise came from a great rent at the end of the basin in which the lake lay. I looked toward the mound, or, rather, toward the place where the mound had been, for it was there no longer, and if I had been in doubt as to what had caused the rent, I was soon in possession of full knowledge. That unearthly crash had been caused by the explosion of those fifteen cases of nitro-glycerine, and there may have been more buried in the sand, when a streak of lightning found its way into the pit in which they were.

"The rocky floor of the pit must have been a sort of pot cover, over the subterranean cavern, or caverns, and the force of the explosion had torn it away rending the rocks and earth into a great tear, extending through the wall which held the lake. It had done even more; it tore out the wall between it and the reservoir, for I found, upon going around the chasm to the dam, that the water was rapidly lowering. While I stood there, amazed at the force of the charge, a large block of concrete from the end of the dam nearest me, broke loose and fell with a splash, into water. Evidently, I thought, the whole dam was being undermined and was liable, at any moment, to fall. I made haste to get away from the place, and I acted wisely, for within ten minutes the whole enormous structure of concrete crumbled and fell; a part of it going completely out of sight in the hole in the bed of the reservoir, while the rest went in the opposite direction.

"It was apparent, since the chasm was enlarging momentarily, that it would not take long to empty both reservoir and lake and, being minded to see the finish, I went back to a point of safety, on the eastern shore, sat down on a rock and waited for the end.

"Sitting there, wondering into what profound depths the waters of the lake and reservoir were plunging, speculating upon the possible truth of some tales I had read concerning people discovered living in a 'World Beneath a World,' I forgot, for a time, what was taking place before my eyes.

"I was aroused from my reverie by a snort, and coming back to actualities, I looked to see what had produced it. There was the great lizard, from whose throat it had emanated, not fifty yards before me.

"At last I saw the monster, and monster it truly was. My powers of description are far too limited to adequately describe that monster. Its body, at least the upper part, was fully exposed. Swanlike in shape, it appeared to be nearly sixty feet from the point where the neck joined the body, to the end of its tail, which resembled, in a way, the tail of a duck. This body, armed or equipped with flappers, similar to those of a seal, but enormously larger, was a greenish black and was covered with what might have been, the slime and ooze of ages. Its neck, flexible as that of the swan, was fully two feet in diameter at its base, tapering slowly to the head, eight feet from the body. The head was a composite of the crocodile and the tyrannosaurus, but much larger, with loosely articulated jaws, permitting of tremendous extension, as is the case with certain snakes. The mouth, armed with teeth fully six inches in length, was at least three feet long from the snout to the angle of the jaws. To add to its frightfulness, the upper canine teeth, or fangs, curved outward and downward over the lower jaw, and were as near as I could judge, at least ten inches long. A more horrible creature I couldn't imagine, and I wondered whether it might be a member of some species that had never been catalogued, or whether it was what it appeared to be, a hybrid. I think it was the latter and, since it was the only one that had come into the light of modern times, I also wondered if the thing could have begun its existence away back there in the mesozoic era. It seemed impossible, and yet, who knows. At any rate it certainly looked ancient enough to have been born long before creation began. Doubtless, I thought, there were others like it, somewhere, for it seemed unlikely that only one specimen would have been caught in one of the cataclysms of those ancient days. But, whether or not I was right, can never be told.

"Apparently the lizard was terrified at something; probably at the idea of being sucked into the chasm, into which the water was pouring, for it was making violent efforts to draw away from that end of the lake. It was a losing game, however, for the suck of the water, powerful as was the reptile, was too strong and, thresh the water as it might, and did, it was slowly being drawn back. Whatever else might be said of the lizard, it was no coward, for, realizing the fact that it was a losing game, it suddenly turned and, with a terrific bellow, using its flippers to accentuate its speed, in a sort of 'devil daring spurt,' it drove head-long into the vortex.

"During the day the waters continued to enlarge the chasm and, by night the lake had nearly vanished, as had also the reservoir.

"The following morning the city engineers were out, and as well as I could, I explained what had happened. As it chanced, I did most of my talking to the man who had supervised the construction of the reservoir, and was therefore the only one who knew about the nitro-glycerine. I realized that my knowledge of its presence in the pit caused him some worry, and he explained that he had given orders for its removal, but they evidently had been forgotten or disregarded by the workmen, so I told him I would not mention the matter to anyone, for which he seemed very grateful. Since it could have done no good to tell about it then, I deemed it best to forget about the matter.

"But I mentioned the lizard to no one. I explained the disappearance of Wilson, by telling them that he had fallen into the lake, from a rowboat, while trying to drive back to the shore a cow that had gone into the water. That also was the story I told the lawyers who settled up the estate.

"As soon as possible I gathered up my traps and came back to the city. I have tried to forget the experience, for it was far from pleasant, but this story in the paper brought it up again and, I repeat, I shall not be surprised to read that those men have found some hold-over from the mesozoic era, for I believe there are specimens still alive. Why not?

REPORT

on the

STATUS QUO

by TERENCE ROBERTS

Introductory

World War III has produced profound changes in our way of life. It has altered the political map of the world out of all recognition; it has given us tools and weapons so amazing and so frightful that despite the current, and it is to be hoped permanent, feeling among all nations that we have now committed the ultimate stupidity and learned our lesson just in time we all stand in dread of the future. However, the most amazing and at the same time the single most important change in our earth has come about from purely natural causes, and would have happened in any case, had we been at war or not. Whether these changes would have reached the proportions that they now have, had we not been engaged in a life and death struggle is another matter and a question that can never be answered.

As we all know, conditions that had been unknown on this planet for about sixty million years, according to the geologists and palaeontologists, have returned to two of the continents—Asia and Africa—and are still likely to spread to the others. The whole balance of animal and plant life has been altered in the short space of three years, and we find ourselves faced with problems so novel and so all-pervasive that humanity as a whole, even working in complete harmony, will be hard put to it to survive. Briefly, we have suddenly been thrown back into the Mesozoic Era, the Age of the Dinosaurs, and unfortunately at a time in geological history when we are entering a warm climatic cycle which will provide a progressively satisfactory environment for the regrowth of this Mesozoic life.

Despite our wonderful modern system of communications, the people as a whole are woefully ignorant of much that is going on in the world today. The reasons for this are threefold. First, military security still demands worldwide censorship for some months. The Communists are not yet by any means under our complete control. Secondly, immense areas of the earth's surface are now debarred from us by official decree or simply because they cannot be penetrated by any expedition. It will take many months of careful planning to equip such forces and despatch them to Africa and central Asia.

Thirdly, and most important, is the widespread residue of that ancient and ingrained scepticism in which, up till this late war, we were all fostered. For this all of us are to blame. The press and the scientific fraternity were but following custom in discrediting anything that in any way smacked of the incredible or the unlikely. Little harm and perhaps much good was achieved thereby in a world divided into national camps of near hysterical people, lacking any religious or other sound emotional guidance, and bewildered by the too rapid progress of the physical sciences. We are suffering now for our age-old obtuseness and complacency.

Six months ago Professor Oswald F. Bristowe's name was not a household word. He was better known to the scientific world, and therein his standing was unsurpassed. It was for this reason that he was chosen by our Government to lead and direct the investigatory mission to Hispaniola, to delve into the real origins of all that has now overtaken the world. Dr. Bristowe is a palaeontologist and a sceptic; that is to say he was always sceptical of the sceptics, and he still has an open mind. The press has carried little else but these matters mentioned in Professor Bristowe's Report for the past year, but yet there has not, so far, been issued or published any overall official statement. This has been a policy on the part of the Government. They long ago decided that the press should retain its right to freedom of speculation, reportage and comment, but at the same time they chose to refrain from issuing any statements of their own until they had the facts before them—facts gathered by real experts.

This publication is an officially sponsored edition of Professor Bristowe's first General Report to the Combined Scientific Societies

of the United States upon what its author very rightly chose to call
"The Status Quo." That is just what it is, as the report only too
clearly shows, because this is the new Status Quo: there is no turning back now.

Finally, the Publishers would like me to add the following brief
words of explanation.

Our planet is now thought to be about three and a half billion
years old. At least, examination of the disintegration patterns of
radioactive materials contained in the oldest known rocks of its
surface strata so indicate. The first two billion of these years were
apparently concerned with the settling down of the planet; lighter
materials composed of silicon, magnesium and aluminum rose to
the surface, and the heavier, composed principally of nickel and
iron, sank to the centre by a simple process of convection result-
ing from the semi-fluid state of the whole, which was produced
not by an initial molten condition, but simply by the excessive pressure of the whole towards the centre caused by gravity. By the end
of this immense period of time, animals had been evolved that had
hard skeletons which could be preserved as fossils. From then on
to the year 1958, there was a steady and apparently uninterrupted
development of life and climate on this earth's surface.

This billion years may be divided into three periods: the Pri-
mary or Palaeozoic, the Secondary or Mesozoic, and the Tertiary
or Caenozoic. The first was the Age of Fishes, the second the Age
of Reptiles, and the third the Age of Mammals. The reptiles for the
most part passed away some sixty million years ago. But they did
not all pass away; the turtles are as old as any, millions of croco-
dilians remained, and one creature known as the Tuatara lingered
on in New Zealand from the misty past even of the reptiles. It was
a pre-dinosaur.

The dinosaurian reptiles vanished simply because they were
superseded, not because anything went wrong with the earth or
their environment upon it. Now they have come back again at a
time when the climate of the earth is particularly suitable to them
and, be it noted well, at a time when a single species of mammal,
e.g. Man, has made space for them by killing off most other large
mammals. Nature, it has been said, abhors a vacuum. Three years

ago there was a vast vacuum in the animal life of this planet caused by pestilence, war, and centuries of slaughter of the natural fauna of the seven continents and the six oceans. There happened to be some Mesozoic life forms resting in their eggs in one small spot on this earth, unknown to us. Occupied by the war, we failed to note the release of this old form of life. When we did wake up to the fact, Mesozoic life forms had already been carried all over the earth and had started to fill the vacuum with a virility unknown among other animals of our time.

No longer do we have to visit museums to gaze upon the mighty Brontosaurus. By next year, scientists assure us, we will be able to travel by plane in a few hours in perfect safety, and watch them wallowing in their swamps. But, let us not forget, they have brought back with them to our time their diseases, their plant food, and the multitudinous life forms that dwelt with them in the swamps of a hundred million years ago. Against these we must be on constant guard. As Professor Bristowe says, let this "remain a taunt to our youth, and a goal of all humanity."

Terence Roberts, May, 1961

* * * * * * * *

April 16, 1961
The Secretary of Science, Washington, D. C.
Sir:
As secretary and official historian of the joint expedition to Hispaniola conducted by the American Government and combined scientific societies, that has just returned after completing an investigation of the original causes of the phenomena that have so utterly disorganized the world during the last three years, I have the honour to submit to you a short and preliminary account of our findings. The full scientific reports are still in the early stages of compilation.

Since the history of events is so crowded with a succession of astounding incidents and entirely novel findings that these technical reports will in all probability run into many volumes before the results are fully told, and since the matter is still foremost in everybody's mind, I will not waste further time in introducing the subject. It would appear that the real cause of all that followed was initiated in the summers of 1958 and 1959 when the rainy season of Haiti—falling as it does normally between May and September because of the island's position on the edge of the Caribbean—was abnormally heavy. The Republic of Haiti, comprising the western half of the great island of Hispaniola, lies within the tropics between 18° and 20° north latitude and 72° and 74° west longitude. Its geographical position is of great significance in the interpretation of recent history, and should be constantly kept in mind while reading this report. Had these events taken place anywhere else, even on an island anywhere else, history might well have taken a much more deplorable turn.

Now there was, it appears, in addition to the usual rains, considerable rainfall during the dry season between September 1958 and April 1959. Such vagaries of the weather were by no means unknown; therefore, on this occasion the results were not expected to be more than a passing phase. Such, however, proved to be very far from the case, at least in one rather limited area—a fact that perhaps hardly needs repeating nowadays.

* * * * * * * *

I will ask you to refer once again to a map of this mysterious tropical island, despite the fact that I am well aware that almost anybody could now probably draw the country in some detail from memory, after constantly viewing its scissor-like appearance on the front pages of newspapers. I would direct your particular attention to what is known as the plateau of Hinche, which forms the hub or cradle of the central block of the country, because we find that an important point has been missed up till now regarding its topography and geological structure.

The island of Hispaniola is really composed of three quite separate and individual blocks of land that happen now to be joined together by two narrow valleys almost at sea level. Not so long ago they were separated by shallow seas and the southernmost block was joined to Jamaica, while prior to this in geological time, the centre block was similarly attached to Puerto Rico. These land masses are mountainous; the northern is small, the centre one is the largest, and the southern is of intermediate dimensions. All three run from east to west, and only the centre block has any real substance, for the Sierra de Monte Christi of the northern land mass is but a single range, and the Morne de la Hotte and the Morne de Celle of the southern block likewise form but a single continuous ridge. The mountains of the centre block, however, comprise several ranges spreading from the Cordillera de Cibao in what used to be Santo Domingo, like the fingers of a hand towards the west into Haitian territory. The palm of this giant hand, moreover, is the upland plateau of Hinche, fifty miles in diameter and completely ringed with rugged mountains. The only outlet for drainage, or anything else for that matter, is the narrow gorge of the Artibonite River which eventually debouches into the Caribbean north of the small town of St. Marc.

This vast bowl, now a glaring white desert, was, as short a time ago as 1957 a rolling green plateau supporting a considerable peasant population, hamlets, small country towns, many herds of domesticated animals, and exceptionally fine crops of cotton, citrus, and other plants. Its fertility appears to have been the result of an ample rainfall on a surface structure of rich, sandy clay, the residue of denuded, soft tertiary strata. These rocks, or rather those immediately below them, hold the key to all the mysterious and terrifying history that follows. It appears that both they and the underlying secondary or Mesozoic deposits lay in horizontal stratification over the whole area, the plateau being in reality a vast bowl sunk into the centre of their geologically level midst by the erosive action of the river system, the headwaters of the Artibonite which is the largest river in the country. This conformity of secondary and tertiary strata, untilted, unfaulted, and apparently unaltered in any way since it was deposited fifty to a hundred million years ago, is apparently, and as far as we know, unique in the world.

* * * * * * * *

The geological structure of the country was known to the scientific staff of the expedition at the time of its inception, but neither

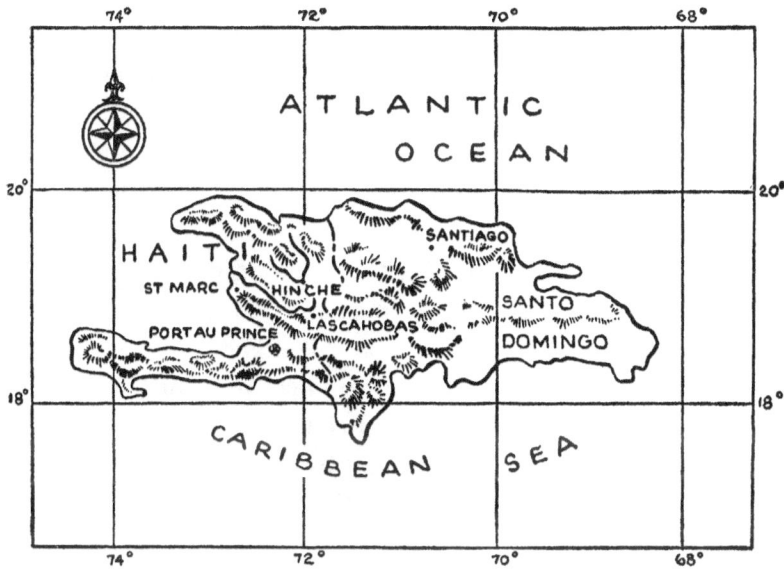

its significance, nor that of the excessive rains that occurred in the seasons 1958-9 were then realized. As a result, had it not been for the first hand reports of the young American sociologist, James Carstairs, and those of his bride, the dauntless flying journalist, Sylvia Rendle—of whose marriage we were all so happy to read only this week—from whom we obtained the only authentic, eye-witness accounts of the happenings at the very centre of the trouble, our work would never have reached such final and definite conclusions.

Mr. Carstairs, who was in the vicinity of Hinche during the whole of 1958 studying a typical rural Haitian community, had ample opportunity of gathering a concise knowledge of the appearance and make-up of the surrounding country. That he fully availed himself of this opportunity may be witnessed by any who hear his tales of the old Haiti, with roads turned to sticky mires by the rain, and its fine steel bridges undermined and overthrown by the swirling, mud-choked rivers in the rainy season. It is not altogether unexpected, therefore, that he, the only American or foreigner of any nationality then in that whole part of the country, and, because of the nature of his work, the only person cognizant with a wide stretch of this territory, should be one of the first—if not the first—to notice the early signs of change that came about.

He asserts, in fact, that it was actually during the later rains of 1958, just after the outbreak of World War III, that he observed a small area of bluish-green earth among the thorns near the native house he was occupying. It should be stressed that although Mr. Carstairs was engaged in an overall study of the Hinche Plateau and its rural community, and although such a study was planned to include not only human activities and customs, but also the vegetation, animal life, soils and the underlying geological structure of the country, his project envisaged at least two years in the field. By the end of the rainy season of 1958 he was still engaged in his preliminary survey, which entailed triangulation and mapping and a rough census of the population. Soil samples had been collected and were packed for shipment and analysis. He had not by then acquired any detailed knowledge of the surface geology of the country. He had, however, naturally taken a keen interest in every aspect of the country around him, and being a trained observer, he had noted the quality and appearance of the typical soils around his headquarters. These soils were, he tells us, of a very distinctive nature, reddish-yellow in colour, clayey, and altogether devoid of stones or concretions.

Mr. Carstairs had discussed the fertility of these surface soils with the local Haitian farmers and a resident agricultural officer of the Haitian Government, and had remarked upon the extraordinary absence of natural ground cover in uncultivated and fallow areas. They had laughed at him good-naturedly and abjured him to await the coming of the rains when they said a profusion of herbage would burst from the ground and be in full bloom within a matter of days. Thus it was that when the rains did begin he took particular note of the land surrounding his house. And sure enough, the earth sprouted just as the Haitians had asserted it would do, and a blanket of greenery covered its face.

However, as the rains continued day after day the water table throughout the whole plateau rose rapidly until extensive areas were flooded. Considerable gutter erosion had been initiated in previous years and the run-off was excessive. Gulleys appeared overnight and were filled with churning torrents of liquid mud. The rains, moreover, were so torrential that the very surface of level areas was gouged out from among the roots of the plants.

Now, the land rose slightly behind the house Mr. Carstairs was occupying, and here the erosion was so excessive that the land surface was washed entirely clean of its fresh herbage. By the end of June several acres of wet, reddish mud stretched away from the back door and this continued to be washed away by the ton daily until suddenly, in the middle of July, Mr. Carstairs awoke one morning to find the whole area covered with a new crop of livid greenery growing upon an entirely different coloured soil. This latter was bluish-green in colour. This new vegetation did not appear to be any different from that covering other open areas among the thorn scrub. It persisted until the end of the rainy season.

Mr. Carstairs explains that he had little time to take note of it, and he would have forgotten the matter entirely had not the unexpected rains in the following November—which should have been the height of the dry season—caused another flood. This drove him out of his house, completely inundated the land behind it, and deposited upon it a deep layer of the ordinary red clay from the surrounding territory. Upon this no greenery appeared and it remained thus naked thereafter. This bit of land, remembered some months later, saved the lives of both Mr. Carstairs and Miss Rendle when they were finally marooned, for it stuck up like a miniature tableland. It also preserved, beneath its protective cap of old clay, evidence without which we would never have arrived at the truth.

Despite the unusual rains during the normally dry period of October to March, 1958-9, the subsequent heavy rains appear to have held off longer than usual. When they did come, in the middle of May, it was with the violence of that great storm which wrecked so much shipping in the Caribbean, and brought down Miss Rendle's plane just as she was commencing her news flight to the African and Asiatic war fronts. Miss Rendle's plane literally fell to pieces in the air after she got over the Morne Cabrit Mountains on her way from Port-au-Prince to Santiago de los Caballeros, in Santo Domingo, as it was then called. Miraculously, she was only slightly hurt, and this more through the violent behaviour of her parachute than the break-up of her plane. She was found near and cared for in Las Cahobas on the plateau of Hinche, but on the south side of the Artibonite. Mr. Carstairs was on the north side. This is an important point.

Neither could get down to or communicate with the capital, Port-au-Prince, because of the complete breakdown of transport and communications in the wake of the storm, and indeed, James Carstairs, as he says, had no cause to wish to go at that time. Neither of them then knew that all communications were already severed and would remain so for many months.

It is now known that the storm caused a tremendous flood on the Hinche plateau, but we can only conjecture that the weight of this water caused some major landslide in the gorge where the Artibonite River leaves the plateau. Certain it is that the water ran off in an incredibly short space of time, carrying with it so much silt, vegetation, and rubbish that a delta was formed at its mouth between Gonaives and St. Marc—a delta that extends five miles into the sea. The storm lasted a whole week.

Perhaps the most amazing aspect of this early course of events is that within the short space of three days after the abatement of the storm, the first Compsognathus was undeniably seen. Mr. Carstairs had a detailed report of it on May 19th from a local farmer. This has been flatly denied, especially by scientists who should have been more circumspect, though they may perhaps be excused when it is realized that they have been working mostly on the theory of reverse evolution in an endeavour to explain this startling phase of history. That the reptile was immature is equally certain from the story here given from details in Mr. Carstairs' diary.

* * * * * * *

Cearnice Heriot, an intelligent peasant farmer, had met Mr. Carstairs during the latter's investigation of his livestock in relation to his status in the village community. Cearnice had noted that Carstairs was a doctor, but mistook this title for that of a doctor of medicine. He therefore brought his infant daughter to him to be treated. The child had apparently been chasing the little 'Zandolites' or fence-lizards that infested the gardens and houses throughout the country in those days. One lizard—bright green in colour— had entered a peach bush and the little girl, observing what she supposed to be its tail, reached out and seized it. The animal—for it was not the Zandolite, though also bright green in colour, turned and lacerated her hand and, as she ran screaming into the house, leapt from the tree, bounded across the compound on stilt-like hind legs and entered a cactus hedge. Cearnice later went in search of it, thinking it to be a novel specimen of Iguana. He came across it still lurking there, but was so amazed at its grotesque appearance— "something between a skinned turkey and a great lizard," as he put it—that he left it and turned his attention to his child.

* * * * * * * *

Now, Miss Rendle was at that time marooned on the other side of the wide and now turbulent Artibonite River, and yet it was before the end of May that she herself, while recuperating at the home of a well-known Haitian family at Las Cahobas, saw what from her description appears to have been another immature Compsognathus, though it was shiny blue black in colour and may have been a very young Struthiomimus.

It is most interesting to note that not only did this particular group of reptiles appear first, but also that it did so on both sides of the river, and in both places before any actual reported appearance of the so-called Nitrogenous Earths. Mr. Carstairs had observed what must have been a small pocket of this blue-green Nitroearth some months before, as has been mentioned above, and it is therefore probable that some other patches were also laid bare before the heavy rains of May 1959. How else could young though well-developed dinosaurs of the Compsognathus and Struthiomimus types be on the prowl only three days after the deluge of May 11th-17th?

From the end of May, however, events moved with greater rapidity. Large areas of country must have been simultaneously denuded not only of vegetation but also of their remaining red, clayey surface soil by the floods, because there is a great volume of entries in the few official Haitian records recovered from the area, showing complaints and pleas for help from peasants in widely separated areas. Conditions at first seem to have been worse round the outer edge of the plateau than at its centre, and this was the cause of Miss Rendle's decision to move to Hinche which is almost exactly at the centre of the great bowl. She made this move on the 10th of June, but the country proved to be already so bad by that time that it took her party ten days to reach the river, where they arrived late on the evening of the 19th. It was apparently upon the advice of one Jules Hermonite that the party endeavoured to cross that night; he believed that the river was going to rise again as a result of a storm they could see to the west.

Luckily, Miss Rendle crossed in the first boat because all the others were lost when the river did so rise. She records that as they crossed, she observed a positive swarm of what she at first mistook for small crocodiles in the river; these surprised the Haitians who said that they had never seen such a thing before. It gave her a first inkling of what was really afoot, because these creatures had flippers in place of clawed feet, and pointed beaks like those of birds.

I understand that a very detailed account of Miss Rendle's sub-sequent adventures up to the time that she was rescued by Mr. Carstairs is even now going to press in a fascinating book written jointly by those two gallant heroes. I will therefore leave this per-sonal story—which will constitute the only first hand observations of these events by scientifically trained people—and return to our more general report.

It was just about the same date that Mr. Carstairs also first became really aware of what was afoot. Having not only the in-tense interest of a scientific investigator in the lives and problems of the Haitians, but also a liberal quota of the very human sympa-thy and compassion of his prominent Quaker forebears, he had thrown his entire energies into almost superhuman efforts to evacuate the peasantry from the farmsteads in the surrounding low-lying areas. The general impression then seems to have been that if only the higher ground around Hinche could be attained, they would be safe. Even then the farmers were very loath to leave their flooded lands. It was while spending a wretched night argu-ing with one such stubborn individual that James Carstairs came face to face with the real danger.

As he tells it, he was sitting on the edge of a table in the sodden, leaky cottage listening to a tremendous tirade in Creole by the old farmer and surrounded by his enormous family when a cow came galloping in through the front door, its eyes rolling and bloodshot. She was giving vent to a noise such as nobody had ever heard a cow make before. So terrified was the beast that it quite missed the back door and charged the wall, carrying away the door-post and several square yards of mud wall in its frenzy. Before the party recovered from its amazement, four curs set up a terrific wailing and came backing into the house, their bellies pressed to the floor. The old farmer seized up his tremendous, short, broad-bladed machete and stepped to the door. As he did so all the womenfolk uttered a united scream, that in Mr. Carstairs' words "would have been worth a thousand a week on radio," and dived for the kitchen.

The amazing thing is that the dogs simply whimpered and crouched at the old farmer's feet, although they were semi-wild pariahs and would normally not even have entered the house. And they stayed there until two of their number were picked out of the lamplight by what appeared to be the head of an unbelievably enormous serpent.

By this time Carstairs had drawn a Colt .45 that he then carried due to the menacing attitude adopted by a few of the farmers, and dashing round the back of the house, he turned a flashlight on to the scene from the corner of the house. What he saw can only be described in his own words.

"There stood in the quagmire that had once been Henri Aurelle's vegetable garden a black, glistening thing that I never thought to see outside a B-Class movie house. In fact, it did not look real at all for its great, arched body bore a crest of spines that ought manifestly to have been hard and sharp, but which bent and flopped to either side as if made of soft rubber. Its clumpy legs were buried knee-deep in the mud and its rear end tapered away into a long tail which was also sunk beneath the mud. It had a long, serpentine neck and a small head with staring, lidless eyes; this probed about between the posts of the verandah for all the world like a giant snake. When I flashed the light upon it, the horrible thing clamped its jaws, together and half a dog fell to the ground with a splash. Then, still chewing the rest of the dog, the two-foot head first withdrew, and then simply waved in my direction. I believe it actually reached the place where I had been standing, but by that time I was halfway back to the kitchen door."

The rest of this extraordinary young man's statement about this incident is so matter of fact that we can gain no idea of just what an effect this terrifying discovery had either upon him or the rest of the people present. By much questioning, however, we have elicited the information that he found an old shotgun in the cottage and, risking death, went out of the front door while the old farmer, himself a more than courageous man, held the flashlight, and put seven shots into the beast. The only reaction on the part of the animal, which he believes was some unknown form of dinosaur related to the herbivorous Diplodocus but apparently of omnivorous feeding habits, was to flop down in the mud and wave its long neck about violently so that he could not get a shot at its head. Seeing that it seemed reluctant either to move or to die, Carstairs gathered the family together at the point of the gun, and putting the old man in the lead, marched them out of the back of the house and no less than three miles through the pitch darkness and torrential downpour to his house.

They appear to have been lucky that no other reptiles happened to be in the intervening area, for marsh conditions had already spread to the path and, as is now known, at least fifty percent of the dinosaurian species then roaming the plateau were nocturnal. Had it not been for James Carstairs these poor people would probably have perished in their home that night, for the Haitian peasants seem to have been rendered completely paralyzed by the appearance of the dinosaurs. Perhaps this was because Haiti had never had any wild animals great, or even small, but had fostered a very strong belief in the occult as an outcome of the common practice of what is called Vaudun, or by the ignorant foreigner "voodoo." They seem to have regarded the whole business as some ghastly make-believe on the part of their ancient African Rain-god, Damballa, and simply to have resigned themselves to their fate. The reactions of domestic animals were little different, for although they ran at first—and strangely enough usually to the nearest human beings—they then simply sat down, howled in their various manners, and waited to be picked off and eaten by the monsters. It is doubtful if so-called civilized communities would have behaved much differently, moreover, for even our most erudite notions of the habits of the dinosaurian reptiles appear to have been entirely erroneous.

* * * * * * *

A fact, of course unknown to the local peasantry, as indeed it was to scientists until that time, caused the first real attack of panic. This 'fact' was that it had never been realized, or even suggested that the vast numbers and individual bulk of Mesozoic Dinosaurs was due not only to a slow evolution over great periods of time, but also to an incredibly rapid growth on the part of the individuals from the time of their emergence from their eggs to the attainment of adult proportions.

On June 14th, a party of officials and labourers were completing the evacuation of people and domestic animals from an area to the north of Hinche. The job was rendered well-nigh impossible by the morass conditions that had set in conditions which are now known to have been caused by the tunnelling and burrowing of countless fossorial reptiles, combined with the growth of giant, subterranean, water-holding fungi and, to some extent, by the deceptive surface-covering of exotic Liverworts and primitive moss-like plants. Only a small knot of people with some goats waited to be drawn across a morass when a tremendous croaking broke out in the tangled growth behind them, and before they could scatter, a group of about thirty young Tyrannosaurs of an as yet unidentified species but already ten to twelve feet tall, burst out and fell upon them.

As an Haitian official who witnessed this episode rather naively reported in Port-au-Prince later, "The spectacle was more gripping than any film. People and goats were torn to shreds in a few seconds. The weight and lightning speed of the great reptiles was unbelievable." (This eye-witness report—the only official Haitian record of this initial period—is being published in our Transactions.)

. . . a black, glistening thing . . . long, serpentine
neck and small head with staring, lidless eyes . . .

It was indeed a grim joke that nature played in bringing forth the carnivorous before the herbivorous types. Had it not been for this many of the inhabitants of the plateau might have been saved. As it was, everyone who did not flee the area—and few did so except Miss Rendle, Mr. Carstairs, and the strange Bravelette brothers, until our investigations entirely unheard of—apparently perished before the end of the year.

When Hinche, or rather the higher ground nearby, was completely surrounded by a morass; when typhoid and cholera had broken out among the wretched people herded together there, and when the evening attacks of the Dinosaurs, now augmented by giant Scorpions, and a genus of terrestrial, soft-bodied animals related to the lowly Rotifera, had already decimated their numbers, Mr. Carstairs and Miss Rendle decided to make a bid for escape, despite the terrible dangers. Their clever device of a punt propelled by a motor and an aerial propeller so rapidly constructed from the remnants of civilization, and in the face of opposition from all the people still alive, was as much the cool-headed act of heroes as the desperate act of terrified people.

They left the settlement at 8:30 a. m. on December 20th. Their machine finally wedged at midday some twelve miles distant, and in an endeavour to retrace their steps and at the same time avoid both morasses and dense vegetation, they reached a river that was still flowing. Mr. Carstairs recognized the clearing beside it as being that near his old house, and they were able to make their way there. It was still covered with the old original soil derived from the erosion of the tertiary clays, but was surrounded by Nitro-earth and underlaid by it, as Mr. Carstairs well knew.

On this patch of land they resided for a year and a half, keeping a perpetual fire fed with dried Selaginellas, living entirely on reptiles caught in ingenious traps, and on fruits the edibility of which they never knew before tasting; surely the greatest feat of endurance ever recorded and only approached by Courtauld's lonely vigil on the ice floes of Greenland in the early thirties, and Pedro Almira's 400 day survival in a rocket ship in free flight round the earth last year.

The remarkable fact that throughout this time the world was quite unaware of their plight, and that even the residents of Port-au-Prince had only the vaguest knowledge of what really was afoot on the Hinche plateau, was due to three things.

First, the world was primarily concerned with the war. After the Russians occupied Europe in January 1958, and began to penetrate Africa, America was concerned only with its own safety. Secondly, the Hinche Plateau is ringed with high mountains, and upon these the new growth of Mesozoic vegetation formed a solid rampart of stinking, sodden, impenetrable jungle. The plateau itself was a dense carpet of green, beneath which the activities of men and beasts were hidden from the few aeroplanes that flew over the area. Thirdly, and most important of all, the Haitian government securely locked up the whole area, because their brilliant chemist, De Blainville, had spotted the value to the belligerent countries of the Nitro-earth, and the whole energy of the state was directed towards mining and exporting this substance and keeping foreigners and non-military nationals from its sources.

And thus this natural phenomenon might have rested for years, until the slow spread of the vegetation carried the Mesozoic life over the whole of Hispaniola, and the civilized nations of the world had exhausted themselves by war, when doubtless the island would have become a wonder zoo for the zoologists of the new generation. That it did not do so is now known to be solely because of the over-zealous commercial enterprise of the deliberate collaborationist activities of the Santo Domingans. Even then, it is probable that spores of various plants and certainly the eggs of some of the invertebrate forms of life would eventually have been carried to the neighbouring Caribbean islands on the feet of migrating water birds. There is also no reason why aquatic species of reptiles should not have taken to the sea and swum to Cuba, Jamaica and Puerto Rico if the Mesozoic conditions had ever reached the coast. There is still danger of this occurring, both on the Indian Ocean and the North Coasts of Africa, and we will have to resign ourselves to the slow infiltration of plants and invertebrates from Africa into Europe along the bird migration routes.

* * * * * * *

Santo Domingo borders the Hinche Plateau on the East—in fact the plateau continues into what was once Santo Domingan territory. The Santo Domingans had come to know of the value of the Nitro-earth, and they were working a surface deposit of it by May, 1960, just one year after the initial deluge. What they had not discovered, or at least failed to adopt, was De Blainville's clever process of refining the Nitro-earth in the old sugar factories. Although hindered by the now excessive rains, they managed to export a considerable quantity in its raw state to Europe whence, of course, it was transported to the Eastern powers. It is interesting, moreover, to note that this unrefined Nitro-earth has only been traced to what were the territories controlled by the Eastern Powers, which in our opinion completely exonerates the Government of Haiti from any complicity in activities subversive to the interest of the Western Powers, but correspondingly implicates the erstwhile Santo Domingan Government. The very knowledge that any Nitro-earth was then reaching the Eastern Powers, combined with the demise of Dr. Forrester, and the tragic end of the First Expeditionary Force, however, caused the deplorable and entirely erroneous accusation that was officially made that year, to the effect that the Haitian Government was in league with the Eastern Powers.

The fact that Nitro-earth had to be moved down to the Haitian coastal plain for refinement, meant, of course—in the light of our present knowledge—that it was only a matter of time before the Mesozoic life would appear both along the route and at the refining plants. It was this sudden appearance—actually of a plague of giant dragonflies, unclassified parasitic worms which were fatal to man, and some cumbersome reptiles related to Protoceratops (which have never appeared again and seem to have been exterminated)—that prompted the American government to send the famous zoolo-gist, Dr. Clemens E. Forrester, to investigate. American officialdom knew practically nothing of the events in Haiti at that time, amazing as that may seem.

Dr. Forrester's first move was to suggest means of coping with the outbreaks near Port-au-Prince. His energies were directed against the animals, though it seems he fully realized the almost greater danger of the plants. Like the great man he was, he then set off at once for the interior and the Hinche plateau to try to discover the

. . . a tremendous croaking broke out in the tangled growth . . . 30 young Tyrannosaurs 10 to 12 feet tall fell upon them . . .

causes of these startling conditions, and see for himself the source from which they were being disseminated.

His death, in the jaws of a reptile now named Forresterosaurus and related to the Triassic form Inostransevia, did not take place on the plateau at all, as is popularly believed. It occurred actually on the maritime plain not more than twenty miles from Port-au-Prince, before the eyes of his military escort, whose rifles and machine guns proved quite useless against the animal's attack. This was, however, misconstrued and added to the fable that he was drawn to his death by the Haitians. In point of fact, the latter put up a most gallant fight and their commander, Lieutenant Auguste, met his death in the jaws of the same animal while trying to rescue Dr. Forrester, virtually with his bare hands.

Nonetheless, as a result of this tragedy, the First Expeditionary Force was hastily dispatched. The grim details of its utter defeat—for we can call it nothing less—are now well known. Had they landed at Port-au-Prince where the Haitians had entrenched themselves, all might have been well, or at least fewer lives would have been lost, but the impression seemed to have been gained that the Haitians were hostile. In consequence, the force landed at St. Marc, some sixty miles northwest of Port-au-Prince. From there they marched round into and up the valley of the Artibonite.

Already, on the second day, new and unimagined diseases of the intestines and lungs had broken out among them, and on the fourth day they were attacked by a vast horde of Ornithopodous Dinosaurs, the very existence of which was then entirely unknown to the troops, and which consequently altogether wrecked their morale.

Their rifles, machine guns and even bazookas were as useless as water-pistols; gas, though thick enough to kill a thousand times over anything then known, was completely ineffectual against the great reptiles because they took upwards of seventy-two hours to succumb. Bombs from aircraft were of little help against such relatively small individual targets on account of the density of the vegetation, and tanks, when eventually brought into action, not only failed to impress the beasts, but were in over a hundred cases trampled almost flat by them. The Tyrannosaurs particularly seem to have flown into paroxysms of rage at the very sight of them, their paltry little brains probably registering them as Sauropodous vegetarian dinosaurs. They rushed at them in hundred foot leaps, never failing to land with all their thirty tons of weight square upon them. In one instance, the whole top of a large tank was ripped cleanly off by the immense, taloned feet of the great beast. The driver and mechanics were then picked out and eaten. Only 240 men and four officers got back to the boats.

The utter lack of planning for this ill-fated expedition—for it can hardly be called a military operation—is indicative not only of the somewhat hysterical state of mind of our Government as a whole at that critical phase of the war, but is also a lesson to all of us of the scientific fraternity. Until then we, and notably the biologists, were smug enough to believe that we had laid down the ultimate laws of nature and that nothing revolutionary would ever occur unless initiated by our own efforts. To us the dinosaurs were dead and could never be revived. Further, we also held to the opinion, now proved ridiculous, that nothing could happen in the world, and especially within that half of it which we still controlled, that would not be known immediately. Yet here were incredible conditions existing for more than two years not more than five hundred miles from our own national borders and on an island of the utmost strategic importance, that even the high command regarded as travellers' tales or simply pure hallucinations. Worse still, we were even then almost wholly dependent upon the supply of Nitro-earth from that area.

* * * * * * * *

Just how lax our whole concept of conditions in Hispaniola really was may perhaps better be gained from the first hand report of Lt. George Roskin who survived the First Expeditionary Force's defeat. This gallant young officer, you will remember, took command of the remnants of the Force and engineered its escape. He writes in his official report as follows:

"As recorded above—Gen. R. 1077 H, Intro. Sec. 1.—the force had advanced west from St. Marc to the new delta of the Artibonite River, and then turned inland. Troops were fatigued due to lack of adequate transport. Further, a gasoline truck had spontaneously exploded, causing a two hour hold up of the column at the heat of the day. The main force bedded down under light canvas at sundown in the narrow gorge, and reconnaissance planes and a helicopter which had been flying over the uplands all day returned to a hastily cleared level area two miles down the valley. They had virtually nothing to report but that the whole interior of the island seemed to be covered with tall forests of an odd nature. The following two days were a nightmare. I sincerely believe that there was not a fit man in the whole Force by nightfall. Although every precaution known to modern science was taken, everybody was vomiting at regular intervals. Our progress was ridiculously slow. Three plane-loads of medical officers arrived from Cuba on the second day, but seemed completely baffled.

"It was on the fourth day that we came upon a saddle in the mountains, after having made a detour over normal arid, old-style, Haitian country with cactuses and thorns. Here we entered a strange forest of immense, pithy plants with green tendrils instead of leaves. Nothing delayed our rapid progress over this level ground. The tanks went ahead, pushing down the vegetation. Just about the time the whole column was well into the tangled mass, the earth began to shake and an avalanche of boulders rolled down upon us from the left side of the valley, and before we had time to deploy or even face about, some two hundred enormous, lizard-shaped forms were among us. They were vivid greenish-blue in colour with red crests, stood about thirty feet tall, and had jaws at least four feet long armed with scimitar-formed teeth about ten inches long. We let go with everything we could bring to bear, but they moved so fast that it was almost impossible to get a sight on them. Also, they were already among us and took leaps of upwards of a hundred feet at a time. The vegetation made matters worse because it crumpled into a semi-liquid mass like a bowl of boiled asparagus, entrapping us, bogging down the mechanized equipment and affording perfect cover for the dinosaurs. The only effective weapons were the AA-Multiple guns on the heavier tanks, brought down and fired horizontally. I regret to have to state, however, that they accounted for more of us than of the reptiles.

. . . a flock of Pterodactyls, tailless . . . with a wingspan of . . . 20 feet . . . wrought ghastly havoc among the sick and wounded . . .

"The attack was continuous and the numbers of the reptiles were constantly augmented. There was no let up till the remnants of our group reached the higher dry ground. More and more dinosaurs of unheard-of forms and sizes kept pouring down the valley. They fought among themselves as well as with us. They seem to have been ravenously hungry. Most amazing was a flock of Pterodactyls, tailless but with a wingspan of about twenty feet, and with long, pointed bills, that came planing down from the hills to land upside down like bats on the tanks, on the giant Tyrannosaurs, and on the vegetation. They drilled at the steel of the tanks like vast woodpeckers and with as little effect. However, they wrought the most ghastly havoc among the sick and wounded, literally tearing them to pieces. They appeared to have the greatest difficulty in flying upwards and could be seen crawling to elevated points and then taking off like gliders to soar aloft on warm air currents."

There follows some fifty pages of technical description both of the reptiles, written in conjunction with Dr. J. F. Fulsom of the U. S. Army Medical Corps, and then thirty pages of observations on the behaviour of tanks, guns and other equipment by Lt. Roskin. I pass on to quote one further passage from this report which speaks for itself:

"After the futile attempt to drive off the animals with gas, and now even further encumbered with gas masks, we managed to gather fourteen tanks together in a rough circle with all the living we could muster by loudspeaker in the centre. About half of these were wounded. We started an orderly retreat across the saddle to the high ground. There was such carnage all about that the larger carnivorous reptiles were for the moment fully occupied. We made more than half the distance virtually unmolested due, I believe, to holding our fire which appeared to me, at least, only to draw their attention and provoke their anger. However, somebody inadvertently let go with a bazooka of an improved type which cut a fiery swathe through the jungle. Immediately every Tyrannosaurus stopped whatever it was doing and rounded upon us. As if at a signal the whole horde came bounding at us. With my own eyes I saw the last remaining medium Roosevelt Tank flattened like a paper carton when a Tyrannosaurus landed full upon it with both of its palm-thick legs of solid bone square on the top. Another, in fury, inserted the claws of its left foot—the central claw is ten inches long and fourteen in circumference at the base—in the fore-visor of a light tank and literally ripped the entire top off of the machine. The steel plates simply tore along the lines of rivets or alongside any welded joints."

* * * * * * *

The significance of this defeat was twofold. Not only was it greatly detrimental to American morale as a whole, but it created a great problem for the Western Allies. More and more we ourselves were becoming dependent upon the Nitro-earth as the only readily available source of fissionable material that required little processing. On the one hand there was now grave danger of this source becoming closed to us, while there were then apparently some real grounds for believing that it might even fall into the hands of the enemy. This the public could not or would not fully realize or believe. That a modern force with rocket planes and artillery could be utterly defeated and almost annihilated, like a Roman legion of old, by mere animals, seemed impossible. Suspicion naturally fell upon the government and the high command.

At about the same time, however—that is, in the spring of 1960—American Intelligence received the first definite intimation that all was not well behind the Communist lines, and particularly in their own home territory. At first, revolt was suspected, but the clue as to what was really wrong, finally came from a British source in East Africa.

A Russian vessel, the motor ship Michurin, which had somehow escaped the western blockade, had been captured carrying a cargo of unrefined Nitro-earth originating from Santo Domingo. Actually the vessel was already incapacitated through a dire sickness that had broken out among her crew. The captured Nitro-earth was unloaded at Mombasa, and moved up to Nairobi in Kenya Colony for refinement and subsequent use at the new fission plant there. It was dumped from sealed trucks into special containers by a railway siding.

A week later, however, these containers were covered with a foam of vivid green liverworts, while their contents, swollen to eight times their previous volume with fungi, were swarming with giant Platyhelminthines, and excavated through and through by strange reptiles of at least eight species. Swift measures were taken against it, but in the absence of experience and suitable chemical weapons, to little effect.

From it, a disease attacking the lungs spread like wild-fire, while the local Africans quickly became infected with a deadly parasitic fluke transmitted to them through eating some of the reptiles, which they hunted on all possible occasions.

That was the first authentic report the allies had of a serious outbreak outside the island of Hispaniola. The spread of Mesozoic conditions seems to have been greater and more rapid in Africa than anywhere else, though little accurate information as to how they got there or concerning this continent generally has been received since the spring of 1960 when the last white people left Capetown. It appears that the whole continent is now again much as it must have been in early Cretaceous times, and it is probable that it will remain so for generations to come and after all the other parts of the world have been completely cleared—that is, if they ever are.

The course of events from then on until now is known to everybody. The collapse of the Eastern Powers was occasioned principally by the ravages of Lung-Hernia—or Gas-chest, as it is more popularly called—now being overcome by the brilliant remedies devised by Drs. Cope and Hindenburg, but which can be traced to spores germinating in the Nitro-earth. This is not generally recognized. We now find also, in studying world reports in conjunction with our own findings at the seat of the trouble, that the real Communist rout took place in their own homelands, for Central Asia had by that time become one vast morass, positively swarming not only with Mesozoic invertebrates and many reptiles and amphibians, but also with great droves of present-day rodents and insects which somehow managed to adapt themselves to and to thrive and multiply in the changed conditions.

And all this, we would stress, was brought about by the admittedly illicit exportation of unrefined Nitro-earth from Hispaniola.

About the time that the President called the first roundtable conference of the Allied Western Powers, the Eastern Powers are now known to have done likewise. The findings and suggestions of both, now that they can be compared, are surprisingly similar, though the whole gruesome state of affairs originated within our jurisdiction. Doubtless there were those on the other side who knew of its real origin in Hispaniola, but the really amazing thing is that until the end, the Russians themselves seem to have thought the Mesozoic life was endemic to Siberia.

It is extremely fortunate that peace was declared when it was, so that all the world's resources could be turned against our new natural enemies—this "tide of fossil ancestors," as the press has so succinctly called it. Had this new war not been declared when it was, it is apparent from our recent researches in Haiti that the battle would have been a losing one from its start to its deplorable finish—none other than the extermination, not only of humanity but also of the whole of quaternary life on this planet, so putting the clock of evolution back just sixty million years.

* * * * * * *

We can state categorically that at the present moment the wound is healing from the inside. Of this you have already been informed through official channels, but from the story of Mr. Carstairs and from our own observations, it is clear that the excessive rainfall engendered on the Hinche plateau by the great increase of moist vegetation has either eroded away or blanketed-over all remaining Nitro-earth of which there was, in any case, originally only a comparatively small amount—geologically speaking, an infinitesimal amount. The supply of fertile, dessicated spores, eggs and seeds is therefore coming to an end, or again being bottled up by new deposits. Much of the Hinche Plateau itself is now a glaring, white, radioactive desert, slightly saline and scoured of all debris by the controlled Lithium bomb dropped there two weeks ago. The only dispersal centres are deltas, outpourings and man-made dumps of Nitro-earth outside this area.

Our researches have elucidated the whole problem as follows: Under the horizontal surface strata of the Hinche Plateau in Haiti, which were of Tertiary age, lay other horizontal strata of still older or Mesozoic rocks. First of these was a belt of early Jurassic clays—akin to Lias—which in the Hinche plateau area, had been formed countless ages ago by slow deposition in a vast stagnant bowl, of swamps of sediment derived from surrounding mountains of still earlier age and of unique chemical constitution. Not only were they rich in uranium, but they also constituted a strange natural preservative for any animal or plant eggs, spores or other remains that happened to be deposited in them.

In that year of excessive rain, 1958, the floods, breaking some natural darn, finally carried denudation to a point to which it had been approaching for countless centuries. The last of the covering Tertiary clays were in many places carried away, and these older sediments, deposited aeons previously in a long-forgotten basin, were exposed. These were the famous Nitrogenous Earths in which countless eggs and spores of Mesozoic animals and plants of sixty million years ago were preserved intact and only awaiting moisture and sunlight to hatch. This clay, or earth, is a concentrate of nitrates and certain extremely rare chemical compounds, but lacks all the carbonates, calcites, aluminates and other common rock-building materials. Be cause of its peculiar constitution and chemical composition, it happened to be an almost perfect preservative, conserving eggs, spores, and seeds better than water-glass or a carbon-dioxide chamber. Coming into contact with air and moisture once again, in a warm and suitable climate, these spores burst into growth, the Dinosaurian eggs lying perfectly preserved therein hatched out, and the reptiles, finding their own food and their own environment around them, thrived.

* * * * * * * *

"But why," countless people have asked, "were there so many? Dinosaurs' eggs and whole seeds in a fossilized condition are few and far between."

*. . . a Russian vessel . . . the Michurin . . . had
been captured carrying unrefined Nitro-earth . . .*

The answer to this, the most puzzling of all questions, we have found. It lies in observations made upon the topography and geological structure of the Hinche plateau. The strata, both Secondary and Tertiary, were horizontal; they were, in fact, just as laid down in the distant past, unaltered by upheaval and little-touched by earth movements. The more ancient Jurassic plateau must have been a great sink in an immense plain. Into it in bygone ages poured many rivers and streams carrying, among other things, spores, seeds, and the more resistant eggs of amphibians and reptiles. Throughout countless ages, whilst the great bowl was slowly filling up with this debris, it was inhabited by the reptilian life of that world. Every so often clutches of their eggs also became sunk in the preservative mud. Chicken's eggs don't get lost every day but if even one is lost in one hundred square miles every day and this continues for a million years, there will be many eggs resting in the region, especially if but few go bad before they are preserved, or are broken. So it came about that beneath the plateau of Hinche lay an almost solid stratum of suspended life awaiting rejuvenation. But with the animals came their diseases also, and a myriad lesser forms of life not previously known in the fossil state because of their soft bodies. Many of them have become plagues to us.

This is the kernel of our findings and the explanation of recent history. Now it only remains for us to concentrate upon the great work before us. That is the final sealing of what pockets of Nitro-earth remain and then a concerted and perhaps prolonged struggle against the varied Mesozoic life that we now find around us in every continent. To this effort every device of modern science and applied biology must be brought to bear.

People must adjust themselves to the new conditions for the world can never be as it was. Many of the ancient forms of life have, we must admit, returned to stay. Moreover, they are exterminating our present-day animals and plants and are retaking their place in the scheme of things. The greater majority are breeding and increasing in numbers. We must expect swarms and plagues but, after all, are they any worse than lions, rats, locusts, the Boll-weevil, the Colorado beetle, or the clothes moth? The Tyrannosaurs, when in large numbers, are the only dinosaurs with which we cannot at present cope, but fortunately they are confined to mountainous tropical areas and doubtless it is only a matter of time before aerial bombing or light, mobile artillery will have cleared them away.

Man's great fight to reconquer the dark continent of Africa seems, until now, to have come to naught, and it now seems "darker" than ever before. However, when we have recuperated from the effects of the senseless war we have ourselves created, we will undoubtedly again be able to tackle this pressing problem with vigour and confidence.

Let it remain a taunt to our youth, and a goal of all humanity.

Signed this 16th day of April, 1961
Oswald F. Bristowe,
Secretary
The Combined Scientific Societies of the
    United States of America

The Lost World

Arthur Conan Doyle

I have wrought my simple plan
If I give one hour of joy
To the boy who's half a man,
Or the man who's half a boy.

Foreword

Mr. E. D. Malone desires to state that both the injunction for restraint and the libel action have been withdrawn unreservedly by Professor G. E. Challenger, who, being satisfied that no criticism or comment in this book is meant in an offensive spirit, has guaranteed that he will place no impediment to its publication and circulation.

1

"There Are Heroisms All Round Us"

Mr. Hungerton, her father, really was the most tactless person upon earth,—a fluffy, feathery, untidy cockatoo of a man, perfectly good-natured, but absolutely centered upon his own silly self. If anything could have driven me from Gladys, it would have been the thought of such a father-in-law. I am convinced that he really believed in his heart that I came round to the Chestnuts three days a week for the pleasure of his company, and very especially to hear his views upon bimetallism, a subject upon which he was by way of being an authority.

For an hour or more that evening I listened to his monotonous chirrup about bad money driving out good, the token value of silver, the depreciation of the rupee, and the true standards of exchange.

"Suppose," he cried with feeble violence, "that all the debts in the world were called up simultaneously, and immediate payment insisted upon,—what under our present conditions would happen then?"

I gave the self-evident answer that I should be a ruined man, upon which he jumped from his chair, reproved me for my habitual levity, which made it impossible for him to discuss any reasonable subject in my presence, and bounced off out of the room to dress for a Masonic meeting.

At last I was alone with Gladys, and the moment of Fate had come! All that evening I had felt like the soldier who awaits the signal which will send him on a forlorn hope; hope of victory and fear of repulse alternating in his mind.

She sat with that proud, delicate profile of hers outlined against the red curtain. How beautiful she was! And yet how aloof! We had been friends, quite good friends; but never could I get beyond the same comradeship which I might have established with one of my fellow-reporters upon the *Gazette*,—perfectly frank, perfectly kindly, and perfectly unsexual. My instincts are all against a woman being too frank and at her ease with me. It is no compliment to a man. Where the real sex feeling begins, timidity and distrust are its companions, heritage from old wicked days when love and violence went often hand in hand. The bent head, the averted eye, the faltering voice, the wincing figure—these, and not the unshrinking gaze and frank reply, are the true signals of passion. Even in my short life I had learned as much as that—or had inherited it in that race memory which we call instinct.

Gladys was full of every womanly quality. Some judged her to be cold and hard; but such a thought was treason. That delicately bronzed skin, almost oriental in its coloring, that raven hair, the large liquid eyes, the full but exquisite lips,—all the stigmata of passion were there. But I was sadly conscious that up to now I had never found the secret of drawing it forth. However, come what might, I should have done with suspense and bring matters to a head to-night. She could but refuse me, and better be a repulsed lover than an accepted brother.

So far my thoughts had carried me, and I was about to break the long and uneasy silence, when two critical, dark eyes looked round at me, and the proud head was shaken in smiling reproof. "I have a presentiment that you are going to propose, Ned. I do wish you wouldn't; for things are so much nicer as they are."

I drew my chair a little nearer. "Now, how did you know that I was going to propose?" I asked in genuine wonder.

"Don't women always know? Do you suppose any woman in the world was ever taken unawares? But—oh, Ned, our friendship has been so good and so pleasant! What a pity to spoil it! Don't you feel how splendid it is that a young man and a young woman should be able to talk face to face as we have talked?"

"I don't know, Gladys. You see, I can talk face to face with—with the station-master." I can't imagine how that official came into the matter; but in he trotted, and set us both laughing. "That does not satisfy me in the least. I want my arms round you, and your head on my breast, and—oh, Gladys, I want—"

She had sprung from her chair, as she saw signs that I proposed to demonstrate some of my wants. "You've spoiled everything, Ned," she said. "It's all so beautiful and natural until this kind of thing comes in! It is such a pity! Why can't you control yourself?"

"I didn't invent it," I pleaded. "It's nature. It's love."

"Well, perhaps if both love, it may be different. I have never felt it."

"But you must—you, with your beauty, with your soul! Oh, Gladys, you were made for love! You must love!"

"One must wait till it comes."

"But why can't you love me, Gladys? Is it my appearance, or what?"

She did unbend a little. She put forward a hand—such a gracious, stooping attitude it was—and she pressed back my head. Then she looked into my upturned face with a very wistful smile.

"No it isn't that," she said at last. "You're not a conceited boy by nature, and so I can safely tell you it is not that. It's deeper."

"My character?"

She nodded severely.

"What can I do to mend it? Do sit down and talk it over. No, really, I won't if you'll only sit down!"

She looked at me with a wondering distrust which was much more to my mind than her whole-hearted confidence. How primitive and bestial it looks when you put it down in black and white!—and perhaps after all it is only a feeling peculiar to myself. Anyhow, she sat down.

"Now tell me what's amiss with me?"

"I'm in love with somebody else," said she.

It was my turn to jump out of my chair.

"It's nobody in particular," she explained, laughing at the expression of my face: "only an ideal. I've never met the kind of man I mean."

"Tell me about him. What does he look like?"

"Oh, he might look very much like you."

"How dear of you to say that! Well, what is it that he does that I don't do? Just say the word,—teetotal, vegetarian, aeronaut, theosophist, superman. I'll have a try at it, Gladys, if you will only give me an idea what would please you."

She laughed at the elasticity of my character. "Well, in the first place, I don't think my ideal would speak like that," said she. "He would be a harder, sterner man, not so ready to adapt himself to a silly girl's whim. But, above all, he must be a man who could do, who could act, who could look Death in the face and have no fear of him, a man of great deeds and strange experiences. It is never a man that I should love, but always the glories he had won; for they would be reflected upon me. Think of Richard Burton! When I read his wife's life of him I could so understand her love! And Lady Stanley! Did you ever read the wonderful last chapter of that book about her husband? These are the sort of men that a woman could worship with all her soul, and yet be the greater, not the less, on account of her love, honored by all the world as the inspirer of noble deeds."

She looked so beautiful in her enthusiasm that I nearly brought down the whole level of the interview. I gripped myself hard, and went on with the argument.

"We can't all be Stanleys and Burtons," said I; "besides, we don't get the chance,—at least, I never had the chance. If I did, I should try to take it."

"But chances are all around you. It is the mark of the kind of man I mean that he makes his own chances. You can't hold him back. I've never met him, and yet I seem to know him so well. There are heroisms all round us waiting to be done. It's for men to do them, and for women to reserve their love as a reward for such men. Look at that young Frenchman who went up last week in a balloon. It was blowing a gale of wind; but because he was announced to go he insisted on starting. The wind blew him fifteen hundred miles in twenty-four hours, and he fell in the middle of Russia. That was the kind of man I mean. Think of the woman he loved, and how other women must have envied her! That's what I should like to be,—envied for my man."

"I'd have done it to please you."

"But you shouldn't do it merely to please me. You should do it because you can't help yourself, because it's natural to you, because the man in you is crying out for heroic expression. Now, when you described the Wigan coal explosion last month, could you not have gone down and helped those people, in spite of the choke-damp?"

"I did."

"You never said so."

"There was nothing worth bucking about."

"I didn't know." She looked at me with rather more interest. "That was brave of you."

"I had to. If you want to write good copy, you must be where the things are."

"What a prosaic motive! It seems to take all the romance out of it. But, still, whatever your motive, I am glad that you went down that mine." She gave me her hand; but with such sweetness and dignity that I could only stoop and kiss it. "I dare say I am merely a foolish woman with a young girl's fancies. And yet it is so real with me, so entirely part of my very self, that I cannot help acting upon it. If I marry, I do want to marry a famous man!"

"Why should you not?" I cried. "It is women like you who brace men up. Give me a chance, and see if I will take it! Besides, as you say, men ought to *make* their own chances, and not wait until they are given. Look at Clive—just a clerk, and he conquered India! By George! I'll do something in the world yet!"

She laughed at my sudden Irish effervescence. "Why not?" she said. "You have everything a man could have,—youth, health, strength, education, energy. I was sorry you spoke. And now I am glad—so glad—if it wakens these thoughts in you!"

"And if I do—"

Her dear hand rested like warm velvet upon my lips. "Not another word, Sir! You should have been at the office for evening duty half an hour ago; only I hadn't the heart to remind you. Some day, perhaps, when you have won your place in the world, we shall talk it over again."

And so it was that I found myself that foggy November evening pursuing the Camberwell tram with my heart glowing within me, and with the eager determination that not another day should elapse before I should find some deed which was worthy of my lady. But who—who in all this wide world could ever have imagined the incredible shape which that deed was to take, or the strange steps by which I was led to the doing of it?

And, after all, this opening chapter will seem to the reader to have nothing to do with my narrative; and yet there would have been no narrative without it, for it is only when a man goes out into the world with the thought that there are heroisms all round him, and with the desire all alive in his heart to follow any which may come within sight of him, that he breaks away as I did from the life he knows, and ventures forth into the wonderful mystic twilight land where lie the great adventures and the great rewards. Behold me, then, at the office of the *Daily Gazette*, on the staff of which I was a most insignificant unit, with the settled determination that very night, if possible, to find the quest which should be worthy of my Gladys! Was it hardness, was it selfishness, that she should ask me to risk my life for her own glorification? Such thoughts may come to middle age; but never to ardent three-and-twenty in the fever of his first love.

2
"Try Your Luck with Professor Challenger"

I always liked McArdle, the crabbed, old, round-backed, red-headed news editor, and I rather hoped that he liked me. Of course, Beaumont was the real boss; but he lived in the rarefied atmosphere of some Olympian height from which he could distinguish nothing smaller than an international crisis or a split in the Cabinet. Sometimes we saw him passing in lonely majesty to his inner sanctum, with his eyes staring vaguely and his mind hovering over the Balkans or the Persian Gulf. He was above and beyond us. But McArdle was his first lieutenant, and it was he that we knew. The old man nodded as I entered the room, and he pushed his spectacles far up on his bald forehead.

"Well, Mr. Malone, from all I hear, you seem to be doing very well," said he in his kindly Scotch accent.

I thanked him.

"The colliery explosion was excellent. So was the Southwark fire. You have the true descreeptive touch. What did you want to see me about?"

"To ask a favor."

He looked alarmed, and his eyes shunned mine. "Tut, tut! What is it?"

"Do you think, Sir, that you could possibly send me on some mission for the paper? I would do my best to put it through and get you some good copy."

"What sort of meesion had you in your mind, Mr. Malone?"

"Well, Sir, anything that had adventure and danger in it. I really would do my very best. The more difficult it was, the better it would suit me."

"You seem very anxious to lose your life."

"To justify my life, Sir."

"Dear me, Mr. Malone, this is very—very exalted. I'm afraid the day for this sort of thing is rather past. The expense of the 'special meesion' business hardly justifies the result, and, of course, in any case it would only be an experienced man with a name that would command public confidence who would get such an order. The big blank spaces in the map are all being filled in, and there's no room for romance anywhere. Wait a bit, though!" he added, with a sudden smile upon his face. "Talking of the blank spaces of the map gives me an idea. What about exposing a fraud—a modern Munchausen—and making him rideeculous? You could show him up as the liar that he is! Eh, man, it would be fine. How does it appeal to you?"

"Anything—anywhere—I care nothing."

McArdle was plunged in thought for some minutes.

"I wonder whether you could get on friendly—or at least on talking terms with the fellow," he said, at last. "You seem to have a sort of genius for establishing relations with people—seempathy, I suppose, or animal magnetism, or youthful vitality, or something. I am conscious of it myself."

"You are very good, sir."

"So why should you not try your luck with Professor Challenger, of Enmore Park?"

I dare say I looked a little startled.

"Challenger!" I cried. "Professor Challenger, the famous zoologist! Wasn't he the man who broke the skull of Blundell, of the *Telegraph*?"

The news editor smiled grimly.

"Do you mind? Didn't you say it was adventures you were after?"

"It is all in the way of business, sir," I answered.

"Exactly. I don't suppose he can always be so violent as that. I'm thinking that Blundell got him at the wrong moment, maybe, or in the wrong fashion. You may have better luck, or more tact in handling him. There's something in your line there, I am sure, and the *Gazette* should work it."

"I really know nothing about him," said I. "I only remember his name in connection with the police-court proceedings, for striking Blundell."

"I have a few notes for your guidance, Mr. Malone. I've had my eye on the Professor for some little time." He took a paper from a drawer. "Here is a summary of his record. I give it you briefly:—

"'Challenger, George Edward. Born: Largs, N. B., 1863. Educ.: Largs Academy; Edinburgh University. British Museum Assistant, 1892. Assistant-Keeper of Comparative Anthropology Department, 1893. Resigned after acrimonious correspondence same year. Winner of Crayston Medal for Zoological Research. Foreign Member of'—well, quite a lot of things, about two inches of small type— 'Societe Belge, American Academy of Sciences, La Plata, etc., etc. Ex-President Palaeontological Society. Section H, British Association'—so on, so on!— 'Publications: *Some Observations Upon a Series of Kalmuck Skulls*; *Outlines of Vertebrate Evolution*; and numerous papers, including *The underlying fallacy of Weissmannism*, which caused heated discussion at the Zoological Congress of Vienna. Recreations: Walking, Alpine climbing. Address: Enmore Park, Kensington, W.'

"There, take it with you. I've nothing more for you to-night."

I pocketed the slip of paper.

"One moment, sir," I said, as I realized that it was a pink bald head, and not a red face, which was fronting me. "I am not very clear yet why I am to interview this gentleman. What has he done?"

The face flashed back again.

"Went to South America on a solitary expedeetion two years ago. Came back last year. Had undoubtedly been to South America, but refused to say exactly where. Began to tell his adventures in a vague way, but somebody started to pick holes, and he just shut up like an oyster. Something wonderful happened—or the man's a champion liar, which is the more probable supposeetion. Had some damaged photographs, said to be fakes. Got so touchy that he assaults anyone who asks questions, and heaves reporters down the stairs. In my opinion he's just a homicidal megalomaniac with a turn for science. That's your man, Mr. Malone. Now, off you run, and see what you can make of him. You're big enough to look after yourself. Anyway, you are all safe. Employers' Liability Act, you know."

A grinning red face turned once more into a pink oval, fringed with gingery fluff; the interview was at an end.

I walked across to the Savage Club, but instead of turning into it I leaned upon the railings of Adelphi Terrace and gazed thoughtfully for a long time at the brown, oily river. I can always think most sanely and clearly in the open air. I took out the list of Professor Challenger's exploits, and I read it over under the electric lamp. Then I had what I can only regard as an inspiration. As a Pressman, I felt sure from what I had been told that I could never hope to get into touch with this cantankerous Professor. But these recriminations, twice mentioned in his skeleton biography, could only mean that he was a fanatic in science. Was there not an exposed margin there upon which he might be accessible? I would try.

I entered the club. It was just after eleven, and the big room was fairly full, though the rush had not yet set in. I noticed a tall, thin, angular man seated in an arm-chair by the fire. He turned as I drew my chair up to him. It was the man of all others whom I should have chosen—Tarp Henry, of the staff of *Nature*, a thin, dry, leathery creature, who was full, to those who knew him, of kindly humanity. I plunged instantly into my subject.

"What do you know of Professor Challenger?"

"Challenger?" He gathered his brows in scientific disapproval. "Challenger was the man who came with some cock-and-bull story from South America."

"What story?"

"Oh, it was rank nonsense about some queer animals he had discovered. I believe he has retracted since. Anyhow, he has suppressed it all. He gave an interview to Reuter's, and there was such a howl that he saw it wouldn't do. It was a discreditable business. There were one or two folk who were inclined to take him seriously, but he soon choked them off."

"How?"

"Well, by his insufferable rudeness and impossible behavior. There was poor old Wadley, of the Zoological Institute. Wadley sent a message: 'The President of the Zoological Institute presents his compliments to Professor Challenger, and would take it as a personal favor if he would do them the honor to come to their next meeting.' The answer was unprintable."

"You don't say?"

"Well, a bowdlerized version of it would run: 'Professor Challenger presents his compliments to the President of the Zoological Institute, and would take it as a personal favor if he would go to the devil.'"

"Good Lord!"

"Yes, I expect that's what old Wadley said. I remember his wail at the meeting, which began: 'In fifty years experience of scientific intercourse—' It quite broke the old man up."

"Anything more about Challenger?"

"Well, I'm a bacteriologist, you know. I live in a nine-hundred-diameter microscope. I can hardly claim to take serious notice of anything that I can see with my naked eye. I'm a frontiersman from the extreme edge of the Knowable, and I feel quite out of place when I leave my study and come into touch with all you great, rough, hulking creatures. I'm too detached to talk scandal, and yet at scientific conversaziones I *have* heard something of Challenger, for he is one of those men whom nobody can ignore. He's as clever as they make 'em—a full-charged battery of force and vitality, but a quarrelsome, ill-conditioned faddist, and unscrupulous at that. He had gone the length of faking some photographs over the South American business."

"You say he is a faddist. What is his particular fad?"

"He has a thousand, but the latest is something about Weissmann and Evolution. He had a fearful row about it in Vienna, I believe."

"Can't you tell me the point?"

"Not at the moment, but a translation of the proceedings exists. We have it filed at the office. Would you care to come?"

"It's just what I want. I have to interview the fellow, and I need some lead up to him. It's really awfully good of you to give me a lift. I'll go with you now, if it is not too late."

Half an hour later I was seated in the newspaper office with a huge tome in front of me, which had been opened at the article "Weissmann versus Darwin," with the sub heading, "Spirited Protest at Vienna. Lively Proceedings." My scientific education having been somewhat neglected, I was unable to follow the whole argument, but it was evident that the English Professor had handled his subject in a very aggressive fashion, and had thoroughly annoyed his Continental colleagues. "Protests," "Uproar," and "General appeal to the Chairman" were three of the first brackets which caught my eye. Most of the matter might have been written in Chinese for any definite meaning that it conveyed to my brain.

"I wish you could translate it into English for me," I said, pathetically, to my help-mate.

"Well, it is a translation."

"Then I'd better try my luck with the original."

"It is certainly rather deep for a layman."

"If I could only get a single good, meaty sentence which seemed to convey some sort of definite human idea, it would serve my turn. Ah, yes, this one will do. I seem in a vague way almost to understand it. I'll copy it out. This shall be my link with the terrible Professor."

"Nothing else I can do?"

"Well, yes; I propose to write to him. If I could frame the letter here, and use your address it would give atmosphere."

"We'll have the fellow round here making a row and breaking the furniture."

"No, no; you'll see the letter—nothing contentious, I assure you."

"Well, that's my chair and desk. You'll find paper there. I'd like to censor it before it goes."

It took some doing, but I flatter myself that it wasn't such a bad job when it was finished. I read it aloud to the critical bacteriologist with some pride in my handiwork.

"Dear Professor Challenger," it said, "As a humble student of Nature, I have always taken the most profound interest in your speculations as to the differences between Darwin and Weissmann. I have recently had occasion to refresh my memory by re-reading—"

"You infernal liar!" murmured Tarp Henry.

— "by re-reading your masterly address at Vienna. That lucid and admirable statement seems to be the last word in the matter. There is one sentence in it, however—namely: 'I protest strongly against the insufferable and entirely dogmatic assertion that each separate id is a microcosm possessed of an historical architecture elaborated slowly through the series of generations.' Have you no desire, in view of later research, to modify this statement? Do you not think that it is over-accentuated? With your permission, I would ask the favor of an interview, as I feel strongly upon the subject, and have certain suggestions which I could only elaborate in a personal conversation. With your consent, I trust to have the honor of calling at eleven o'clock the day after to-morrow (Wednesday) morning.

"I remain, Sir, with assurances of profound respect, yours very truly, Edward D. Malone."

"How's that?" I asked, triumphantly.

"Well if your conscience can stand it—"

"It has never failed me yet."

"But what do you mean to do?"

"To get there. Once I am in his room I may see some opening. I may even go the length of open confession. If he is a sportsman he will be tickled."

"Tickled, indeed! He's much more likely to do the tickling. Chain mail, or an American football suit—that's what you'll want. Well, good-bye. I'll have the answer for you here on Wednesday morning—if he ever deigns to answer you. He is a violent, dangerous, cantankerous character, hated by everyone who comes across him, and the butt of the students, so far as they dare take a liberty with him. Perhaps it would be best for you if you never heard from the fellow at all."

3
"He is a Perfectly Impossible Person"

My friend's fear or hope was not destined to be realized. When I called on Wednesday there was a letter with the West Kensington postmark upon it, and my name scrawled across the envelope in a handwriting which looked like a barbed-wire railing. The contents were as follows:—

"Enmore Park, W.

"Sir,—I have duly received your note, in which you claim to endorse my views, although I am not aware that they are dependent upon endorsement either from you or anyone else. You have ventured to use the word 'speculation' with regard to my statement upon the subject of Darwinism, and I would call your attention to the fact that such a word in such a connection is offensive to a degree. The context convinces me, however, that you have sinned rather through ignorance and tactlessness than through malice, so I am content to pass the matter by. You quote an isolated sentence from my lecture, and appear to have some difficulty in understanding it. I should have thought that only a sub-human intelligence could have failed to grasp the point, but if it really needs amplification I shall consent to see you at the hour named, though visits and visitors of every sort are exceeding distasteful to me. As to your suggestion that I may modify my opinion, I would have you know that it is not my habit to do so after a deliberate expression of my mature views. You will kindly show the envelope of this letter to my man, Austin, when you call, as he has to take every precaution to shield me from the intrusive rascals who call themselves 'journalists.'

"Yours faithfully,

"George Edward Challenger."

This was the letter that I read aloud to Tarp Henry, who had come down early to hear the result of my venture. His only remark was, "There's some new stuff, cuticura or something, which is better than arnica." Some people have such extraordinary notions of humor.

It was nearly half-past ten before I had received my message, but a taxicab took me round in good time for my appointment. It was an imposing porticoed house at which we stopped, and the heavily-curtained windows gave every indication of wealth upon the part of this formidable Professor. The door was opened by an odd, swarthy, dried-up person of uncertain age, with a dark pilot jacket and brown leather gaiters. I found afterwards that he was the chauffeur, who filled the gaps left by a succession of fugitive butlers. He looked me up and down with a searching light blue eye.

"Expected?" he asked.

"An appointment."

"Got your letter?"

I produced the envelope.

"Right!" He seemed to be a person of few words. Following him down the passage I was suddenly interrupted by a small woman, who stepped out from what proved to be the dining-room door. She was a bright, vivacious, dark-eyed lady, more French than English in her type.

"One moment," she said. "You can wait, Austin. Step in here, sir. May I ask if you have met my husband before?"

"No, madam, I have not had the honor."

"Then I apologize to you in advance. I must tell you that he is a perfectly impossible person—absolutely impossible. If you are forewarned you will be the more ready to make allowances."

"It is most considerate of you, madam."

"Get quickly out of the room if he seems inclined to be violent. Don't wait to argue with him. Several people have been injured through doing that. Afterwards there is a public scandal and it reflects upon me and all of us. I suppose it wasn't about South America you wanted to see him?"

I could not lie to a lady.

"Dear me! That is his most dangerous subject. You won't believe a word he says—I'm sure I don't wonder. But don't tell him so, for it makes him very violent. Pretend to believe him, and you may get through all right. Remember he believes it himself. Of that you may be assured. A more honest man never lived. Don't wait any longer or he may suspect. If you find him dangerous—really dangerous—ring the bell and hold him off until I come. Even at his worst I can usually control him."

With these encouraging words the lady handed me over to the taciturn Austin, who had waited like a bronze statue of discretion during our short interview, and I was conducted to the end of the passage. There was a tap at a door, a bull's bellow from within, and I was face to face with the Professor.

He sat in a rotating chair behind a broad table, which was covered with books, maps, and diagrams. As I entered, his seat spun round to face me. His appearance made me gasp. I was prepared for something strange, but not for so overpowering a personality as this. It was his size which took one's breath away—his size and his imposing presence. His head was enormous, the largest I have ever seen upon a human being. I am sure that his top-hat, had I ever ventured to don it, would have slipped over me entirely and rested on my shoulders. He had the face and beard which I associate with an Assyrian bull; the former florid, the latter so black as almost to have a suspicion of blue, spade-shaped and rippling down over his chest. The hair was peculiar, plastered down in front in a long, curving wisp over his massive forehead. The eyes were blue-gray under great black tufts, very clear, very critical, and very masterful. A huge spread of shoulders and a chest like a barrel were the other parts of him which appeared above the table, save for two enormous hands covered with long black hair. This and a bellowing, roaring, rumbling voice made up my first impression of the notorious Professor Challenger.

"Well?" said he, with a most insolent stare. "What now?"

I must keep up my deception for at least a little time longer, otherwise here was evidently an end of the interview.

"You were good enough to give me an appointment, sir," said I, humbly, producing his envelope.

He took my letter from his desk and laid it out before him.

"Oh, you are the young person who cannot understand plain English, are you? My general conclusions you are good enough to approve, as I understand?"

"Entirely, sir—entirely!" I was very emphatic.

"Dear me! That strengthens my position very much, does it not? Your age and appearance make your support doubly valuable. Well, at least you are better than that herd of swine in Vienna, whose gregarious grunt is, however, not more offensive than the isolated effort of the British hog." He glared at me as the present representative of the beast.

"They seem to have behaved abominably," said I.

"I assure you that I can fight my own battles, and that I have no possible need of your sympathy. Put me alone, sir, and with my back to the wall. G. E. C. is happiest then. Well, sir, let us do what we can to curtail this visit, which can hardly be agreeable to you, and is inexpressibly irksome to me. You had, as I have been led to believe, some comments to make upon the proposition which I advanced in my thesis."

There was a brutal directness about his methods which made evasion difficult. I must still make play and wait for a better opening. It had seemed simple enough at a distance. Oh, my Irish wits, could they not help me now, when I needed help so sorely? He transfixed me with two sharp, steely eyes. "Come, come!" he rumbled.

"I am, of course, a mere student," said I, with a fatuous smile, "hardly more, I might say, than an earnest inquirer. At the same time, it seemed to me that you were a little severe upon Weissmann in this matter. Has not the general evidence since that date tended to—well, to strengthen his position?"

"What evidence?" He spoke with a menacing calm.

"Well, of course, I am aware that there is not any what you might call *definite* evidence. I alluded merely to the trend of modern thought and the general scientific point of view, if I might so express it."

He leaned forward with great earnestness.

"I suppose you are aware," said he, checking off points upon his fingers, "that the cranial index is a constant factor?"

"Naturally," said I.

"And that telegony is still *sub judice*?"

"Undoubtedly."

"And that the germ plasm is different from the parthenogenetic egg?"

"Why, surely!" I cried, and gloried in my own audacity.

"But what does that prove?" he asked, in a gentle, persuasive voice.

"Ah, what indeed?" I murmured. "What does it prove?"

"Shall I tell you?" he cooed.

"Pray do."

"It proves," he roared, with a sudden blast of fury, "that you are the damnedest imposter in London—a vile, crawling journalist, who has no more science than he has decency in his composition!"

He had sprung to his feet with a mad rage in his eyes. Even at that moment of tension I found time for amazement at the discovery that he was quite a short man, his head not higher than my shoulder—a stunted Hercules whose tremendous vitality had all run to depth, breadth, and brain.

"Gibberish!" he cried, leaning forward, with his fingers on the table and his face projecting. "That's what I have been talking to you, sir—scientific gibberish! Did you think you could match cunning with me—you with your walnut of a brain? You think you are omnipotent, you infernal scribblers, don't you? That your praise can make a man and your blame can break him? We must all bow to you, and try to get a favorable word, must we? This man shall have a leg up, and this man shall have a dressing down! Creeping vermin, I know you! You've got out of your station. Time was when your ears were clipped. You've lost your sense of proportion. Swollen gas-bags! I'll keep you in your proper place. Yes, sir, you haven't got over G. E. C. There's one man who is still your master. He warned you off, but if you *will* come, by the Lord you do it at your own risk. Forfeit, my good Mr. Malone, I claim forfeit! You have played a rather dangerous game, and it strikes me that you have lost it."

"Look here, sir," said I, backing to the door and opening it; "you can be as abusive as you like. But there is a limit. You shall not assault me."

"Shall I not?" He was slowly advancing in a peculiarly menacing way, but he stopped now and put his big hands into the side-pockets of a rather boyish short jacket which he wore. "I have thrown several of you out of the house. You will be the fourth or fifth. Three pound fifteen each—that is how it averaged. Expensive, but very necessary. Now, sir, why should you not follow your brethren? I rather think you must." He resumed his unpleasant and stealthy advance, pointing his toes as he walked, like a dancing master.

I could have bolted for the hall door, but it would have been too ignominious. Besides, a little glow of righteous anger was springing up within me. I had been hopelessly in the wrong before, but this man's menaces were putting me in the right.

"I'll trouble you to keep your hands off, sir. I'll not stand it."

"Dear me!" His black moustache lifted and a white fang twinkled in a sneer. "You won't stand it, eh?"

"Don't be such a fool, Professor!" I cried. "What can you hope for? I'm fifteen stone, as hard as nails, and play center three-quarter every Saturday for the London Irish. I'm not the man—"

It was at that moment that he rushed me. It was lucky that I had opened the door, or we should have gone through it. We did a Catharine-wheel together down the passage. Somehow we gathered up a chair upon our way, and bounded on with it towards the street. My mouth was full of his beard, our arms were locked, our bodies intertwined, and that infernal chair radiated its legs all round us. The watchful Austin had thrown open the hall door. We went with a back somersault down the front steps. I have seen the two Macs attempt something of the kind at the halls, but it appears to take some practise to do it without hurting oneself. The chair went to matchwood at the bottom, and we rolled apart into the gutter. He sprang to his feet, waving his fists and wheezing like an asthmatic.

"Had enough?" he panted.

"You infernal bully!" I cried, as I gathered myself together.

Then and there we should have tried the thing out, for he was effervescing with fight, but fortunately I was rescued from an odious situation. A policeman was beside us, his notebook in his hand.

"What's all this? You ought to be ashamed" said the policeman. It was the most rational remark which I had heard in Enmore Park. "Well," he insisted, turning to me, "what is it, then?"

"This man attacked me," said I.

"Did you attack him?" asked the policeman.

The Professor breathed hard and said nothing.

"It's not the first time, either," said the policeman, severely, shaking his head. "You were in trouble last month for the same thing. You've blackened this young man's eye. Do you give him in charge, sir?"

I relented.

"No," said I, "I do not."

"What's that?" said the policeman.

"I was to blame myself. I intruded upon him. He gave me fair warning."

The policeman snapped up his notebook.

"Don't let us have any more such goings-on," said he. "Now, then! Move on, there, move on!" This to a butcher's boy, a maid, and one or two loafers who had collected. He clumped heavily down the street, driving this little flock before him. The Professor looked at me, and there was something humorous at the back of his eyes.

"Come in!" said he. "I've not done with you yet."

The speech had a sinister sound, but I followed him none the less into the house. The man-servant, Austin, like a wooden image, closed the door behind us.

4
"It's Just the very Biggest Thing in the World"

Hardly was it shut when Mrs. Challenger darted out from the dining-room. The small woman was in a furious temper. She barred her husband's way like an enraged chicken in front of a bulldog. It was evident that she had seen my exit, but had not observed my return.

"You brute, George!" she screamed. "You've hurt that nice young man."

He jerked backwards with his thumb.

"Here he is, safe and sound behind me."

She was confused, but not unduly so.

"I am so sorry, I didn't see you."

"I assure you, madam, that it is all right."

"He has marked your poor face! Oh, George, what a brute you are! Nothing but scandals from one end of the week to the other. Everyone hating and making fun of you. You've finished my patience. This ends it."

"Dirty linen," he rumbled.

"It's not a secret," she cried. "Do you suppose that the whole street—the whole of London, for that matter—Get away, Austin, we don't want you here. Do you suppose they don't all talk about you? Where is your dignity? You, a man who should have been Regius Professor at a great University with a thousand students all revering you. Where is your dignity, George?"

"How about yours, my dear?"

"You try me too much. A ruffian—a common brawling ruffian—that's what you have become."

"Be good, Jessie."

"A roaring, raging bully!"

"That's done it! Stool of penance!" said he.

To my amazement he stooped, picked her up, and placed her sitting upon a high pedestal of black marble in the angle of the hall. It was at least seven feet high, and so thin that she could hardly balance upon it. A more absurd object than she presented cocked up there with her face convulsed with anger, her feet dangling, and her body rigid for fear of an upset, I could not imagine.

"Let me down!" she wailed.

"Say 'please.'"

"You brute, George! Let me down this instant!"

"Come into the study, Mr. Malone."

"Really, sir—!" said I, looking at the lady.

"Here's Mr. Malone pleading for you, Jessie. Say 'please,' and down you come."

"Oh, you brute! Please! please!"

"You must behave yourself, dear. Mr. Malone is a Pressman. He will have it all in his rag to-morrow, and sell an extra dozen among our neighbors. 'Strange story of high life'—you felt fairly high on that pedestal, did you not? Then a sub-title, 'Glimpse of a singular *menage*.' He's a foul feeder, is Mr. Malone, a carrion eater, like all of his kind—*porcus ex grege diaboli*—a swine from the devil's herd. That's it, Malone—what?"

"You are really intolerable!" said I, hotly.

He bellowed with laughter.

"We shall have a coalition presently," he boomed, looking from his wife to me and puffing out his enormous chest. Then, suddenly altering his tone, "Excuse this frivolous family badinage, Mr. Malone. I called you back for some more serious purpose than to mix you up with our little domestic pleasantries. Run away, little woman, and don't fret." He placed a huge hand upon each of her shoulders. "All that you say is perfectly true. I should be a better man if I did what you advise, but I shouldn't be quite George Edward Challenger. There are plenty of better men, my dear, but only one G. E. C. So make the best of him." He suddenly gave her a resounding kiss, which embarrassed me even more than his violence

had done. "Now, Mr. Malone," he continued, with a great acces-
sion of dignity, "this way, if *you* please."

We re-entered the room which we had left so tumultuously ten
minutes before. The Professor closed the door carefully behind us,
motioned me into an arm-chair, and pushed a cigar-box under my
nose.

"Real San Juan Colorado," he said. "Excitable people like you
are the better for narcotics. Heavens! don't bite it! Cut—and cut
with reverence! Now lean back, and listen attentively to whatever
I may care to say to you. If any remark should occur to you, you
can reserve it for some more opportune time.

"First of all, as to your return to my house after your most jus-
tifiable expulsion"—he protruded his beard, and stared at me as
one who challenges and invites contradiction— "after, as I say, your
well-merited expulsion. The reason lay in your answer to that most
officious policeman, in which I seemed to discern some glimmer-
ing of good feeling upon your part—more, at any rate, than I am
accustomed to associate with your profession. In admitting that
the fault of the incident lay with you, you gave some evidence of a
certain mental detachment and breadth of view which attracted
my favorable notice. The sub-species of the human race to which
you unfortunately belong has always been below my mental horizon. Your words brought you suddenly above it. You swam up into
my serious notice. For this reason I asked you to return with me,
as I was minded to make your further acquaintance. You will kindly
deposit your ash in the small Japanese tray on the bamboo table
which stands at your left elbow."

All this he boomed forth like a professor addressing his class.
He had swung round his revolving chair so as to face me, and he
sat all puffed out like an enormous bull-frog, his head laid back
and his eyes half-covered by supercilious lids. Now he suddenly
turned himself sideways, and all I could see of him was tangled
hair with a red, protruding ear. He was scratching about among
the litter of papers upon his desk. He faced me presently with what
looked like a very tattered sketch-book in his hand.

"I am going to talk to you about South America," said he. "No
comments if you please. First of all, I wish you to understand that

nothing I tell you now is to be repeated in any public way unless you have my express permission. That permission will, in all human probability, never be given. Is that clear?"

"It is very hard," said I. "Surely a judicious account—"

He replaced the notebook upon the table.

"That ends it," said he. "I wish you a very good morning."

"No, no!" I cried. "I submit to any conditions. So far as I can see, I have no choice."

"None in the world," said he.

"Well, then, I promise."

"Word of honor?"

"Word of honor."

He looked at me with doubt in his insolent eyes.

"After all, what do I know about your honor?" said he.

"Upon my word, sir," I cried, angrily, "you take very great liberties! I have never been so insulted in my life."

He seemed more interested than annoyed at my outbreak.

"Round-headed," he muttered. "Brachycephalic, gray-eyed, black-haired, with suggestion of the negroid. Celtic, I presume?"

"I am an Irishman, sir."

"Irish Irish?"

"Yes, sir."

"That, of course, explains it. Let me see; you have given me your promise that my confidence will be respected? That confidence, I may say, will be far from complete. But I am prepared to give you a few indications which will be of interest. In the first place, you are probably aware that two years ago I made a journey to South America—one which will be classical in the scientific history of the world? The object of my journey was to verify some conclusions of Wallace and of Bates, which could only be done by observing their reported facts under the same conditions in which they had themselves noted them. If my expedition had no other results it would still have been noteworthy, but a curious incident occurred to me while there which opened up an entirely fresh line of inquiry.

"You are aware—or probably, in this half-educated age, you are not aware—that the country round some parts of the Amazon is still only partially explored, and that a great number of tributaries, some of them entirely uncharted, run into the main river. It was my business to visit this little-known back-country and to examine its fauna, which furnished me with the materials for several chapters for that great and monumental work upon zoology which will be my life's justification. I was returning, my work accomplished, when I had occasion to spend a night at a small Indian village at a point where a certain tributary—the name and position of which I withhold—opens into the main river. The natives were Cucama Indians, an amiable but degraded race, with mental powers hardly superior to the average Londoner. I had effected some cures among them upon my way up the river, and had impressed them considerably with my personality, so that I was not surprised to find myself eagerly awaited upon my return. I gathered from their signs that someone had urgent need of my medical services, and I followed the chief to one of his huts. When I entered I found that the sufferer to whose aid I had been summoned had that instant expired. He was, to my surprise, no Indian, but a white man; indeed, I may say a very white man, for he was flaxen-haired and had some characteristics of an albino. He was clad in rags, was very emaciated, and bore every trace of prolonged hardship. So far as I could understand the account of the natives, he was a complete stranger to them, and had come upon their village through the woods alone and in the last stage of exhaustion.

"The man's knapsack lay beside the couch, and I examined the contents. His name was written upon a tab within it—Maple White, Lake Avenue, Detroit, Michigan. It is a name to which I am prepared always to lift my hat. It is not too much to say that it will rank level with my own when the final credit of this business comes to be apportioned.

"From the contents of the knapsack it was evident that this man had been an artist and poet in search of effects. There were scraps of verse. I do not profess to be a judge of such things, but they appeared to me to be singularly wanting in merit. There were also some rather commonplace pictures of river scenery, a paint-box, a box of colored chalks, some brushes, that curved bone which lies upon my inkstand, a volume of Baxter's *Moths and Butterflies*, a cheap revolver, and a few cartridges. Of personal equipment he either had none or he had lost it in his journey. Such were the total effects of this strange American Bohemian.

"I was turning away from him when I observed that something projected from the front of his ragged jacket. It was this sketchbook, which was as dilapidated then as you see it now. Indeed, I can assure you that a first folio of Shakespeare could not be treated with greater reverence than this relic has been since it came into my possession. I hand it to you now, and I ask you to take it page by page and to examine the contents."

He helped himself to a cigar and leaned back with a fiercely critical pair of eyes, taking note of the effect which this document would produce.

I had opened the volume with some expectation of a revelation, though of what nature I could not imagine. The first page was disappointing, however, as it contained nothing but the picture of a very fat man in a pea-jacket, with the legend, "Jimmy Colver on the Mail-boat," written beneath it. There followed several pages which were filled with small sketches of Indians and their ways.

Then came a picture of a cheerful and corpulent ecclesiastic in a shovel hat, sitting opposite a very thin European, and the inscription: "Lunch with Fra Cristofero at Rosario." Studies of women and babies accounted for several more pages, and then there was an unbroken series of animal drawings with such explanations as "Manatee upon Sandbank," "Turtles and Their Eggs," "Black Ajouti under a Miriti Palm"—the matter disclosing some sort of pig-like animal; and finally came a double page of studies of long-snouted and very unpleasant saurians. I could make nothing of it, and said so to the Professor.

"Surely these are only crocodiles?"

"Alligators! Alligators! There is hardly such a thing as a true crocodile in South America. The distinction between them—"

"I meant that I could see nothing unusual—nothing to justify what you have said."

He smiled serenely.

"Try the next page," said he.

I was still unable to sympathize. It was a full-page sketch of a landscape roughly tinted in color—the kind of painting which an open-air artist takes as a guide to a future more elaborate effort. There was a pale-green foreground of feathery vegetation, which sloped upwards and ended in a line of cliffs dark red in color, and curiously ribbed like some basaltic formations which I have seen. They extended in an unbroken wall right across the background. At one point was an isolated pyramidal rock, crowned by a great tree, which appeared to be separated by a cleft from the main crag. Behind it all, a blue tropical sky. A thin green line of vegetation fringed the summit of the ruddy cliff.

"Well?" he asked.

"It is no doubt a curious formation," said I "but I am not geologist enough to say that it is wonderful."

"Wonderful!" he repeated. "It is unique. It is incredible. No one on earth has ever dreamed of such a possibility. Now the next."

I turned it over, and gave an exclamation of surprise. There was a full-page picture of the most extraordinary creature that I had ever seen. It was the wild dream of an opium smoker, a vision of delirium.

The head was like that of a fowl, the body that of a bloated lizard, the trailing tail was furnished with upward-turned spikes, and the curved back was edged with a high serrated fringe, which looked like a dozen cocks' wattles placed behind each other. In front of this creature was an absurd mannikin, or dwarf, in human form, who stood staring at it.

"Well, what do you think of that?" cried the Professor, rubbing his hands with an air of triumph.

"It is monstrous—grotesque."

"But what made him draw such an animal?"

"Trade gin, I should think."

"Oh, that's the best explanation you can give, is it?"

"Well, sir, what is yours?"

"The obvious one that the creature exists. That is actually sketched from the life."

I should have laughed only that I had a vision of our doing another Catharine-wheel down the passage.

"No doubt," said I, "no doubt," as one humors an imbecile. "I confess, however," I added, "that this tiny human figure puzzles me. If it were an Indian we could set it down as evidence of some pigmy race in America, but it appears to be a European in a sun-hat."

The Professor snorted like an angry buffalo. "You really touch the limit," said he. "You enlarge my view of the possible. Cerebral paresis! Mental inertia! Wonderful!"

He was too absurd to make me angry. Indeed, it was a waste of energy, for if you were going to be angry with this man you would be angry all the time. I contented myself with smiling wearily. "It struck me that the man was small," said I.

"Look here!" he cried, leaning forward and dabbing a great hairy sausage of a finger on to the picture. "You see that plant behind the animal; I suppose you thought it was a dandelion or a Brussels sprout—what? Well, it is a vegetable ivory palm, and they run to about fifty or sixty feet. Don't you see that the man is put in for a purpose? He couldn't really have stood in front of that brute and lived to draw it. He sketched himself in to give a scale of heights. He was, we will say, over five feet high. The tree is ten times bigger, which is what one would expect."

"Good heavens!" I cried. "Then you think the beast was—Why, Charing Cross station would hardly make a kennel for such a brute!"

"Apart from exaggeration, he is certainly a well-grown specimen," said the Professor, complacently.

"But," I cried, "surely the whole experience of the human race is not to be set aside on account of a single sketch"—I had turned over the leaves and ascertained that there was nothing more in the book— "a single sketch by a wandering American artist who may have done it under hashish, or in the delirium of fever, or simply in order to gratify a freakish imagination. You can't, as a man of science, defend such a position as that."

For answer the Professor took a book down from a shelf.

"This is an excellent monograph by my gifted friend, Ray Lankester!" said he. "There is an illustration here which would interest you. Ah, yes, here it is! The inscription beneath it runs:

'Probable appearance in life of the Jurassic Dinosaur Stegosaurus. The hind leg alone is twice as tall as a full-grown man.' Well, what do you make of that?"

He handed me the open book. I started as I looked at the picture. In this reconstructed animal of a dead world there was certainly a very great resemblance to the sketch of the unknown artist.

"That is certainly remarkable," said I.

"But you won't admit that it is final?"

"Surely it might be a coincidence, or this American may have seen a picture of the kind and carried it in his memory. It would be likely to recur to a man in a delirium."

"Very good," said the Professor, indulgently; "we leave it at that. I will now ask you to look at this bone." He handed over the one which he had already described as part of the dead man's possessions. It was about six inches long, and thicker than my thumb, with some indications of dried cartilage at one end of it.

"To what known creature does that bone belong?" asked the Professor.

I examined it with care and tried to recall some half-forgotten knowledge.

"It might be a very thick human collar-bone," I said.

My companion waved his hand in contemptuous deprecation.

"The human collar-bone is curved. This is straight. There is a groove upon its surface showing that a great tendon played across it, which could not be the case with a clavicle."

"Then I must confess that I don't know what it is."

"You need not be ashamed to expose your ignorance, for I don't suppose the whole South Kensington staff could give a name to it." He took a little bone the size of a bean out of a pill-box. "So far as I am a judge this human bone is the analogue of the one which you hold in your hand. That will give you some idea of the size of the creature. You will observe from the cartilage that this is no fossil specimen, but recent. What do you say to that?"

"Surely in an elephant—"

He winced as if in pain.

"Don't! Don't talk of elephants in South America. Even in these days of Board schools—"

"Well," I interrupted, "any large South American animal—a tapir, for example."

"You may take it, young man, that I am versed in the elements of my business. This is not a conceivable bone either of a tapir or of any other creature known to zoology. It belongs to a very large, a very strong, and, by all analogy, a very fierce animal which exists upon the face of the earth, but has not yet come under the notice of science. You are still unconvinced?"

"I am at least deeply interested."

"Then your case is not hopeless. I feel that there is reason lurking in you somewhere, so we will patiently grope round for it. We will now leave the dead American and proceed with my narrative. You can imagine that I could hardly come away from the Amazon without probing deeper into the matter. There were indications as to the direction from which the dead traveler had come. Indian legends would alone have been my guide, for I found that rumors of a strange land were common among all the riverine tribes. You have heard, no doubt, of Curupuri?"

"Never."

"Curupuri is the spirit of the woods, something terrible, something malevolent, something to be avoided. None can describe its shape or nature, but it is a word of terror along the Amazon. Now all tribes agree as to the direction in which Curupuri lives. It was the same direction from which the American had come. Something terrible lay that way. It was my business to find out what it was."

"What did you do?" My flippancy was all gone. This massive man compelled one's attention and respect.

"I overcame the extreme reluctance of the natives—a reluctance which extends even to talk upon the subject—and by judicious persuasion and gifts, aided, I will admit, by some threats of coercion, I got two of them to act as guides. After many adventures which I need not describe, and after traveling a distance which I will not mention, in a direction which I withhold, we came at last to a tract of country which has never been described, nor, indeed, visited save by my unfortunate predecessor. Would you kindly look at this?"

He handed me a photograph—half-plate size.

"The unsatisfactory appearance of it is due to the fact," said he, "that on descending the river the boat was upset and the case which contained the undeveloped films was broken, with disastrous results. Nearly all of them were totally ruined—an irreparable loss. This is one of the few which partially escaped. This explanation of deficiencies or abnormalities you will kindly accept. There was talk of faking. I am not in a mood to argue such a point."

The photograph was certainly very off-colored. An unkind critic might easily have misinterpreted that dim surface. It was a dull gray landscape, and as I gradually deciphered the details of it I realized that it represented a long and enormously high line of cliffs exactly like an immense cataract seen in the distance, with a sloping, tree-clad plain in the foreground.

"I believe it is the same place as the painted picture," said I.

"It is the same place," the Professor answered. "I found traces of the fellow's camp. Now look at this."

It was a nearer view of the same scene, though the photograph was extremely defective. I could distinctly see the isolated, tree-crowned pinnacle of rock which was detached from the crag.

"I have no doubt of it at all," said I.

"Well, that is something gained," said he. "We progress, do we not? Now, will you please look at the top of that rocky pinnacle? Do you observe something there?"

"An enormous tree."

"But on the tree?"

"A large bird," said I.

He handed me a lens.

"Yes," I said, peering through it, "a large bird stands on the tree. It appears to have a considerable beak. I should say it was a pelican."

"I cannot congratulate you upon your eyesight," said the Professor. "It is not a pelican, nor, indeed, is it a bird. It may interest you to know that I succeeded in shooting that particular specimen. It was the only absolute proof of my experiences which I was able to bring away with me."

"You have it, then?" Here at last was tangible corroboration.

"I had it. It was unfortunately lost with so much else in the same boat accident which ruined my photographs. I clutched at it as it disappeared in the swirl of the rapids, and part of its wing was left in my hand. I was insensible when washed ashore, but the miserable remnant of my superb specimen was still intact; I now lay it before you."

From a drawer he produced what seemed to me to be the upper portion of the wing of a large bat. It was at least two feet in length, a curved bone, with a membranous veil beneath it.

"A monstrous bat!" I suggested.

"Nothing of the sort," said the Professor, severely. "Living, as I do, in an educated and scientific atmosphere, I could not have conceived that the first principles of zoology were so little known. Is it possible that you do not know the elementary fact in comparative anatomy, that the wing of a bird is really the forearm, while the wing of a bat consists of three elongated fingers with membranes between? Now, in this case, the bone is certainly not the forearm, and you can see for yourself that this is a single membrane hanging upon a single bone, and therefore that it cannot belong to a bat. But if it is neither bird nor bat, what is it?"

My small stock of knowledge was exhausted.

"I really do not know," said I.

He opened the standard work to which he had already referred me.

"Here," said he, pointing to the picture of an extraordinary flying monster, "is an excellent reproduction of the dimorphodon, or pterodactyl, a flying reptile of the Jurassic period. On the next page is a diagram of the mechanism of its wing. Kindly compare it with the specimen in your hand."

A wave of amazement passed over me as I looked. I was convinced. There could be no getting away from it. The cumulative proof was overwhelming. The sketch, the photographs, the narrative, and now the actual specimen—the evidence was complete. I said so—I said so warmly, for I felt that the Professor was an ill-used man. He leaned back in his chair with drooping eyelids and a tolerant smile, basking in this sudden gleam of sunshine.

"It's just the very biggest thing that I ever heard of!" said I, though it was my journalistic rather than my scientific enthusiasm that was roused. "It is colossal. You are a Columbus of science who has discovered a lost world. I'm awfully sorry if I seemed to doubt you. It was all so unthinkable. But I understand evidence when I see it, and this should be good enough for anyone."

The Professor purred with satisfaction.

"And then, sir, what did you do next?"

"It was the wet season, Mr. Malone, and my stores were exhausted. I explored some portion of this huge cliff, but I was unable to find any way to scale it. The pyramidal rock upon which I saw and shot the pterodactyl was more accessible. Being something of a cragsman, I did manage to get half way to the top of that. From that height I had a better idea of the plateau upon the top of the crags. It appeared to be very large; neither to east nor to west could I see any end to the vista of green-capped cliffs. Below, it is a swampy, jungly region, full of snakes, insects, and fever. It is a natural protection to this singular country."

"Did you see any other trace of life?"

"No, sir, I did not; but during the week that we lay encamped at the base of the cliff we heard some very strange noises from above."

"But the creature that the American drew? How do you account for that?"

"We can only suppose that he must have made his way to the summit and seen it there. We know, therefore, that there is a way up. We know equally that it must be a very difficult one, otherwise the creatures would have come down and overrun the surrounding country. Surely that is clear?"

"But how did they come to be there?"

"I do not think that the problem is a very obscure one," said the Professor; "there can only be one explanation. South America is, as you may have heard, a granite continent. At this single point in the interior there has been, in some far distant age, a great, sudden volcanic upheaval. These cliffs, I may remark, are basaltic, and therefore plutonic. An area, as large perhaps as Sussex, has been lifted up en bloc with all its living contents, and cut off by perpendicular precipices of a hardness which defies erosion from all the rest of the continent. What is the result? Why, the ordinary laws of Nature are suspended. The various checks which influence the struggle for existence in the world at large are all neutralized or altered. Creatures survive which would otherwise disappear. You will observe that both the pterodactyl and the stegosaurus are Jurassic, and therefore of a great age in the order of life. They have been artificially conserved by those strange accidental conditions."

"But surely your evidence is conclusive. You have only to lay it before the proper authorities."

"So in my simplicity, I had imagined," said the Professor, bitterly. "I can only tell you that it was not so, that I was met at every turn by incredulity, born partly of stupidity and partly of jealousy. It is not my nature, sir, to cringe to any man, or to seek to prove a fact if my word has been doubted. After the first I have not condescended to show such corroborative proofs as I possess. The subject became hateful to me—I would not speak of it. When men like yourself, who represent the foolish curiosity of the public, came to disturb my privacy I was unable to meet them with dignified reserve. By nature I am, I admit, somewhat fiery, and under provocation I am inclined to be violent. I fear you may have remarked it."

I nursed my eye and was silent.

"My wife has frequently remonstrated with me upon the subject, and yet I fancy that any man of honor would feel the same. To-night, however, I propose to give an extreme example of the control of the will over the emotions. I invite you to be present at the exhibition." He handed me a card from his desk. "You will perceive that Mr. Percival Waldron, a naturalist of some popular repute, is announced to lecture at eight-thirty at the Zoological Institute's Hall upon 'The Record of the Ages.' I have been specially invited to be present upon the platform, and to move a vote of thanks to the lecturer. While doing so, I shall make it my business, with infinite tact and delicacy, to throw out a few remarks which may arouse the interest of the audience and cause some of them to desire to go more deeply into the matter. Nothing contentious, you understand, but only an indication that there are greater deeps beyond. I shall hold myself strongly in leash, and see whether by this self-restraint I attain a more favorable result."

"And I may come?" I asked eagerly.

"Why, surely," he answered, cordially. He had an enormously massive genial manner, which was almost as overpowering as his violence. His smile of benevolence was a wonderful thing, when his cheeks would suddenly bunch into two red apples, between his half-closed eyes and his great black beard. "By all means, come. It will be a comfort to me to know that I have one ally in the hall, however inefficient and ignorant of the subject he may be. I fancy there will be a large audience, for Waldron, though an absolute charlatan, has a considerable popular following. Now, Mr. Malone, I have given you rather more of my time than I had intended. The individual must not monopolize what is meant for the world. I shall be pleased to see you at the lecture to-night. In the meantime, you will understand that no public use is to be made of any of the material that I have given you."

"But Mr. McArdle—my news editor, you know—will want to know what I have done."

"Tell him what you like. You can say, among other things, that if he sends anyone else to intrude upon me I shall call upon him with a riding-whip. But I leave it to you that nothing of all this appears in print. Very good. Then the Zoological Institute's Hall at eight-thirty to-night." I had a last impression of red cheeks, blue rippling beard, and intolerant eyes, as he waved me out of the room.

5
"Question!"

What with the physical shocks incidental to my first interview with Professor Challenger and the mental ones which accompanied the second, I was a somewhat demoralized journalist by the time I found myself in Enmore Park once more. In my aching head the one thought was throbbing that there really was truth in this man's story, that it was of tremendous consequence, and that it would work up into inconceivable copy for the *Gazette* when I could obtain permission to use it. A taxicab was waiting at the end of the road, so I sprang into it and drove down to the office. McArdle was at his post as usual.

"Well," he cried, expectantly, "what may it run to? I'm thinking, young man, you have been in the wars. Don't tell me that he assaulted you."

"We had a little difference at first."

"What a man it is! What did you do?"

"Well, he became more reasonable and we had a chat. But I got nothing out of him—nothing for publication."

"I'm not so sure about that. You got a black eye out of him, and that's for publication. We can't have this reign of terror, Mr. Malone. We must bring the man to his bearings. I'll have a leaderette on him to-morrow that will raise a blister. Just give me the material and I will engage to brand the fellow for ever. Professor Munchausen—how's that for an inset headline? Sir John Mandeville redivivus—Cagliostro—all the imposters and bullies in history. I'll show him up for the fraud he is."

"I wouldn't do that, sir."

"Why not?"

"Because he is not a fraud at all."

"What!" roared McArdle. "You don't mean to say you really believe this stuff of his about mammoths and mastodons and great sea sairpents?"

"Well, I don't know about that. I don't think he makes any claims of that kind. But I do believe he has got something new."

"Then for Heaven's sake, man, write it up!"

"I'm longing to, but all I know he gave me in confidence and on condition that I didn't." I condensed into a few sentences the Professor's narrative. "That's how it stands."

McArdle looked deeply incredulous.

"Well, Mr. Malone," he said at last, "about this scientific meeting to-night; there can be no privacy about that, anyhow. I don't suppose any paper will want to report it, for Waldron has been reported already a dozen times, and no one is aware that Challenger will speak. We may get a scoop, if we are lucky. You'll be there in any case, so you'll just give us a pretty full report. I'll keep space up to midnight."

My day was a busy one, and I had an early dinner at the Savage Club with Tarp Henry, to whom I gave some account of my adventures. He listened with a sceptical smile on his gaunt face, and roared with laughter on hearing that the Professor had convinced me.

"My dear chap, things don't happen like that in real life. People don't stumble upon enormous discoveries and then lose their evidence. Leave that to the novelists. The fellow is as full of tricks as the monkey-house at the Zoo. It's all bosh."

"But the American poet?"

"He never existed."

"I saw his sketch-book."

"Challenger's sketch-book."

"You think he drew that animal?"

"Of course he did. Who else?"

"Well, then, the photographs?"

"There was nothing in the photographs. By your own admission you only saw a bird."

"A pterodactyl."

"That's what *he* says. He put the pterodactyl into your head."

"Well, then, the bones?"

"First one out of an Irish stew. Second one vamped up for the occasion. If you are clever and know your business you can fake a bone as easily as you can a photograph."

I began to feel uneasy. Perhaps, after all, I had been premature in my acquiescence. Then I had a sudden happy thought.

"Will you come to the meeting?" I asked.

Tarp Henry looked thoughtful.

"He is not a popular person, the genial Challenger," said he. "A lot of people have accounts to settle with him. I should say he is about the best-hated man in London. If the medical students turn out there will be no end of a rag. I don't want to get into a bear-garden."

"You might at least do him the justice to hear him state his own case."

"Well, perhaps it's only fair. All right. I'm your man for the evening."

When we arrived at the hall we found a much greater concourse than I had expected. A line of electric broughams discharged their little cargoes of white-bearded professors, while the dark stream of humbler pedestrians, who crowded through the arched door-way, showed that the audience would be popular as well as scientific. Indeed, it became evident to us as soon as we had taken our seats that a youthful and even boyish spirit was abroad in the gallery and the back portions of the hall. Looking behind me, I could see rows of faces of the familiar medical student type. Apparently the great hospitals had each sent down their contingent. The behavior of the audience at present was good-humored, but mischievous. Scraps of popular songs were chorused with an enthusiasm which was a strange prelude to a scientific lecture, and there was already a tendency to personal chaff which promised a jovial evening to others, however embarrassing it might be to the recipients of these dubious honors.

Thus, when old Doctor Meldrum, with his well-known curly-brimmed opera-hat, appeared upon the platform, there was such a universal query of "Where *did* you get that tile?" that he hurriedly removed it, and concealed it furtively under his chair. When gouty Professor Wadley limped down to his seat there were general affectionate inquiries from all parts of the hall as to the exact state of his poor toe, which caused him obvious embarrassment. The greatest demonstration of all, however, was at the entrance of my new acquaintance, Professor Challenger, when he passed down to take his place at the extreme end of the front row of the platform. Such a yell of welcome broke forth when his black beard first protruded round the corner that I began to suspect Tarp Henry was right in his surmise, and that this assemblage was there not merely for the sake of the lecture, but because it had got rumored abroad that the famous Professor would take part in the proceedings.

There was some sympathetic laughter on his entrance among the front benches of well-dressed spectators, as though the demonstration of the students in this instance was not unwelcome to them. That greeting was, indeed, a frightful outburst of sound, the uproar of the carnivora cage when the step of the bucket-bearing keeper is heard in the distance. There was an offensive tone in it, perhaps, and yet in the main it struck me as mere riotous outcry, the noisy reception of one who amused and interested them, rather than of one they disliked or despised. Challenger smiled with weary and tolerant contempt, as a kindly man would meet the yapping of a litter of puppies. He sat slowly down, blew out his chest, passed his hand caressingly down his beard, and looked with drooping eyelids and supercilious eyes at the crowded hall before him. The uproar of his advent had not yet died away when Professor Ronald Murray, the chairman, and Mr. Waldron, the lecturer, threaded their way to the front, and the proceedings began.

Professor Murray will, I am sure, excuse me if I say that he has the common fault of most Englishmen of being inaudible. Why on earth people who have something to say which is worth hearing should not take the slight trouble to learn how to make it heard is one of the strange mysteries of modern life. Their methods are as reasonable as to try to pour some precious stuff from the spring to the reservoir through a non-conducting pipe, which could by the least effort be opened. Professor Murray made several profound remarks to his white tie and to the water-carafe upon the table, with a humorous, twinkling aside to the silver candlestick upon his right. Then he sat down, and Mr. Waldron, the famous popular lecturer, rose amid a general murmur of applause. He was a stern, gaunt man, with a harsh voice, and an aggressive manner, but he had the merit of knowing how to assimilate the ideas of other men, and to pass them on in a way which was intelligible and even interesting to the lay public, with a happy knack of being funny about the most unlikely objects, so that the precession of the Equinox or the formation of a vertebrate became a highly humorous process as treated by him.

It was a bird's-eye view of creation, as interpreted by science, which, in language always clear and sometimes picturesque, he unfolded before us. He told us of the globe, a huge mass of flaming gas, flaring through the heavens. Then he pictured the solidification, the cooling, the wrinkling which formed the mountains, the steam which turned to water, the slow preparation of the stage upon which was to be played the inexplicable drama of life. On the origin of life itself he was discreetly vague. That the germs of it could hardly have survived the original roasting was, he declared, fairly certain. Therefore it had come later. Had it built itself out of the cooling, inorganic elements of the globe? Very likely. Had the germs of it arrived from outside upon a meteor? It was hardly conceivable. On the whole, the wisest man was the least dogmatic upon the point. We could not—or at least we had not succeeded up to date in making organic life in our laboratories out of inorganic materials. The gulf between the dead and the living was something which our chemistry could not as yet bridge. But there was a higher and subtler chemistry of Nature, which, working with great forces over long epochs, might well produce results which were impossible for us. There the matter must be left.

This brought the lecturer to the great ladder of animal life, beginning low down in molluscs and feeble sea creatures, then up rung by rung through reptiles and fishes, till at last we came to a kangaroo-rat, a creature which brought forth its young alive, the direct ancestor of all mammals, and presumably, therefore, of everyone in the audience. ("No, no," from a sceptical student in the back row.) If the young gentleman in the red tie who cried "No, no," and who presumably claimed to have been hatched out of an egg, would wait upon him after the lecture, he would be glad to see such a curiosity. (Laughter.) It was strange to think that the climax of all the age-long process of Nature had been the creation of that gentleman in the red tie. But had the process stopped? Was this gentleman to be taken as the final type—the be-all and end-all of development? He hoped that he would not hurt the feelings of the gentleman in the red tie if he maintained that, whatever virtues that gentleman might possess in private life, still the vast processes of the universe were not fully justified if they were to end entirely in his production. Evolution was not a spent force, but one still working, and even greater achievements were in store.

Having thus, amid a general titter, played very prettily with his interrupter, the lecturer went back to his picture of the past, the drying of the seas, the emergence of the sand-bank, the sluggish, viscous life which lay upon their margins, the overcrowded lagoons, the tendency of the sea creatures to take refuge upon the mud-flats, the abundance of food awaiting them, their consequent enormous growth. "Hence, ladies and gentlemen," he added, "that frightful brood of saurians which still affright our eyes when seen in the Wealden or in the Solenhofen slates, but which were fortunately extinct long before the first appearance of mankind upon this planet."

"Question!" boomed a voice from the platform.

Mr. Waldron was a strict disciplinarian with a gift of acid humor, as exemplified upon the gentleman with the red tie, which made it perilous to interrupt him. But this interjection appeared to him so absurd that he was at a loss how to deal with it. So looks the Shakespearean who is confronted by a rancid Baconian, or the astronomer who is assailed by a flat-earth fanatic. He paused for a moment, and then, raising his voice, repeated slowly the words: "Which were extinct before the coming of man."

"Question!" boomed the voice once more.

Waldron looked with amazement along the line of professors upon the platform until his eyes fell upon the figure of Challenger, who leaned back in his chair with closed eyes and an amused expression, as if he were smiling in his sleep.

"I see!" said Waldron, with a shrug. "It is my friend Professor Challenger," and amid laughter he renewed his lecture as if this was a final explanation and no more need be said.

But the incident was far from being closed. Whatever path the lecturer took amid the wilds of the past seemed invariably to lead him to some assertion as to extinct or prehistoric life which instantly brought the same bulls' bellow from the Professor. The audience began to anticipate it and to roar with delight when it came. The packed benches of students joined in, and every time Challenger's beard opened, before any sound could come forth, there was a yell of "Question!" from a hundred voices, and an answering counter cry of "Order!" and "Shame!" from as many more. Waldron, though a hardened lecturer and a strong man, became rattled. He hesitated, stammered, repeated himself, got snarled in a long sentence, and finally turned furiously upon the cause of his troubles.

"This is really intolerable!" he cried, glaring across the platform. "I must ask you, Professor Challenger, to cease these ignorant and unmannerly interruptions."

There was a hush over the hall, the students rigid with delight at seeing the high gods on Olympus quarrelling among themselves. Challenger levered his bulky figure slowly out of his chair.

"I must in turn ask you, Mr. Waldron," he said, "to cease to make assertions which are not in strict accordance with scientific fact."

The words unloosed a tempest. "Shame! Shame!" "Give him a hearing!" "Put him out!" "Shove him off the platform!" "Fair play!" emerged from a general roar of amusement or execration. The chairman was on his feet flapping both his hands and bleating excitedly. "Professor Challenger—personal—views—later," were the solid peaks above his clouds of inaudible mutter. The interrupter bowed, smiled, stroked his beard, and relapsed into his chair. Waldron, very flushed and warlike, continued his observations. Now and then, as he made an assertion, he shot a venomous glance at his opponent, who seemed to be slumbering deeply, with the same broad, happy smile upon his face.

At last the lecture came to an end—I am inclined to think that it was a premature one, as the peroration was hurried and disconnected.

The thread of the argument had been rudely broken, and the audience was restless and expectant. Waldron sat down, and, after a chirrup from the chairman, Professor Challenger rose and advanced to the edge of the platform. In the interests of my paper I took down his speech verbatim.

"Ladies and Gentlemen," he began, amid a sustained interruption from the back. "I beg pardon—Ladies, Gentlemen, and Children—I must apologize, I had inadvertently omitted a considerable section of this audience" (tumult, during which the Professor stood with one hand raised and his enormous head nodding sympathetically, as if he were bestowing a pontifical blessing upon the crowd), "I have been selected to move a vote of thanks to Mr. Waldron for the very picturesque and imaginative address to which we have just listened. There are points in it with which I disagree, and it has been my duty to indicate them as they arose, but, none the less, Mr. Waldron has accomplished his object well, that object being to give a simple and interesting account of what he conceives to have been the history of our planet. Popular lectures are the easiest to listen to, but Mr. Waldron" (here he beamed and blinked at the lecturer) "will excuse me when I say that they are necessarily both superficial and misleading, since they have to be graded to the comprehension of an ignorant audience." (Ironical cheering.) "Popular lecturers are in their nature parasitic." (Angry gesture of protest from Mr. Waldron.) "They exploit for fame or cash the work which has been done by their indigent and unknown brethren. One smallest new fact obtained in the laboratory, one brick built into the temple of science, far outweighs any second-hand exposition which passes an idle hour, but can leave no useful result behind it. I put forward this obvious reflection, not out of any desire to disparage Mr. Waldron in particular, but that you may not lose your sense of proportion and mistake the acolyte for the high priest." (At this point Mr. Waldron whispered to the chairman, who half rose and said something severely to his water-carafe.) "But enough of this!" (Loud and prolonged cheers.) "Let me pass to some subject of wider interest. What is the particular point upon which I, as an original investigator, have challenged our lecturer's accuracy? It is upon the permanence of certain types of animal life upon the earth. I do not speak upon this subject as an amateur, nor, I may add, as a popular lecturer, but I speak as one whose scientific conscience compels him to adhere closely to facts, when I say that Mr. Waldron is very wrong in supposing that because he has never himself seen a so-called prehistoric animal, therefore these creatures no longer exist. They are indeed, as he has said, our ancestors, but they are, if I may use the expression, our contemporary ancestors, who can still be found with all their hideous and formidable characteristics if one has but the energy and hardihood to seek their haunts. Creatures which were supposed to be Jurassic, monsters who would hunt down and devour our largest and fiercest mammals, still exist." (Cries of "Bosh!" "Prove it!" "How do *you* know?" "Question!") "How do I know, you ask me? I know because I have visited their secret haunts. I know because I have seen some of them." (Applause, uproar, and a voice, "Liar!") "Am I a liar?" (General hearty and noisy assent.) "Did I hear someone say that I was a liar? Will the person who called me a liar kindly stand up that I may know him?" (A voice, "Here he is, sir!" and an inoffensive little person in spectacles, struggling violently, was held up among a group of students.) "Did you venture to call me a liar?" ("No, sir, no!" shouted the accused, and disappeared like a jack-in-the-box.) "If any person in this hall dares to doubt my veracity, I shall be glad to have a few words with him after the lecture." ("Liar!") "Who said that?" (Again the inoffensive one plunging desperately, was elevated high into the air.) "If I come down among you—" (General chorus of "Come, love, come!" which interrupted the proceedings for some moments, while the chairman, standing up and waving both his arms, seemed to be conducting the music. The Professor, with his face flushed, his nostrils dilated, and his beard bristling, was now in a proper Berserk mood.) "Every great discoverer has been met with the same incredulity—the sure brand of a generation of fools. When great facts are laid before you, you have not the intuition, the imagination which would help you to understand them. You can only throw mud at the men who have risked their lives to open new fields to science. You persecute the prophets! Galileo! Darwin, and I—" (Prolonged cheering and complete interruption.)

All this is from my hurried notes taken at the time, which give little notion of the absolute chaos to which the assembly had by this time been reduced. So terrific was the uproar that several ladies had already beaten a hurried retreat. Grave and reverend seniors seemed to have caught the prevailing spirit as badly as the students, and I saw white-bearded men rising and shaking their fists at the obdurate Professor. The whole great audience seethed and simmered like a boiling pot. The Professor took a step forward and raised both his hands. There was something so big and arresting and virile in the man that the clatter and shouting died gradually away before his commanding gesture and his masterful eyes. He seemed to have a definite message. They hushed to hear it.

"I will not detain you," he said. "It is not worth it. Truth is truth, and the noise of a number of foolish young men—and, I fear I must add, of their equally foolish seniors—cannot affect the matter. I claim that I have opened a new field of science. You dispute it." (Cheers.) "Then I put you to the test. Will you accredit one or more of your own number to go out as your representatives and test my statement in your name?"

Mr. Summerlee, the veteran Professor of Comparative Anatomy, rose among the audience, a tall, thin, bitter man, with the withered aspect of a theologian. He wished, he said, to ask Professor Challenger whether the results to which he had alluded in his remarks had been obtained during a journey to the headwaters of the Amazon made by him two years before.

Professor Challenger answered that they had.

Mr. Summerlee desired to know how it was that Professor Challenger claimed to have made discoveries in those regions which had been overlooked by Wallace, Bates, and other previous explorers of established scientific repute.

Professor Challenger answered that Mr. Summerlee appeared to be confusing the Amazon with the Thames; that it was in reality a somewhat larger river; that Mr. Summerlee might be interested to know that with the Orinoco, which communicated with it, some fifty thousand miles of country were opened up, and that in so vast a space it was not impossible for one person to find what another had missed.

Mr. Summerlee declared, with an acid smile, that he fully appreciated the difference between the Thames and the Amazon, which lay in the fact that any assertion about the former could be tested, while about the latter it could not. He would be obliged if Professor Challenger would give the latitude and the longitude of the country in which prehistoric animals were to be found.

Professor Challenger replied that he reserved such information for good reasons of his own, but would be prepared to give it with proper precautions to a committee chosen from the audience. Would Mr. Summerlee serve on such a committee and test his story in person?

Mr. Summerlee: "Yes, I will." (Great cheering.)

Professor Challenger: "Then I guarantee that I will place in your hands such material as will enable you to find your way. It is only right, however, since Mr. Summerlee goes to check my statement that I should have one or more with him who may check his. I will not disguise from you that there are difficulties and dangers. Mr. Summerlee will need a younger colleague. May I ask for volunteers?"

It is thus that the great crisis of a man's life springs out at him. Could I have imagined when I entered that hall that I was about to pledge myself to a wilder adventure than had ever come to me in my dreams? But Gladys—was it not the very opportunity of which she spoke? Gladys would have told me to go. I had sprung to my feet. I was speaking, and yet I had prepared no words. Tarp Henry, my companion, was plucking at my skirts and I heard him whispering, "Sit down, Malone! Don't make a public ass of yourself." At the same time I was aware that a tall, thin man, with dark gingery hair, a few seats in front of me, was also upon his feet. He glared back at me with hard angry eyes, but I refused to give way.

"I will go, Mr. Chairman," I kept repeating over and over again.

"Name! Name!" cried the audience.

"My name is Edward Dunn Malone. I am the reporter of the *Daily Gazette*. I claim to be an absolutely unprejudiced witness."

"What is *your* name, sir?" the chairman asked of my tall rival.

"I am Lord John Roxton. I have already been up the Amazon, I know all the ground, and have special qualifications for this investigation."

"Lord John Roxton's reputation as a sportsman and a traveler is, of course, world-famous," said the chairman; "at the same time it would certainly be as well to have a member of the Press upon such an expedition."

"Then I move," said Professor Challenger, "that both these gentlemen be elected, as representatives of this meeting, to accompany Professor Summerlee upon his journey to investigate and to report upon the truth of my statements."

And so, amid shouting and cheering, our fate was decided, and I found myself borne away in the human current which swirled towards the door, with my mind half stunned by the vast new project which had risen so suddenly before it. As I emerged from the hall I was conscious for a moment of a rush of laughing students—down the pavement, and of an arm wielding a heavy umbrella, which rose and fell in the midst of them. Then, amid a mixture of groans and cheers, Professor Challenger's electric brougham slid from the curb, and I found myself walking under the silvery lights of Regent Street, full of thoughts of Gladys and of wonder as to my future.

Suddenly there was a touch at my elbow. I turned, and found myself looking into the humorous, masterful eyes of the tall, thin man who had volunteered to be my companion on this strange quest.

"Mr. Malone, I understand," said he. "We are to be companions—what? My rooms are just over the road, in the Albany. Perhaps you would have the kindness to spare me half an hour, for there are one or two things that I badly want to say to you."

6
"I was the Flail of the Lord"

Lord John Roxton and I turned down Vigo Street together and through the dingy portals of the famous aristocratic rookery. At the end of a long drab passage my new acquaintance pushed open a door and turned on an electric switch. A number of lamps shining through tinted shades bathed the whole great room before us in a ruddy radiance. Standing in the doorway and glancing round me, I had a general impression of extraordinary comfort and elegance combined with an atmosphere of masculine virility. Everywhere there were mingled the luxury of the wealthy man of taste and the careless untidiness of the bachelor. Rich furs and strange irides-cent mats from some Oriental bazaar were scattered upon the floor. Pictures and prints which even my unpractised eyes could recog-nize as being of great price and rarity hung thick upon the walls. Sketches of boxers, of ballet-girls, and of racehorses alternated with a sensuous Fragonard, a martial Girardet, and a dreamy Turner. But amid these varied ornaments there were scattered the trophies which brought back strongly to my recollection the fact that Lord John Roxton was one of the great all-round sportsmen and ath-letes of his day. A dark-blue oar crossed with a cherry-pink one above his mantel-piece spoke of the old Oxonian and Leander man, while the foils and boxing-gloves above and below them were the tools of a man who had won supremacy with each. Like a dado round the room was the jutting line of splendid heavy game-heads, the best of their sort from every quarter of the world, with the rare white rhinoceros of the Lado Enclave drooping its supercilious lip above them all.

In the center of the rich red carpet was a black and gold Louis Quinze table, a lovely antique, now sacrilegiously desecrated with marks of glasses and the scars of cigar-stumps. On it stood a silver tray of smokables and a burnished spirit-stand, from which and an adjacent siphon my silent host proceeded to charge two high glasses. Having indicated an arm-chair to me and placed my refreshment near it, he handed me a long, smooth Havana. Then, seating himself opposite to me, he looked at me long and fixedly with his strange, twinkling, reckless eyes—eyes of a cold light blue, the color of a glacier lake.

Through the thin haze of my cigar-smoke I noted the details of a face which was already familiar to me from many photographs— the strongly-curved nose, the hollow, worn cheeks, the dark, ruddy hair, thin at the top, the crisp, virile moustaches, the small, aggressive tuft upon his projecting chin. Something there was of Napoleon III., something of Don Quixote, and yet again something which was the essence of the English country gentleman, the keen, alert, open-air lover of dogs and of horses. His skin was of a rich flower-pot red from sun and wind. His eyebrows were tufted and overhanging, which gave those naturally cold eyes an almost ferocious aspect, an impression which was increased by his strong and furrowed brow. In figure he was spare, but very strongly built— indeed, he had often proved that there were few men in England capable of such sustained exertions. His height was a little over six feet, but he seemed shorter on account of a peculiar rounding of the shoulders.

Such was the famous Lord John Roxton as he sat opposite to me, biting hard upon his cigar and watching me steadily in a long and embarrassing silence.

"Well," said he, at last, "we've gone and done it, young fellah my lad." (This curious phrase he pronounced as if it were all one word— "young-fellah-me-lad.") "Yes, we've taken a jump, you an' me. I suppose, now, when you went into that room there was no such notion in your head—what?"

"No thought of it."

"The same here. No thought of it. And here we are, up to our necks in the tureen. Why, I've only been back three weeks from

Uganda, and taken a place in Scotland, and signed the lease and all. Pretty goin's on—what? How does it hit you?"

"Well, it is all in the main line of my business. I am a journalist on the *Gazette*."

"Of course—you said so when you took it on. By the way, I've got a small job for you, if you'll help me."

"With pleasure."

"Don't mind takin' a risk, do you?"

"What is the risk?"

"Well, it's Ballinger—he's the risk. You've heard of him?"

"No."

"Why, young fellah, where *have* you lived? Sir John Ballinger is the best gentleman jock in the north country. I could hold him on the flat at my best, but over jumps he's my master. Well, it's an open secret that when he's out of trainin' he drinks hard—strikin' an average, he calls it. He got delirium on Toosday, and has been ragin' like a devil ever since. His room is above this. The doctors say that it is all up with the old dear unless some food is got into him, but as he lies in bed with a revolver on his coverlet, and swears he will put six of the best through anyone that comes near him, there's been a bit of a strike among the serving-men. He's a hard nail, is Jack, and a dead shot, too, but you can't leave a Grand National winner to die like that—what?"

"What do you mean to do, then?" I asked.

"Well, my idea was that you and I could rush him. He may be dozin', and at the worst he can only wing one of us, and the other should have him. If we can get his bolster-cover round his arms and then 'phone up a stomach-pump, we'll give the old dear the supper of his life."

It was a rather desperate business to come suddenly into one's day's work. I don't think that I am a particularly brave man. I have an Irish imagination which makes the unknown and the untried more terrible than they are. On the other hand, I was brought up with a horror of cowardice and with a terror of such a stigma. I dare say that I could throw myself over a precipice, like the Hun in the history books, if my courage to do it were questioned, and yet it would surely be pride and fear, rather than courage, which would be my inspiration. Therefore, although every nerve in my body shrank from the whisky-maddened figure which I pictured in the room above, I still answered, in as careless a voice as I could command, that I was ready to go. Some further remark of Lord Roxton's about the danger only made me irritable.

"Talking won't make it any better," said I. "Come on."

I rose from my chair and he from his. Then with a little confidential chuckle of laughter, he patted me two or three times on the chest, finally pushing me back into my chair.

"All right, sonny my lad—you'll do," said he. I looked up in surprise.

"I saw after Jack Ballinger myself this mornin'. He blew a hole in the skirt of my kimono, bless his shaky old hand, but we got a jacket on him, and he's to be all right in a week. I say, young fellah, I hope you don't mind—what? You see, between you an' me close-tiled, I look on this South American business as a mighty serious thing, and if I have a pal with me I want a man I can bank on. So I sized you down, and I'm bound to say that you came well out of it. You see, it's all up to you and me, for this old Summerlee man will want dry-nursin' from the first. By the way, are you by any chance the Malone who is expected to get his Rugby cap for Ireland?"

"A reserve, perhaps."

"I thought I remembered your face. Why, I was there when you got that try against Richmond—as fine a swervin' run as I saw the whole season. I never miss a Rugby match if I can help it, for it is the manliest game we have left. Well, I didn't ask you in here just to talk sport. We've got to fix our business. Here are the sailin's, on the first page of the *Times*. There's a Booth boat for Para next Wednesday week, and if the Professor and you can work it, I think we should take it—what? Very good, I'll fix it with him. What about your outfit?"

"My paper will see to that."

"Can you shoot?"

"About average Territorial standard."

"Good Lord! as bad as that? It's the last thing you young fellahs think of learnin'. You're all bees without stings, so far as lookin' after the hive goes. You'll look silly, some o' these days, when someone comes along an' sneaks the honey. But you'll need to hold your gun straight in South America, for, unless our friend the Professor is a madman or a liar, we may see some queer things before we get back. What gun have you?"

He crossed to an oaken cupboard, and as he threw it open I caught a glimpse of glistening rows of parallel barrels, like the pipes of an organ.

"I'll see what I can spare you out of my own battery," said he.

One by one he took out a succession of beautiful rifles, opening and shutting them with a snap and a clang, and then patting them as he put them back into the rack as tenderly as a mother would fondle her children.

"This is a Bland's .577 axite express," said he. "I got that big fellow with it." He glanced up at the white rhinoceros. "Ten more yards, and he'd would have added me to *his* collection.

> 'On that conical bullet his one chance hangs,
> 'Tis the weak one's advantage fair.'

"Hope you know your Gordon, for he's the poet of the horse and the gun and the man that handles both. Now, here's a useful tool—.470, telescopic sight, double ejector, point-blank up to three-fifty. That's the rifle I used against the Peruvian slave-drivers three years ago. I was the flail of the Lord up in those parts, I may tell you, though you won't find it in any Blue-book. There are times, young fellah, when every one of us must make a stand for human right and justice, or you never feel clean again. That's why I made a little war on my own. Declared it myself, waged it myself, ended it myself. Each of those nicks is for a slave murderer—a good row of them—what? That big one is for Pedro Lopez, the king of them all, that I killed in a backwater of the Putomayo River. Now, here's something that would do for you." He took out a beautiful brown-and-silver rifle. "Well rubbered at the stock, sharply sighted, five cartridges to the clip. You can trust your life to that." He handed it to me and closed the door of his oak cabinet.

"By the way," he continued, coming back to his chair, "what do you know of this Professor Challenger?"

"I never saw him till to-day."

"Well, neither did I. It's funny we should both sail under sealed orders from a man we don't know. He seemed an uppish old bird. His brothers of science don't seem too fond of him, either. How came you to take an interest in the affair?"

I told him shortly my experiences of the morning, and he listened intently. Then he drew out a map of South America and laid it on the table.

"I believe every single word he said to you was the truth," said he, earnestly, "and, mind you, I have something to go on when I speak like that. South America is a place I love, and I think, if you take it right through from Darien to Fuego, it's the grandest, richest, most wonderful bit of earth upon this planet. People don't know it yet, and don't realize what it may become. I've been up an' down it from end to end, and had two dry seasons in those very parts, as I told you when I spoke of the war I made on the slave-dealers. Well, when I was up there I heard some yarns of the same kind—traditions of Indians and the like, but with somethin' behind them, no doubt. The more you knew of that country, young fellah, the more you would understand that anythin' was possible—*Anythin'*! There are just some narrow water-lanes along which folk travel, and outside that it is all darkness. Now, down here in the Matto Grande"—he swept his cigar over a part of the map— "or up in this corner where three countries meet, nothin' would surprise me. As that chap said to-night, there are fifty-thousand miles of water-way runnin' through a forest that is very near the size of Europe. You and I could be as far away from each other as Scotland is from Constantinople, and yet each of us be in the same great Brazilian forest. Man has just made a track here and a scrape there in the maze. Why, the river rises and falls the best part of forty feet, and half the country is a morass that you can't pass over. Why shouldn't somethin' new and wonderful lie in such a country? And why shouldn't we be the men to find it out? Besides," he added, his queer, gaunt face shining with delight, "there's a sportin' risk in every mile of it. I'm like an old golf-ball—I've had all the white paint knocked off me long ago. Life can whack me about now, and it can't leave a mark. But a sportin' risk, young fellah, that's the salt of existence. Then it's worth livin' again. We're all gettin' a deal too soft and dull and comfy. Give me the great waste lands and the wide spaces, with a gun in my fist and somethin' to look for that's worth findin'. I've tried war and steeplechasin' and aeroplanes, but this huntin' of beasts that look like a lobster-supper dream is a brand-new sensation." He chuckled with glee at the prospect.

Perhaps I have dwelt too long upon this new acquaintance, but he is to be my comrade for many a day, and so I have tried to set him down as I first saw him, with his quaint personality and his queer little tricks of speech and of thought. It was only the need of getting in the account of my meeting which drew me at last from his company. I left him seated amid his pink radiance, oiling the lock of his favorite rifle, while he still chuckled to himself at the thought of the adventures which awaited us. It was very clear to me that if dangers lay before us I could not in all England have found a cooler head or a braver spirit with which to share them.

That night, wearied as I was after the wonderful happenings of the day, I sat late with McArdle, the news editor, explaining to him the whole situation, which he thought important enough to bring next morning before the notice of Sir George Beaumont, the chief. It was agreed that I should write home full accounts of my adventures in the shape of successive letters to McArdle, and that these should either be edited for the *Gazette* as they arrived, or held back to be published later, according to the wishes of Professor Challenger, since we could not yet know what conditions he might attach to those directions which should guide us to the unknown land. In response to a telephone inquiry, we received nothing more definite than a fulmination against the Press, ending up with the remark that if we would notify our boat he would hand us any directions which he might think it proper to give us at the moment of starting. A second question from us failed to elicit any answer at all, save a plaintive bleat from his wife to the effect that her husband was in a very violent temper already, and that she hoped we would do nothing to make it worse. A third attempt, later in the day, provoked a terrific crash, and a subsequent message from the Central Exchange that Professor Challenger's receiver had been shattered. After that we abandoned all attempt at communication.

And now my patient readers, I can address you directly no longer. From now onwards (if, indeed, any continuation of this narrative should ever reach you) it can only be through the paper which I represent. In the hands of the editor I leave this account of the events which have led up to one of the most remarkable expeditions of all time, so that if I never return to England there shall be some record as to how the affair came about. I am writing these last lines in the saloon of the Booth liner *Francisca*, and they will go back by the pilot to the keeping of Mr. McArdle. Let me draw one last picture before I close the notebook—a picture which is the last memory of the old country which I bear away with me. It is a wet, foggy morning in the late spring; a thin, cold rain is falling. Three shining mackintoshed figures are walking down the quay, making for the gang-plank of the great liner from which the blue-peter is flying. In front of them a porter pushes a trolley piled high with trunks, wraps, and gun-cases. Professor Summerlee, a long, melancholy figure, walks with dragging steps and drooping head, as one who is already profoundly sorry for himself. Lord John Roxton steps briskly, and his thin, eager face beams forth between his hunting-cap and his muffler. As for myself, I am glad to have got the bustling days of preparation and the pangs of leave-taking behind me, and I have no doubt that I show it in my bearing. Suddenly, just as we reach the vessel, there is a shout behind us. It is Professor Challenger, who had promised to see us off. He runs after us, a puffing, red-faced, irascible figure.

"No thank you," says he; "I should much prefer not to go aboard. I have only a few words to say to you, and they can very well be said where we are. I beg you not to imagine that I am in any way indebted to you for making this journey. I would have you to understand that it is a matter of perfect indifference to me, and I refuse to entertain the most remote sense of personal obligation. Truth is truth, and nothing which you can report can affect it in any way, though it may excite the emotions and allay the curiosity of a number of very ineffectual people. My directions for your instruction and guidance are in this sealed envelope. You will open it when you reach a town upon the Amazon which is called Manaos, but not until the date and hour which is marked upon the outside. Have

I made myself clear? I leave the strict observance of my conditions entirely to your honor. No, Mr. Malone, I will place no restriction upon your correspondence, since the ventilation of the facts is the object of your journey; but I demand that you shall give no particulars as to your exact destination, and that nothing be actually published until your return. Good-bye, sir. You have done something to mitigate my feelings for the loathsome profession to which you unhappily belong. Good-bye, Lord John. Science is, as I understand, a sealed book to you; but you may congratulate yourself upon the hunting-field which awaits you. You will, no doubt, have the opportunity of describing in the *Field* how you brought down the rocketing dimorphodon. And good-bye to you also, Professor Summerlee. If you are still capable of self-improvement, of which I am frankly unconvinced, you will surely return to London a wiser man."

So he turned upon his heel, and a minute later from the deck I could see his short, squat figure bobbing about in the distance as he made his way back to his train. Well, we are well down Channel now. There's the last bell for letters, and it's good-bye to the pilot. We'll be "down, hull-down, on the old trail" from now on. God bless all we leave behind us, and send us safely back.

7
"To-morrow we Disappear into the Unknown"

I will not bore those whom this narrative may reach by an account of our luxurious voyage upon the Booth liner, nor will I tell of our week's stay at Para (save that I should wish to acknowledge the great kindness of the Pereira da Pinta Company in helping us to get together our equipment). I will also allude very briefly to our river journey, up a wide, slow-moving, clay-tinted stream, in a steamer which was little smaller than that which had carried us across the Atlantic. Eventually we found ourselves through the narrows of Obidos and reached the town of Manaos. Here we were rescued from the limited attractions of the local inn by Mr. Shortman, the representative of the British and Brazilian Trading Company. In his hospital Fazenda we spent our time until the day when we were empowered to open the letter of instructions given to us by Professor Challenger. Before I reach the surprising events of that date I would desire to give a clearer sketch of my comrades in this enterprise, and of the associates whom we had already gathered together in South America. I speak freely, and I leave the use of my material to your own discretion, Mr. McArdle, since it is through your hands that this report must pass before it reaches the world.

The scientific attainments of Professor Summerlee are too well known for me to trouble to recapitulate them. He is better equipped for a rough expedition of this sort than one would imagine at first sight. His tall, gaunt, stringy figure is insensible to fatigue, and his dry, half-sarcastic, and often wholly unsympathetic manner is uninfluenced by any change in his surroundings. Though in his sixty-sixth year, I have never heard him express any dissatisfaction at the occasional hardships which we have had to encounter. I had regarded his presence as an encumbrance to the expedition, but, as a matter of fact, I am now well convinced that his power of endurance is as great as my own. In temper he is naturally acid and sceptical. From the beginning he has never concealed his belief that Professor Challenger is an absolute fraud, that we are all embarked upon an absurd wild-goose chase and that we are likely to reap nothing but disappointment and danger in South America, and corresponding ridicule in England. Such are the views which, with much passionate distortion of his thin features and wagging of his thin, goat-like beard, he poured into our ears all the way from Southampton to Manaos. Since landing from the boat he has obtained some consolation from the beauty and variety of the insect and bird life around him, for he is absolutely whole-hearted in his devotion to science. He spends his days flitting through the woods with his shot-gun and his butterfly-net, and his evenings in mounting the many specimens he has acquired. Among his minor peculiarities are that he is careless as to his attire, unclean in his person, exceedingly absent-minded in his habits, and addicted to smoking a short briar pipe, which is seldom out of his mouth. He has been upon several scientific expeditions in his youth (he was with Robertson in Papua), and the life of the camp and the canoe is nothing fresh to him.

Lord John Roxton has some points in common with Professor Summerlee, and others in which they are the very antithesis to each other. He is twenty years younger, but has something of the same spare, scraggy physique. As to his appearance, I have, as I recollect, described it in that portion of my narrative which I have left behind me in London. He is exceedingly neat and prim in his ways, dresses always with great care in white drill suits and high brown mosquito-boots, and shaves at least once a day. Like most men of action, he is laconic in speech, and sinks readily into his own thoughts, but he is always quick to answer a question or join in a conversation, talking in a queer, jerky, half-humorous fashion. His knowledge of the world, and very especially of South America, is surprising, and he has a whole-hearted belief in the possibilities of our journey which is not to be dashed by the sneers of Professor Summerlee. He has a gentle voice and a quiet manner, but behind his twinkling blue eyes there lurks a capacity for furious wrath and implacable resolution, the more dangerous because they are held in leash. He spoke little of his own exploits in Brazil and Peru, but it was a revelation to me to find the excitement which was caused by his presence among the riverine natives, who looked upon him as their champion and protector. The exploits of the Red Chief, as they called him, had become legends among them, but the real facts, as far as I could learn them, were amazing enough.

These were that Lord John had found himself some years before in that no-man's-land which is formed by the half-defined frontiers between Peru, Brazil, and Columbia. In this great district the wild rubber tree flourishes, and has become, as in the Congo, a curse to the natives which can only be compared to their forced labor under the Spaniards upon the old silver mines of Darien. A handful of villainous half-breeds dominated the country, armed such Indians as would support them, and turned the rest into slaves, terrorizing them with the most inhuman tortures in order to force them to gather the india-rubber, which was then floated down the river to Para. Lord John Roxton expostulated on behalf of the wretched victims, and received nothing but threats and insults for his pains. He then formally declared war against Pedro Lopez, the leader of the slave-drivers, enrolled a band of runaway slaves in his service, armed them, and conducted a campaign, which ended by his killing with his own hands the notorious half-breed and breaking down the system which he represented.

No wonder that the ginger-headed man with the silky voice and the free and easy manners was now looked upon with deep interest upon the banks of the great South American river, though the feelings he inspired were naturally mixed, since the gratitude of the natives was equaled by the resentment of those who desired to exploit them. One useful result of his former experiences was that he could talk fluently in the Lingoa Geral, which is the peculiar talk, one-third Portuguese and two-thirds Indian, which is current all over Brazil.

I have said before that Lord John Roxton was a South Americo-maniac. He could not speak of that great country without ardor, and this ardor was infectious, for, ignorant as I was, he fixed my attention and stimulated my curiosity. How I wish I could reproduce the glamour of his discourses, the peculiar mixture of accurate knowledge and of racy imagination which gave them their fascination, until even the Professor's cynical and sceptical smile would gradually vanish from his thin face as he listened. He would tell the history of the mighty river so rapidly explored (for some of the first conquerors of Peru actually crossed the entire continent upon its waters), and yet so unknown in regard to all that lay behind its ever-changing banks.

"What is there?" he would cry, pointing to the north. "Wood and marsh and unpenetrated jungle. Who knows what it may shelter? And there to the south? A wilderness of swampy forest, where no white man has ever been. The unknown is up against us on every side. Outside the narrow lines of the rivers what does anyone know? Who will say what is possible in such a country? Why should old man Challenger not be right?" At which direct defiance the stubborn sneer would reappear upon Professor Summerlee's face, and he would sit, shaking his sardonic head in unsympathetic silence, behind the cloud of his briar-root pipe.

So much, for the moment, for my two white companions, whose characters and limitations will be further exposed, as surely as my own, as this narrative proceeds. But already we have enrolled certain retainers who may play no small part in what is to come. The first is a gigantic negro named Zambo, who is a black Hercules, as willing as any horse, and about as intelligent. Him we enlisted at Para, on the recommendation of the steamship company, on whose vessels he had learned to speak a halting English.

It was at Para also that we engaged Gomez and Manuel, two half-breeds from up the river, just come down with a cargo of red-wood. They were swarthy fellows, bearded and fierce, as active and wiry as panthers. Both of them had spent their lives in those upper waters of the Amazon which we were about to explore, and it was this recommendation which had caused Lord John to engage them.

One of them, Gomez, had the further advantage that he could speak excellent English. These men were willing to act as our personal servants, to cook, to row, or to make themselves useful in any way at a payment of fifteen dollars a month. Besides these, we had engaged three Mojo Indians from Bolivia, who are the most skilful at fishing and boat work of all the river tribes. The chief of these we called Mojo, after his tribe, and the others are known as Jose and Fernando. Three white men, then, two half-breeds, one negro, and three Indians made up the personnel of the little expedition which lay waiting for its instructions at Manaos before starting upon its singular quest.

At last, after a weary week, the day had come and the hour. I ask you to picture the shaded sitting-room of the Fazenda St. Ignatio, two miles inland from the town of Manaos. Outside lay the yellow, brassy glare of the sunshine, with the shadows of the palm trees as black and definite as the trees themselves. The air was calm, full of the eternal hum of insects, a tropical chorus of many octaves, from the deep drone of the bee to the high, keen pipe of the mosquito. Beyond the veranda was a small cleared garden, bounded with cactus hedges and adorned with clumps of flowering shrubs, round which the great blue butterflies and the tiny humming-birds fluttered and darted in crescents of sparkling light. Within we were seated round the cane table, on which lay a sealed envelope. Inscribed upon it, in the jagged handwriting of Professor Challenger, were the words:—

"Instructions to Lord John Roxton and party. To be opened at Manaos upon July 15th, at 12 o'clock precisely."

Lord John had placed his watch upon the table beside him.

"We have seven more minutes," said he. "The old dear is very precise."

Professor Summerlee gave an acid smile as he picked up the envelope in his gaunt hand.

"What can it possibly matter whether we open it now or in seven minutes?" said he. "It is all part and parcel of the same system of quackery and nonsense, for which I regret to say that the writer is notorious."

"Oh, come, we must play the game accordin' to rules," said Lord John. "It's old man Challenger's show and we are here by his good will, so it would be rotten bad form if we didn't follow his instructions to the letter."

"A pretty business it is!" cried the Professor, bitterly. "It struck me as preposterous in London, but I'm bound to say that it seems even more so upon closer acquaintance. I don't know what is inside this envelope, but, unless it is something pretty definite, I shall be much tempted to take the next down-river boat and catch the Bolivia at Para. After all, I have some more responsible work in the world than to run about disproving the assertions of a lunatic. Now, Roxton, surely it is time."

"Time it is," said Lord John. "You can blow the whistle." He took up the envelope and cut it with his penknife. From it he drew a folded sheet of paper. This he carefully opened out and flattened on the table. It was a blank sheet. He turned it over. Again it was blank. We looked at each other in a bewildered silence, which was broken by a discordant burst of derisive laughter from Professor Summerlee.

"It is an open admission," he cried. "What more do you want? The fellow is a self-confessed humbug. We have only to return home and report him as the brazen imposter that he is."

"Invisible ink!" I suggested.

"I don't think!" said Lord Roxton, holding the paper to the light. "No, young fellah my lad, there is no use deceiving yourself. I'll go bail for it that nothing has ever been written upon this paper."

"May I come in?" boomed a voice from the veranda.

The shadow of a squat figure had stolen across the patch of sunlight. That voice! That monstrous breadth of shoulder! We sprang to our feet with a gasp of astonishment as Challenger, in a round, boyish straw-hat with a colored ribbon—Challenger, with his hands in his jacket-pockets and his canvas shoes daintily pointing as he walked—appeared in the open space before us. He threw back his head, and there he stood in the golden glow with all his old Assyrian luxuriance of beard, all his native insolence of drooping eyelids and intolerant eyes.

"I fear," said he, taking out his watch, "that I am a few minutes too late. When I gave you this envelope I must confess that I had never intended that you should open it, for it had been my fixed intention to be with you before the hour. The unfortunate delay can be apportioned between a blundering pilot and an intrusive sandbank. I fear that it has given my colleague, Professor Summerlee, occasion to blaspheme."

"I am bound to say, sir," said Lord John, with some sternness of voice, "that your turning up is a considerable relief to us, for our mission seemed to have come to a premature end. Even now I can't for the life of me understand why you should have worked it in so extraordinary a manner."

Instead of answering, Professor Challenger entered, shook hands with myself and Lord John, bowed with ponderous insolence to Professor Summerlee, and sank back into a basket-chair, which creaked and swayed beneath his weight.

"Is all ready for your journey?" he asked.

"We can start to-morrow."

"Then so you shall. You need no chart of directions now, since you will have the inestimable advantage of my own guidance. From the first I had determined that I would myself preside over your investigation. The most elaborate charts would, as you will readily admit, be a poor substitute for my own intelligence and advice. As to the small ruse which I played upon you in the matter of the envelope, it is clear that, had I told you all my intentions, I should have been forced to resist unwelcome pressure to travel out with you."

"Not from me, sir!" exclaimed Professor Summerlee, heartily. "So long as there was another ship upon the Atlantic."

Challenger waved him away with his great hairy hand.

"Your common sense will, I am sure, sustain my objection and realize that it was better that I should direct my own movements and appear only at the exact moment when my presence was needed. That moment has now arrived. You are in safe hands. You will not now fail to reach your destination. From henceforth I take command of this expedition, and I must ask you to complete your preparations to-night, so that we may be able to make an early start in the morning. My time is of value, and the same thing may be said, no doubt, in a lesser degree of your own. I propose, therefore, that we push on as rapidly as possible, until I have demonstrated what you have come to see."

Lord John Roxton has chartered a large steam launch, the Esmeralda, which was to carry us up the river. So far as climate goes, it was immaterial what time we chose for our expedition, as the temperature ranges from seventy-five to ninety degrees both summer and winter, with no appreciable difference in heat. In moisture, however, it is otherwise; from December to May is the period of the rains, and during this time the river slowly rises until it attains a height of nearly forty feet above its low-water mark. It floods the banks, extends in great lagoons over a monstrous waste of country, and forms a huge district, called locally the Gapo, which is for the most part too marshy for foot-travel and too shallow for boating. About June the waters begin to fall, and are at their lowest at October or November. Thus our expedition was at the time of the dry season, when the great river and its tributaries were more or less in a normal condition.

The current of the river is a slight one, the drop being not greater than eight inches in a mile. No stream could be more convenient for navigation, since the prevailing wind is south-east, and sailing boats may make a continuous progress to the Peruvian frontier, dropping down again with the current. In our own case the excellent engines of the Esmeralda could disregard the sluggish flow of the stream, and we made as rapid progress as if we were navigating a stagnant lake. For three days we steamed north-westwards up a stream which even here, a thousand miles from its mouth, was still so enormous that from its center the two banks were mere shadows upon the distant skyline. On the fourth day after leaving Manaos we turned into a tributary which at its mouth was little smaller than the main stream. It narrowed rapidly, however, and after two more days' steaming we reached an Indian village, where the Professor insisted that we should land, and that the Esmeralda should be sent back to Manaos. We should soon come upon rapids, he explained, which would make its further use impossible. He added privately that we were now approaching the door of the unknown country, and that the fewer whom we took into our confidence the better it would be. To this end also he made each of us give our word of honor that we would publish or say nothing which would give any exact clue as to the whereabouts of our travels, while the servants were all solemnly sworn to the same effect. It is for this reason that I am compelled to be vague in my narrative, and I would warn my readers that in any map or diagram which I may give the relation of places to each other may be correct, but the points of the compass are carefully confused, so that in no way can it be taken as an actual guide to the country. Professor Challenger's reasons for secrecy may be valid or not, but we had no choice but to adopt them, for he was prepared to abandon the whole expedition rather than modify the conditions upon which he would guide us.

It was August 2nd when we snapped our last link with the outer world by bidding farewell to the Esmeralda. Since then four days have passed, during which we have engaged two large canoes from the Indians, made of so light a material (skins over a bamboo framework) that we should be able to carry them round any obstacle. These we have loaded with all our effects, and have engaged two additional Indians to help us in the navigation. I understand that they are the very two—Ataca and Ipetu by name—who accompanied Professor Challenger upon his previous journey. They appeared to be terrified at the prospect of repeating it, but the chief has patriarchal powers in these countries, and if the bargain is good in his eyes the clansman has little choice in the matter.

So to-morrow we disappear into the unknown. This account I am transmitting down the river by canoe, and it may be our last word to those who are interested in our fate. I have, according to our arrangement, addressed it to you, my dear Mr. McArdle, and I leave it to your discretion to delete, alter, or do what you like with it. From the assurance of Professor Challenger's manner—and in spite of the continued scepticism of Professor Summerlee—I have no doubt that our leader will make good his statement, and that we are really on the eve of some most remarkable experiences.

8
"The Outlying Pickets of the New World"

Our friends at home may well rejoice with us, for we are at our goal, and up to a point, at least, we have shown that the statement of Professor Challenger can be verified. We have not, it is true, ascended the plateau, but it lies before us, and even Professor Summerlee is in a more chastened mood. Not that he will for an instant admit that his rival could be right, but he is less persistent in his incessant objections, and has sunk for the most part into an observant silence. I must hark back, however, and continue my narrative from where I dropped it. We are sending home one of our local Indians who is injured, and I am committing this letter to his charge, with considerable doubts in my mind as to whether it will ever come to hand.

When I wrote last we were about to leave the Indian village where we had been deposited by the Esmeralda. I have to begin my report by bad news, for the first serious personal trouble (I pass over the incessant bickerings between the Professors) occurred this evening, and might have had a tragic ending. I have spoken of our English-speaking half-breed, Gomez—a fine worker and a willing fellow, but afflicted, I fancy, with the vice of curiosity, which is common enough among such men. On the last evening he seems to have hid himself near the hut in which we were discussing our plans, and, being observed by our huge negro Zambo, who is as faithful as a dog and has the hatred which all his race bear to the half-breeds, he was dragged out and carried into our presence. Gomez whipped out his knife, however, and but for the huge strength of his captor, which enabled him to disarm him with one hand, he would certainly have stabbed him. The matter has ended in reprimands, the opponents have been compelled to shake hands, and there is every hope that all will be well. As to the feuds of the two learned men, they are continuous and bitter. It must be admitted that Challenger is provocative in the last degree, but Summerlee has an acid tongue, which makes matters worse. Last night Challenger said that he never cared to walk on the Thames Embankment and look up the river, as it was always sad to see one's own eventual goal. He is convinced, of course, that he is destined for Westminster Abbey. Summerlee rejoined, however, with a sour smile, by saying that he understood that Millbank Prison had been pulled down. Challenger's conceit is too colossal to allow him to be really annoyed. He only smiled in his beard and repeated "Really! Really!" in the pitying tone one would use to a child. Indeed, they are children both—the one wizened and cantankerous, the other formidable and overbearing, yet each with a brain which has put him in the front rank of his scientific age. Brain, character, soul—only as one sees more of life does one understand how distinct is each.

The very next day we did actually make our start upon this remarkable expedition. We found that all our possessions fitted very easily into the two canoes, and we divided our personnel, six in each, taking the obvious precaution in the interests of peace of putting one Professor into each canoe. Personally, I was with Challenger, who was in a beatific humor, moving about as one in a silent ecstasy and beaming benevolence from every feature. I have had some experience of him in other moods, however, and shall be the less surprised when the thunderstorms suddenly come up amidst the sunshine. If it is impossible to be at your ease, it is equally impossible to be dull in his company, for one is always in a state of half-tremulous doubt as to what sudden turn his formidable temper may take.

For two days we made our way up a good-sized river some hundreds of yards broad, and dark in color, but transparent, so that one could usually see the bottom. The affluents of the Amazon are, half of them, of this nature, while the other half are whitish and opaque, the difference depending upon the class of country through which they have flowed. The dark indicate vegetable decay, while the others point to clayey soil. Twice we came across rapids, and in each case made a portage of half a mile or so to avoid them. The woods on either side were primeval, which are more easily penetrated than woods of the second growth, and we had no great difficulty in carrying our canoes through them. How shall I ever forget the solemn mystery of it? The height of the trees and the thickness of the boles exceeded anything which I in my town-bred life could have imagined, shooting upwards in magnificent columns until, at an enormous distance above our heads, we could dimly discern the spot where they threw out their side-branches into Gothic upward curves which coalesced to form one great matted roof of verdure, through which only an occasional golden ray of sunshine shot downwards to trace a thin dazzling line of light amidst the majestic obscurity. As we walked noiselessly amid the thick, soft carpet of decaying vegetation the hush fell upon our souls which comes upon us in the twilight of the Abbey, and even Professor Challenger's full-chested notes sank into a whisper. Alone, I should have been ignorant of the names of these giant growths, but our men of science pointed out the cedars, the great silk cotton trees, and the redwood trees, with all that profusion of various plants which has made this continent the chief supplier to the human race of those gifts of Nature which depend upon the vegetable world, while it is the most backward in those products which come from animal life. Vivid orchids and wonderful colored lichens smoldered upon the swarthy tree-trunks and where a wandering shaft of light fell full upon the golden allamanda, the scarlet star-clusters of the tacsonia, or the rich deep blue of ipomaea, the effect was as a dream of fairyland. In these great wastes of forest, life, which abhors darkness, struggles ever upwards to the light. Every plant, even the smaller ones, curls and writhes to the green surface, twining itself round its stronger and taller brethren in the effort. Climbing plants are monstrous and luxuriant, but others which have never been known to climb elsewhere learn the art as an escape from that somber shadow, so that the common nettle, the jasmine, and even the jacitara palm tree can be seen circling the stems of the cedars and striving to reach their crowns. Of animal life there was no movement amid the majestic vaulted aisles which stretched from us as we walked, but a constant movement far above our heads told of that multitudinous world of snake and monkey, bird and sloth, which lived in the sunshine, and looked down in wonder at our tiny, dark, stumbling figures in the obscure depths immeasurably below them. At dawn and at sunset the howler monkeys screamed together and the parakeets broke into shrill chatter, but during the hot hours of the day only the full drone of insects, like the beat of a distant surf, filled the ear, while nothing moved amid the solemn vistas of stupendous trunks, fading away into the darkness which held us in. Once some bandy-legged, lurching creature, an ant-eater or a bear, scuttled clumsily amid the shadows. It was the only sign of earth life which I saw in this great Amazonian forest.

And yet there were indications that even human life itself was not far from us in those mysterious recesses. On the third day out we were aware of a singular deep throbbing in the air, rhythmic and solemn, coming and going fitfully throughout the morning. The two boats were paddling within a few yards of each other when first we heard it, and our Indians remained motionless, as if they had been turned to bronze, listening intently with expressions of terror upon their faces.

"What is it, then?" I asked.

"Drums," said Lord John, carelessly; "war drums. I have heard them before."

"Yes, sir, war drums," said Gomez, the half-breed. "Wild Indians, bravos, not mansos; they watch us every mile of the way; kill us if they can."

"How can they watch us?" I asked, gazing into the dark, motionless void.

The half-breed shrugged his broad shoulders.

"The Indians know. They have their own way. They watch us. They talk the drum talk to each other. Kill us if they can."

By the afternoon of that day—my pocket diary shows me that it was Tuesday, August 18th—at least six or seven drums were throbbing from various points. Sometimes they beat quickly, sometimes slowly, sometimes in obvious question and answer, one far to the east breaking out in a high staccato rattle, and being followed after a pause by a deep roll from the north. There was something indescribably nerve-shaking and menacing in that constant mutter, which seemed to shape itself into the very syllables of the half-breed, endlessly repeated, "We will kill you if we can. We will kill you if we can." No one ever moved in the silent woods. All the peace and soothing of quiet Nature lay in that dark curtain of vegetation, but away from behind there came ever the one message from our fellow-man. "We will kill you if we can," said the men in the east. "We will kill you if we can," said the men in the north.

All day the drums rumbled and whispered, while their menace reflected itself in the faces of our colored companions. Even the hardy, swaggering half-breed seemed cowed. I learned, however, that day once for all that both Summerlee and Challenger possessed that highest type of bravery, the bravery of the scientific mind. Theirs was the spirit which upheld Darwin among the gauchos of the Argentine or Wallace among the head-hunters of Malaya. It is decreed by a merciful Nature that the human brain cannot think of two things simultaneously, so that if it be steeped in curiosity as to science it has no room for merely personal considerations. All day amid that incessant and mysterious menace our two Professors watched every bird upon the wing, and every shrub upon the bank, with many a sharp wordy contention, when the snarl of Summerlee came quick upon the deep growl of Challenger, but with no more sense of danger and no more reference to drum-beating Indians than if they were seated together in the smoking-room of the Royal Society's Club in St. James's Street. Once only did they condescend to discuss them.

"Miranha or Amajuaca cannibals," said Challenger, jerking his thumb towards the reverberating wood.

"No doubt, sir," Summerlee answered. "Like all such tribes, I shall expect to find them of polysynthetic speech and of Mongolian type."

"Polysynthetic certainly," said Challenger, indulgently. "I am not aware that any other type of language exists in this continent, and I have notes of more than a hundred. The Mongolian theory I regard with deep suspicion."

"I should have thought that even a limited knowledge of comparative anatomy would have helped to verify it," said Summerlee, bitterly.

Challenger thrust out his aggressive chin until he was all beard and hat-rim. "No doubt, sir, a limited knowledge would have that effect. When one's knowledge is exhaustive, one comes to other conclusions." They glared at each other in mutual defiance, while all round rose the distant whisper, "We will kill you—we will kill you if we can."

That night we moored our canoes with heavy stones for anchors in the center of the stream, and made every preparation for a possible attack. Nothing came, however, and with the dawn we pushed upon our way, the drum-beating dying out behind us. About three o'clock in the afternoon we came to a very steep rapid, more than a mile long—the very one in which Professor Challenger had suffered disaster upon his first journey. I confess that the sight of it consoled me, for it was really the first direct corroboration, slight as it was, of the truth of his story. The Indians carried first our canoes and then our stores through the brushwood, which is very thick at this point, while we four whites, our rifles on our shoulders, walked between them and any danger coming from the woods. Before evening we had successfully passed the rapids, and made our way some ten miles above them, where we anchored for the night. At this point I reckoned that we had come not less than a hundred miles up the tributary from the main stream.

It was in the early forenoon of the next day that we made the great departure. Since dawn Professor Challenger had been acutely uneasy, continually scanning each bank of the river. Suddenly he gave an exclamation of satisfaction and pointed to a single tree, which projected at a peculiar angle over the side of the stream.

"What do you make of that?" he asked.

"It is surely an Assai palm," said Summerlee.

"Exactly. It was an Assai palm which I took for my landmark. The secret opening is half a mile onwards upon the other side of the river. There is no break in the trees. That is the wonder and the mystery of it. There where you see light-green rushes instead of dark-green undergrowth, there between the great cotton woods, that is my private gate into the unknown. Push through, and you will understand."

It was indeed a wonderful place. Having reached the spot marked by a line of light-green rushes, we poled out two canoes through them for some hundreds of yards, and eventually emerged into a placid and shallow stream, running clear and transparent over a sandy bottom. It may have been twenty yards across, and was banked in on each side by most luxuriant vegetation. No one who had not observed that for a short distance reeds had taken the place of shrubs, could possibly have guessed the existence of such a stream or dreamed of the fairyland beyond.

For a fairyland it was—the most wonderful that the imagination of man could conceive. The thick vegetation met overhead, interlacing into a natural pergola, and through this tunnel of verdure in a golden twilight flowed the green, pellucid river, beautiful in itself, but marvelous from the strange tints thrown by the vivid light from above filtered and tempered in its fall. Clear as crystal, motionless as a sheet of glass, green as the edge of an iceberg, it stretched in front of us under its leafy archway, every stroke of our paddles sending a thousand ripples across its shining surface. It was a fitting avenue to a land of wonders. All sign of the Indians had passed away, but animal life was more frequent, and the tameness of the creatures showed that they knew nothing of the hunter. Fuzzy little black-velvet monkeys, with snow-white teeth and gleaming, mocking eyes, chattered at us as we passed. With a dull, heavy splash an occasional cayman plunged in from the bank. Once a dark, clumsy tapir stared at us from a gap in the bushes, and then lumbered away through the forest; once, too, the yellow, sinuous form of a great puma whisked amid the brushwood, and its green, baleful eyes glared hatred at us over its tawny shoulder. Bird life was abundant, especially the wading birds, stork, heron, and ibis gathering in little groups, blue, scarlet, and white, upon every log which jutted from the bank, while beneath us the crystal water was alive with fish of every shape and color.

For three days we made our way up this tunnel of hazy green sunshine. On the longer stretches one could hardly tell as one looked ahead where the distant green water ended and the distant green archway began. The deep peace of this strange waterway was unbroken by any sign of man.

"No Indian here. Too much afraid. Curupuri," said Gomez.

"Curupuri is the spirit of the woods," Lord John explained. "It's a name for any kind of devil. The poor beggars think that there is something fearsome in this direction, and therefore they avoid it."

On the third day it became evident that our journey in the canoes could not last much longer, for the stream was rapidly growing more shallow. Twice in as many hours we stuck upon the bottom. Finally we pulled the boats up among the brushwood and spent the night on the bank of the river. In the morning Lord John and I made our way for a couple of miles through the forest, keeping parallel with the stream; but as it grew ever shallower we returned and reported, what Professor Challenger had already suspected, that we had reached the highest point to which the canoes could be brought. We drew them up, therefore, and concealed them among the bushes, blazing a tree with our axes, so that we should find them again. Then we distributed the various burdens among us—guns, ammunition, food, a tent, blankets, and the rest—and, shouldering our packages, we set forth upon the more laborious stage of our journey.

An unfortunate quarrel between our pepper-pots marked the outset of our new stage. Challenger had from the moment of joining us issued directions to the whole party, much to the evident discontent of Summerlee. Now, upon his assigning some duty to his fellow-Professor (it was only the carrying of an aneroid barometer), the matter suddenly came to a head.

"May I ask, sir," said Summerlee, with vicious calm, "in what capacity you take it upon yourself to issue these orders?"

Challenger glared and bristled.

"I do it, Professor Summerlee, as leader of this expedition."

"I am compelled to tell you, sir, that I do not recognize you in that capacity."

"Indeed!" Challenger bowed with unwieldy sarcasm. "Perhaps you would define my exact position."

"Yes, sir. You are a man whose veracity is upon trial, and this committee is here to try it. You walk, sir, with your judges."

"Dear me!" said Challenger, seating himself on the side of one of the canoes. "In that case you will, of course, go on your way, and I will follow at my leisure. If I am not the leader you cannot expect me to lead."

Thank heaven that there were two sane men—Lord John Roxton and myself—to prevent the petulance and folly of our learned Professors from sending us back empty-handed to London. Such arguing and pleading and explaining before we could get them mollified! Then at last Summerlee, with his sneer and his pipe, would move forwards, and Challenger would come rolling and grumbling after. By some good fortune we discovered about this time that both our savants had the very poorest opinion of Dr. Illingworth of Edinburgh. Thenceforward that was our one safety, and every strained situation was relieved by our introducing the name of the Scotch zoologist, when both our Professors would form a temporary alliance and friendship in their detestation and abuse of this common rival.

Advancing in single file along the bank of the stream, we soon found that it narrowed down to a mere brook, and finally that it lost itself in a great green morass of sponge-like mosses, into which we sank up to our knees. The place was horribly haunted by clouds of mosquitoes and every form of flying pest, so we were glad to find solid ground again and to make a circuit among the trees, which enabled us to outflank this pestilent morass, which droned like an organ in the distance, so loud was it with insect life.

On the second day after leaving our canoes we found that the whole character of the country changed. Our road was persistently upwards, and as we ascended the woods became thinner and lost their tropical luxuriance. The huge trees of the alluvial Amazonian plain gave place to the Phoenix and coco palms, growing in scattered clumps, with thick brushwood between. In the damper hollows the Mauritia palms threw out their graceful drooping fronds. We traveled entirely by compass, and once or twice there were differences of opinion between Challenger and the two Indians, when, to quote the Professor's indignant words, the whole party agreed to "trust the fallacious instincts of undeveloped savages rather than the highest product of modern European culture." That we were justified in doing so was shown upon the third day, when Challenger admitted that he recognized several landmarks of his former journey, and in one spot we actually came upon four fire-blackened stones, which must have marked a camping-place.

The road still ascended, and we crossed a rock-studded slope which took two days to traverse. The vegetation had again changed, and only the vegetable ivory tree remained, with a great profusion of wonderful orchids, among which I learned to recognize the rare *Nuttonia Vexillaria* and the glorious pink and scarlet blossoms of *Cattleya* and *Odontoglossum*. Occasional brooks with pebbly bottoms and fern-draped banks gurgled down the shallow gorges in the hill, and offered good camping-grounds every evening on the banks of some rock-studded pool, where swarms of little blue-backed fish, about the size and shape of English trout, gave us a delicious supper.

On the ninth day after leaving the canoes, having done, as I reckon, about a hundred and twenty miles, we began to emerge from the trees, which had grown smaller until they were mere shrubs. Their place was taken by an immense wilderness of bamboo, which grew so thickly that we could only penetrate it by cutting a pathway with the machetes and billhooks of the Indians. It took us a long day, traveling from seven in the morning till eight at night, with only two breaks of one hour each, to get through this obstacle. Anything more monotonous and wearying could not be imagined, for, even at the most open places, I could not see more than ten or twelve yards, while usually my vision was limited to the back of Lord John's cotton jacket in front of me, and to the yellow wall within a foot of me on either side. From above came one thin knife-edge of sunshine, and fifteen feet over our heads one saw the tops of the reeds swaying against the deep blue sky. I do not know what kind of creatures inhabit such a thicket, but several times we heard the plunging of large, heavy animals quite close to us. From their sounds Lord John judged them to be some form of wild cattle. Just as night fell we cleared the belt of bamboos, and at once formed our camp, exhausted by the interminable day.

Early next morning we were again afoot, and found that the character of the country had changed once again. Behind us was the wall of bamboo, as definite as if it marked the course of a river. In front was an open plain, sloping slightly upwards and dotted with clumps of tree-ferns, the whole curving before us until it ended in a long, whale-backed ridge. This we reached about midday, only to find a shallow valley beyond, rising once again into a gentle incline which led to a low, rounded sky-line. It was here, while we crossed the first of these hills, that an incident occurred which may or may not have been important.

Professor Challenger, who with the two local Indians was in the van of the party, stopped suddenly and pointed excitedly to the right. As he did so we saw, at the distance of a mile or so, something which appeared to be a huge gray bird flap slowly up from the ground and skim smoothly off, flying very low and straight, until it was lost among the tree-ferns.

"Did you see it?" cried Challenger, in exultation. "Summerlee, did you see it?"

His colleague was staring at the spot where the creature had disappeared.

"What do you claim that it was?" he asked.

"To the best of my belief, a pterodactyl."

Summerlee burst into derisive laughter "A pter-fiddlestick!" said he. "It was a stork, if ever I saw one."

Challenger was too furious to speak. He simply swung his pack upon his back and continued upon his march. Lord John came abreast of me, however, and his face was more grave than was his wont. He had his Zeiss glasses in his hand.

"I focused it before it got over the trees," said he. "I won't undertake to say what it was, but I'll risk my reputation as a sportsman that it wasn't any bird that ever I clapped eyes on in my life."

So there the matter stands. Are we really just at the edge of the unknown, encountering the outlying pickets of this lost world of which our leader speaks? I give you the incident as it occurred and you will know as much as I do. It stands alone, for we saw nothing more which could be called remarkable.

And now, my readers, if ever I have any, I have brought you up the broad river, and through the screen of rushes, and down the green tunnel, and up the long slope of palm trees, and through the bamboo brake, and across the plain of tree-ferns. At last our destination lay in full sight of us. When we had crossed the second ridge we saw before us an irregular, palm-studded plain, and then the line of high red cliffs which I have seen in the picture. There it lies, even as I write, and there can be no question that it is the same. At the nearest point it is about seven miles from our present camp, and it curves away, stretching as far as I can see. Challenger struts about like a prize peacock, and Summerlee is silent, but still sceptical. Another day should bring some of our doubts to an end. Meanwhile, as Jose, whose arm was pierced by a broken bamboo, insists upon returning, I send this letter back in his charge, and only hope that it may eventually come to hand. I will write again as the occasion serves. I have enclosed with this a rough chart of our journey, which may have the effect of making the account rather easier to understand.

9

"Who could have Foreseen it?"

A dreadful thing has happened to us. Who could have foreseen it? I cannot foresee any end to our troubles. It may be that we are condemned to spend our whole lives in this strange, inaccessible place. I am still so confused that I can hardly think clearly of the facts of the present or of the chances of the future. To my astounded senses the one seems most terrible and the other as black as night.

No men have ever found themselves in a worse position; nor is there any use in disclosing to you our exact geographical situation and asking our friends for a relief party. Even if they could send one, our fate will in all human probability be decided long before it could arrive in South America.

We are, in truth, as far from any human aid as if we were in the moon. If we are to win through, it is only our own qualities which can save us. I have as companions three remarkable men, men of great brain-power and of unshaken courage. There lies our one and only hope. It is only when I look upon the untroubled faces of my comrades that I see some glimmer through the darkness. Outwardly I trust that I appear as unconcerned as they. Inwardly I am filled with apprehension.

Let me give you, with as much detail as I can, the sequence of events which have led us to this catastrophe.

When I finished my last letter I stated that we were within seven miles from an enormous line of ruddy cliffs, which encircled, beyond all doubt, the plateau of which Professor Challenger spoke. Their height, as we approached them, seemed to me in some places to be greater than he had stated—running up in parts to at least a thousand feet—and they were curiously striated, in a manner which is, I believe, characteristic of basaltic upheavals. Something of the sort is to be seen in Salisbury Crags at Edinburgh. The summit showed every sign of a luxuriant vegetation, with bushes near the edge, and farther back many high trees. There was no indication of any life that we could see.

That night we pitched our camp immediately under the cliff—a most wild and desolate spot. The crags above us were not merely perpendicular, but curved outwards at the top, so that ascent was out of the question. Close to us was the high thin pinnacle of rock which I believe I mentioned earlier in this narrative. It is like a broad red church spire, the top of it being level with the plateau, but a great chasm gaping between. On the summit of it there grew one high tree. Both pinnacle and cliff were comparatively low— some five or six hundred feet, I should think.

"It was on that," said Professor Challenger, pointing to this tree, "that the pterodactyl was perched. I climbed half-way up the rock before I shot him. I am inclined to think that a good mountaineer like myself could ascend the rock to the top, though he would, of course, be no nearer to the plateau when he had done so."

As Challenger spoke of his pterodactyl I glanced at Professor Summerlee, and for the first time I seemed to see some signs of a dawning credulity and repentance. There was no sneer upon his thin lips, but, on the contrary, a gray, drawn look of excitement and amazement. Challenger saw it, too, and reveled in the first taste of victory.

"Of course," said he, with his clumsy and ponderous sarcasm, "Professor Summerlee will understand that when I speak of a ptero-dactyl I mean a stork—only it is the kind of stork which has no feathers, a leathery skin, membranous wings, and teeth in its jaws." He grinned and blinked and bowed until his colleague turned and walked away.

In the morning, after a frugal breakfast of coffee and manioc— we had to be economical of our stores—we held a council of war as to the best method of ascending to the plateau above us.

Challenger presided with a solemnity as if he were the Lord Chief Justice on the Bench. Picture him seated upon a rock, his absurd boyish straw hat tilted on the back of his head, his super-cilious eyes dominating us from under his drooping lids, his great black beard wagging as he slowly defined our present situation and our future movements.

Beneath him you might have seen the three of us—myself, sun-burnt, young, and vigorous after our open-air tramp; Summerlee, solemn but still critical, behind his eternal pipe; Lord John, as keen as a razor-edge, with his supple, alert figure leaning upon his rifle, and his eager eyes fixed eagerly upon the speaker. Behind us were grouped the two swarthy half-breeds and the little knot of Indi-ans, while in front and above us towered those huge, ruddy ribs of rocks which kept us from our goal.

"I need not say," said our leader, "that on the occasion of my last visit I exhausted every means of climbing the cliff, and where I failed I do not think that anyone else is likely to succeed, for I am something of a mountaineer. I had none of the appliances of a rock-climber with me, but I have taken the precaution to bring them now. With their aid I am positive I could climb that detached pin-nacle to the summit; but so long as the main cliff overhangs, it is vain to attempt ascending that. I was hurried upon my last visit by the approach of the rainy season and by the exhaustion of my sup-plies. These considerations limited my time, and I can only claim that I have surveyed about six miles of the cliff to the east of us, finding no possible way up. What, then, shall we now do?"

"There seems to be only one reasonable course," said Profes-sor Summerlee. "If you have explored the east, we should travel along the base of the cliff to the west, and seek for a practicable point for our ascent."

"That's it," said Lord John. "The odds are that this plateau is of no great size, and we shall travel round it until we either find an easy way up it, or come back to the point from which we started."

"I have already explained to our young friend here," said Chal-lenger (he has a way of alluding to me as if I were a school child ten years old), "that it is quite impossible that there should be an easy way up anywhere, for the simple reason that if there were the summit would not be isolated, and those conditions would not obtain which have effected so singular an interference with the general laws of survival. Yet I admit that there may very well be places where an expert human climber may reach the summit, and yet a cumbrous and heavy animal be unable to descend. It is certain that there is a point where an ascent is possible."

"How do you know that, sir?" asked Summerlee, sharply.

"Because my predecessor, the American Maple White, actually made such an ascent. How otherwise could he have seen the monster which he sketched in his notebook?"

"There you reason somewhat ahead of the proved facts," said the stubborn Summerlee. "I admit your plateau, because I have seen it; but I have not as yet satisfied myself that it contains any form of life whatever."

"What you admit, sir, or what you do not admit, is really of inconceivably small importance. I am glad to perceive that the plateau itself has actually obtruded itself upon your intelligence." He glanced up at it, and then, to our amazement, he sprang from his rock, and, seizing Summerlee by the neck, he tilted his face into the air. "Now sir!" he shouted, hoarse with excitement. "Do I help you to realize that the plateau contains some animal life?"

I have said that a thick fringe of green overhung the edge of the cliff. Out of this there had emerged a black, glistening object. As it came slowly forth and overhung the chasm, we saw that it was a very large snake with a peculiar flat, spade-like head. It wavered and quivered above us for a minute, the morning sun gleaming upon its sleek, sinuous coils. Then it slowly drew inwards and disappeared.

Summerlee had been so interested that he had stood unresisting while Challenger tilted his head into the air. Now he shook his colleague off and came back to his dignity.

"I should be glad, Professor Challenger," said he, "if you could see your way to make any remarks which may occur to you without seizing me by the chin. Even the appearance of a very ordinary rock python does not appear to justify such a liberty."

"But there is life upon the plateau all the same," his colleague replied in triumph. "And now, having demonstrated this important conclusion so that it is clear to anyone, however prejudiced or obtuse, I am of opinion that we cannot do better than break up our camp and travel to westward until we find some means of ascent."

The ground at the foot of the cliff was rocky and broken so that the going was slow and difficult. Suddenly we came, however, upon something which cheered our hearts. It was the site of an old encampment, with several empty Chicago meat tins, a bottle labeled "Brandy," a broken tin-opener, and a quantity of other travelers' debris. A crumpled, disintegrated newspaper revealed itself as the Chicago Democrat, though the date had been obliterated.

"Not mine," said Challenger. "It must be Maple White's."

Lord John had been gazing curiously at a great tree-fern which overshadowed the encampment. "I say, look at this," said he. "I believe it is meant for a sign-post."

A slip of hard wood had been nailed to the tree in such a way as to point to the westward.

"Most certainly a sign-post," said Challenger. "What else? Finding himself upon a dangerous errand, our pioneer has left this sign so that any party which follows him may know the way he has taken. Perhaps we shall come upon some other indications as we proceed."

We did indeed, but they were of a terrible and most unexpected nature. Immediately beneath the cliff there grew a considerable patch of high bamboo, like that which we had traversed in our journey. Many of these stems were twenty feet high, with sharp, strong tops, so that even as they stood they made formidable spears. We were passing along the edge of this cover when my eye was caught by the gleam of something white within it. Thrusting in my head between the stems, I found myself gazing at a fleshless skull. The whole skeleton was there, but the skull had detached itself and lay some feet nearer to the open.

With a few blows from the machetes of our Indians we cleared the spot and were able to study the details of this old tragedy. Only a few shreds of clothes could still be distinguished, but there were the remains of boots upon the bony feet, and it was very clear that the dead man was a European.

A gold watch by Hudson, of New York, and a chain which held a stylographic pen, lay among the bones. There was also a silver cigarette-case, with "J. C., from A. E. S.," upon the lid. The state of the metal seemed to show that the catastrophe had occurred no great time before.

"Who can he be?" asked Lord John. "Poor devil! every bone in his body seems to be broken."

"And the bamboo grows through his smashed ribs," said Summerlee. "It is a fast-growing plant, but it is surely inconceivable that this body could have been here while the canes grew to be twenty feet in length."

"As to the man's identity," said Professor Challenger, "I have no doubt whatever upon that point. As I made my way up the river before I reached you at the fazenda I instituted very particular inquiries about Maple White. At Para they knew nothing. Fortunately, I had a definite clew, for there was a particular picture in his sketch-book which showed him taking lunch with a certain ecclesiastic at Rosario. This priest I was able to find, and though he proved a very argumentative fellow, who took it absurdly amiss that I should point out to him the corrosive effect which modern science must have upon his beliefs, he none the less gave me some positive information. Maple White passed Rosario four years ago, or two years before I saw his dead body. He was not alone at the time, but there was a friend, an American named James Colver, who remained in the boat and did not meet this ecclesiastic. I think, therefore, that there can be no doubt that we are now looking upon the remains of this James Colver."

"Nor," said Lord John, "is there much doubt as to how he met his death. He has fallen or been chucked from the top, and so been impaled. How else could he come by his broken bones, and how could he have been stuck through by these canes with their points so high above our heads?"

A hush came over us as we stood round these shattered remains and realized the truth of Lord John Roxton's words. The beetling head of the cliff projected over the cane-brake. Undoubtedly he had fallen from above. But had he fallen? Had it been an accident? Or—already ominous and terrible possibilities began to form round that unknown land.

We moved off in silence, and continued to coast round the line of cliffs, which were as even and unbroken as some of those monstrous

Antarctic ice-fields which I have seen depicted as stretching from horizon to horizon and towering high above the mast-heads of the exploring vessel.

In five miles we saw no rift or break. And then suddenly we perceived something which filled us with new hope. In a hollow of the rock, protected from rain, there was drawn a rough arrow in chalk, pointing still to the westwards.

"Maple White again," said Professor Challenger. "He had some presentiment that worthy footsteps would follow close behind him."

"He had chalk, then?"

"A box of colored chalks was among the effects I found in his knapsack. I remember that the white one was worn to a stump."

"That is certainly good evidence," said Summerlee. "We can only accept his guidance and follow on to the westward."

We had proceeded some five more miles when again we saw a white arrow upon the rocks. It was at a point where the face of the cliff was for the first time split into a narrow cleft. Inside the cleft was a second guidance mark, which pointed right up it with the tip somewhat elevated, as if the spot indicated were above the level of the ground.

It was a solemn place, for the walls were so gigantic and the slit of blue sky so narrow and so obscured by a double fringe of verdure, that only a dim and shadowy light penetrated to the bottom. We had had no food for many hours, and were very weary with the stony and irregular journey, but our nerves were too strung to allow us to halt. We ordered the camp to be pitched, however, and, leaving the Indians to arrange it, we four, with the two half-breeds, proceeded up the narrow gorge.

It was not more than forty feet across at the mouth, but it rapidly closed until it ended in an acute angle, too straight and smooth for an ascent. Certainly it was not this which our pioneer had attempted to indicate. We made our way back—the whole gorge was not more than a quarter of a mile deep—and then suddenly the quick eyes of Lord John fell upon what we were seeking. High up above our heads, amid the dark shadows, there was one circle of deeper gloom. Surely it could only be the opening of a cave.

The base of the cliff was heaped with loose stones at the spot, and it was not difficult to clamber up. When we reached it, all doubt was removed. Not only was it an opening into the rock, but on the side of it there was marked once again the sign of the arrow. Here was the point, and this the means by which Maple White and his ill-fated comrade had made their ascent.

We were too excited to return to the camp, but must make our first exploration at once. Lord John had an electric torch in his knapsack, and this had to serve us as light. He advanced, throwing his little clear circlet of yellow radiance before him, while in single file we followed at his heels.

The cave had evidently been water-worn, the sides being smooth and the floor covered with rounded stones. It was of such a size that a single man could just fit through by stooping. For fifty yards it ran almost straight into the rock, and then it ascended at an angle of forty-five. Presently this incline became even steeper, and we found ourselves climbing upon hands and knees among loose rubble which slid from beneath us. Suddenly an exclamation broke from Lord Roxton.

"It's blocked!" said he.

Clustering behind him we saw in the yellow field of light a wall of broken basalt which extended to the ceiling.

"The roof has fallen in!"

In vain we dragged out some of the pieces. The only effect was that the larger ones became detached and threatened to roll down the gradient and crush us. It was evident that the obstacle was far beyond any efforts which we could make to remove it. The road by which Maple White had ascended was no longer available.

Too much cast down to speak, we stumbled down the dark tunnel and made our way back to the camp.

One incident occurred, however, before we left the gorge, which is of importance in view of what came afterwards.

We had gathered in a little group at the bottom of the chasm, some forty feet beneath the mouth of the cave, when a huge rock rolled suddenly downwards—and shot past us with tremendous force. It was the narrowest escape for one or all of us. We could not ourselves see whence the rock had come, but our half-breed servants, who were still at the opening of the cave, said that it had flown past them, and must therefore have fallen from the summit. Looking upwards, we could see no sign of movement above us amidst the green jungle which topped the cliff. There could be little doubt, however, that the stone was aimed at us, so the incident surely pointed to humanity—and malevolent humanity—upon the plateau.

We withdrew hurriedly from the chasm, our minds full of this new development and its bearing upon our plans. The situation was difficult enough before, but if the obstructions of Nature were increased by the deliberate opposition of man, then our case was indeed a hopeless one. And yet, as we looked up at that beautiful fringe of verdure only a few hundreds of feet above our heads, there was not one of us who could conceive the idea of returning to London until we had explored it to its depths.

On discussing the situation, we determined that our best course was to continue to coast round the plateau in the hope of finding some other means of reaching the top. The line of cliffs, which had decreased considerably in height, had already begun to trend from west to north, and if we could take this as representing the arc of a circle, the whole circumference could not be very great. At the worst, then, we should be back in a few days at our starting-point.

We made a march that day which totaled some two-and-twenty miles, without any change in our prospects. I may mention that our aneroid shows us that in the continual incline which we have ascended since we abandoned our canoes we have risen to no less than three thousand feet above sea-level. Hence there is a considerable change both in the temperature and in the vegetation. We have shaken off some of that horrible insect life which is the bane of tropical travel. A few palms still survive, and many tree-ferns, but the Amazonian trees have been all left behind. It was pleasant to see the convolvulus, the passion-flower, and the begonia, all reminding me of home, here among these inhospitable rocks. There was a red begonia just the same color as one that is kept in a pot in the window of a certain villa in Streatham—but I am drifting into private reminiscence.

That night—I am still speaking of the first day of our circumnavigation of the plateau—a great experience awaited us, and one

which for ever set at rest any doubt which we could have had as to
the wonders so near us.

You will realize as you read it, my dear Mr. McArdle, and possibly for the first time that the paper has not sent me on a wild-
goose chase, and that there is inconceivably fine copy waiting for
the world whenever we have the Professor's leave to make use of
it. I shall not dare to publish these articles unless I can bring back
my proofs to England, or I shall be hailed as the journalistic
Munchausen of all time. I have no doubt that you feel the same
way yourself, and that you would not care to stake the whole credit
of the Gazette upon this adventure until we can meet the chorus of
criticism and scepticism which such articles must of necessity elicit.
So this wonderful incident, which would make such a headline for
the old paper, must still wait its turn in the editorial drawer.

And yet it was all over in a flash, and there was no sequel to it,
save in our own convictions.

What occurred was this. Lord John had shot an ajouti—which
is a small, pig-like animal—and, half of it having been given to the
Indians, we were cooking the other half upon our fire. There is a
chill in the air after dark, and we had all drawn close to the blaze.
The night was moonless, but there were some stars, and one could
see for a little distance across the plain. Well, suddenly out of the
darkness, out of the night, there swooped something with a swish
like an aeroplane. The whole group of us were covered for an instant by a canopy of leathery wings, and I had a momentary vision
of a long, snake-like neck, a fierce, red, greedy eye, and a great
snapping beak, filled, to my amazement, with little, gleaming teeth.
The next instant it was gone—and so was our dinner. A huge black
shadow, twenty feet across, skimmed up into the air; for an instant the monster wings blotted out the stars, and then it vanished
over the brow of the cliff above us.

We all sat in amazed silence round the fire, like the heroes of
Virgil when the Harpies came down upon them. It was Summerlee
who was the first to speak.

"Professor Challenger," said he, in a solemn voice, which qua-
vered with emotion, "I owe you an apology. Sir, I am very much in
the wrong, and I beg that you will forget what is past."

It was handsomely said, and the two men for the first time shook hands. So much we have gained by this clear vision of our first pterodactyl. It was worth a stolen supper to bring two such men together.

But if prehistoric life existed upon the plateau it was not superabundant, for we had no further glimpse of it during the next three days. During this time we traversed a barren and forbidding country, which alternated between stony desert and desolate marshes full of many wild-fowl, upon the north and east of the cliffs. From that direction the place is really inaccessible, and, were it not for a hardish ledge which runs at the very base of the precipice, we should have had to turn back. Many times we were up to our waists in the slime and blubber of an old, semi-tropical swamp. To make matters worse, the place seemed to be a favorite breeding-place of the Jaracaca snake, the most venomous and aggressive in South America. Again and again these horrible creatures came writhing and springing towards us across the surface of this putrid bog, and it was only by keeping our shot-guns for ever ready that we could feel safe from them. One funnel-shaped depression in the morass, of a livid green in color from some lichen which festered in it, will always remain as a nightmare memory in my mind. It seems to have been a special nest of these vermins, and the slopes were alive with them, all writhing in our direction, for it is a peculiarity of the Jaracaca that he will always attack man at first sight. There were too many for us to shoot, so we fairly took to our heels and ran until we were exhausted. I shall always remember as we looked back how far behind we could see the heads and necks of our horrible pursuers rising and falling amid the reeds. Jaracaca Swamp we named it in the map which we are constructing.

The cliffs upon the farther side had lost their ruddy tint, being chocolate-brown in color; the vegetation was more scattered along the top of them, and they had sunk to three or four hundred feet in height, but in no place did we find any point where they could be ascended. If anything, they were more impossible than at the first point where we had met them. Their absolute steepness is indicated in the photograph which I took over the stony desert.

"Surely," said I, as we discussed the situation, "the rain must find its way down somehow. There are bound to be water-channels in the rocks."

"Our young friend has glimpses of lucidity," said Professor Challenger, patting me upon the shoulder.

"The rain must go somewhere," I repeated.

"He keeps a firm grip upon actuality. The only drawback is that we have conclusively proved by ocular demonstration that there are no water channels down the rocks."

"Where, then, does it go?" I persisted.

"I think it may be fairly assumed that if it does not come outwards it must run inwards."

"Then there is a lake in the center."

"So I should suppose."

"It is more than likely that the lake may be an old crater," said Summerlee. "The whole formation is, of course, highly volcanic. But, however that may be, I should expect to find the surface of the plateau slope inwards with a considerable sheet of water in the center, which may drain off, by some subterranean channel, into the marshes of the Jaracaca Swamp."

"Or evaporation might preserve an equilibrium," remarked Challenger, and the two learned men wandered off into one of their usual scientific arguments, which were as comprehensible as Chinese to the layman.

On the sixth day we completed our first circuit of the cliffs, and found ourselves back at the first camp, beside the isolated pinnacle of rock. We were a disconsolate party, for nothing could have been more minute than our investigation, and it was absolutely certain that there was no single point where the most active human being could possibly hope to scale the cliff. The place which Maple White's chalk-marks had indicated as his own means of access was now entirely impassable.

What were we to do now? Our stores of provisions, supplemented by our guns, were holding out well, but the day must come when they would need replenishment. In a couple of months the rains might be expected, and we should be washed out of our camp. The rock was harder than marble, and any attempt at cutting a path for so great a height was more than our time or resources would admit. No wonder that we looked gloomily at each other that night, and sought our blankets with hardly a word exchanged. I remember that as I dropped off to sleep my last recollection was that Challenger was squatting, like a monstrous bull-frog, by the fire, his huge head in his hands, sunk apparently in the deepest thought, and entirely oblivious to the good-night which I wished him.

But it was a very different Challenger who greeted us in the morning—a Challenger with contentment and self-congratulation shining from his whole person. He faced us as we assembled for breakfast with a deprecating false modesty in his eyes, as who should say, "I know that I deserve all that you can say, but I pray you to spare my blushes by not saying it." His beard bristled exultantly, his chest was thrown out, and his hand was thrust into the front of his jacket. So, in his fancy, may he see himself sometimes, gracing the vacant pedestal in Trafalgar Square, and adding one more to the horrors of the London streets.

"Eureka!" he cried, his teeth shining through his beard. "Gentlemen, you may congratulate me and we may congratulate each other. The problem is solved."

"You have found a way up?"

"I venture to think so."

"And where?"

For answer he pointed to the spire-like pinnacle upon our right.

Our faces—or mine, at least—fell as we surveyed it. That it could be climbed we had our companion's assurance. But a horrible abyss lay between it and the plateau.

"We can never get across," I gasped.

"We can at least all reach the summit," said he. "When we are up I may be able to show you that the resources of an inventive mind are not yet exhausted."

After breakfast we unpacked the bundle in which our leader had brought his climbing accessories. From it he took a coil of the strongest and lightest rope, a hundred and fifty feet in length, with climbing irons, clamps, and other devices. Lord John was an experienced mountaineer, and Summerlee had done some rough climbing at various times, so that I was really the novice at rock-work of the party; but my strength and activity may have made up for my want of experience.

It was not in reality a very stiff task, though there were moments which made my hair bristle upon my head. The first half was perfectly easy, but from there upwards it became continually steeper until, for the last fifty feet, we were literally clinging with our fingers and toes to tiny ledges and crevices in the rock. I could not have accomplished it, nor could Summerlee, if Challenger had not gained the summit (it was extraordinary to see such activity in so unwieldy a creature) and there fixed the rope round the trunk of the considerable tree which grew there. With this as our support, we were soon able to scramble up the jagged wall until we found ourselves upon the small grassy platform, some twenty-five feet each way, which formed the summit.

The first impression which I received when I had recovered my breath was of the extraordinary view over the country which we had traversed. The whole Brazilian plain seemed to lie beneath us, extending away and away until it ended in dim blue mists upon the farthest sky-line. In the foreground was the long slope, strewn with rocks and dotted with tree-ferns; farther off in the middle distance, looking over the saddle-back hill, I could just see the yellow and green mass of bamboos through which we had passed; and then, gradually, the vegetation increased until it formed the huge forest which extended as far as the eyes could reach, and for a good two thousand miles beyond.

I was still drinking in this wonderful panorama when the heavy hand of the Professor fell upon my shoulder.

"This way, my young friend," said he; "*vestigia nulla retrorsum.* Never look rearwards, but always to our glorious goal."

The level of the plateau, when I turned, was exactly that on which we stood, and the green bank of bushes, with occasional trees, was so near that it was difficult to realize how inaccessible it remained. At a rough guess the gulf was forty feet across, but, so far as I could see, it might as well have been forty miles. I placed one arm round the trunk of the tree and leaned over the abyss. Far down were the small dark figures of our servants, looking up at us. The wall was absolutely precipitous, as was that which faced me.

"This is indeed curious," said the creaking voice of Professor Summerlee.

I turned, and found that he was examining with great interest the tree to which I clung. That smooth bark and those small, ribbed leaves seemed familiar to my eyes. "Why," I cried, "it's a beech!"

"Exactly," said Summerlee. "A fellow-countryman in a far land."

"Not only a fellow-countryman, my good sir," said Challenger, "but also, if I may be allowed to enlarge your simile, an ally of the first value. This beech tree will be our saviour."

"By George!" cried Lord John, "a bridge!"

"Exactly, my friends, a bridge! It is not for nothing that I expended an hour last night in focusing my mind upon the situation. I have some recollection of once remarking to our young friend here that G. E. C. is at his best when his back is to the wall. Last night you will admit that all our backs were to the wall. But where will-power and intellect go together, there is always a way out. A drawbridge had to be found which could be dropped across the abyss. Behold it!"

It was certainly a brilliant idea. The tree was a good sixty feet in height, and if it only fell the right way it would easily cross the chasm. Challenger had slung the camp axe over his shoulder when he ascended. Now he handed it to me.

"Our young friend has the thews and sinews," said he. "I think he will be the most useful at this task. I must beg, however, that you will kindly refrain from thinking for yourself, and that you will do exactly what you are told."

Under his direction I cut such gashes in the sides of the trees as would ensure that it should fall as we desired. It had already a strong, natural tilt in the direction of the plateau, so that the matter was not difficult. Finally I set to work in earnest upon the trunk, taking turn and turn with Lord John. In a little over an hour there was a loud crack, the tree swayed forward, and then crashed over, burying its branches among the bushes on the farther side. The severed trunk rolled to the very edge of our platform, and for one terrible second we all thought it was over. It balanced itself, however, a few inches from the edge, and there was our bridge to the unknown.

All of us, without a word, shook hands with Professor Challenger, who raised his straw hat and bowed deeply to each in turn.

"I claim the honor," said he, "to be the first to cross to the unknown land—a fitting subject, no doubt, for some future historical painting."

He had approached the bridge when Lord John laid his hand upon his coat.

"My dear chap," said he, "I really cannot allow it."

"Cannot allow it, sir!" The head went back and the beard forward.

"When it is a matter of science, don't you know, I follow your lead because you are by way of bein' a man of science. But it's up to you to follow me when you come into my department."

"Your department, sir?"

"We all have our professions, and soldierin' is mine. We are, accordin' to my ideas, invadin' a new country, which may or may not be chock-full of enemies of sorts. To barge blindly into it for want of a little common sense and patience isn't my notion of management."

The remonstrance was too reasonable to be disregarded. Challenger tossed his head and shrugged his heavy shoulders.

"Well, sir, what do you propose?"

"For all I know there may be a tribe of cannibals waitin' for lunch-time among those very bushes," said Lord John, looking across the bridge. "It's better to learn wisdom before you get into a cookin'-pot; so we will content ourselves with hopin' that there is no trouble waitin' for us, and at the same time we will act as if there were. Malone and I will go down again, therefore, and we will fetch up the four rifles, together with Gomez and the other. One man can then go across and the rest will cover him with guns, until he sees that it is safe for the whole crowd to come along."

Challenger sat down upon the cut stump and groaned his impatience; but Summerlee and I were of one mind that Lord John was our leader when such practical details were in question. The climb was a more simple thing now that the rope dangled down the face of the worst part of the ascent. Within an hour we had brought up the rifles and a shot-gun. The half-breeds had ascended also, and under Lord John's orders they had carried up a bale of provisions in case our first exploration should be a long one. We had each bandoliers of cartridges.

"Now, Challenger, if you really insist upon being the first man in," said Lord John, when every preparation was complete.

"I am much indebted to you for your gracious permission," said the angry Professor; for never was a man so intolerant of every form of authority. "Since you are good enough to allow it, I shall most certainly take it upon myself to act as pioneer upon this occasion."

Seating himself with a leg overhanging the abyss on each side, and his hatchet slung upon his back, Challenger hopped his way across the trunk and was soon at the other side. He clambered up and waved his arms in the air.

"At last!" he cried; "at last!"

I gazed anxiously at him, with a vague expectation that some terrible fate would dart at him from the curtain of green behind him. But all was quiet, save that a strange, many-colored bird flew up from under his feet and vanished among the trees.

Summerlee was the second. His wiry energy is wonderful in so frail a frame. He insisted upon having two rifles slung upon his back, so that both Professors were armed when he had made his transit. I came next, and tried hard not to look down into the horrible gulf over which I was passing. Summerlee held out the butt-end of his rifle, and an instant later I was able to grasp his hand. As to Lord John, he walked across—actually walked without support! He must have nerves of iron.

And there we were, the four of us, upon the dreamland, the lost world, of Maple White. To all of us it seemed the moment of our supreme triumph. Who could have guessed that it was the prelude to our supreme disaster? Let me say in a few words how the crushing blow fell upon us.

We had turned away from the edge, and had penetrated about fifty yards of close brushwood, when there came a frightful rending crash from behind us. With one impulse we rushed back the way that we had come. The bridge was gone!

Far down at the base of the cliff I saw, as I looked over, a tangled mass of branches and splintered trunk. It was our beech tree. Had the edge of the platform crumbled and let it through? For a moment this explanation was in all our minds. The next, from the farther side of the rocky pinnacle before us a swarthy face, the face of Gomez the half-breed, was slowly protruded. Yes, it was Gomez, but no longer the Gomez of the demure smile and the mask-like expression. Here was a face with flashing eyes and distorted features, a face convulsed with hatred and with the mad joy of gratified revenge.

"Lord Roxton!" he shouted. "Lord John Roxton!"

"Well," said our companion, "here I am."

A shriek of laughter came across the abyss.

"Yes, there you are, you English dog, and there you will remain! I have waited and waited, and now has come my chance. You found it hard to get up; you will find it harder to get down. You cursed fools, you are trapped, every one of you!"

We were too astounded to speak. We could only stand there staring in amazement. A great broken bough upon the grass showed whence he had gained his leverage to tilt over our bridge. The face had vanished, but presently it was up again, more frantic than before.

"We nearly killed you with a stone at the cave," he cried; "but this is better. It is slower and more terrible. Your bones will whiten up there, and none will know where you lie or come to cover them. As you lie dying, think of Lopez, whom you shot five years ago on the Putomayo River. I am his brother, and, come what will I will die happy now, for his memory has been avenged." A furious hand was shaken at us, and then all was quiet.

Had the half-breed simply wrought his vengeance and then escaped, all might have been well with him. It was that foolish, irresistible Latin impulse to be dramatic which brought his own downfall. Roxton, the man who had earned himself the name of the Flail of the Lord through three countries, was not one who could be safely taunted. The half-breed was descending on the farther side of the pinnacle; but before he could reach the ground Lord John had run along the edge of the plateau and gained a point from which he could see his man. There was a single crack of his rifle, and, though we saw nothing, we heard the scream and then the distant thud of the falling body. Roxton came back to us with a face of granite.

"I have been a blind simpleton," said he, bitterly, "It's my folly that has brought you all into this trouble. I should have remembered that these people have long memories for blood-feuds, and have been more upon my guard."

"What about the other one? It took two of them to lever that tree over the edge."

"I could have shot him, but I let him go. He may have had no part in it. Perhaps it would have been better if I had killed him, for he must, as you say, have lent a hand."

Now that we had the clue to his action, each of us could cast back and remember some sinister act upon the part of the half-breed—his constant desire to know our plans, his arrest outside our tent when he was over-hearing them, the furtive looks of hatred which from time to time one or other of us had surprised. We were still discussing it, endeavoring to adjust our minds to these new conditions, when a singular scene in the plain below arrested our attention.

A man in white clothes, who could only be the surviving half-breed, was running as one does run when Death is the pacemaker. Behind him, only a few yards in his rear, bounded the huge ebony figure of Zambo, our devoted negro. Even as we looked, he sprang upon the back of the fugitive and flung his arms round his neck. They rolled on the ground together. An instant afterwards Zambo rose, looked at the prostrate man, and then, waving his hand joyously to us, came running in our direction. The white figure lay motionless in the middle of the great plain.

Our two traitors had been destroyed, but the mischief that they had done lived after them. By no possible means could we get back to the pinnacle. We had been natives of the world; now we were natives of the plateau. The two things were separate and apart. There was the plain which led to the canoes. Yonder, beyond the violet, hazy horizon, was the stream which led back to civilization. But the link between was missing. No human ingenuity could suggest a means of bridging the chasm which yawned between ourselves and our past lives. One instant had altered the whole conditions of our existence.

It was at such a moment that I learned the stuff of which my three comrades were composed. They were grave, it is true, and thoughtful, but of an invincible serenity. For the moment we could only sit among the bushes in patience and wait the coming of Zambo.

Presently his honest black face topped the rocks and his Herculean figure emerged upon the top of the pinnacle.

"What I do now?" he cried. "You tell me and I do it."

It was a question which it was easier to ask than to answer. One thing only was clear. He was our one trusty link with the outside world. On no account must he leave us.

"No no!" he cried. "I not leave you. Whatever come, you always find me here. But no able to keep Indians. Already they say too much Curupuri live on this place, and they go home. Now you leave them me no able to keep them."

It was a fact that our Indians had shown in many ways of late that they were weary of their journey and anxious to return. We realized that Zambo spoke the truth, and that it would be impossible for him to keep them.

"Make them wait till to-morrow, Zambo," I shouted; "then I can send letter back by them."

"Very good, sarr! I promise they wait till to-morrow," said the negro. "But what I do for you now?"

There was plenty for him to do, and admirably the faithful fellow did it. First of all, under our directions, he undid the rope from the tree-stump and threw one end of it across to us. It was not thicker than a clothes-line, but it was of great strength, and though we could not make a bridge of it, we might well find it invaluable if we had any climbing to do. He then fastened his end of the rope to the package of supplies which had been carried up, and we were able to drag it across. This gave us the means of life for at least a week, even if we found nothing else. Finally he descended and carried up two other packets of mixed goods—a box of ammunition and a number of other things, all of which we got across by throwing our rope to him and hauling it back. It was evening when he at last climbed down, with a final assurance that he would keep the Indians till next morning.

And so it is that I have spent nearly the whole of this our first night upon the plateau writing up our experiences by the light of a single candle-lantern.

We supped and camped at the very edge of the cliff, quenching our thirst with two bottles of Apollinaris which were in one of the cases. It is vital to us to find water, but I think even Lord John himself had had adventures enough for one day, and none of us felt inclined to make the first push into the unknown. We forbore to light a fire or to make any unnecessary sound.

To-morrow (or to-day, rather, for it is already dawn as I write) we shall make our first venture into this strange land. When I shall be able to write again—or if I ever shall write again—I know not. Meanwhile, I can see that the Indians are still in their place, and I am sure that the faithful Zambo will be here presently to get my letter. I only trust that it will come to hand.

P.S.—The more I think the more desperate does our position seem. I see no possible hope of our return. If there were a high tree near the edge of the plateau we might drop a return bridge across, but there is none within fifty yards. Our united strength could not carry a trunk which would serve our purpose. The rope, of course, is far too short that we could descend by it. No, our position is hopeless—hopeless!

10

"The Most Wonderful Things have Happened"

The most wonderful things have happened and are continually happening to us. All the paper that I possess consists of five old note-books and a lot of scraps, and I have only the one stylographic pencil; but so long as I can move my hand I will continue to set down our experiences and impressions, for, since we are the only men of the whole human race to see such things, it is of enormous importance that I should record them whilst they are fresh in my memory and before that fate which seems to be constantly impending does actually overtake us. Whether Zambo can at last take these letters to the river, or whether I shall myself in some miraculous way carry them back with me, or, finally, whether some daring explorer, coming upon our tracks with the advantage, perhaps, of a perfected monoplane, should find this bundle of manuscript, in any case I can see that what I am writing is destined to immortality as a classic of true adventure.

On the morning after our being trapped upon the plateau by the villainous Gomez we began a new stage in our experiences. The first incident in it was not such as to give me a very favorable opinion of the place to which we had wandered. As I roused myself from a short nap after day had dawned, my eyes fell upon a most singular appearance upon my own leg. My trouser had slipped up, exposing a few inches of my skin above my sock. On this there rested a large, purplish grape. Astonished at the sight, I leaned forward to pick it off, when, to my horror, it burst between my finger and thumb, squirting blood in every direction. My cry of disgust had brought the two professors to my side.

"Most interesting," said Summerlee, bending over my shin. "An enormous blood-tick, as yet, I believe, unclassified."

"The first-fruits of our labors," said Challenger in his booming, pedantic fashion. "We cannot do less than call it *Ixodes Maloni*. The very small inconvenience of being bitten, my young friend, cannot, I am sure, weigh with you as against the glorious privilege of having your name inscribed in the deathless roll of zoology. Unhappily you have crushed this fine specimen at the moment of satiation."

"Filthy vermin!" I cried.

Professor Challenger raised his great eyebrows in protest, and placed a soothing paw upon my shoulder.

"You should cultivate the scientific eye and the detached scientific mind," said he. "To a man of philosophic temperament like myself the blood-tick, with its lancet-like proboscis and its distending stomach, is as beautiful a work of Nature as the peacock or, for that matter, the aurora borealis. It pains me to hear you speak of it in so unappreciative a fashion. No doubt, with due diligence, we can secure some other specimen."

"There can be no doubt of that," said Summerlee, grimly, "for one has just disappeared behind your shirt-collar."

Challenger sprang into the air bellowing like a bull, and tore frantically at his coat and shirt to get them off. Summerlee and I laughed so that we could hardly help him. At last we exposed that monstrous torso (fifty-four inches, by the tailor's tape). His body was all matted with black hair, out of which jungle we picked the wandering tick before it had bitten him. But the bushes round were full of the horrible pests, and it was clear that we must shift our camp.

But first of all it was necessary to make our arrangements with the faithful negro, who appeared presently on the pinnacle with a number of tins of cocoa and biscuits, which he tossed over to us. Of the stores which remained below he was ordered to retain as much as would keep him for two months. The Indians were to have the remainder as a reward for their services and as payment for taking our letters back to the Amazon. Some hours later we saw them in single file far out upon the plain, each with a bundle on his head, making their way back along the path we had come. Zambo occupied our little tent at the base of the pinnacle, and there he remained, our one link with the world below.

And now we had to decide upon our immediate movements. We shifted our position from among the tick-laden bushes until we came to a small clearing thickly surrounded by trees upon all sides. There were some flat slabs of rock in the center, with an excellent well close by, and there we sat in cleanly comfort while we made our first plans for the invasion of this new country. Birds were calling among the foliage—especially one with a peculiar whooping cry which was new to us—but beyond these sounds there were no signs of life.

Our first care was to make some sort of list of our own stores, so that we might know what we had to rely upon. What with the things we had ourselves brought up and those which Zambo had sent across on the rope, we were fairly well supplied. Most important of all, in view of the dangers which might surround us, we had our four rifles and one thousand three hundred rounds, also a shotgun, but not more than a hundred and fifty medium pellet cartridges. In the matter of provisions we had enough to last for several weeks, with a sufficiency of tobacco and a few scientific implements, including a large telescope and a good field-glass. All these things we collected together in the clearing, and as a first precaution, we cut down with our hatchet and knives a number of thorny bushes, which we piled round in a circle some fifteen yards in diameter. This was to be our headquarters for the time—our place of refuge against sudden danger and the guard-house for our stores. Fort Challenger, we called it.

It was midday before we had made ourselves secure, but the heat was not oppressive, and the general character of the plateau, both in its temperature and in its vegetation, was almost temperate. The beech, the oak, and even the birch were to be found among the tangle of trees which girt us in. One huge gingko tree, topping all the others, shot its great limbs and maidenhair foliage over the fort which we had constructed. In its shade we continued our discussion, while Lord John, who had quickly taken command in the hour of action, gave us his views.

"So long as neither man nor beast has seen or heard us, we are safe," said he. "From the time they know we are here our troubles begin. There are no signs that they have found us out as yet. So our game surely is to lie low for a time and spy out the land. We want to have a good look at our neighbors before we get on visitin' terms."

"But we must advance," I ventured to remark.

"By all means, sonny my boy! We will advance. But with common sense. We must never go so far that we can't get back to our base. Above all, we must never, unless it is life or death, fire off our guns."

"But *you* fired yesterday," said Summerlee.

"Well, it couldn't be helped. However, the wind was strong and blew outwards. It is not likely that the sound could have traveled far into the plateau. By the way, what shall we call this place? I suppose it is up to us to give it a name?"

There were several suggestions, more or less happy, but Challenger's was final.

"It can only have one name," said he. "It is called after the pioneer who discovered it. It is Maple White Land."

Maple White Land it became, and so it is named in that chart which has become my special task. So it will, I trust, appear in the atlas of the future.

The peaceful penetration of Maple White Land was the pressing subject before us. We had the evidence of our own eyes that the place was inhabited by some unknown creatures, and there was that of Maple White's sketch-book to show that more dreadful and more dangerous monsters might still appear. That there might also prove to be human occupants and that they were of a malevolent character was suggested by the skeleton impaled upon the bamboos, which could not have got there had it not been dropped from above. Our situation, stranded without possibility of escape in such a land, was clearly full of danger, and our reasons endorsed every measure of caution which Lord John's experience could suggest. Yet it was surely impossible that we should halt on the edge of this world of mystery when our very souls were tingling with impatience to push forward and to pluck the heart from it.

We therefore blocked the entrance to our *zareba* by filling it up with several thorny bushes, and left our camp with the stores entirely surrounded by this protecting hedge. We then slowly and cautiously set forth into the unknown, following the course of the little stream which flowed from our spring, as it should always serve us as a guide on our return.

Hardly had we started when we came across signs that there were indeed wonders awaiting us. After a few hundred yards of thick forest, containing many trees which were quite unknown to me, but which Summerlee, who was the botanist of the party, recognized as forms of conifera and of cycadaceous plants which have long passed away in the world below, we entered a region where the stream widened out and formed a considerable bog. High reeds of a peculiar type grew thickly before us, which were pronounced to be equisetacea, or mare's-tails, with tree-ferns scattered amongst them, all of them swaying in a brisk wind. Suddenly Lord John, who was walking first, halted with uplifted hand.

"Look at this!" said he. "By George, this must be the trail of the father of all birds!"

An enormous three-toed track was imprinted in the soft mud before us. The creature, whatever it was, had crossed the swamp and had passed on into the forest. We all stopped to examine that monstrous spoor. If it were indeed a bird—and what animal could leave such a mark?—its foot was so much larger than an ostrich's that its height upon the same scale must be enormous. Lord John looked eagerly round him and slipped two cartridges into his elephant-gun.

"I'll stake my good name as a shikarree," said he, "that the track is a fresh one. The creature has not passed ten minutes. Look how the water is still oozing into that deeper print! By Jove! See, here is the mark of a little one!"

Sure enough, smaller tracks of the same general form were running parallel to the large ones.

"But what do you make of this?" cried Professor Summerlee, triumphantly, pointing to what looked like the huge print of a five-fingered human hand appearing among the three-toed marks.

"Wealden!" cried Challenger, in an ecstasy. "I've seen them in the Wealden clay. It is a creature walking erect upon three-toed feet, and occasionally putting one of its five-fingered forepaws upon the ground. Not a bird, my dear Roxton—not a bird."

"A beast?"

"No; a reptile—a dinosaur. Nothing else could have left such a track. They puzzled a worthy Sussex doctor some ninety years ago; but who in the world could have hoped—hoped—to have seen a sight like that?"

His words died away into a whisper, and we all stood in motionless amazement. Following the tracks, we had left the morass and passed through a screen of brushwood and trees. Beyond was an open glade, and in this were five of the most extraordinary creatures that I have ever seen. Crouching down among the bushes, we observed them at our leisure.

There were, as I say, five of them, two being adults and three young ones. In size they were enormous. Even the babies were as big as elephants, while the two large ones were far beyond all creatures I have ever seen. They had slate-colored skin, which was scaled like a lizard's and shimmered where the sun shone upon it. All five were sitting up, balancing themselves upon their broad, powerful tails and their huge three-toed hind-feet, while with their small five-fingered front-feet they pulled down the branches upon which they browsed. I do not know that I can bring their appearance home to you better than by saying that they looked like monstrous kangaroos, twenty feet in length, and with skins like black crocodiles.

I do not know how long we stayed motionless gazing at this marvelous spectacle. A strong wind blew towards us and we were well concealed, so there was no chance of discovery. From time to time the little ones played round their parents in unwieldy gambols, the great beasts bounding into the air and falling with dull thuds upon the earth. The strength of the parents seemed to be limitless, for one of them, having some difficulty in reaching a bunch of foliage which grew upon a considerable-sized tree, put his fore-legs round the trunk and tore it down as if it had been a sapling. The action seemed, as I thought, to show not only the great development of its muscles, but also the small one of its brain, for the whole weight came crashing down upon the top of it, and it uttered a series of shrill yelps to show that, big as it was, there was a limit to what it could endure. The incident made it think, apparently, that the neighborhood was dangerous, for it slowly lurched off through the wood, followed by its mate and its three enormous infants. We saw the shimmering slaty gleam of their skins between the tree-trunks, and their heads undulating high above the brushwood. Then they vanished from our sight.

I looked at my comrades. Lord John was standing at gaze with his finger on the trigger of his elephant-gun, his eager hunter's soul shining from his fierce eyes. What would he not give for one such head to place between the two crossed oars above the mantelpiece in his snuggery at the Albany! And yet his reason held him in, for all our exploration of the wonders of this unknown land depended upon our presence being concealed from its inhabitants. The two professors were in silent ecstasy. In their excitement they had unconsciously seized each other by the hand, and stood like two little children in the presence of a marvel, Challenger's cheeks bunched up into a seraphic smile, and Summerlee's sardonic face softening for the moment into wonder and reverence.

"*Nunc dimittis!*" he cried at last. "What will they say in England of this?"

"My dear Summerlee, I will tell you with great confidence exactly what they will say in England," said Challenger. "They will say that you are an infernal liar and a scientific charlatan, exactly as you and others said of me."

"In the face of photographs?"

"Faked, Summerlee! Clumsily faked!"

"In the face of specimens?"

"Ah, there we may have them! Malone and his filthy Fleet Street crew may be all yelping our praises yet. August the twenty-eighth— the day we saw five live iguanodons in a glade of Maple White Land. Put it down in your diary, my young friend, and send it to your rag."

"And be ready to get the toe-end of the editorial boot in return," said Lord John. "Things look a bit different from the latitude of London, young fellah my lad. There's many a man who never tells his adventures, for he can't hope to be believed. Who's to blame them? For this will seem a bit of a dream to ourselves in a month or two. *What* did you say they were?"

"Iguanodons," said Summerlee. "You'll find their footmarks all over the Hastings sands, in Kent, and in Sussex. The South of England was alive with them when there was plenty of good lush green-stuff to keep them going. Conditions have changed, and the beasts died. Here it seems that the conditions have not changed, and the beasts have lived."

"If ever we get out of this alive, I must have a head with me," said Lord John. "Lord, how some of that Somaliland-Uganda crowd would turn a beautiful pea-green if they saw it! I don't know what you chaps think, but it strikes me that we are on mighty thin ice all this time."

I had the same feeling of mystery and danger around us. In the gloom of the trees there seemed a constant menace and as we looked up into their shadowy foliage vague terrors crept into one's heart. It is true that these monstrous creatures which we had seen were lumbering, inoffensive brutes which were unlikely to hurt anyone, but in this world of wonders what other survivals might there not be—what fierce, active horrors ready to pounce upon us from their lair among the rocks or brushwood? I knew little of prehistoric life, but I had a clear remembrance of one book which I had read in which it spoke of creatures who would live upon our lions and tigers as a cat lives upon mice. What if these also were to be found in the woods of Maple White Land!

It was destined that on this very morning—our first in the new country—we were to find out what strange hazards lay around us. It was a loathsome adventure, and one of which I hate to think. If, as Lord John said, the glade of the iguanodons will remain with us as a dream, then surely the swamp of the pterodactyls will forever be our nightmare. Let me set down exactly what occurred.

We passed very slowly through the woods, partly because Lord Roxton acted as scout before he would let us advance, and partly because at every second step one or other of our professors would fall, with a cry of wonder, before some flower or insect which presented him with a new type. We may have traveled two or three miles in all, keeping to the right of the line of the stream, when we came upon a considerable opening in the trees. A belt of brushwood led up to a tangle of rocks—the whole plateau was strewn with boulders. We were walking slowly towards these rocks, among bushes which reached over our waists, when we became aware of a strange low gabbling and whistling sound, which filled the air with a constant clamor and appeared to come from some spot immediately before us. Lord John held up his hand as a signal for us to stop, and he made his way swiftly, stooping and running, to the line of rocks. We saw him peep over them and give a gesture of amazement. Then he stood staring as if forgetting us, so utterly entranced was he by what he saw. Finally he waved us to come on, holding up his hand as a signal for caution. His whole bearing made me feel that something wonderful but dangerous lay before us.

Creeping to his side, we looked over the rocks. The place into which we gazed was a pit, and may, in the early days, have been one of the smaller volcanic blow-holes of the plateau. It was bowl-shaped and at the bottom, some hundreds of yards from where we lay, were pools of green-scummed, stagnant water, fringed with bullrushes. It was a weird place in itself, but its occupants made it seem like a scene from the Seven Circles of Dante. The place was a rookery of pterodactyls. There were hundreds of them congregated within view. All the bottom area round the water-edge was alive with their young ones, and with hideous mothers brooding upon their leathery, yellowish eggs. From this crawling flapping mass of obscene reptilian life came the shocking clamor which filled the air and the mephitic, horrible, musty odor which turned us sick. But above, perched each upon its own stone, tall, gray, and withered, more like dead and dried specimens than actual living creatures, sat the horrible males, absolutely motionless save for the rolling of their red eyes or an occasional snap of their rat-trap beaks as a dragon-fly went past them. Their huge, membranous wings were closed by folding their fore-arms, so that they sat like gigantic old women, wrapped in hideous web-colored shawls, and with their ferocious heads protruding above them. Large and small, not less than a thousand of these filthy creatures lay in the hollow before us.

Our professors would gladly have stayed there all day, so entranced were they by this opportunity of studying the life of a prehistoric age. They pointed out the fish and dead birds lying about

among the rocks as proving the nature of the food of these creatures, and I heard them congratulating each other on having
cleared up the point why the bones of this flying dragon are found
in such great numbers in certain well-defined areas, as in the Cam-
bridge Green-sand, since it was now seen that, like penguins, they
lived in gregarious fashion.

Finally, however, Challenger, bent upon proving some point
which Summerlee had contested, thrust his head over the rock and
nearly brought destruction upon us all. In an instant the nearest
male gave a shrill, whistling cry, and flapped its twenty-foot span
of leathery wings as it soared up into the air. The females and young
ones huddled together beside the water, while the whole circle of
sentinels rose one after the other and sailed off into the sky. It was
a wonderful sight to see at least a hundred creatures of such enormous size and hideous appearance all swooping like swallows with
swift, shearing wing-strokes above us; but soon we realized that it
was not one on which we could afford to linger. At first the great
brutes flew round in a huge ring, as if to make sure what the exact
extent of the danger might be. Then, the flight grew lower and the
circle narrower, until they were whizzing round and round us, the
dry, rustling flap of their huge slate-colored wings filling the air
with a volume of sound that made me think of Hendon aerodrome
upon a race day.

"Make for the wood and keep together," cried Lord John, club-
bing his rifle. "The brutes mean mischief."

The moment we attempted to retreat the circle closed in upon
us, until the tips of the wings of those nearest to us nearly touched
our faces. We beat at them with the stocks of our guns, but there
was nothing solid or vulnerable to strike. Then suddenly out of the
whizzing, slate-colored circle a long neck shot out, and a fierce beak
made a thrust at us. Another and another followed. Summerlee
gave a cry and put his hand to his face, from which the blood was
streaming. I felt a prod at the back of my neck, and turned dizzy
with the shock. Challenger fell, and as I stooped to pick him up I
was again struck from behind and dropped on the top of him. At the
same instant I heard the crash of Lord John's elephant-gun, and,
looking up, saw one of the creatures with a broken wing struggling

upon the ground, spitting and gurgling at us with a wide-opened beak and blood-shot, goggled eyes, like some devil in a medieval picture. Its comrades had flown higher at the sudden sound, and were circling above our heads.

"Now," cried Lord John, "now for our lives!"

We staggered through the brushwood, and even as we reached the trees the harpies were on us again. Summerlee was knocked down, but we tore him up and rushed among the trunks. Once there we were safe, for those huge wings had no space for their sweep beneath the branches. As we limped homewards, sadly mauled and discomfited, we saw them for a long time flying at a great height against the deep blue sky above our heads, soaring round and round, no bigger than wood-pigeons, with their eyes no doubt still following our progress. At last, however, as we reached the thicker woods they gave up the chase, and we saw them no more.

"A most interesting and convincing experience," said Challenger, as we halted beside the brook and he bathed a swollen knee. "We are exceptionally well informed, Summerlee, as to the habits of the enraged pterodactyl."

Summerlee was wiping the blood from a cut in his forehead, while I was tying up a nasty stab in the muscle of the neck. Lord John had the shoulder of his coat torn away, but the creature's teeth had only grazed the flesh.

"It is worth noting," Challenger continued, "that our young friend has received an undoubted stab, while Lord John's coat could only have been torn by a bite. In my own case, I was beaten about the head by their wings, so we have had a remarkable exhibition of their various methods of offence."

"It has been touch and go for our lives," said Lord John, gravely, "and I could not think of a more rotten sort of death than to be outed by such filthy vermin. I was sorry to fire my rifle, but, by Jove! there was no great choice."

"We should not be here if you hadn't," said I, with conviction.

"It may do no harm," said he. "Among these woods there must be many loud cracks from splitting or falling trees which would be just like the sound of a gun. But now, if you are of my opinion, we have had thrills enough for one day, and had best get back to the surgical box at the camp for some carbolic. Who knows what venom these beasts may have in their hideous jaws?"

But surely no men ever had just such a day since the world began. Some fresh surprise was ever in store for us. When, following the course of our brook, we at last reached our glade and saw the thorny barricade of our camp, we thought that our adventures were at an end. But we had something more to think of before we could rest. The gate of Fort Challenger had been untouched, the walls were unbroken, and yet it had been visited by some strange and powerful creature in our absence. No foot-mark showed a trace of its nature, and only the overhanging branch of the enormous ginko tree suggested how it might have come and gone; but of its malevolent strength there was ample evidence in the condition of our stores. They were strewn at random all over the ground, and one tin of meat had been crushed into pieces so as to extract the contents. A case of cartridges had been shattered into matchwood, and one of the brass shells lay shredded into pieces beside it. Again the feeling of vague horror came upon our souls, and we gazed round with frightened eyes at the dark shadows which lay around us, in all of which some fearsome shape might be lurking. How good it was when we were hailed by the voice of Zambo, and, going to the edge of the plateau, saw him sitting grinning at us upon the top of the opposite pinnacle.

"All well, Massa Challenger, all well!" he cried. "Me stay here. No fear. You always find me when you want."

His honest black face, and the immense view before us, which carried us half-way back to the affluent of the Amazon, helped us to remember that we really were upon this earth in the twentieth century, and had not by some magic been conveyed to some raw planet in its earliest and wildest state. How difficult it was to realize that the violet line upon the far horizon was well advanced to that great river upon which huge steamers ran, and folk talked of the small affairs of life, while we, marooned among the creatures of a bygone age, could but gaze towards it and yearn for all that it meant!

One other memory remains with me of this wonderful day, and with it I will close this letter. The two professors, their tempers aggravated no doubt by their injuries, had fallen out as to whether our assailants were of the genus pterodactylus or dimorphodon, and high words had ensued. To avoid their wrangling I moved some little way apart, and was seated smoking upon the trunk of a fallen tree, when Lord John strolled over in my direction.

"I say, Malone," said he, "do you remember that place where those beasts were?"

"Very clearly."

"A sort of volcanic pit, was it not?"

"Exactly," said I.

"Did you notice the soil?"

"Rocks."

"But round the water—where the reeds were?"

"It was a bluish soil. It looked like clay."

"Exactly. A volcanic tube full of blue clay."

"What of that?" I asked.

"Oh, nothing, nothing," said he, and strolled back to where the voices of the contending men of science rose in a prolonged duet, the high, strident note of Summerlee rising and falling to the sonorous bass of Challenger. I should have thought no more of Lord John's remark were it not that once again that night I heard him mutter to himself: "Blue clay—clay in a volcanic tube!" They were the last words I heard before I dropped into an exhausted sleep.

11

"For once I was the Hero"

Lord John Roxton was right when he thought that some specially toxic quality might lie in the bite of the horrible creatures which had attacked us. On the morning after our first adventure upon the plateau, both Summerlee and I were in great pain and fever, while Challenger's knee was so bruised that he could hardly limp. We kept to our camp all day, therefore, Lord John busying himself, with such help as we could give him, in raising the height and thickness of the thorny walls which were our only defense. I remember that during the whole long day I was haunted by the feeling that we were closely observed, though by whom or whence I could give no guess.

So strong was the impression that I told Professor Challenger of it, who put it down to the cerebral excitement caused by my fever. Again and again I glanced round swiftly, with the conviction that I was about to see something, but only to meet the dark tangle of our hedge or the solemn and cavernous gloom of the great trees which arched above our heads. And yet the feeling grew ever stronger in my own mind that something observant and something malevolent was at our very elbow. I thought of the Indian superstition of the Curupuri—the dreadful, lurking spirit of the woods—and I could have imagined that his terrible presence haunted those who had invaded his most remote and sacred retreat.

That night (our third in Maple White Land) we had an experience which left a fearful impression upon our minds, and made us thankful that Lord John had worked so hard in making our retreat impregnable. We were all sleeping round our dying fire when we

were aroused—or, rather, I should say, shot out of our slumbers—
by a succession of the most frightful cries and screams to which I
have ever listened. I know no sound to which I could compare this
amazing tumult, which seemed to come from some spot within a
few hundred yards of our camp. It was as ear-splitting as any
whistle of a railway-engine; but whereas the whistle is a clear,
mechanical, sharp-edged sound, this was far deeper in volume and
vibrant with the uttermost strain of agony and horror. We clapped
our hands to our ears to shut out that nerve-shaking appeal. A cold
sweat broke out over my body, and my heart turned sick at the
misery of it. All the woes of tortured life, all its stupendous indict-
ment of high heaven, its innumerable sorrows, seemed to be centered and condensed into that one dreadful, agonized cry. And then,
under this high-pitched, ringing sound there was another, more
intermittent, a low, deep-chested laugh, a growling, throaty gurgle
of merriment which formed a grotesque accompaniment to the
shriek with which it was blended. For three or four minutes on
end the fearsome duet continued, while all the foliage rustled with
the rising of startled birds. Then it shut off as suddenly as it began.

For a long time we sat in horrified silence. Then Lord John
threw a bundle of twigs upon the fire, and their red glare lit up the
intent faces of my companions and flickered over the great boughs
above our heads.

"What was it?" I whispered.

"We shall know in the morning," said Lord John. "It was close
to us—not farther than the glade."

"We have been privileged to overhear a prehistoric tragedy, the
sort of drama which occurred among the reeds upon the border of
some Jurassic lagoon, when the greater dragon pinned the lesser
among the slime," said Challenger, with more solemnity than I had
ever heard in his voice. "It was surely well for man that he came
late in the order of creation. There were powers abroad in earlier
days which no courage and no mechanism of his could have met.
What could his sling, his throwing-stick, or his arrow avail him
against such forces as have been loose to-night? Even with a modern rifle it would be all odds on the monster."

"I think I should back my little friend," said Lord John, caressing his Express. "But the beast would certainly have a good sporting chance."

Summerlee raised his hand.

"Hush!" he cried. "Surely I hear something?"

From the utter silence there emerged a deep, regular pat-pat. It was the tread of some animal—the rhythm of soft but heavy pads placed cautiously upon the ground. It stole slowly round the camp, and then halted near our gateway. There was a low, sibilant rise and fall—the breathing of the creature. Only our feeble hedge separated us from this horror of the night. Each of us had seized his rifle, and Lord John had pulled out a small bush to make an embrasure in the hedge.

"By George!" he whispered. "I think I can see it!"

I stooped and peered over his shoulder through the gap. Yes, I could see it, too. In the deep shadow of the tree there was a deeper shadow yet, black, inchoate, vague—a crouching form full of savage vigor and menace. It was no higher than a horse, but the dim outline suggested vast bulk and strength. That hissing pant, as regular and full-volumed as the exhaust of an engine, spoke of a monstrous organism. Once, as it moved, I thought I saw the glint of two terrible, greenish eyes. There was an uneasy rustling, as if it were crawling slowly forward.

"I believe it is going to spring!" said I, cocking my rifle.

"Don't fire! Don't fire!" whispered Lord John. "The crash of a gun in this silent night would be heard for miles. Keep it as a last card."

"If it gets over the hedge we're done," said Summerlee, and his voice crackled into a nervous laugh as he spoke.

"No, it must not get over," cried Lord John; "but hold your fire to the last. Perhaps I can make something of the fellow. I'll chance it, anyhow."

It was as brave an act as ever I saw a man do. He stooped to the fire, picked up a blazing branch, and slipped in an instant through a sallyport which he had made in our gateway. The thing moved forward with a dreadful snarl. Lord John never hesitated, but, running towards it with a quick, light step, he dashed the flaming wood into the brute's face. For one moment I had a vision of a horrible mask like a giant toad's, of a warty, leprous skin, and of a loose mouth all beslobbered with fresh blood. The next, there was a crash in the underwood and our dreadful visitor was gone.

"I thought he wouldn't face the fire," said Lord John, laughing, as he came back and threw his branch among the faggots.

"You should not have taken such a risk!" we all cried.

"There was nothin' else to be done. If he had got among us we should have shot each other in tryin' to down him. On the other hand, if we had fired through the hedge and wounded him he would soon have been on the top of us—to say nothin' of giving ourselves away. On the whole, I think that we are jolly well out of it. What was he, then?"

Our learned men looked at each other with some hesitation.

"Personally, I am unable to classify the creature with any certainty," said Summerlee, lighting his pipe from the fire.

"In refusing to commit yourself you are but showing a proper scientific reserve," said Challenger, with massive condescension. "I am not myself prepared to go farther than to say in general terms that we have almost certainly been in contact to-night with some form of carnivorous dinosaur. I have already expressed my anticipation that something of the sort might exist upon this plateau."

"We have to bear in mind," remarked Summerlee, "that there are many prehistoric forms which have never come down to us. It would be rash to suppose that we can give a name to all that we are likely to meet."

"Exactly. A rough classification may be the best that we can attempt. To-morrow some further evidence may help us to an identification. Meantime we can only renew our interrupted slumbers."

"But not without a sentinel," said Lord John, with decision. "We can't afford to take chances in a country like this. Two-hour spells in the future, for each of us."

"Then I'll just finish my pipe in starting the first one," said Professor Summerlee; and from that time onwards we never trusted ourselves again without a watchman.

In the morning it was not long before we discovered the source of the hideous uproar which had aroused us in the night. The iguanodon glade was the scene of a horrible butchery. From the pools of blood and the enormous lumps of flesh scattered in every direction over the green sward we imagined at first that a number of animals had been killed, but on examining the remains more closely we discovered that all this carnage came from one of these unwieldy monsters, which had been literally torn to pieces by some creature not larger, perhaps, but far more ferocious, than itself.

Our two professors sat in absorbed argument, examining piece after piece, which showed the marks of savage teeth and of enormous claws.

"Our judgment must still be in abeyance," said Professor Challenger, with a huge slab of whitish-colored flesh across his knee. "The indications would be consistent with the presence of a saber-toothed tiger, such as are still found among the breccia of our caverns; but the creature actually seen was undoubtedly of a larger and more reptilian character. Personally, I should pronounce for allosaurus."

"Or megalosaurus," said Summerlee.

"Exactly. Any one of the larger carnivorous dinosaurs would meet the case. Among them are to be found all the most terrible types of animal life that have ever cursed the earth or blessed a museum." He laughed sonorously at his own conceit, for, though he had little sense of humor, the crudest pleasantry from his own lips moved him always to roars of appreciation.

"The less noise the better," said Lord Roxton, curtly. "We don't know who or what may be near us. If this fellah comes back for his breakfast and catches us here we won't have so much to laugh at. By the way, what is this mark upon the iguanodon's hide?"

On the dull, scaly, slate-colored skin somewhere above the shoulder, there was a singular black circle of some substance which looked like asphalt. None of us could suggest what it meant, though Summerlee was of opinion that he had seen something similar upon one of the young ones two days before. Challenger said nothing, but looked pompous and puffy, as if he could if he would, so that finally Lord John asked his opinion direct.

"If your lordship will graciously permit me to open my mouth, I shall be happy to express my sentiments," said he, with elaborate sarcasm. "I am not in the habit of being taken to task in the fashion which seems to be customary with your lordship. I was not aware that it was necessary to ask your permission before smiling at a harmless pleasantry."

It was not until he had received his apology that our touchy friend would suffer himself to be appeased. When at last his ruffled feelings were at ease, he addressed us at some length from his seat upon a fallen tree, speaking, as his habit was, as if he were imparting most precious information to a class of a thousand.

"With regard to the marking," said he, "I am inclined to agree with my friend and colleague, Professor Summerlee, that the stains are from asphalt. As this plateau is, in its very nature, highly volcanic, and as asphalt is a substance which one associates with Plutonic forces, I cannot doubt that it exists in the free liquid state, and that the creatures may have come in contact with it. A much more important problem is the question as to the existence of the carnivorous monster which has left its traces in this glade. We know roughly that this plateau is not larger than an average English county. Within this confined space a certain number of creatures, mostly types which have passed away in the world below, have lived together for innumerable years. Now, it is very clear to me that in so long a period one would have expected that the carnivorous creatures, multiplying unchecked, would have exhausted their food supply and have been compelled to either modify their flesh-eating habits or die of hunger. This we see has not been so. We can only imagine, therefore, that the balance of Nature is preserved by some check which limits the numbers of these ferocious creatures. One of the many interesting problems, therefore, which await our solution is to discover what that check may be and how it operates. I venture to trust that we may have some future opportunity for the closer study of the carnivorous dinosaurs."

"And I venture to trust we may not," I observed.

The Professor only raised his great eyebrows, as the schoolmaster meets the irrelevant observation of the naughty boy.

"Perhaps Professor Summerlee may have an observation to make," he said, and the two savants ascended together into some rarefied scientific atmosphere, where the possibilities of a modification of the birth-rate were weighed against the decline of the food supply as a check in the struggle for existence.

That morning we mapped out a small portion of the plateau, avoiding the swamp of the pterodactyls, and keeping to the east of our brook instead of to the west. In that direction the country was still thickly wooded, with so much undergrowth that our progress was very slow.

I have dwelt up to now upon the terrors of Maple White Land; but there was another side to the subject, for all that morning we wandered among lovely flowers—mostly, as I observed, white or yellow in color, these being, as our professors explained, the primitive flower-shades. In many places the ground was absolutely covered with them, and as we walked ankle-deep on that wonderful yielding carpet, the scent was almost intoxicating in its sweetness and intensity. The homely English bee buzzed everywhere around us. Many of the trees under which we passed had their branches bowed down with fruit, some of which were of familiar sorts, while other varieties were new. By observing which of them were pecked by the birds we avoided all danger of poison and added a delicious variety to our food reserve.

In the jungle which we traversed were numerous hard-trodden paths made by the wild beasts, and in the more marshy places we saw a profusion of strange footmarks, including many of the iguanodon. Once in a grove we observed several of these great creatures grazing, and Lord John, with his glass, was able to report that they also were spotted with asphalt, though in a different place to the one which we had examined in the morning. What this phenomenon meant we could not imagine.

We saw many small animals, such as porcupines, a scaly anteater, and a wild pig, piebald in color and with long curved tusks. Once, through a break in the trees, we saw a clear shoulder of green hill some distance away, and across this a large dun-colored animal was traveling at a considerable pace. It passed so swiftly that we were unable to say what it was; but if it were a deer, as was claimed by Lord John, it must have been as large as those monstrous Irish elk which are still dug up from time to time in the bogs of my native land.

Ever since the mysterious visit which had been paid to our camp we always returned to it with some misgivings. However, on this occasion we found everything in order.

That evening we had a grand discussion upon our present situation and future plans, which I must describe at some length, as it led to a new departure by which we were enabled to gain a more complete knowledge of Maple White Land than might have come in many weeks of exploring. It was Summerlee who opened the debate. All day he had been querulous in manner, and now some remark of Lord John's as to what we should do on the morrow brought all his bitterness to a head.

"What we ought to be doing to-day, to-morrow, and all the time," said he, "is finding some way out of the trap into which we have fallen. You are all turning your brains towards getting into this country. I say that we should be scheming how to get out of it."

"I am surprised, sir," boomed Challenger, stroking his majestic beard, "that any man of science should commit himself to so ignoble a sentiment. You are in a land which offers such an inducement to the ambitious naturalist as none ever has since the world began, and you suggest leaving it before we have acquired more than the most superficial knowledge of it or of its contents. I expected better things of you, Professor Summerlee."

"You must remember," said Summerlee, sourly, "that I have a large class in London who are at present at the mercy of an extremely inefficient *locum tenens*. This makes my situation different from yours, Professor Challenger, since, so far as I know, you have never been entrusted with any responsible educational work."

"Quite so," said Challenger. "I have felt it to be a sacrilege to divert a brain which is capable of the highest original research to any lesser object. That is why I have sternly set my face against any proffered scholastic appointment."

"For example?" asked Summerlee, with a sneer; but Lord John hastened to change the conversation.

"I must say," said he, "that I think it would be a mighty poor thing to go back to London before I know a great deal more of this place than I do at present."

"I could never dare to walk into the back office of my paper and face old McArdle," said I. (You will excuse the frankness of this report, will you not, sir?) "He'd never forgive me for leaving such unexhausted copy behind me. Besides, so far as I can see it is not worth discussing, since we can't get down, even if we wanted."

"Our young friend makes up for many obvious mental lacunae by some measure of primitive common sense," remarked Challenger. "The interests of his deplorable profession are immaterial to us; but, as he observes, we cannot get down in any case, so it is a waste of energy to discuss it."

"It is a waste of energy to do anything else," growled Summerlee from behind his pipe. "Let me remind you that we came here upon a perfectly definite mission, entrusted to us at the meeting of the Zoological Institute in London. That mission was to test the truth of Professor Challenger's statements. Those statements, as I am bound to admit, we are now in a position to endorse. Our ostensible work is therefore done. As to the detail which remains to be worked out upon this plateau, it is so enormous that only a large expedition, with a very special equipment, could hope to cope with it. Should we attempt to do so ourselves, the only possible result must be that we shall never return with the important contribution to science which we have already gained. Professor Challenger has devised means for getting us on to this plateau when it appeared to be inaccessible; I think that we should now call upon him to use the same ingenuity in getting us back to the world from which we came."

I confess that as Summerlee stated his view it struck me as altogether reasonable. Even Challenger was affected by the consideration that his enemies would never stand confuted if the confirmation of his statements should never reach those who had doubted them.

"The problem of the descent is at first sight a formidable one," said he, "and yet I cannot doubt that the intellect can solve it. I am prepared to agree with our colleague that a protracted stay in Maple White Land is at present inadvisable, and that the question of our return will soon have to be faced. I absolutely refuse to leave, however, until we have made at least a superficial examination of this country, and are able to take back with us something in the nature of a chart."

Professor Summerlee gave a snort of impatience.

"We have spent two long days in exploration," said he, "and we are no wiser as to the actual geography of the place than when we started. It is clear that it is all thickly wooded, and it would take months to penetrate it and to learn the relations of one part to another. If there were some central peak it would be different, but it all slopes downwards, so far as we can see. The farther we go the less likely it is that we will get any general view."

It was at that moment that I had my inspiration. My eyes chanced to light upon the enormous gnarled trunk of the gingko tree which cast its huge branches over us. Surely, if its bole exceeded that of all others, its height must do the same. If the rim of the plateau was indeed the highest point, then why should this mighty tree not prove to be a watchtower which commanded the whole country? Now, ever since I ran wild as a lad in Ireland I have been a bold and skilled tree-climber. My comrades might be my masters on the rocks, but I knew that I would be supreme among those branches. Could I only get my legs on to the lowest of the giant off-shoots, then it would be strange indeed if I could not make my way to the top. My comrades were delighted at my idea.

"Our young friend," said Challenger, bunching up the red apples of his cheeks, "is capable of acrobatic exertions which would be impossible to a man of a more solid, though possibly of a more commanding, appearance. I applaud his resolution."

"By George, young fellah, you've put your hand on it!" said Lord John, clapping me on the back. "How we never came to think of it before I can't imagine! There's not more than an hour of daylight left, but if you take your notebook you may be able to get some rough sketch of the place. If we put these three ammunition cases under the branch, I will soon hoist you on to it."

He stood on the boxes while I faced the trunk, and was gently raising me when Challenger sprang forward and gave me such a thrust with his huge hand that he fairly shot me into the tree. With both arms clasping the branch, I scrambled hard with my feet until I had worked, first my body, and then my knees, onto it. There were three excellent off-shoots, like huge rungs of a ladder, above my head, and a tangle of convenient branches beyond, so that I clambered onwards with such speed that I soon lost sight of the ground and had nothing but foliage beneath me. Now and then I encountered a check, and once I had to shin up a creeper for eight or ten feet, but I made excellent progress, and the booming of Challenger's voice seemed to be a great distance beneath me. The tree was, however, enormous, and, looking upwards, I could see no thinning of the leaves above my head. There was some thick, bush-like clump which seemed to be a parasite upon a branch up which I was swarming. I leaned my head round it in order to see what was beyond, and I nearly fell out of the tree in my surprise and horror at what I saw.

A face was gazing into mine—at the distance of only a foot or two. The creature that owned it had been crouching behind the parasite, and had looked round it at the same instant that I did. It was a human face—or at least it was far more human than any monkey's that I have ever seen. It was long, whitish, and blotched with pimples, the nose flattened, and the lower jaw projecting, with a bristle of coarse whiskers round the chin. The eyes, which were under thick and heavy brows, were bestial and ferocious, and as it opened its mouth to snarl what sounded like a curse at me I observed that it had curved, sharp canine teeth. For an instant I read hatred and menace in the evil eyes. Then, as quick as a flash, came an expression of overpowering fear. There was a crash of broken boughs as it dived wildly down into the tangle of green. I caught a glimpse of a hairy body like that of a reddish pig, and then it was gone amid a swirl of leaves and branches.

"What's the matter?" shouted Roxton from below. "Anything wrong with you?"

"Did you see it?" I cried, with my arms round the branch and all my nerves tingling.

"We heard a row, as if your foot had slipped. What was it?"

I was so shocked at the sudden and strange appearance of this ape-man that I hesitated whether I should not climb down again and tell my experience to my companions. But I was already so far up the great tree that it seemed a humiliation to return without having carried out my mission.

After a long pause, therefore, to recover my breath and my courage, I continued my ascent. Once I put my weight upon a rotten
branch and swung for a few seconds by my hands, but in the main
it was all easy climbing. Gradually the leaves thinned around me,
and I was aware, from the wind upon my face, that I had topped all
the trees of the forest. I was determined, however, not to look about
me before I had reached the very highest point, so I scrambled on
until I had got so far that the topmost branch was bending beneath
my weight. There I settled into a convenient fork, and, balancing
myself securely, I found myself looking down at a most wonderful
panorama of this strange country in which we found ourselves.

The sun was just above the western sky-line, and the evening
was a particularly bright and clear one, so that the whole extent of
the plateau was visible beneath me. It was, as seen from this height,
of an oval contour, with a breadth of about thirty miles and a width
of twenty. Its general shape was that of a shallow funnel, all the
sides sloping down to a considerable lake in the center. This lake
may have been ten miles in circumference, and lay very green and
beautiful in the evening light, with a thick fringe of reeds at its
edges, and with its surface broken by several yellow sandbanks,
which gleamed golden in the mellow sunshine. A number of long
dark objects, which were too large for alligators and too long for
canoes, lay upon the edges of these patches of sand. With my glass
I could clearly see that they were alive, but what their nature might
be I could not imagine.

From the side of the plateau on which we were, slopes of wood-
land, with occasional glades, stretched down for five or six miles
to the central lake. I could see at my very feet the glade of the iguanodons, and farther off was a round opening in the trees which
marked the swamp of the pterodactyls. On the side facing me, however, the plateau presented a very different aspect. There the basalt cliffs of the outside were reproduced upon the inside, forming
an escarpment about two hundred feet high, with a woody slope
beneath it. Along the base of these red cliffs, some distance above
the ground, I could see a number of dark holes through the glass,
which I conjectured to be the mouths of caves. At the opening of
one of these something white was shimmering, but I was unable to

make out what it was. I sat charting the country until the sun had set and it was so dark that I could no longer distinguish details. Then I climbed down to my companions waiting for me so eagerly at the bottom of the great tree. For once I was the hero of the expedition. Alone I had thought of it, and alone I had done it; and here was the chart which would save us a month's blind groping among unknown dangers. Each of them shook me solemnly by the hand.

But before they discussed the details of my map I had to tell them of my encounter with the ape-man among the branches.

"He has been there all the time," said I.

"How do you know that?" asked Lord John.

"Because I have never been without that feeling that something malevolent was watching us. I mentioned it to you, Professor Challenger."

"Our young friend certainly said something of the kind. He is also the one among us who is endowed with that Celtic temperament which would make him sensitive to such impressions."

"The whole theory of telepathy—" began Summerlee, filling his pipe.

"Is too vast to be now discussed," said Challenger, with decision. "Tell me, now," he added, with the air of a bishop addressing a Sunday-school, "did you happen to observe whether the creature could cross its thumb over its palm?"

"No, indeed."

"Had it a tail?"

"No."

"Was the foot prehensile?"

"I do not think it could have made off so fast among the branches if it could not get a grip with its feet."

"In South America there are, if my memory serves me—you will check the observation, Professor Summerlee—some thirty-six species of monkeys, but the anthropoid ape is unknown. It is clear, however, that he exists in this country, and that he is not the hairy, gorilla-like variety, which is never seen out of Africa or the East." (I was inclined to interpolate, as I looked at him, that I had seen his first cousin in Kensington.) "This is a whiskered and colorless type, the latter characteristic pointing to the fact that he spends his days in arboreal seclusion. The question which we have to face is whether he approaches more closely to the ape or the man. In the latter case, he may well approximate to what the vulgar have called the 'missing link.' The solution of this problem is our immediate duty."

"It is nothing of the sort," said Summerlee, abruptly. "Now that, through the intelligence and activity of Mr. Malone" (I cannot help quoting the words), "we have got our chart, our one and only immediate duty is to get ourselves safe and sound out of this awful place."

"The flesh-pots of civilization," groaned Challenger.

"The ink-pots of civilization, sir. It is our task to put on record what we have seen, and to leave the further exploration to others. You all agreed as much before Mr. Malone got us the chart."

"Well," said Challenger, "I admit that my mind will be more at ease when I am assured that the result of our expedition has been conveyed to our friends. How we are to get down from this place I have not as yet an idea. I have never yet encountered any problem, however, which my inventive brain was unable to solve, and I promise you that to-morrow I will turn my attention to the question of our descent." And so the matter was allowed to rest.

But that evening, by the light of the fire and of a single candle, the first map of the lost world was elaborated. Every detail which I had roughly noted from my watch-tower was drawn out in its relative place. Challenger's pencil hovered over the great blank which marked the lake.

"What shall we call it?" he asked.

"Why should you not take the chance of perpetuating your own name?" said Summerlee, with his usual touch of acidity.

"I trust, sir, that my name will have other and more personal claims upon posterity," said Challenger, severely. "Any ignoramus can hand down his worthless memory by imposing it upon a mountain or a river. I need no such monument."

Summerlee, with a twisted smile, was about to make some fresh assault when Lord John hastened to intervene.

"It's up to you, young fellah, to name the lake," said he. "You saw it first, and, by George, if you choose to put 'Lake Malone' on it, no one has a better right."

"By all means. Let our young friend give it a name," said Challenger.

"Then," said I, blushing, I dare say, as I said it, "let it be named Lake Gladys."

"Don't you think the Central Lake would be more descriptive?" remarked Summerlee.

"I should prefer Lake Gladys."

Challenger looked at me sympathetically, and shook his great head in mock disapproval. "Boys will be boys," said he. "Lake Gladys let it be."

12

"It was Dreadful in the Forest"

I have said—or perhaps I have not said, for my memory plays me sad tricks these days—that I glowed with pride when three such men as my comrades thanked me for having saved, or at least greatly helped, the situation. As the youngster of the party, not merely in years, but in experience, character, knowledge, and all that goes to make a man, I had been overshadowed from the first. And now I was coming into my own. I warmed at the thought. Alas! for the pride which goes before a fall! That little glow of self-satisfaction, that added measure of self-confidence, were to lead me on that very night to the most dreadful experience of my life, ending with a shock which turns my heart sick when I think of it.

It came about in this way. I had been unduly excited by the adventure of the tree, and sleep seemed to be impossible. Summerlee was on guard, sitting hunched over our small fire, a quaint, angular figure, his rifle across his knees and his pointed, goat-like beard wagging with each weary nod of his head. Lord John lay silent, wrapped in the South American poncho which he wore, while Challenger snored with a roll and rattle which reverberated through the woods. The full moon was shining brightly, and the air was crisply cold. What a night for a walk! And then suddenly came the thought, "Why not?" Suppose I stole softly away, suppose I made my way down to the central lake, suppose I was back at breakfast with some record of the place—would I not in that case be thought an even more worthy associate? Then, if Summerlee carried the day and some means of escape were found, we should return to London with first-hand knowledge of the central mystery of the plateau, to which I alone, of all men, would have penetrated. I thought of Gladys, with her "There are heroisms all round us." I seemed to hear her voice as she said it. I thought also of McArdle. What a three column article for the paper! What a foundation for a career! A correspondentship in the next great war might be within my reach. I clutched at a gun—my pockets were full of cartridges—and, parting the thorn bushes at the gate of our *zareba*, quickly slipped out. My last glance showed me the unconscious Summerlee, most futile of sentinels, still nodding away like a queer mechanical toy in front of the smouldering fire.

I had not gone a hundred yards before I deeply repented my rashness. I may have said somewhere in this chronicle that I am too imaginative to be a really courageous man, but that I have an overpowering fear of seeming afraid. This was the power which now carried me onwards. I simply could not slink back with nothing done. Even if my comrades should not have missed me, and should never know of my weakness, there would still remain some intolerable self-shame in my own soul. And yet I shuddered at the position in which I found myself, and would have given all I possessed at that moment to have been honorably free of the whole business.

It was dreadful in the forest. The trees grew so thickly and their foliage spread so widely that I could see nothing of the moon-light save that here and there the high branches made a tangled filigree against the starry sky. As the eyes became more used to the obscurity one learned that there were different degrees of darkness among the trees—that some were dimly visible, while between and among them there were coal-black shadowed patches, like the mouths of caves, from which I shrank in horror as I passed. I thought of the despairing yell of the tortured iguanodon—that dreadful cry which had echoed through the woods. I thought, too, of the glimpse I had in the light of Lord John's torch of that bloated, warty, blood-slavering muzzle. Even now I was on its hunting-ground. At any instant it might spring upon me from the shadows—this nameless and horrible monster. I stopped, and, picking a cartridge from my pocket, I opened the breech of my gun. As I touched the lever my heart leaped within me. It was the shot-gun, not the rifle, which I had taken!

Again the impulse to return swept over me. Here, surely, was a most excellent reason for my failure—one for which no one would think the less of me. But again the foolish pride fought against that very word. I could not—must not—fail. After all, my rifle would probably have been as useless as a shot-gun against such dangers as I might meet. If I were to go back to camp to change my weapon I could hardly expect to enter and to leave again without being seen. In that case there would be explanations, and my attempt would no longer be all my own. After a little hesitation, then, I screwed up my courage and continued upon my way, my useless gun under my arm.

The darkness of the forest had been alarming, but even worse was the white, still flood of moonlight in the open glade of the iguanodons. Hid among the bushes, I looked out at it. None of the great brutes were in sight. Perhaps the tragedy which had befallen one of them had driven them from their feeding-ground. In the misty, silvery night I could see no sign of any living thing. Taking courage, therefore, I slipped rapidly across it, and among the jungle on the farther side I picked up once again the brook which was my guide. It was a cheery companion, gurgling and chuckling as it ran, like the dear old trout-stream in the West Country where I have fished at night in my boyhood. So long as I followed it down I must come to the lake, and so long as I followed it back I must come to the camp. Often I had to lose sight of it on account of the tangled brush-wood, but I was always within earshot of its tinkle and splash.

As one descended the slope the woods became thinner, and bushes, with occasional high trees, took the place of the forest. I could make good progress, therefore, and I could see without being seen. I passed close to the pterodactyl swamp, and as I did so, with a dry, crisp, leathery rattle of wings, one of these great creatures— it was twenty feet at least from tip to tip—rose up from somewhere near me and soared into the air. As it passed across the face of the moon the light shone clearly through the membranous wings, and it looked like a flying skeleton against the white, tropical radiance. I crouched low among the bushes, for I knew from past experience that with a single cry the creature could bring a hundred of its loathsome mates about my ears. It was not until it had settled again that I dared to steal onwards upon my journey.

The night had been exceedingly still, but as I advanced I became conscious of a low, rumbling sound, a continuous murmur, somewhere in front of me. This grew louder as I proceeded, until at last it was clearly quite close to me. When I stood still the sound was constant, so that it seemed to come from some stationary cause. It was like a boiling kettle or the bubbling of some great pot. Soon I came upon the source of it, for in the center of a small clearing I found a lake—or a pool, rather, for it was not larger than the basin of the Trafalgar Square fountain—of some black, pitch-like stuff, the surface of which rose and fell in great blisters of bursting gas. The air above it was shimmering with heat, and the ground round was so hot that I could hardly bear to lay my hand on it. It was clear that the great volcanic outburst which had raised this strange plateau so many years ago had not yet entirely spent its forces. Blackened rocks and mounds of lava I had already seen everywhere peeping out from amid the luxuriant vegetation which draped them, but this asphalt pool in the jungle was the first sign that we had of actual existing activity on the slopes of the ancient crater. I had no time to examine it further for I had need to hurry if I were to be back in camp in the morning.

It was a fearsome walk, and one which will be with me so long as memory holds. In the great moonlight clearings I slunk along among the shadows on the margin. In the jungle I crept forward, stopping with a beating heart whenever I heard, as I often did, the crash of breaking branches as some wild beast went past. Now and then great shadows loomed up for an instant and were gone—great, silent shadows which seemed to prowl upon padded feet. How often I stopped with the intention of returning, and yet every time my pride conquered my fear, and sent me on again until my object should be attained.

At last (my watch showed that it was one in the morning) I saw the gleam of water amid the openings of the jungle, and ten minutes later I was among the reeds upon the borders of the central lake. I was exceedingly dry, so I lay down and took a long draught of its waters, which were fresh and cold. There was a broad pathway with many tracks upon it at the spot which I had found, so that it was clearly one of the drinking-places of the animals. Close to the water's edge there was a huge isolated block of lava. Up this I climbed, and, lying on the top, I had an excellent view in every direction.

The first thing which I saw filled me with amazement. When I described the view from the summit of the great tree, I said that on the farther cliff I could see a number of dark spots, which appeared to be the mouths of caves. Now, as I looked up at the same cliffs, I saw discs of light in every direction, ruddy, clearly-defined patches, like the port-holes of a liner in the darkness. For a moment I thought it was the lava-glow from some volcanic action; but this could not be so. Any volcanic action would surely be down in the hollow and not high among the rocks. What, then, was the alternative? It was wonderful, and yet it must surely be. These ruddy spots must be the reflection of fires within the caves—fires which could only be lit by the hand of man. There were human beings, then, upon the plateau. How gloriously my expedition was justified! Here was news indeed for us to bear back with us to London!

For a long time I lay and watched these red, quivering blotches of light. I suppose they were ten miles off from me, yet even at that distance one could observe how, from time to time, they twinkled or were obscured as someone passed before them. What would I not have given to be able to crawl up to them, to peep in, and to take back some word to my comrades as to the appearance and character of the race who lived in so strange a place! It was out of the question for the moment, and yet surely we could not leave the plateau until we had some definite knowledge upon the point.

Lake Gladys—my own lake—lay like a sheet of quicksilver before me, with a reflected moon shining brightly in the center of it. It was shallow, for in many places I saw low sandbanks protruding above the water. Everywhere upon the still surface I could see signs of life, sometimes mere rings and ripples in the water, sometimes the gleam of a great silver-sided fish in the air, sometimes the arched, slate-colored back of some passing monster. Once upon a yellow sandbank I saw a creature like a huge swan, with a clumsy body and a high, flexible neck, shuffling about upon the margin. Presently it plunged in, and for some time I could see the arched neck and darting head undulating over the water. Then it dived, and I saw it no more.

My attention was soon drawn away from these distant sights and brought back to what was going on at my very feet. Two creatures like large armadillos had come down to the drinking-place, and were squatting at the edge of the water, their long, flexible tongues like red ribbons shooting in and out as they lapped. A huge deer, with branching horns, a magnificent creature which carried itself like a king, came down with its doe and two fawns and drank beside the armadillos. No such deer exist anywhere else upon earth, for the moose or elks which I have seen would hardly have reached its shoulders. Presently it gave a warning snort, and was off with its family among the reeds, while the armadillos also scuttled for shelter. A new-comer, a most monstrous animal, was coming down the path.

For a moment I wondered where I could have seen that ungainly shape, that arched back with triangular fringes along it, that strange bird-like head held close to the ground. Then it came back, to me. It was the stegosaurus—the very creature which Maple White had preserved in his sketch-book, and which had been the first object which arrested the attention of Challenger! There he was—perhaps the very specimen which the American artist had encountered. The ground shook beneath his tremendous weight, and his gulpings of water resounded through the still night. For five minutes he was so close to my rock that by stretching out my hand I could have touched the hideous waving hackles upon his back. Then he lumbered away and was lost among the boulders.

Looking at my watch, I saw that it was half-past two o'clock, and high time, therefore, that I started upon my homeward journey. There was no difficulty about the direction in which I should return for all along I had kept the little brook upon my left, and it opened into the central lake within a stone's-throw of the boulder upon which I had been lying. I set off, therefore, in high spirits, for I felt that I had done good work and was bringing back a fine budget of news for my companions. Foremost of all, of course, were the sight of the fiery caves and the certainty that some troglodytic race inhabited them. But besides that I could speak from experience of the central lake. I could testify that it was full of strange creatures, and I had seen several land forms of primeval life which we had not before encountered. I reflected as I walked that few men in the world could have spent a stranger night or added more to human knowledge in the course of it.

I was plodding up the slope, turning these thoughts over in my mind, and had reached a point which may have been half-way to home, when my mind was brought back to my own position by a strange noise behind me. It was something between a snore and a growl, low, deep, and exceedingly menacing. Some strange creature was evidently near me, but nothing could be seen, so I hastened more rapidly upon my way. I had traversed half a mile or so when suddenly the sound was repeated, still behind me, but louder and more menacing than before. My heart stood still within me as it flashed across me that the beast, whatever it was, must surely be after *me*. My skin grew cold and my hair rose at the thought. That these monsters should tear each other to pieces was a part of the strange struggle for existence, but that they should turn upon modern man, that they should deliberately track and hunt down the predominant human, was a staggering and fearsome thought. I remembered again the blood-beslobbered face which we had seen in the glare of Lord John's torch, like some horrible vision from the deepest circle of Dante's hell. With my knees shaking beneath me, I stood and glared with starting eyes down the moonlit path which lay behind me. All was quiet as in a dream landscape. Silver clearings and the black patches of the bushes—nothing else could I see. Then from out of the silence, imminent and threatening, there came once more that low, throaty croaking, far louder and closer than before. There could no longer be a doubt. Something was on my trail, and was closing in upon me every minute.

I stood like a man paralyzed, still staring at the ground which I had traversed. Then suddenly I saw it. There was movement among the bushes at the far end of the clearing which I had just traversed. A great dark shadow disengaged itself and hopped out into the clear moonlight. I say "hopped" advisedly, for the beast moved like a kangaroo, springing along in an erect position upon its powerful hind legs, while its front ones were held bent in front of it. It was of enormous size and power, like an erect elephant, but its movements, in spite of its bulk, were exceedingly alert. For a moment, as I saw its shape, I hoped that it was an iguanodon, which I knew to be harmless, but, ignorant as I was, I soon saw that this was a very different creature. Instead of the gentle, deer-shaped head of the great three-toed leaf-eater, this beast had a broad, squat, toad-like face like that which had alarmed us in our camp. His ferocious cry and the horrible energy of his pursuit both assured me that this was surely one of the great flesh-eating dinosaurs, the most terrible beasts which have ever walked this earth. As the huge brute loped along it dropped forward upon its fore-paws and brought its nose to the ground every twenty yards or so. It was smelling out my trail. Sometimes, for an instant, it was at fault. Then it would catch it up again and come bounding swiftly along the path I had taken.

Even now when I think of that nightmare the sweat breaks out upon my brow. What could I do? My useless fowling-piece was in my hand. What help could I get from that? I looked desperately round for some rock or tree, but I was in a bushy jungle with nothing higher than a sapling within sight, while I knew that the creature behind me could tear down an ordinary tree as though it were a reed. My only possible chance lay in flight. I could not move swiftly over the rough, broken ground, but as I looked round me in despair I saw a well-marked, hard-beaten path which ran across in front of me. We had seen several of the sort, the runs of various wild beasts, during our expeditions. Along this I could perhaps hold my own, for I was a fast runner, and in excellent condition. Flinging away my useless gun, I set myself to do such a half-mile as I have never done before or since. My limbs ached, my chest heaved, I felt that my throat would burst for want of air, and yet with that horror behind me I ran and I ran and ran. At last I paused, hardly able to move. For a moment I thought that I had thrown him off. The path lay still behind me. And then suddenly, with a crashing and a rending, a thudding of giant feet and a panting of monster lungs the beast was upon me once more. He was at my very heels. I was lost.

Madman that I was to linger so long before I fled! Up to then he had hunted by scent, and his movement was slow. But he had actually seen me as I started to run. From then onwards he had hunted by sight, for the path showed him where I had gone. Now, as he came round the curve, he was springing in great bounds. The moonlight shone upon his huge projecting eyes, the row of enormous teeth in his open mouth, and the gleaming fringe of claws upon his short, powerful forearms. With a scream of terror I turned and rushed wildly down the path. Behind me the thick, gasping breathing of the creature sounded louder and louder. His heavy footfall was beside me. Every instant I expected to feel his grip upon my back. And then suddenly there came a crash—I was falling through space, and everything beyond was darkness and rest.

As I emerged from my unconsciousness—which could not, I think, have lasted more than a few minutes—I was aware of a most dreadful and penetrating smell. Putting out my hand in the darkness I came upon something which felt like a huge lump of meat, while my other hand closed upon a large bone. Up above me there was a circle of starlit sky, which showed me that I was lying at the bottom of a deep pit. Slowly I staggered to my feet and felt myself all over. I was stiff and sore from head to foot, but there was no limb which would not move, no joint which would not bend. As the circumstances of my fall came back into my confused brain, I looked up in terror, expecting to see that dreadful head silhouetted against the paling sky. There was no sign of the monster, however, nor could I hear any sound from above. I began to walk slowly round, therefore, feeling in every direction to find out what this strange place could be into which I had been so opportunely precipitated.

It was, as I have said, a pit, with sharply-sloping walls and a level bottom about twenty feet across. This bottom was littered with great gobbets of flesh, most of which was in the last state of putridity. The atmosphere was poisonous and horrible. After tripping and stumbling over these lumps of decay, I came suddenly against something hard, and I found that an upright post was firmly fixed in the center of the hollow. It was so high that I could not reach the top of it with my hand, and it appeared to be covered with grease.

Suddenly I remembered that I had a tin box of wax-vestas in my pocket. Striking one of them, I was able at last to form some opinion of this place into which I had fallen. There could be no question as to its nature. It was a trap—made by the hand of man. The post in the center, some nine feet long, was sharpened at the upper end, and was black with the stale blood of the creatures who had been impaled upon it. The remains scattered about were fragments of the victims, which had been cut away in order to clear the stake for the next who might blunder in. I remembered that Challenger had declared that man could not exist upon the plateau, since with his feeble weapons he could not hold his own against the monsters who roamed over it. But now it was clear enough how it could be done. In their narrow-mouthed caves the natives, whoever they might be, had refuges into which the huge saurians could not penetrate, while with their developed brains they were capable of setting such traps, covered with branches, across the paths which marked the run of the animals as would destroy them in spite of all their strength and activity. Man was always the master.

The sloping wall of the pit was not difficult for an active man to climb, but I hesitated long before I trusted myself within reach of the dreadful creature which had so nearly destroyed me. How did I know that he was not lurking in the nearest clump of bushes, waiting for my reappearance? I took heart, however, as I recalled a conversation between Challenger and Summerlee upon the habits of the great saurians. Both were agreed that the monsters were practically brainless, that there was no room for reason in their tiny cranial cavities, and that if they have disappeared from the rest of the world it was assuredly on account of their own stupidity, which made it impossible for them to adapt themselves to changing conditions.

To lie in wait for me now would mean that the creature had appreciated what had happened to me, and this in turn would argue some power connecting cause and effect. Surely it was more likely that a brainless creature, acting solely by vague predatory instinct, would give up the chase when I disappeared, and, after a pause of astonishment, would wander away in search of some other prey? I clambered to the edge of the pit and looked over. The stars were fading, the sky was whitening, and the cold wind of morning blew pleasantly upon my face. I could see or hear nothing of my enemy. Slowly I climbed out and sat for a while upon the ground, ready to spring back into my refuge if any danger should appear. Then, re-assured by the absolute stillness and by the growing light, I took my courage in both hands and stole back along the path which I had come. Some distance down it I picked up my gun, and shortly afterwards struck the brook which was my guide. So, with many a frightened backward glance, I made for home.

And suddenly there came something to remind me of my absent companions. In the clear, still morning air there sounded far away the sharp, hard note of a single rifle-shot. I paused and listened, but there was nothing more. For a moment I was shocked at the thought that some sudden danger might have befallen them. But then a simpler and more natural explanation came to my mind. It was now broad daylight. No doubt my absence had been noticed. They had imagined, that I was lost in the woods, and had fired this shot to guide me home. It is true that we had made a strict resolution against firing, but if it seemed to them that I might be in danger they would not hesitate. It was for me now to hurry on as fast as possible, and so to reassure them.

I was weary and spent, so my progress was not so fast as I wished; but at last I came into regions which I knew. There was the swamp of the pterodactyls upon my left; there in front of me was the glade of the iguanodons. Now I was in the last belt of trees which separated me from Fort Challenger. I raised my voice in a cheery shout to allay their fears. No answering greeting came back to me. My heart sank at that ominous stillness. I quickened my pace into a run. The *zareba* rose before me, even as I had left it, but the gate was open. I rushed in. In the cold, morning light it was a fearful sight which met my eyes. Our effects were scattered in wild confusion over the ground; my comrades had disappeared, and close to the smouldering ashes of our fire the grass was stained crimson with a hideous pool of blood.

I was so stunned by this sudden shock that for a time I must have nearly lost my reason. I have a vague recollection, as one remembers a bad dream, of rushing about through the woods all round the empty camp, calling wildly for my companions. No answer came back from the silent shadows. The horrible thought that I might never see them again, that I might find myself abandoned all alone in that dreadful place, with no possible way of descending into the world below, that I might live and die in that nightmare country, drove me to desperation. I could have torn my hair and beaten my head in my despair. Only now did I realize how I had learned to lean upon my companions, upon the serene self-confidence of Challenger, and upon the masterful, humorous coolness of Lord John Roxton. Without them I was like a child in the dark, helpless and powerless. I did not know which way to turn or what I should do first.

After a period, during which I sat in bewilderment, I set myself to try and discover what sudden misfortune could have befallen my companions. The whole disordered appearance of the camp showed that there had been some sort of attack, and the rifle-shot no doubt marked the time when it had occurred. That there should have been only one shot showed that it had been all over in an instant. The rifles still lay upon the ground, and one of them—Lord John's—had the empty cartridge in the breech. The blankets of Challenger and of Summerlee beside the fire suggested that they had been asleep at the time. The cases of ammunition and of food were scattered about in a wild litter, together with our unfortunate cameras and plate-carriers, but none of them were missing. On the other hand, all the exposed provisions—and I remembered that there were a considerable quantity of them—were gone. They were animals, then, and not natives, who had made the inroad, for surely the latter would have left nothing behind.

But if animals, or some single terrible animal, then what had become of my comrades? A ferocious beast would surely have destroyed them and left their remains. It is true that there was that one hideous pool of blood, which told of violence. Such a monster as had pursued me during the night could have carried away a victim as easily as a cat would a mouse. In that case the others would have followed in pursuit. But then they would assuredly have taken their rifles with them. The more I tried to think it out with my confused and weary brain the less could I find any plausible explanation. I searched round in the forest, but could see no tracks which could help me to a conclusion. Once I lost myself, and it was only by good luck, and after an hour of wandering, that I found the camp once more.

Suddenly a thought came to me and brought some little comfort to my heart. I was not absolutely alone in the world. Down at the bottom of the cliff, and within call of me, was waiting the faithful Zambo. I went to the edge of the plateau and looked over. Sure enough, he was squatting among his blankets beside his fire in his little camp. But, to my amazement, a second man was seated in front of him. For an instant my heart leaped for joy, as I thought that one of my comrades had made his way safely down. But a second glance dispelled the hope. The rising sun shone red upon the man's skin. He was an Indian. I shouted loudly and waved my handkerchief. Presently Zambo looked up, waved his hand, and turned to ascend the pinnacle. In a short time he was standing close to me and listening with deep distress to the story which I told him.

"Devil got them for sure, Massa Malone," said he. "You got into the devil's country, sah, and he take you all to himself. You take advice, Massa Malone, and come down quick, else he get you as well."

"How can I come down, Zambo?"

"You get creepers from trees, Massa Malone. Throw them over here. I make fast to this stump, and so you have bridge."

"We have thought of that. There are no creepers here which could bear us."

"Send for ropes, Massa Malone."

"Who can I send, and where?"

"Send to Indian villages, sah. Plenty hide rope in Indian village. Indian down below; send him."

"Who is he?

"One of our Indians. Other ones beat him and take away his pay. He come back to us. Ready now to take letter, bring rope,—anything."

To take a letter! Why not? Perhaps he might bring help; but in any case he would ensure that our lives were not spent for nothing, and that news of all that we had won for Science should reach our friends at home. I had two completed letters already waiting. I would spend the day in writing a third, which would bring my experiences absolutely up to date. The Indian could bear this back to the world. I ordered Zambo, therefore, to come again in the evening, and I spent my miserable and lonely day in recording my own adventures of the night before. I also drew up a note, to be given to any white merchant or captain of a steam-boat whom the Indian could find, imploring them to see that ropes were sent to us, since our lives must depend upon it. These documents I threw to Zambo in the evening, and also my purse, which contained three English sovereigns. These were to be given to the Indian, and he was promised twice as much if he returned with the ropes.

So now you will understand, my dear Mr. McArdle, how this communication reaches you, and you will also know the truth, in case you never hear again from your unfortunate correspondent. To-night I am too weary and too depressed to make my plans. To-morrow I must think out some way by which I shall keep in touch with this camp, and yet search round for any traces of my unhappy friends.

13

"A Sight Which I Shall Never Forget"

Just as the sun was setting upon that melancholy night I saw the lonely figure of the Indian upon the vast plain beneath me, and I watched him, our one faint hope of salvation, until he disappeared in the rising mists of evening which lay, rose-tinted from the setting sun, between the far-off river and me.

It was quite dark when I at last turned back to our stricken camp, and my last vision as I went was the red gleam of Zambo's fire, the one point of light in the wide world below, as was his faithful presence in my own shadowed soul. And yet I felt happier than I had done since this crushing blow had fallen upon me, for it was good to think that the world should know what we had done, so that at the worst our names should not perish with our bodies, but should go down to posterity associated with the result of our labors.

It was an awesome thing to sleep in that ill-fated camp; and yet it was even more unnerving to do so in the jungle. One or the other it must be. Prudence, on the one hand, warned me that I should remain on guard, but exhausted Nature, on the other, declared that I should do nothing of the kind. I climbed up on to a limb of the great gingko tree, but there was no secure perch on its rounded surface, and I should certainly have fallen off and broken my neck the moment I began to doze. I got down, therefore, and pondered over what I should do. Finally, I closed the door of the zareba, lit three separate fires in a triangle, and having eaten a hearty supper dropped off into a profound sleep, from which I had a strange and most welcome awakening. In the early morning, just as day was breaking, a hand was laid upon my arm, and starting up, with all my nerves in a tingle and my hand feeling for a rifle, I gave a cry of joy as in the cold gray light I saw Lord John Roxton kneeling beside me.

It was he—and yet it was not he. I had left him calm in his bearing, correct in his person, prim in his dress. Now he was pale and wild-eyed, gasping as he breathed like one who has run far and fast. His gaunt face was scratched and bloody, his clothes were hanging in rags, and his hat was gone. I stared in amazement, but he gave me no chance for questions. He was grabbing at our stores all the time he spoke.

"Quick, young fellah! Quick!" he cried. "Every moment counts. Get the rifles, both of them. I have the other two. Now, all the cartridges you can gather. Fill up your pockets. Now, some food. Half a dozen tins will do. That's all right! Don't wait to talk or think. Get a move on, or we are done!"

Still half-awake, and unable to imagine what it all might mean, I found myself hurrying madly after him through the wood, a rifle under each arm and a pile of various stores in my hands. He dodged in and out through the thickest of the scrub until he came to a dense clump of brush-wood. Into this he rushed, regardless of thorns, and threw himself into the heart of it, pulling me down by his side.

"There!" he panted. "I think we are safe here. They'll make for the camp as sure as fate. It will be their first idea. But this should puzzle 'em."

"What is it all?" I asked, when I had got my breath. "Where are the professors? And who is it that is after us?"

"The ape-men," he cried. "My God, what brutes! Don't raise your voice, for they have long ears—sharp eyes, too, but no power of scent, so far as I could judge, so I don't think they can sniff us out. Where have you been, young fellah? You were well out of it."

In a few sentences I whispered what I had done.

"Pretty bad," said he, when he had heard of the dinosaur and the pit. "It isn't quite the place for a rest cure. What? But I had no idea what its possibilities were until those devils got hold of us. The man-eatin' Papuans had me once, but they are Chesterfields compared to this crowd."

"How did it happen?" I asked.

"It was in the early mornin'. Our learned friends were just stirrin'. Hadn't even begun to argue yet. Suddenly it rained apes. They came down as thick as apples out of a tree. They had been assemblin' in the dark, I suppose, until that great tree over our heads was heavy with them. I shot one of them through the belly, but before we knew where we were they had us spread-eagled on our backs. I call them apes, but they carried sticks and stones in their hands and jabbered talk to each other, and ended up by tyin' our hands with creepers, so they are ahead of any beast that I have seen in my wanderin's. Ape-men—that's what they are—Missin' Links, and I wish they had stayed missin'. They carried off their wounded comrade—he was bleedin' like a pig—and then they sat around us, and if ever I saw frozen murder it was in their faces. They were big fellows, as big as a man and a deal stronger. Curious glassy gray eyes they have, under red tufts, and they just sat and gloated and gloated. Challenger is no chicken, but even he was cowed. He managed to struggle to his feet, and yelled out at them to have done with it and get it over. I think he had gone a bit off his head at the suddenness of it, for he raged and cursed at them like a lunatic. If they had been a row of his favorite Pressmen he could not have slanged them worse."

"Well, what did they do?" I was enthralled by the strange story which my companion was whispering into my ear, while all the time his keen eyes were shooting in every direction and his hand grasping his cocked rifle.

"I thought it was the end of us, but instead of that it started them on a new line. They all jabbered and chattered together. Then one of them stood out beside Challenger. You'll smile, young fellah, but 'pon my word they might have been kinsmen. I couldn't have believed it if I hadn't seen it with my own eyes. This old ape-man— he was their chief—was a sort of red Challenger, with every one of our friend's beauty points, only just a trifle more so. He had the short body, the big shoulders, the round chest, no neck, a great ruddy frill of a beard, the tufted eyebrows, the 'What do you want, damn you!' look about the eyes, and the whole catalogue. When the ape-man stood by Challenger and put his paw on his shoulder, the thing was complete. Summerlee was a bit hysterical, and he laughed till he cried. The ape-men laughed too—or at least they put up the devil of a cacklin'—and they set to work to drag us off through the forest. They wouldn't touch the guns and things— thought them dangerous, I expect—but they carried away all our loose food. Summerlee and I got some rough handlin' on the way— there's my skin and my clothes to prove it—for they took us a bee-line through the brambles, and their own hides are like leather. But Challenger was all right. Four of them carried him shoulder high, and he went like a Roman emperor. What's that?"

It was a strange clicking noise in the distance not unlike casta-nets.

"There they go!" said my companion, slipping cartridges into the second double-barrelled "Express." "Load them all up, young fellah my lad, for we're not going to be taken alive, and don't you think it! That's the row they make when they are excited. By George! they'll have something to excite them if they put us up. The 'Last Stand of the Grays' won't be in it. 'With their rifles grasped in their stiffened hands, mid a ring of the dead and dyin',' as some fathead sings. Can you hear them now?"

"Very far away."

"That little lot will do no good, but I expect their search parties are all over the wood. Well, I was telling you my tale of woe. They got us soon to this town of theirs—about a thousand huts of branches and leaves in a great grove of trees near the edge of the cliff. It's three or four miles from here. The filthy beasts fingered me all over, and I feel as if I should never be clean again. They tied us up—the fellow who handled me could tie like a bosun—and there we lay with our toes up, beneath a tree, while a great brute stood guard over us with a club in his hand. When I say 'we' I mean Summerlee and myself. Old Challenger was up a tree, eatin' pines and havin' the time of his life. I'm bound to say that he managed to get some fruit to us, and with his own hands he loosened our bonds. If you'd seen him sitting up in that tree hob-nobbin' with his twin brother—and singin' in that rollin' bass of his, 'Ring out, wild bells,' 'cause music of any kind seemed to put 'em in a good humor, you'd have smiled; but we weren't in much mood for laughin', as you can guess. They were inclined, within limits, to let him do what he liked, but they drew the line pretty sharply at us. It was a mighty consolation to us all to know that you were runnin' loose and had the archives in your keepin'.

"Well, now, young fellah, I'll tell you what will surprise you. You say you saw signs of men, and fires, traps, and the like. Well, we have seen the natives themselves. Poor devils they were, down-faced little chaps, and had enough to make them so. It seems that the humans hold one side of this plateau—over yonder, where you saw the caves—and the ape-men hold this side, and there is bloody war between them all the time. That's the situation, so far as I could follow it. Well, yesterday the ape-men got hold of a dozen of the humans and brought them in as prisoners. You never heard such a jabberin' and shriekin' in your life. The men were little red fellows, and had been bitten and clawed so that they could hardly walk. The ape-men put two of them to death there and then—fairly pulled the arm off one of them—it was perfectly beastly. Plucky little chaps they are, and hardly gave a squeak. But it turned us absolutely sick. Summerlee fainted, and even Challenger had as much as he could stand. I think they have cleared, don't you?"

We listened intently, but nothing save the calling of the birds broke the deep peace of the forest. Lord Roxton went on with his story.

"I think you have had the escape of your life, young fellah my lad. It was catchin' those Indians that put you clean out of their heads, else they would have been back to the camp for you as sure as fate and gathered you in. Of course, as you said, they have been watchin' us from the beginnin' out of that tree, and they knew perfectly well that we were one short. However, they could think only of this new haul; so it was I, and not a bunch of apes, that dropped in on you in the morning. Well, we had a horrid business afterwards. My God! what a nightmare the whole thing is! You remember the great bristle of sharp canes down below where we found the skeleton of the American? Well, that is just under ape-town, and that's the jumpin'-off place of their prisoners. I expect there's heaps of skeletons there, if we looked for 'em. They have a sort of clear parade-ground on the top, and they make a proper ceremony about it. One by one the poor devils have to jump, and the game is to see whether they are merely dashed to pieces or whether they get skewered on the canes. They took us out to see it, and the whole tribe lined up on the edge. Four of the Indians jumped, and the canes went through 'em like knittin' needles through a pat of butter. No wonder we found that poor Yankee's skeleton with the canes growin' between his ribs. It was horrible—but it was doocedly interestin' too. We were all fascinated to see them take the dive, even when we thought it would be our turn next on the spring-board.

"Well, it wasn't. They kept six of the Indians up for to-day—that's how I understood it—but I fancy we were to be the star performers in the show. Challenger might get off, but Summerlee and I were in the bill. Their language is more than half signs, and it was not hard to follow them. So I thought it was time we made a break for it. I had been plottin' it out a bit, and had one or two things clear in my mind. It was all on me, for Summerlee was useless and Challenger not much better. The only time they got together they got slangin' because they couldn't agree upon the scientific classification of these red-headed devils that had got hold of us. One said it was the dryopithecus of Java, the other said it was pithecanthropus. Madness, I call it—Loonies, both. But, as I say, I had thought out one or two points that were helpful. One was that these brutes could not run as fast as a man in the open. They have short, bandy legs, you see, and heavy bodies. Even Challenger could give a few yards in a hundred to the best of them, and you or I would be a perfect Shrubb. Another point was that they knew nothin' about guns. I don't believe they ever understood how the fellow I shot came by his hurt. If we could get at our guns there was no sayin' what we could do.

"So I broke away early this mornin', gave my guard a kick in the tummy that laid him out, and sprinted for the camp. There I got you and the guns, and here we are."

"But the professors!" I cried, in consternation.

"Well, we must just go back and fetch 'em. I couldn't bring 'em with me. Challenger was up the tree, and Summerlee was not fit for the effort. The only chance was to get the guns and try a rescue. Of course they may scupper them at once in revenge. I don't think they would touch Challenger, but I wouldn't answer for Summerlee. But they would have had him in any case. Of that I am certain. So I haven't made matters any worse by boltin'. But we are honor bound to go back and have them out or see it through with them. So you can make up your soul, young fellah my lad, for it will be one way or the other before evenin'."

I have tried to imitate here Lord Roxton's jerky talk, his short, strong sentences, the half-humorous, half-reckless tone that ran through it all. But he was a born leader. As danger thickened his jaunty manner would increase, his speech become more racy, his cold eyes glitter into ardent life, and his Don Quixote moustache bristle with joyous excitement. His love of danger, his intense appreciation of the drama of an adventure—all the more intense for being held tightly in—his consistent view that every peril in life is a form of sport, a fierce game betwixt you and Fate, with Death as a forfeit, made him a wonderful companion at such hours. If it were not for our fears as to the fate of our companions, it would have been a positive joy to throw myself with such a man into such an affair. We were rising from our brushwood hiding-place when suddenly I felt his grip upon my arm.

"By George!" he whispered, "here they come!"

From where we lay we could look down a brown aisle, arched with green, formed by the trunks and branches. Along this a party of the ape-men were passing. They went in single file, with bent legs and rounded backs, their hands occasionally touching the ground, their heads turning to left and right as they trotted along. Their crouching gait took away from their height, but I should put them at five feet or so, with long arms and enormous chests. Many of them carried sticks, and at the distance they looked like a line of very hairy and deformed human beings. For a moment I caught this clear glimpse of them. Then they were lost among the bushes.

"Not this time," said Lord John, who had caught up his rifle. "Our best chance is to lie quiet until they have given up the search. Then we shall see whether we can't get back to their town and hit 'em where it hurts most. Give 'em an hour and we'll march."

We filled in the time by opening one of our food tins and making sure of our breakfast. Lord Roxton had had nothing but some fruit since the morning before and ate like a starving man. Then, at last, our pockets bulging with cartridges and a rifle in each hand, we started off upon our mission of rescue. Before leaving it we carefully marked our little hiding-place among the brush-wood and its bearing to Fort Challenger, that we might find it again if we needed it. We slunk through the bushes in silence until we came to the very edge of the cliff, close to the old camp. There we halted, and Lord John gave me some idea of his plans.

"So long as we are among the thick trees these swine are our masters," said he. "They can see us and we cannot see them. But in the open it is different. There we can move faster than they. So we must stick to the open all we can. The edge of the plateau has fewer large trees than further inland. So that's our line of advance. Go slowly, keep your eyes open and your rifle ready. Above all, never let them get you prisoner while there is a cartridge left—that's my last word to you, young fellah."

When we reached the edge of the cliff I looked over and saw our good old black Zambo sitting smoking on a rock below us. I would have given a great deal to have hailed him and told him how we were placed, but it was too dangerous, lest we should be heard. The woods seemed to be full of the ape-men; again and again we heard their curious clicking chatter. At such times we plunged into the nearest clump of bushes and lay still until the sound had passed away. Our advance, therefore, was very slow, and two hours at least must have passed before I saw by Lord John's cautious movements that we must be close to our destination. He motioned to me to lie still, and he crawled forward himself. In a minute he was back again, his face quivering with eagerness.

"Come!" said he. "Come quick! I hope to the Lord we are not too late already!"

I found myself shaking with nervous excitement as I scrambled forward and lay down beside him, looking out through the bushes at a clearing which stretched before us.

It was a sight which I shall never forget until my dying day—so weird, so impossible, that I do not know how I am to make you realize it, or how in a few years I shall bring myself to believe in it if I live to sit once more on a lounge in the Savage Club and look

out on the drab solidity of the Embankment. I know that it will
seem then to be some wild nightmare, some delirium of fever. Yet
I will set it down now, while it is still fresh in my memory, and one
at least, the man who lay in the damp grasses by my side, will know
if I have lied.

A wide, open space lay before us—some hundreds of yards
across—all green turf and low bracken growing to the very edge of
the cliff. Round this clearing there was a semi-circle of trees with
curious huts built of foliage piled one above the other among the
branches. A rookery, with every nest a little house, would best convey the idea. The openings of these huts and the branches of the
trees were thronged with a dense mob of ape-people, whom from
their size I took to be the females and infants of the tribe. They
formed the background of the picture, and were all looking out with
eager interest at the same scene which fascinated and bewildered
us.

In the open, and near the edge of the cliff, there had assembled
a crowd of some hundred of these shaggy, red-haired creatures,
many of them of immense size, and all of them horrible to look
upon. There was a certain discipline among them, for none of them
attempted to break the line which had been formed. In front there
stood a small group of Indians—little, clean-limbed, red fellows,
whose skins glowed like polished bronze in the strong sunlight. A
tall, thin white man was standing beside them, his head bowed,
his arms folded, his whole attitude expressive of his horror and
dejection. There was no mistaking the angular form of Professor
Summerlee.

In front of and around this dejected group of prisoners were
several ape-men, who watched them closely and made all escape
impossible. Then, right out from all the others and close to the
edge of the cliff, were two figures, so strange, and under other circumstances so ludicrous, that they absorbed my attention. The one
was our comrade, Professor Challenger. The remains of his coat
still hung in strips from his shoulders, but his shirt had been all
torn out, and his great beard merged itself in the black tangle which
covered his mighty chest. He had lost his hat, and his hair, which
had grown long in our wanderings, was flying in wild disorder. A

single day seemed to have changed him from the highest product of modern civilization to the most desperate savage in South America. Beside him stood his master, the king of the ape-men. In all things he was, as Lord John had said, the very image of our Professor, save that his coloring was red instead of black. The same short, broad figure, the same heavy shoulders, the same forward hang of the arms, the same bristling beard merging itself in the hairy chest. Only above the eyebrows, where the sloping forehead and low, curved skull of the ape-man were in sharp contrast to the broad brow and magnificent cranium of the European, could one see any marked difference. At every other point the king was an absurd parody of the Professor.

All this, which takes me so long to describe, impressed itself upon me in a few seconds. Then we had very different things to think of, for an active drama was in progress. Two of the ape-men had seized one of the Indians out of the group and dragged him forward to the edge of the cliff. The king raised his hand as a signal. They caught the man by his leg and arm, and swung him three times backwards and forwards with tremendous violence. Then, with a frightful heave they shot the poor wretch over the precipice. With such force did they throw him that he curved high in the air before beginning to drop. As he vanished from sight, the whole assembly, except the guards, rushed forward to the edge of the precipice, and there was a long pause of absolute silence, broken by a mad yell of delight. They sprang about, tossing their long, hairy arms in the air and howling with exultation. Then they fell back from the edge, formed themselves again into line, and waited for the next victim.

This time it was Summerlee. Two of his guards caught him by the wrists and pulled him brutally to the front..His thin figure and long limbs struggled and fluttered like a chicken being dragged from a coop. Challenger had turned to the king and waved his hands frantically before him. He was begging, pleading, imploring for his comrade's life. The ape-man pushed him roughly aside and shook his head. It was the last conscious movement he was to make upon earth. Lord John's rifle cracked, and the king sank down, a tangled red sprawling thing, upon the ground.

"Shoot into the thick of them! Shoot! sonny, shoot!" cried my companion.

There are strange red depths in the soul of the most common-place man. I am tenderhearted by nature, and have found my eyes moist many a time over the scream of a wounded hare. Yet the blood lust was on me now. I found myself on my feet emptying one magazine, then the other, clicking open the breech to re-load, snap-ping it to again, while cheering and yelling with pure ferocity and joy of slaughter as I did so. With our four guns the two of us made a horrible havoc. Both the guards who held Summerlee were down, and he was staggering about like a drunken man in his amazement, unable to realize that he was a free man. The dense mob of ape-men ran about in bewilderment, marveling whence this storm of death was coming or what it might mean. They waved, gesticulated, screamed, and tripped up over those who had fallen. Then, with a sudden impulse, they all rushed in a howling crowd to the trees for shelter, leaving the ground behind them spotted with their stricken comrades. The prisoners were left for the moment stand-ing alone in the middle of the clearing.

Challenger's quick brain had grasped the situation. He seized the bewildered Summerlee by the arm, and they both ran towards us. Two of their guards bounded after them and fell to two bullets from Lord John. We ran forward into the open to meet our friends, and pressed a loaded rifle into the hands of each. But Summerlee was at the end of his strength. He could hardly totter. Already the ape-men were recovering from their panic. They were coming through the brushwood and threatening to cut us off. Challenger and I ran Summerlee along, one at each of his elbows, while Lord John covered our retreat, firing again and again as savage heads snarled at us out of the bushes. For a mile or more the chattering brutes were at our very heels. Then the pursuit slackened, for they learned our power and would no longer face that unerring rifle. When we had at last reached the camp, we looked back and found ourselves alone.

So it seemed to us; and yet we were mistaken. We had hardly closed the thornbush door of our *zareba*, clasped each other's hands, and thrown ourselves panting upon the ground beside our spring, when we heard a patter of feet and then a gentle, plaintive crying from outside our entrance. Lord Roxton rushed forward, rifle in hand, and threw it open. There, prostrate upon their faces, lay the little red figures of the four surviving Indians, trembling with fear of us and yet imploring our protection. With an expressive sweep of his hands one of them pointed to the woods around them, and indicated that they were full of danger. Then, darting forward, he threw his arms round Lord John's legs, and rested his face upon them.

"By George!" cried our peer, pulling at his moustache in great perplexity, "I say—what the deuce are we to do with these people? Get up, little chappie, and take your face off my boots."

Summerlee was sitting up and stuffing some tobacco into his old briar.

"We've got to see them safe," said he. "You've pulled us all out of the jaws of death. My word! it was a good bit of work!"

"Admirable!" cried Challenger. "Admirable! Not only we as individuals, but European science collectively, owe you a deep debt of gratitude for what you have done. I do not hesitate to say that the disappearance of Professor Summerlee and myself would have left an appreciable gap in modern zoological history. Our young friend here and you have done most excellently well."

He beamed at us with the old paternal smile, but European science would have been somewhat amazed could they have seen their chosen child, the hope of the future, with his tangled, unkempt head, his bare chest, and his tattered clothes. He had one of the meat-tins between his knees, and sat with a large piece of cold Australian mutton between his fingers. The Indian looked up at him, and then, with a little yelp, cringed to the ground and clung to Lord John's leg.

"Don't you be scared, my bonnie boy," said Lord John, patting the matted head in front of him. "He can't stick your appearance, Challenger; and, by George! I don't wonder. All right, little chap, he's only a human, just the same as the rest of us."

"Really, sir!" cried the Professor.

"Well, it's lucky for you, Challenger, that you *are* a little out of the ordinary. If you hadn't been so like the king—"

"Upon my word, Lord John, you allow yourself great latitude."

"Well, it's a fact."

"I beg, sir, that you will change the subject. Your remarks are irrelevant and unintelligible. The question before us is what are we to do with these Indians? The obvious thing is to escort them home, if we knew where their home was."

"There is no difficulty about that," said I. "They live in the caves on the other side of the central lake."

"Our young friend here knows where they live. I gather that it is some distance."

"A good twenty miles," said I.

Summerlee gave a groan.

"I, for one, could never get there. Surely I hear those brutes still howling upon our track."

As he spoke, from the dark recesses of the woods we heard far away the jabbering cry of the ape-men. The Indians once more set up a feeble wail of fear.

"We must move, and move quick!" said Lord John. "You help Summerlee, young fellah. These Indians will carry stores. Now, then, come along before they can see us."

In less than half-an-hour we had reached our brushwood retreat and concealed ourselves. All day we heard the excited calling of the ape-men in the direction of our old camp, but none of them came our way, and the tired fugitives, red and white, had a long, deep sleep. I was dozing myself in the evening when someone plucked my sleeve, and I found Challenger kneeling beside me.

"You keep a diary of these events, and you expect eventually to publish it, Mr. Malone," said he, with solemnity.

"I am only here as a Press reporter," I answered.

"Exactly. You may have heard some rather fatuous remarks of Lord John Roxton's which seemed to imply that there was some—some resemblance—"

"Yes, I heard them."

"I need not say that any publicity given to such an idea—any levity in your narrative of what occurred—would be exceedingly offensive to me."

"I will keep well within the truth."

"Lord John's observations are frequently exceedingly fanciful, and he is capable of attributing the most absurd reasons to the respect which is always shown by the most undeveloped races to dignity and character. You follow my meaning?"

"Entirely."

"I leave the matter to your discretion." Then, after a long pause, he added: "The king of the ape-men was really a creature of great distinction—a most remarkably handsome and intelligent personality. Did it not strike you?"

"A most remarkable creature," said I.

And the Professor, much eased in his mind, settled down to his slumber once more.

14

"Those Were the Real Conquests"

We had imagined that our pursuers, the ape-men, knew nothing of our brush-wood hiding-place, but we were soon to find out our mistake. There was no sound in the woods—not a leaf moved upon the trees, and all was peace around us—but we should have been warned by our first experience how cunningly and how patiently these creatures can watch and wait until their chance comes. Whatever fate may be mine through life, I am very sure that I shall never be nearer death than I was that morning. But I will tell you the thing in its due order.

We all awoke exhausted after the terrific emotions and scanty food of yesterday. Summerlee was still so weak that it was an effort for him to stand; but the old man was full of a sort of surly courage which would never admit defeat. A council was held, and it was agreed that we should wait quietly for an hour or two where we were, have our much-needed breakfast, and then make our way across the plateau and round the central lake to the caves where my observations had shown that the Indians lived. We relied upon the fact that we could count upon the good word of those whom we had rescued to ensure a warm welcome from their fellows. Then, with our mission accomplished and possessing a fuller knowledge of the secrets of Maple White Land, we should turn our whole thoughts to the vital problem of our escape and return. Even Challenger was ready to admit that we should then have done all for which we had come, and that our first duty from that time onwards was to carry back to civilization the amazing discoveries we had made.

We were able now to take a more leisurely view of the Indians whom we had rescued. They were small men, wiry, active, and well-built, with lank black hair tied up in a bunch behind their heads with a leathern thong, and leathern also were their loin-clothes. Their faces were hairless, well formed, and good-humored. The lobes of their ears, hanging ragged and bloody, showed that they had been pierced for some ornaments which their captors had torn out. Their speech, though unintelligible to us, was fluent among themselves, and as they pointed to each other and uttered the word "Accala" many times over, we gathered that this was the name of the nation. Occasionally, with faces which were convulsed with fear and hatred, they shook their clenched hands at the woods round and cried: "Doda! Doda!" which was surely their term for their enemies.

"What do you make of them, Challenger?" asked Lord John. "One thing is very clear to me, and that is that the little chap with the front of his head shaved is a chief among them."

It was indeed evident that this man stood apart from the others, and that they never ventured to address him without every sign of deep respect. He seemed to be the youngest of them all, and yet, so proud and high was his spirit that, upon Challenger laying his great hand upon his head, he started like a spurred horse and, with a quick flash of his dark eyes, moved further away from the Professor. Then, placing his hand upon his breast and holding himself with great dignity, he uttered the word "Maretas" several times. The Professor, unabashed, seized the nearest Indian by the shoulder and proceeded to lecture upon him as if he were a potted specimen in a class-room.

"The type of these people," said he in his sonorous fashion, "whether judged by cranial capacity, facial angle, or any other test, cannot be regarded as a low one; on the contrary, we must place it as considerably higher in the scale than many South American tribes which I can mention. On no possible supposition can we explain the evolution of such a race in this place. For that matter, so great a gap separates these ape-men from the primitive animals which have survived upon this plateau, that it is inadmissible to think that they could have developed where we find them."

"Then where the dooce did they drop from?" asked Lord John.

"A question which will, no doubt, be eagerly discussed in every scientific society in Europe and America," the Professor answered. "My own reading of the situation for what it is worth—" he inflated his chest enormously and looked insolently around him at the words— "is that evolution has advanced under the peculiar conditions of this country up to the vertebrate stage, the old types surviving and living on in company with the newer ones. Thus we find such modern creatures as the tapir—an animal with quite a respectable length of pedigree—the great deer, and the ant-eater in the companionship of reptilian forms of jurassic type. So much is clear. And now come the ape-men and the Indian. What is the scientific mind to think of their presence? I can only account for it by an invasion from outside. It is probable that there existed an anthropoid ape in South America, who in past ages found his way to this place, and that he developed into the creatures we have seen, some of which"—here he looked hard at me— "were of an appearance and shape which, if it had been accompanied by corresponding intelligence, would, I do not hesitate to say, have reflected credit upon any living race. As to the Indians I cannot doubt that they are more recent immigrants from below. Under the stress of famine or of conquest they have made their way up here. Faced by ferocious creatures which they had never before seen, they took refuge in the caves which our young friend has described, but they have no doubt had a bitter fight to hold their own against wild beasts, and especially against the ape-men who would regard them as intruders, and wage a merciless war upon them with a cunning which the larger beasts would lack. Hence the fact that their numbers appear to be limited. Well, gentlemen, have I read you the riddle aright, or is there any point which you would query?"

Professor Summerlee for once was too depressed to argue, though he shook his head violently as a token of general disagreement. Lord John merely scratched his scanty locks with the remark that he couldn't put up a fight as he wasn't in the same weight or class. For my own part I performed my usual role of bringing things down to a strictly prosaic and practical level by the remark that one of the Indians was missing.

"He has gone to fetch some water," said Lord Roxton. "We fitted him up with an empty beef tin and he is off."

"To the old camp?" I asked.

"No, to the brook. It's among the trees there. It can't be more than a couple of hundred yards. But the beggar is certainly taking his time."

"I'll go and look after him," said I. I picked up my rifle and strolled in the direction of the brook, leaving my friends to lay out the scanty breakfast. It may seem to you rash that even for so short a distance I should quit the shelter of our friendly thicket, but you will remember that we were many miles from Ape-town, that so far as we knew the creatures had not discovered our retreat, and that in any case with a rifle in my hands I had no fear of them. I had not yet learned their cunning or their strength.

I could hear the murmur of our brook somewhere ahead of me, but there was a tangle of trees and brushwood between me and it. I was making my way through this at a point which was just out of sight of my companions, when, under one of the trees, I noticed something red huddled among the bushes. As I approached it, I was shocked to see that it was the dead body of the missing Indian. He lay upon his side, his limbs drawn up, and his head screwed round at a most unnatural angle, so that he seemed to be looking straight over his own shoulder. I gave a cry to warn my friends that something was amiss, and running forwards I stooped over the body. Surely my guardian angel was very near me then, for some instinct of fear, or it may have been some faint rustle of leaves, made me glance upwards. Out of the thick green foliage which hung low over my head, two long muscular arms covered with reddish hair were slowly descending. Another instant and the great stealthy hands would have been round my throat. I sprang backwards, but quick as I was, those hands were quicker still. Through my sudden spring they missed a fatal grip, but one of them caught the back of my neck and the other one my face. I threw my hands up to protect my throat, and the next moment the huge paw had slid down my face and closed over them. I was lifted lightly from the ground, and I felt an intolerable pressure forcing my head back and back until the strain upon the cervical spine was more than I could bear. My senses swam, but I still tore at the hand and forced it out from my chin. Looking up I saw a frightful face with cold inexorable light blue eyes looking down into mine. There was something hypnotic in those terrible eyes. I could struggle no longer. As the creature felt me grow limp in his grasp, two white canines gleamed for a moment at each side of the vile mouth, and the grip tightened still more upon my chin, forcing it always upwards and back. A thin, oval-tinted mist formed before my eyes and little silvery bells tinkled in my ears. Dully and far off I heard the crack of a rifle and was feebly aware of the shock as I was dropped to the earth, where I lay without sense or motion.

I awoke to find myself on my back upon the grass in our lair within the thicket. Someone had brought the water from the brook, and Lord John was sprinkling my head with it, while Challenger and Summerlee were propping me up, with concern in their faces. For a moment I had a glimpse of the human spirits behind their scientific masks. It was really shock, rather than any injury, which had prostrated me, and in half-an-hour, in spite of aching head and stiff neck, I was sitting up and ready for anything.

"But you've had the escape of your life, young fellah my lad," said Lord Roxton. "When I heard your cry and ran forward, and saw your head twisted half-off and your stohwassers kickin' in the air, I thought we were one short. I missed the beast in my flurry, but he dropped you all right and was off like a streak. By George! I wish I had fifty men with rifles. I'd clear out the whole infernal gang of them and leave this country a bit cleaner than we found it."

It was clear now that the ape-men had in some way marked us down, and that we were watched on every side. We had not so much to fear from them during the day, but they would be very likely to rush us by night; so the sooner we got away from their neighborhood the better. On three sides of us was absolute forest, and there we might find ourselves in an ambush. But on the fourth side— that which sloped down in the direction of the lake—there was only low scrub, with scattered trees and occasional open glades. It was, in fact, the route which I had myself taken in my solitary journey, and it led us straight for the Indian caves. This then must for every reason be our road.

One great regret we had, and that was to leave our old camp behind us, not only for the sake of the stores which remained there, but even more because we were losing touch with Zambo, our link with the outside world. However, we had a fair supply of cartridges and all our guns, so, for a time at least, we could look after ourselves, and we hoped soon to have a chance of returning and restoring our communications with our negro. He had faithfully promised to stay where he was, and we had not a doubt that he would be as good as his word.

It was in the early afternoon that we started upon our journey. The young chief walked at our head as our guide, but refused indignantly to carry any burden. Behind him came the two surviving Indians with our scanty possessions upon their backs. We four white men walked in the rear with rifles loaded and ready. As we started there broke from the thick silent woods behind us a sudden great ululation of the ape-men, which may have been a cheer of triumph at our departure or a jeer of contempt at our flight. Looking back we saw only the dense screen of trees, but that long-drawn yell told us how many of our enemies lurked among them. We saw no sign of pursuit, however, and soon we had got into more open country and beyond their power.

As I tramped along, the rearmost of the four, I could not help smiling at the appearance of my three companions in front. Was this the luxurious Lord John Roxton who had sat that evening in the Albany amidst his Persian rugs and his pictures in the pink radiance of the tinted lights? And was this the imposing Professor who had swelled behind the great desk in his massive study at Enmore Park? And, finally, could this be the austere and prim figure which had risen before the meeting at the Zoological Institute? No three tramps that one could have met in a Surrey lane could have looked more hopeless and bedraggled. We had, it is true, been only a week or so upon the top of the plateau, but all our spare clothing was in our camp below, and the one week had been a severe one upon us all, though least to me who had not to endure the handling of the ape-men. My three friends had all lost their hats, and had now bound handkerchiefs round their heads, their clothes hung in ribbons about them, and their unshaven grimy faces were hardly to be recognized. Both Summerlee and Challenger were limping heavily, while I still dragged my feet from weakness after the shock of the morning, and my neck was as stiff as a board from the murderous grip that held it. We were indeed a sorry crew, and I did not wonder to see our Indian companions glance back at us occasionally with horror and amazement on their faces.

In the late afternoon we reached the margin of the lake, and as we emerged from the bush and saw the sheet of water stretching before us our native friends set up a shrill cry of joy and pointed eagerly in front of them. It was indeed a wonderful sight which lay before us. Sweeping over the glassy surface was a great flotilla of canoes coming straight for the shore upon which we stood. They were some miles out when we first saw them, but they shot forward with great swiftness, and were soon so near that the rowers could distinguish our persons. Instantly a thunderous shout of delight burst from them, and we saw them rise from their seats, waving their paddles and spears madly in the air. Then bending to their work once more, they flew across the intervening water, beached their boats upon the sloping sand, and rushed up to us, prostrating themselves with loud cries of greeting before the young chief. Finally one of them, an elderly man, with a necklace and bracelet of great lustrous glass beads and the skin of some beautiful mottled amber-colored animal slung over his shoulders, ran forward and embraced most tenderly the youth whom we had saved. He then looked at us and asked some questions, after which he stepped up with much dignity and embraced us also each in turn. Then, at his order, the whole tribe lay down upon the ground before us in homage. Personally I felt shy and uncomfortable at this obsequious adoration, and I read the same feeling in the faces of Roxton and Summerlee, but Challenger expanded like a flower in the sun.

"They may be undeveloped types," said he, stroking his beard and looking round at them, "but their deportment in the presence of their superiors might be a lesson to some of our more advanced Europeans. Strange how correct are the instincts of the natural man!"

It was clear that the natives had come out upon the war-path, for every man carried his spear—a long bamboo tipped with bone—

his bow and arrows, and some sort of club or stone battle-axe slung at his side. Their dark, angry glances at the woods from which we had come, and the frequent repetition of the word "Doda," made it clear enough that this was a rescue party who had set forth to save or revenge the old chief's son, for such we gathered that the youth must be. A council was now held by the whole tribe squatting in a circle, whilst we sat near on a slab of basalt and watched their proceedings. Two or three warriors spoke, and finally our young friend made a spirited harangue with such eloquent features and gestures that we could understand it all as clearly as if we had known his language.

"What is the use of returning?" he said. "Sooner or later the thing must be done. Your comrades have been murdered. What if I have returned safe? These others have been done to death. There is no safety for any of us. We are assembled now and ready." Then he pointed to us. "These strange men are our friends. They are great fighters, and they hate the ape-men even as we do. They command," here he pointed up to heaven, "the thunder and the lightning. When shall we have such a chance again? Let us go forward, and either die now or live for the future in safety. How else shall we go back unashamed to our women?"

The little red warriors hung upon the words of the speaker, and when he had finished they burst into a roar of applause, waving their rude weapons in the air. The old chief stepped forward to us, and asked us some questions, pointing at the same time to the woods. Lord John made a sign to him that he should wait for an answer and then he turned to us.

"Well, it's up to you to say what you will do," said he; "for my part I have a score to settle with these monkey-folk, and if it ends by wiping them off the face of the earth I don't see that the earth need fret about it. I'm goin' with our little red pals and I mean to see them through the scrap. What do you say, young fellah?"

"Of course I will come."

"And you, Challenger?"

"I will assuredly co-operate."

"And you, Summerlee?"

"We seem to be drifting very far from the object of this expedition, Lord John. I assure you that I little thought when I left my

professional chair in London that it was for the purpose of heading a raid of savages upon a colony of anthropoid apes."

"To such base uses do we come," said Lord John, smiling. "But
we are up against it, so what's the decision?"

"It seems a most questionable step," said Summerlee, argumentative to the last, "but if you are all going, I hardly see how I can
remain behind."

"Then it is settled," said Lord John, and turning to the chief he
nodded and slapped his rifle.

The old fellow clasped our hands, each in turn, while his men
cheered louder than ever. It was too late to advance that night, so
the Indians settled down into a rude bivouac. On all sides their
fires began to glimmer and smoke. Some of them who had disappeared into the jungle came back presently driving a young iguanodon before them. Like the others, it had a daub of asphalt upon
its shoulder, and it was only when we saw one of the natives step
forward with the air of an owner and give his consent to the beast's
slaughter that we understood at last that these great creatures were
as much private property as a herd of cattle, and that these symbols which had so perplexed us were nothing more than the marks
of the owner. Helpless, torpid, and vegetarian, with great limbs
but a minute brain, they could be rounded up and driven by a child.
In a few minutes the huge beast had been cut up and slabs of him
were hanging over a dozen camp fires, together with great scaly
ganoid fish which had been speared in the lake.

Summerlee had lain down and slept upon the sand, but we others
roamed round the edge of the water, seeking to learn something
more of this strange country. Twice we found pits of blue clay, such
as we had already seen in the swamp of the pterodactyls. These
were old volcanic vents, and for some reason excited the greatest
interest in Lord John. What attracted Challenger, on the other
hand, was a bubbling, gurgling mud geyser, where some strange
gas formed great bursting bubbles upon the surface. He thrust a
hollow reed into it and cried out with delight like a schoolboy then
he was able, on touching it with a lighted match, to cause a sharp
explosion and a blue flame at the far end of the tube. Still more
pleased was he when, inverting a leathern pouch over the end of

the reed, and so filling it with the gas, he was able to send it soaring up into the air.

"An inflammable gas, and one markedly lighter than the atmosphere. I should say beyond doubt that it contained a considerable proportion of free hydrogen. The resources of G. E. C. are not yet exhausted, my young friend. I may yet show you how a great mind molds all Nature to its use." He swelled with some secret purpose, but would say no more.

There was nothing which we could see upon the shore which seemed to me so wonderful as the great sheet of water before us. Our numbers and our noise had frightened all living creatures away, and save for a few pterodactyls, which soared round high above our heads while they waited for the carrion, all was still around the camp. But it was different out upon the rose-tinted waters of the central lake. It boiled and heaved with strange life. Great slate-colored backs and high serrated dorsal fins shot up with a fringe of silver, and then rolled down into the depths again. The sand-banks far out were spotted with uncouth crawling forms, huge turtles, strange saurians, and one great flat creature like a writhing, palpitating mat of black greasy leather, which flopped its way slowly to the lake. Here and there high serpent heads projected out of the water, cutting swiftly through it with a little collar of foam in front, and a long swirling wake behind, rising and falling in graceful, swan-like undulations as they went. It was not until one of these creatures wriggled on to a sand-bank within a few hundred yards of us, and exposed a barrel-shaped body and huge flippers behind the long serpent neck, that Challenger, and Summerlee, who had joined us, broke out into their duet of wonder and admiration.

"Plesiosaurus! A fresh-water plesiosaurus!" cried Summerlee. "That I should have lived to see such a sight! We are blessed, my dear Challenger, above all zoologists since the world began!"

It was not until the night had fallen, and the fires of our savage allies glowed red in the shadows, that our two men of science could be dragged away from the fascinations of that primeval lake. Even in the darkness as we lay upon the strand, we heard from time to time the snort and plunge of the huge creatures who lived therein.

At earliest dawn our camp was astir and an hour later we had started upon our memorable expedition. Often in my dreams have I thought that I might live to be a war correspondent. In what wildest one could I have conceived the nature of the campaign which it should be my lot to report! Here then is my first despatch from a field of battle:

Our numbers had been reinforced during the night by a fresh batch of natives from the caves, and we may have been four or five hundred strong when we made our advance. A fringe of scouts was thrown out in front, and behind them the whole force in a solid column made their way up the long slope of the bush country until we were near the edge of the forest. Here they spread out into a long straggling line of spearmen and bowmen. Roxton and Summerlee took their position upon the right flank, while Challenger and I were on the left. It was a host of the stone age that we were accompanying to battle—we with the last word of the gunsmith's art from St. James' Street and the Strand.

We had not long to wait for our enemy. A wild shrill clamor rose from the edge of the wood and suddenly a body of ape-men rushed out with clubs and stones, and made for the center of the Indian line. It was a valiant move but a foolish one, for the great bandy-legged creatures were slow of foot, while their opponents were as active as cats. It was horrible to see the fierce brutes with foaming mouths and glaring eyes, rushing and grasping, but forever missing their elusive enemies, while arrow after arrow buried itself in their hides. One great fellow ran past me roaring with pain, with a dozen darts sticking from his chest and ribs. In mercy I put a bullet through his skull, and he fell sprawling among the aloes. But this was the only shot fired, for the attack had been on the center of the line, and the Indians there had needed no help of ours in repulsing it. Of all the ape-men who had rushed out into the open, I do not think that one got back to cover.

But the matter was more deadly when we came among the trees. For an hour or more after we entered the wood, there was a desperate struggle in which for a time we hardly held our own. Springing out from among the scrub the ape-men with huge clubs broke in upon the Indians and often felled three or four of them before they could be speared. Their frightful blows shattered everything upon which they fell. One of them knocked Summerlee's rifle to matchwood and the next would have crushed his skull had an Indian not stabbed the beast to the heart. Other ape-men in the trees above us hurled down stones and logs of wood, occasionally dropping bodily on to our ranks and fighting furiously until they were felled. Once our allies broke under the pressure, and had it not been for the execution done by our rifles they would certainly have taken to their heels. But they were gallantly rallied by their old chief and came on with such a rush that the ape-men began in turn to give way. Summerlee was weaponless, but I was emptying my magazine as quick as I could fire, and on the further flank we heard the continuous cracking of our companion's rifles.

Then in a moment came the panic and the collapse. Screaming and howling, the great creatures rushed away in all directions through the brushwood, while our allies yelled in their savage delight, following swiftly after their flying enemies. All the feuds of countless generations, all the hatreds and cruelties of their narrow history, all the memories of ill-usage and persecution were to be purged that day. At last man was to be supreme and the man-beast to find forever his allotted place. Fly as they would the fugitives were too slow to escape from the active savages, and from every side in the tangled woods we heard the exultant yells, the twanging of bows, and the crash and thud as ape-men were brought down from their hiding-places in the trees.

I was following the others, when I found that Lord John and Challenger had come across to join us.

"It's over," said Lord John. "I think we can leave the tidying up to them. Perhaps the less we see of it the better we shall sleep."

Challenger's eyes were shining with the lust of slaughter.

"We have been privileged," he cried, strutting about like a gamecock, "to be present at one of the typical decisive battles of history—the battles which have determined the fate of the world. What, my friends, is the conquest of one nation by another? It is meaningless. Each produces the same result. But those fierce fights, when in the dawn of the ages the cave-dwellers held their own against the tiger folk, or the elephants first found that they had a master, those were the real conquests—the victories that count. By this strange turn of fate we have seen and helped to decide even such a contest. Now upon this plateau the future must ever be for man."

It needed a robust faith in the end to justify such tragic means. As we advanced together through the woods we found the ape-men lying thick, transfixed with spears or arrows. Here and there a little group of shattered Indians marked where one of the anthropoids had turned to bay, and sold his life dearly. Always in front of us we heard the yelling and roaring which showed the direction of the pursuit. The ape-men had been driven back to their city, they had made a last stand there, once again they had been broken, and now we were in time to see the final fearful scene of all. Some eighty or a hundred males, the last survivors, had been driven across that same little clearing which led to the edge of the cliff, the scene of our own exploit two days before. As we arrived the Indians, a semi-circle of spearmen, had closed in on them, and in a minute it was over. Thirty or forty died where they stood. The others, screaming and clawing, were thrust over the precipice, and went hurtling down, as their prisoners had of old, on to the sharp bamboos six hundred feet below. It was as Challenger had said, and the reign of man was assured forever in Maple White Land. The males were exterminated, Ape Town was destroyed, the females and young were driven away to live in bondage, and the long rivalry of untold centuries had reached its bloody end.

For us the victory brought much advantage. Once again we were able to visit our camp and get at our stores. Once more also we were able to communicate with Zambo, who had been terrified by the spectacle from afar of an avalanche of apes falling from the edge of the cliff.

"Come away, Massas, come away!" he cried, his eyes starting from his head. "The debbil get you sure if you stay up there."

"It is the voice of sanity!" said Summerlee with conviction. "We have had adventures enough and they are neither suitable to our character or our position. I hold you to your word, Challenger. From now onwards you devote your energies to getting us out of this horrible country and back once more to civilization."

15

"Our Eyes have seen Great Wonders"

I write this from day to day, but I trust that before I come to the end of it, I may be able to say that the light shines, at last, through our clouds. We are held here with no clear means of making our escape, and bitterly we chafe against it. Yet, I can well imagine that the day may come when we may be glad that we were kept, against our will, to see something more of the wonders of this singular place, and of the creatures who inhabit it.

The victory of the Indians and the annihilation of the ape-men, marked the turning point of our fortunes. From then onwards, we were in truth masters of the plateau, for the natives looked upon us with a mixture of fear and gratitude, since by our strange powers we had aided them to destroy their hereditary foe. For their own sakes they would, perhaps, be glad to see the departure of such formidable and incalculable people, but they have not themselves suggested any way by which we may reach the plains below. There had been, so far as we could follow their signs, a tunnel by which the place could be approached, the lower exit of which we had seen from below. By this, no doubt, both ape-men and Indians had at different epochs reached the top, and Maple White with his companion had taken the same way.

Only the year before, however, there had been a terrific earthquake, and the upper end of the tunnel had fallen in and completely disappeared. The Indians now could only shake their heads and shrug their shoulders when we expressed by signs our desire to descend. It may be that they cannot, but it may also be that they will not, help us to get away.

At the end of the victorious campaign the surviving ape-folk were driven across the plateau (their wailings were horrible) and established in the neighborhood of the Indian caves, where they would, from now onwards, be a servile race under the eyes of their masters. It was a rude, raw, primeval version of the Jews in Babylon or the Israelites in Egypt. At night we could hear from amid the trees the long-drawn cry, as some primitive Ezekiel mourned for fallen greatness and recalled the departed glories of Ape Town. Hewers of wood and drawers of water, such were they from now onwards.

We had returned across the plateau with our allies two days after the battle, and made our camp at the foot of their cliffs. They would have had us share their caves with them, but Lord John would by no means consent to it considering that to do so would put us in their power if they were treacherously disposed. We kept our independence, therefore, and had our weapons ready for any emergency, while preserving the most friendly relations. We also continually visited their caves, which were most remarkable places, though whether made by man or by Nature we have never been able to determine. They were all on the one stratum, hollowed out of some soft rock which lay between the volcanic basalt forming the ruddy cliffs above them, and the hard granite which formed their base.

The openings were about eighty feet above the ground, and were led up to by long stone stairs, so narrow and steep that no large animal could mount them. Inside they were warm and dry, running in straight passages of varying length into the side of the hill, with smooth gray walls decorated with many excellent pictures done with charred sticks and representing the various animals of the plateau. If every living thing were swept from the country the future explorer would find upon the walls of these caves ample evidence of the strange fauna—the dinosaurs, iguanodons, and fish lizards—which had lived so recently upon earth.

Since we had learned that the huge iguanodons were kept as tame herds by their owners, and were simply walking meat-stores, we had conceived that man, even with his primitive weapons, had established his ascendancy upon the plateau. We were soon to discover that it was not so, and that he was still there upon tolerance.

It was on the third day after our forming our camp near the Indian caves that the tragedy occurred. Challenger and Summerlee had gone off together that day to the lake where some of the natives, under their direction, were engaged in harpooning specimens of the great lizards. Lord John and I had remained in our camp, while a number of the Indians were scattered about upon the grassy slope in front of the caves engaged in different ways. Suddenly there was a shrill cry of alarm, with the word "Stoa" resounding from a hundred tongues. From every side men, women, and children were rushing wildly for shelter, swarming up the staircases and into the caves in a mad stampede.

Looking up, we could see them waving their arms from the rocks above and beckoning to us to join them in their refuge. We had both seized our magazine rifles and ran out to see what the danger could be. Suddenly from the near belt of trees there broke forth a group of twelve or fifteen Indians, running for their lives, and at their very heels two of those frightful monsters which had disturbed our camp and pursued me upon my solitary journey. In shape they were like horrible toads, and moved in a succession of springs, but in size they were of an incredible bulk, larger than the largest elephant. We had never before seen them save at night, and indeed they are nocturnal animals save when disturbed in their lairs, as these had been. We now stood amazed at the sight, for their blotched and warty skins were of a curious fish-like iridescence, and the sunlight struck them with an ever-varying rainbow bloom as they moved.

We had little time to watch them, however, for in an instant they had overtaken the fugitives and were making a dire slaughter among them. Their method was to fall forward with their full weight upon each in turn, leaving him crushed and mangled, to bound on after the others. The wretched Indians screamed with terror, but were helpless, run as they would, before the relentless purpose and horrible activity of these monstrous creatures. One after another they went down, and there were not half-a-dozen surviving by the time my companion and I could come to their help. But our aid was of little avail and only involved us in the same peril. At the range of a couple of hundred yards we emptied our magazines, firing bullet after bullet into the beasts, but with no more effect than if we were pelting them with pellets of paper. Their slow reptilian natures cared nothing for wounds, and the springs of their lives, with no special brain center but scattered throughout their spinal cords, could not be tapped by any modern weapons. The most that we could do was to check their progress by distracting their attention with the flash and roar of our guns, and so to give both the natives and ourselves time to reach the steps which led to safety. But where the conical explosive bullets of the twentieth century were of no avail, the poisoned arrows of the natives, dipped in the juice of strophanthus and steeped afterwards in decayed carrion, could succeed. Such arrows were of little avail to the hunter who attacked the beast, because their action in that torpid circulation was slow, and before its powers failed it could certainly overtake and slay its assailant. But now, as the two monsters hounded us to the very foot of the stairs, a drift of darts came whistling from every chink in the cliff above them. In a minute they were feathered with them, and yet with no sign of pain they clawed and slobbered with impotent rage at the steps which would lead them to their victims, mounting clumsily up for a few yards and then sliding down again to the ground. But at last the poison worked. One of them gave a deep rumbling groan and dropped his huge squat head on to the earth. The other bounded round in an eccentric circle with shrill, wailing cries, and then lying down writhed in agony for some minutes before it also stiffened and lay still. With yells of triumph the Indians came flocking down from their caves and danced a frenzied dance of victory round the dead bodies, in mad joy that two more of the most dangerous of all their enemies had been slain. That night they cut up and removed the bodies, not to eat—for the poison was still active—but lest they should breed a pestilence. The great reptilian hearts, however, each as large as a cushion, still lay there, beating slowly and steadily, with a gentle rise and fall, in horrible independent life. It was only upon the third day that the ganglia ran down and the dreadful things were still.

Some day, when I have a better desk than a meat-tin and more helpful tools than a worn stub of pencil and a last, tattered notebook, I will write some fuller account of the Accala Indians—of our life amongst them, and of the glimpses which we had of the strange conditions of wondrous Maple White Land. Memory, at least, will never fail me, for so long as the breath of life is in me, every hour and every action of that period will stand out as hard and clear as do the first strange happenings of our childhood. No new impressions could efface those which are so deeply cut.

When the time comes I will describe that wondrous moonlit night upon the great lake when a young ichthyosaurus—a strange creature, half seal, half fish, to look at, with bone-covered eyes on each side of his snout, and a third eye fixed upon the top of his head—was entangled in an Indian net, and nearly upset our canoe before we towed it ashore; the same night that a green water-snake shot out from the rushes and carried off in its coils the steersman of Challenger's canoe. I will tell, too, of the great nocturnal white thing—to this day we do not know whether it was beast or reptile—which lived in a vile swamp to the east of the lake, and flitted about with a faint phosphorescent glimmer in the darkness. The Indians were so terrified at it that they would not go near the place, and, though we twice made expeditions and saw it each time, we could not make our way through the deep marsh in which it lived. I can only say that it seemed to be larger than a cow and had the strangest musky odor.

I will tell also of the huge bird which chased Challenger to the shelter of the rocks one day—a great running bird, far taller than an ostrich, with a vulture-like neck and cruel head which made it a walking death. As Challenger climbed to safety one dart of that savage curving beak shore off the heel of his boot as if it had been cut with a chisel. This time at least modern weapons prevailed and the great creature, twelve feet from head to foot—phororachus its name, according to our panting but exultant Professor—went down before Lord Roxton's rifle in a flurry of waving feathers and kicking limbs, with two remorseless yellow eyes glaring up from the midst of it. May I live to see that flattened vicious skull in its own niche amid the trophies of the Albany. Finally, I will assuredly give some account of the toxodon, the giant ten-foot guinea pig, with projecting chisel teeth, which we killed as it drank in the gray of the morning by the side of the lake.

All this I shall some day write at fuller length, and amidst these more stirring days I would tenderly sketch in these lovely summer evenings, when with the deep blue sky above us we lay in good comradeship among the long grasses by the wood and marveled at the strange fowl that swept over us and the quaint new creatures which crept from their burrows to watch us, while above us the boughs of the bushes were heavy with luscious fruit, and below us strange and lovely flowers peeped at us from among the herbage; or those long moonlit nights when we lay out upon the shimmering surface of the great lake and watched with wonder and awe the huge circles rippling out from the sudden splash of some fantastic monster; or the greenish gleam, far down in the deep water, of some strange creature upon the confines of darkness. These are the scenes which my mind and my pen will dwell upon in every detail at some future day.

But, you will ask, why these experiences and why this delay, when you and your comrades should have been occupied day and night in the devising of some means by which you could return to the outer world? My answer is, that there was not one of us who was not working for this end, but that our work had been in vain. One fact we had very speedily discovered: The Indians would do nothing to help us. In every other way they were our friends—one might almost say our devoted slaves—but when it was suggested that they should help us to make and carry a plank which would bridge the chasm, or when we wished to get from them thongs of leather or liana to weave ropes which might help us, we were met by a good-humored, but an invincible, refusal. They would smile, twinkle their eyes, shake their heads, and there was the end of it. Even the old chief met us with the same obstinate denial, and it was only Maretas, the youngster whom we had saved, who looked wistfully at us and told us by his gestures that he was grieved for our thwarted wishes. Ever since their crowning triumph with the ape-men they looked upon us as supermen, who bore victory in the tubes of strange weapons, and they believed that so long as we remained with them good fortune would be theirs. A little red-skinned wife and a cave of our own were freely offered to each of us if we would but forget our own people and dwell forever upon the plateau. So far all had been kindly, however far apart our desires might be; but we felt well assured that our actual plans of a descent must be kept secret, for we had reason to fear that at the last they might try to hold us by force.

In spite of the danger from dinosaurs (which is not great save at night, for, as I may have said before, they are mostly nocturnal in their habits) I have twice in the last three weeks been over to our old camp in order to see our negro who still kept watch and ward below the cliff. My eyes strained eagerly across the great plain in the hope of seeing afar off the help for which we had prayed. But the long cactus-strewn levels still stretched away, empty and bare, to the distant line of the cane-brake.

"They will soon come now, Massa Malone. Before another week pass Indian come back and bring rope and fetch you down." Such was the cheery cry of our excellent Zambo.

I had one strange experience as I came from this second visit which had involved my being away for a night from my companions. I was returning along the well-remembered route, and had reached a spot within a mile or so of the marsh of the pterodactyls, when I saw an extraordinary object approaching me. It was a man who walked inside a framework made of bent canes so that he was enclosed on all sides in a bell-shaped cage. As I drew nearer I was more amazed still to see that it was Lord John Roxton. When he saw me he slipped from under his curious protection and came towards me laughing, and yet, as I thought, with some confusion in his manner.

"Well, young fellah," said he, "who would have thought of meetin' you up here?"

"What in the world are you doing?" I asked.

"Visitin' my friends, the pterodactyls," said he.

"But why?"

"Interestin' beasts, don't you think? But unsociable! Nasty rude ways with strangers, as you may remember. So I rigged this framework which keeps them from bein' too pressin' in their attentions."

"But what do you want in the swamp?"

He looked at me with a very questioning eye, and I read hesitation in his face.

"Don't you think other people besides Professors can want to know things?" he said at last. "I'm studyin' the pretty dears. That's enough for you."

"No offense," said I.

His good-humor returned and he laughed.

"No offense, young fellah. I'm goin' to get a young devil chick for Challenger. That's one of my jobs. No, I don't want your company. I'm safe in this cage, and you are not. So long, and I'll be back in camp by night-fall."

He turned away and I left him wandering on through the wood with his extraordinary cage around him.

If Lord John's behavior at this time was strange, that of Challenger was more so. I may say that he seemed to possess an extraordinary fascination for the Indian women, and that he always carried a large spreading palm branch with which he beat them off as if they were flies, when their attentions became too pressing. To see him walking like a comic opera Sultan, with this badge of authority in his hand, his black beard bristling in front of him, his toes pointing at each step, and a train of wide-eyed Indian girls behind him, clad in their slender drapery of bark cloth, is one of the most grotesque of all the pictures which I will carry back with me. As to Summerlee, he was absorbed in the insect and bird life of the plateau, and spent his whole time (save that considerable portion which was devoted to abusing Challenger for not getting us out of our difficulties) in cleaning and mounting his specimens.

Challenger had been in the habit of walking off by himself every morning and returning from time to time with looks of portentous solemnity, as one who bears the full weight of a great enterprise upon his shoulders. One day, palm branch in hand, and his crowd of adoring devotees behind him, he led us down to his hidden workshop and took us into the secret of his plans.

The place was a small clearing in the center of a palm grove. In this was one of those boiling mud geysers which I have already described. Around its edge were scattered a number of leathern thongs cut from iguanodon hide, and a large collapsed membrane which proved to be the dried and scraped stomach of one of the great fish lizards from the lake. This huge sack had been sewn up at one end and only a small orifice left at the other. Into this opening several bamboo canes had been inserted and the other ends of these canes were in contact with conical clay funnels which collected the gas bubbling up through the mud of the geyser. Soon the flaccid organ began to slowly expand and show such a tendency to upward movements that Challenger fastened the cords which held it to the trunks of the surrounding trees. In half an hour a good-sized gas-bag had been formed, and the jerking and straining upon the thongs showed that it was capable of considerable lift. Challenger, like a glad father in the presence of his first-born, stood smiling and stroking his beard, in silent, self-satisfied content as he gazed at the creation of his brain. It was Summerlee who first broke the silence.

"You don't mean us to go up in that thing, Challenger?" said he, in an acid voice.

"I mean, my dear Summerlee, to give you such a demonstration of its powers that after seeing it you will, I am sure, have no hesitation in trusting yourself to it."

"You can put it right out of your head now, at once," said Summerlee with decision, "nothing on earth would induce me to commit such a folly. Lord John, I trust that you will not countenance such madness?"

"Dooced ingenious, I call it," said our peer. "I'd like to see how it works."

"So you shall," said Challenger. "For some days I have exerted my whole brain force upon the problem of how we shall descend from these cliffs. We have satisfied ourselves that we cannot climb down and that there is no tunnel. We are also unable to construct any kind of bridge which may take us back to the pinnacle from which we came. How then shall I find a means to convey us? Some little time ago I had remarked to our young friend here that free hydrogen was evolved from the geyser. The idea of a balloon naturally followed. I was, I will admit, somewhat baffled by the difficulty of discovering an envelope to contain the gas, but the contemplation of the immense entrails of these reptiles supplied me with a solution to the problem. Behold the result!"

He put one hand in the front of his ragged jacket and pointed proudly with the other.

By this time the gas-bag had swollen to a goodly rotundity and was jerking strongly upon its lashings.

"Midsummer madness!" snorted Summerlee.

Lord John was delighted with the whole idea. "Clever old dear, ain't he?" he whispered to me, and then louder to Challenger. "What about a car?"

"The car will be my next care. I have already planned how it is to be made and attached. Meanwhile I will simply show you how capable my apparatus is of supporting the weight of each of us."

"All of us, surely?"

"No, it is part of my plan that each in turn shall descend as in a parachute, and the balloon be drawn back by means which I shall have no difficulty in perfecting. If it will support the weight of one and let him gently down, it will have done all that is required of it. I will now show you its capacity in that direction."

He brought out a lump of basalt of a considerable size, constructed in the middle so that a cord could be easily attached to it. This cord was the one which we had brought with us on to the plateau after we had used it for climbing the pinnacle. It was over a hundred feet long, and though it was thin it was very strong. He had prepared a sort of collar of leather with many straps depending from it. This collar was placed over the dome of the balloon, and the hanging thongs were gathered together below, so that the pressure of any weight would be diffused over a considerable surface. Then the lump of basalt was fastened to the thongs, and the rope was allowed to hang from the end of it, being passed three times round the Professor's arm.

"I will now," said Challenger, with a smile of pleased anticipation, "demonstrate the carrying power of my balloon." As he said so he cut with a knife the various lashings that held it.

Never was our expedition in more imminent danger of complete annihilation. The inflated membrane shot up with frightful velocity into the air. In an instant Challenger was pulled off his feet and dragged after it. I had just time to throw my arms round his ascending waist when I was myself whipped up into the air. Lord John had me with a rat-trap grip round the legs, but I felt that he also was coming off the ground. For a moment I had a vision of four adventurers floating like a string of sausages over the land that they had explored. But, happily, there were limits to the strain which the rope would stand, though none apparently to the lifting powers of this infernal machine. There was a sharp crack, and we were in a heap upon the ground with coils of rope all over us. When we were able to stagger to our feet we saw far off in the deep blue sky one dark spot where the lump of basalt was speeding upon its way.

"Splendid!" cried the undaunted Challenger, rubbing his injured arm. "A most thorough and satisfactory demonstration! I could not have anticipated such a success. Within a week, gentlemen, I promise that a second balloon will be prepared, and that you can count upon taking in safety and comfort the first stage of our homeward journey." So far I have written each of the foregoing events as it occurred. Now I am rounding off my narrative from the old camp, where Zambo has waited so long, with all our difficulties and dangers left like a dream behind us upon the summit of those vast ruddy crags which tower above our heads. We have descended in safety, though in a most unexpected fashion, and all is well with us. In six weeks or two months we shall be in London, and it is possible that this letter may not reach you much earlier than we do ourselves. Already our hearts yearn and our spirits fly towards the great mother city which holds so much that is dear to us.

It was on the very evening of our perilous adventure with Challenger's home-made balloon that the change came in our fortunes. I have said that the one person from whom we had had some sign of sympathy in our attempts to get away was the young chief whom we had rescued. He alone had no desire to hold us against our will in a strange land. He had told us as much by his expressive language of signs. That evening, after dusk, he came down to our little camp, handed me (for some reason he had always shown his attentions to me, perhaps because I was the one who was nearest his age) a small roll of the bark of a tree, and then pointing solemnly up at the row of caves above him, he had put his finger to his lips as a sign of secrecy and had stolen back again to his people.

I took the slip of bark to the firelight and we examined it together. It was about a foot square, and on the inner side there was a singular arrangement of lines, which I here reproduce:

⊤ ⊺⊤'⊤'⊤⊺⊧⊤⋏⊤'⊤ ⊤⊤⋌⊼⊤

They were neatly done in charcoal upon the white surface, and looked to me at first sight like some sort of rough musical score.

"Whatever it is, I can swear that it is of importance to us," said I. "I could read that on his face as he gave it."

"Unless we have come upon a primitive practical joker," Summerlee suggested, "which I should think would be one of the most elementary developments of man."

"It is clearly some sort of script," said Challenger.

"Looks like a guinea puzzle competition," remarked Lord John, craning his neck to have a look at it. Then suddenly he stretched out his hand and seized the puzzle.

"By George!" he cried, "I believe I've got it. The boy guessed right the very first time. See here! How many marks are on that paper? Eighteen. Well, if you come to think of it there are eighteen cave openings on the hill-side above us."

"He pointed up to the caves when he gave it to me," said I.

"Well, that settles it. This is a chart of the caves. What! Eighteen of them all in a row, some short, some deep, some branching, same as we saw them. It's a map, and here's a cross on it. What's the cross for? It is placed to mark one that is much deeper than the others."

"One that goes through," I cried.

"I believe our young friend has read the riddle," said Challenger. "If the cave does not go through I do not understand why this person, who has every reason to mean us well, should have drawn our attention to it. But if it does go through and comes out at the corresponding point on the other side, we should not have more than a hundred feet to descend."

"A hundred feet!" grumbled Summerlee.

"Well, our rope is still more than a hundred feet long," I cried. "Surely we could get down."

"How about the Indians in the cave?" Summerlee objected.

"There are no Indians in any of the caves above our heads," said I. "They are all used as barns and store-houses. Why should we not go up now at once and spy out the land?"

There is a dry bituminous wood upon the plateau—a species of araucaria, according to our botanist—which is always used by the Indians for torches. Each of us picked up a faggot of this, and we made our way up weed-covered steps to the particular cave which was marked in the drawing. It was, as I had said, empty, save for a great number of enormous bats, which flapped round our heads as we advanced into it. As we had no desire to draw the attention of the Indians to our proceedings, we stumbled along in the dark until we had gone round several curves and penetrated a considerable distance into the cavern. Then, at last, we lit our torches. It was a beautiful dry tunnel with smooth gray walls covered with native symbols, a curved roof which arched over our heads, and white glistening sand beneath our feet. We hurried eagerly along it until, with a deep groan of bitter disappointment, we were brought to a halt. A sheer wall of rock had appeared before us, with no chink through which a mouse could have slipped. There was no escape for us there.

We stood with bitter hearts staring at this unexpected obstacle. It was not the result of any convulsion, as in the case of the ascending tunnel. The end wall was exactly like the side ones. It was, and had always been, a cul-de-sac.

"Never mind, my friends," said the indomitable Challenger. "You have still my firm promise of a balloon."

Summerlee groaned.

"Can we be in the wrong cave?" I suggested.

"No use, young fellah," said Lord John, with his finger on the chart. "Seventeen from the right and second from the left. This is the cave sure enough."

I looked at the mark to which his finger pointed, and I gave a sudden cry of joy.

"I believe I have it! Follow me! Follow me!"

I hurried back along the way we had come, my torch in my hand. "Here," said I, pointing to some matches upon the ground, "is where we lit up."

"Exactly."

"Well, it is marked as a forked cave, and in the darkness we passed the fork before the torches were lit. On the right side as we go out we should find the longer arm."

It was as I had said. We had not gone thirty yards before a great black opening loomed in the wall. We turned into it to find that we were in a much larger passage than before. Along it we hurried in breathless impatience for many hundreds of yards. Then, suddenly, in the black darkness of the arch in front of us we saw a gleam of dark red light. We stared in amazement. A sheet of steady flame seemed to cross the passage and to bar our way. We hastened towards it. No sound, no heat, no movement came from it, but still the great luminous curtain glowed before us, silvering all the cave and turning the sand to powdered jewels, until as we drew closer it discovered a circular edge.

"The moon, by George!" cried Lord John. "We are through, boys! We are through!"

It was indeed the full moon which shone straight down the aperture which opened upon the cliffs. It was a small rift, not larger than a window, but it was enough for all our purposes. As we craned our necks through it we could see that the descent was not a very difficult one, and that the level ground was no very great way below us. It was no wonder that from below we had not observed the place, as the cliffs curved overhead and an ascent at the spot would have seemed so impossible as to discourage close inspection. We satisfied ourselves that with the help of our rope we could find our way down, and then returned, rejoicing, to our camp to make our preparations for the next evening.

What we did we had to do quickly and secretly, since even at this last hour the Indians might hold us back. Our stores we would leave behind us, save only our guns and cartridges. But Challenger had some unwieldy stuff which he ardently desired to take with him, and one particular package, of which I may not speak, which gave us more labor than any. Slowly the day passed, but when the darkness fell we were ready for our departure. With much labor we got our things up the steps, and then, looking back, took one last long survey of that strange land, soon I fear to be vulgarized, the prey of hunter and prospector, but to each of us a dreamland of glamour and romance, a land where we had dared much, suffered much, and learned much—*our* land, as we shall ever fondly call it. Along upon our left the neighboring caves each threw out its ruddy cheery firelight into the gloom. From the slope below us rose the voices of the Indians as they laughed and sang. Beyond was the long sweep of the woods, and in the center, shimmering vaguely through the gloom, was the great lake, the mother of strange monsters. Even as we looked a high whickering cry, the call of some weird animal, rang clear out of the darkness. It was the very voice of Maple White Land bidding us good-bye. We turned and plunged into the cave which led to home.

Two hours later, we, our packages, and all we owned, were at the foot of the cliff. Save for Challenger's luggage we had never a difficulty. Leaving it all where we descended, we started at once for Zambo's camp. In the early morning we approached it, but only to find, to our amazement, not one fire but a dozen upon the plain. The rescue party had arrived. There were twenty Indians from the river, with stakes, ropes, and all that could be useful for bridging the chasm. At least we shall have no difficulty now in carrying our packages, when to-morrow we begin to make our way back to the Amazon.

And so, in humble and thankful mood, I close this account. Our eyes have seen great wonders and our souls are chastened by what we have endured. Each is in his own way a better and deeper man. It may be that when we reach Para we shall stop to refit. If we do, this letter will be a mail ahead. If not, it will reach London on the very day that I do. In either case, my dear Mr. McArdle, I hope very soon to shake you by the hand.

16

"A Procession! A Procession!"

I should wish to place upon record here our gratitude to all our friends upon the Amazon for the very great kindness and hospitality which was shown to us upon our return journey. Very particularly would I thank Senhor Penalosa and other officials of the Brazilian Government for the special arrangements by which we were helped upon our way, and Senhor Pereira of Para, to whose forethought we owe the complete outfit for a decent appearance in the civilized world which we found ready for us at that town. It seemed a poor return for all the courtesy which we encountered that we should deceive our hosts and benefactors, but under the circumstances we had really no alternative, and I hereby tell them that they will only waste their time and their money if they attempt to follow upon our traces. Even the names have been altered in our accounts, and I am very sure that no one, from the most careful study of them, could come within a thousand miles of our unknown land.

The excitement which had been caused through those parts of South America which we had to traverse was imagined by us to be purely local, and I can assure our friends in England that we had no notion of the uproar which the mere rumor of our experiences had caused through Europe.

It was not until the Ivernia was within five hundred miles of Southampton that the wireless messages from paper after paper and agency after agency, offering huge prices for a short return message as to our actual results, showed us how strained was the attention not only of the scientific world but of the general public. It was agreed among us, however, that no definite statement should be given to the Press until we had met the members of the Zoological Institute, since as delegates it was our clear duty to give our first report to the body from which we had received our commission of investigation.

Thus, although we found Southampton full of Pressmen, we absolutely refused to give any information, which had the natural effect of focusing public attention upon the meeting which was advertised for the evening of November 7th. For this gathering, the Zoological Hall which had been the scene of the inception of our task was found to be far too small, and it was only in the Queen's Hall in Regent Street that accommodation could be found. It is now common knowledge the promoters might have ventured upon the Albert Hall and still found their space too scanty.

It was for the second evening after our arrival that the great meeting had been fixed. For the first, we had each, no doubt, our own pressing personal affairs to absorb us. Of mine I cannot yet speak. It may be that as it stands further from me I may think of it, and even speak of it, with less emotion. I have shown the reader in the beginning of this narrative where lay the springs of my action. It is but right, perhaps, that I should carry on the tale and show also the results. And yet the day may come when I would not have it otherwise. At least I have been driven forth to take part in a wondrous adventure, and I cannot but be thankful to the force that drove me.

And now I turn to the last supreme eventful moment of our adventure. As I was racking my brain as to how I should best describe it, my eyes fell upon the issue of my own Journal for the morning of the 8th of November with the full and excellent account of my friend and fellow-reporter Macdona. What can I do better than transcribe his narrative—head-lines and all? I admit that the paper was exuberant in the matter, out of compliment to its own enterprise in sending a correspondent, but the other great dailies were hardly less full in their account. Thus, then, friend Mac in his report:

THE NEW WORLD
GREAT MEETING AT THE QUEEN'S HALL
SCENES OF UPROAR
EXTRAORDINARY INCIDENT
WHAT WAS IT?
NOCTURNAL RIOT IN REGENT STREET
(Special)

"The much-discussed meeting of the Zoological Institute, convened to hear the report of the Committee of Investigation sent out last year to South America to test the assertions made by Professor Challenger as to the continued
existence of prehistoric life upon that Continent, was held
last night in the greater Queen's Hall, and it is safe to say
that it is likely to be a red letter date in the history of Science, for the proceedings were of so remarkable and sensational a character that no one present is ever likely to forget them." (Oh, brother scribe Macdona, what a monstrous
opening sentence!) "The tickets were theoretically confined
to members and their friends, but the latter is an elastic
term, and long before eight o'clock, the hour fixed for the
commencement of the proceedings, all parts of the Great
Hall were tightly packed. The general public, however, which
most unreasonably entertained a grievance at having been
excluded, stormed the doors at a quarter to eight, after a
prolonged melee in which several people were injured, including Inspector Scoble of H. Division, whose leg was unfortunately broken. After this unwarrantable invasion,
which not only filled every passage, but even intruded upon
the space set apart for the Press, it is estimated that nearly
five thousand people awaited the arrival of the travelers.
When they eventually appeared, they took their places in
the front of a platform which already contained all the leading scientific men, not only of this country, but of France
and of Germany. Sweden was also represented, in the person of Professor Sergius, the famous Zoologist of the University of Upsala. The entrance of the four heroes of the

occasion was the signal for a remarkable demonstration of welcome, the whole audience rising and cheering for some minutes. An acute observer might, however, have detected some signs of dissent amid the applause, and gathered that the proceedings were likely to become more lively than harmonious. It may safely be prophesied, however, that no one could have foreseen the extraordinary turn which they were actually to take.

"Of the appearance of the four wanderers little need be said, since their photographs have for some time been appearing in all the papers. They bear few traces of the hardships which they are said to have undergone. Professor Challenger's beard may be more shaggy, Professor Summerlee's features more ascetic, Lord John Roxton's figure more gaunt, and all three may be burned to a darker tint than when they left our shores, but each appeared to be in most excellent health. As to our own representative, the well-known athlete and international Rugby football player, E. D. Malone, he looks trained to a hair, and as he surveyed the crowd a smile of good-humored contentment pervaded his honest but homely face." (All right, Mac, wait till I get you alone!)

"When quiet had been restored and the audience resumed their seats after the ovation which they had given to the travelers, the chairman, the Duke of Durham, addressed the meeting. 'He would not,' he said, 'stand for more than a moment between that vast assembly and the treat which lay before them. It was not for him to anticipate what Professor Summerlee, who was the spokesman of the committee, had to say to them, but it was common rumor that their expedition had been crowned by extraordinary success.' (Applause.) 'Apparently the age of romance was not dead, and there was common ground upon which the wildest imaginings of the novelist could meet the actual scientific investigations of the searcher for truth. He would only add, before he sat down, that he rejoiced—and all of them would rejoice—that these gentlemen had returned safe and sound

from their difficult and dangerous task, for it cannot be
denied that any disaster to such an expedition would have
inflicted a well-nigh irreparable loss to the cause of Zoological science.' (Great applause, in which Professor Challenger was observed to join.)

"Professor Summerlee's rising was the signal for another
extraordinary outbreak of enthusiasm, which broke out
again at intervals throughout his address. That address will
not be given *in extenso* in these columns, for the reason that
a full account of the whole adventures of the expedition is
being published as a supplement from the pen of our own
special correspondent. Some general indications will therefore suffice. Having described the genesis of their journey,
and paid a handsome tribute to his friend Professor Challenger, coupled with an apology for the incredulity with
which his assertions, now fully vindicated, had been received, he gave the actual course of their journey, carefully
withholding such information as would aid the public in any
attempt to locate this remarkable plateau. Having described,
in general terms, their course from the main river up to the
time that they actually reached the base of the cliffs, he
enthralled his hearers by his account of the difficulties encountered by the expedition in their repeated attempts to
mount them, and finally described how they succeeded in
their desperate endeavors, which cost the lives of their two
devoted half-breed servants." (This amazing reading of the
affair was the result of Summerlee's endeavors to avoid raising any questionable matter at the meeting.)

"Having conducted his audience in fancy to the summit,
and marooned them there by reason of the fall of their
bridge, the Professor proceeded to describe both the horrors
and the attractions of that remarkable land. Of personal adventures he said little, but laid stress upon the rich harvest
reaped by Science in the observations of the wonderful
beast, bird, insect, and plant life of the plateau. Peculiarly
rich in the coleoptera and in the lepidoptera, forty-six new
species of the one and ninety-four of the other had been

secured in the course of a few weeks. It was, however, in
the larger animals, and especially in the larger animals supposed to have been long extinct, that the interest of the
public was naturally centered. Of these he was able to give
a goodly list, but had little doubt that it would be largely
extended when the place had been more thoroughly investigated. He and his companions had seen at least a dozen
creatures, most of them at a distance, which corresponded
with nothing at present known to Science. These would in
time be duly classified and examined. He instanced a snake,
the cast skin of which, deep purple in color, was fifty-one
feet in length, and mentioned a white creature, supposed
to be mammalian, which gave forth well-marked phosphorescence in the darkness; also a large black moth, the bite
of which was supposed by the Indians to be highly poisonous. Setting aside these entirely new forms of life, the plateau was very rich in known prehistoric forms, dating back
in some cases to early Jurassic times. Among these he mentioned the gigantic and grotesque stegosaurus, seen once
by Mr. Malone at a drinking-place by the lake, and drawn
in the sketch-book of that adventurous American who had
first penetrated this unknown world. He described also the
iguanodon and the pterodactyl—two of the first of the wonders which they had encountered. He then thrilled the assembly by some account of the terrible carnivorous dinosaurs, which had on more than one occasion pursued members of the party, and which were the most formidable of
all the creatures which they had encountered. Thence he
passed to the huge and ferocious bird, the phororachus, and
to the great elk which still roams upon this upland. It was
not, however, until he sketched the mysteries of the central
lake that the full interest and enthusiasm of the audience
were aroused. One had to pinch oneself to be sure that one
was awake as one heard this sane and practical Professor
in cold measured tones describing the monstrous three-eyed
fish-lizards and the huge water-snakes which inhabit this
enchanted sheet of water. Next he touched upon the Indians,

and upon the extraordinary colony of anthropoid apes, which might be looked upon as an advance upon the pithecanthropus of Java, and as coming therefore nearer than any known form to that hypothetical creation, the missing link. Finally he described, amongst some merriment, the ingenious but highly dangerous aeronautic invention of Professor Challenger, and wound up a most memorable address by an account of the methods by which the committee did at last find their way back to civilization.

"It had been hoped that the proceedings would end there, and that a vote of thanks and congratulation, moved by Professor Sergius, of Upsala University, would be duly seconded and carried; but it was soon evident that the course of events was not destined to flow so smoothly. Symptoms of opposition had been evident from time to time during the evening, and now Dr. James Illingworth, of Edinburgh, rose in the center of the hall. Dr. Illingworth asked whether an amendment should not be taken before a resolution.

"THE CHAIRMAN: 'Yes, sir, if there must be an amendment.'

"DR. ILLINGWORTH: 'Your Grace, there must be an amendment.'

"THE CHAIRMAN: 'Then let us take it at once.'

"PROFESSOR SUMMERLEE (springing to his feet): 'Might I explain, your Grace, that this man is my personal enemy ever since our controversy in the *Quarterly Journal of Science* as to the true nature of Bathybius?'

"THE CHAIRMAN: 'I fear I cannot go into personal matters. Proceed.'

"Dr. Illingworth was imperfectly heard in part of his remarks on account of the strenuous opposition of the friends of the explorers. Some attempts were also made to pull him down. Being a man of enormous physique, however, and possessed of a very powerful voice, he dominated the tumult and succeeded in finishing his speech. It was clear, from the moment of his rising, that he had a number of friends and sympathizers in the hall, though they formed a minority in the audience. The attitude of the greater part of the public might be described as one of attentive neutrality.

"Dr. Illingworth began his remarks by expressing his high appreciation of the scientific work both of Professor Challenger and of Professor Summerlee. He much regretted that any personal bias should have been read into his remarks, which were entirely dictated by his desire for scientific truth. His position, in fact, was substantially the same as that taken up by Professor Summerlee at the last meeting. At that last meeting Professor Challenger had made certain assertions which had been queried by his colleague. Now this colleague came forward himself with the same assertions and expected them to remain unquestioned. Was this reasonable? ('Yes,' 'No,' and prolonged interruption, during which Professor Challenger was heard from the Press box to ask leave from the chairman to put Dr. Illingworth into the street.) A year ago one man said certain things. Now four men said other and more startling ones. Was this to constitute a final proof where the matters in question were of the most revolutionary and incredible character? There had been recent examples of travelers arriving from the unknown with certain tales which had been too readily accepted. Was the London Zoological Institute to place itself in this position? He admitted that the members of the committee were men of character. But human nature was very complex. Even Professors might be misled by the desire for notoriety. Like moths, we all love best to flutter in the light. Heavy-game shots liked to be in a position to cap the tales of their rivals, and journalists were not averse from sensational coups, even when imagination had to aid fact in the process. Each member of the committee had his own motive for making the most of his results. ('Shame! shame!') He had no desire to be offensive. ('You are!' and interruption.) The corroboration of these wondrous tales was really of the most slender description. What did it amount to? Some photographs. {Was it possible that in this age of ingenious manipulation photographs could be accepted as evidence?} What more? We have a story of a flight and a descent by ropes which precluded the production of larger specimens. It was ingenious, but not convincing. It was understood that Lord John Roxton claimed to have the skull of a phororachus. He could only say that he would like to see that skull.

"LORD JOHN ROXTON: 'Is this fellow calling me a liar?' (Uproar.)

"THE CHAIRMAN: 'Order! order! Dr. Illingworth, I must direct you to bring your remarks to a conclusion and to move your amendment.'

"DR. ILLINGWORTH: 'Your Grace, I have more to say, but I bow to your ruling. I move, then, that, while Professor Summerlee be thanked for his interesting address, the whole matter shall be regarded as 'non-proven,' and shall be referred back to a larger, and possibly more reliable Committee of Investigation.'

"It is difficult to describe the confusion caused by this amendment. A large section of the audience expressed their indignation at such a slur upon the travelers by noisy shouts of dissent and cries of, 'Don't put it!' 'Withdraw!' 'Turn him out!' On the other hand, the malcontents—and it cannot be denied that they were fairly numerous—cheered for the amendment, with cries of 'Order!' 'Chair!' and 'Fair play!' A scuffle broke out in the back benches, and blows were freely exchanged among the medical students who crowded that part of the hall. It was only the moderating influence of the presence of large numbers of ladies which prevented an absolute riot. Suddenly, however, there was a pause, a hush, and then complete silence. Professor Challenger was on his feet. His appearance and manner are peculiarly arresting, and as he raised his hand for order the whole audience settled down expectantly to give him a hearing.

"'It will be within the recollection of many present,' said Professor Challenger, 'that similar foolish and unmannerly scenes marked the last meeting at which I have been able to address them. On that occasion Professor Summerlee was the chief offender, and though he is now chastened and contrite, the matter could not be entirely forgotten. I have heard to-night similar, but even more offensive, sentiments from the person who has just sat down, and though it is a conscious effort of self-effacement to come down to that person's mental level, I will endeavor to do so, in order to allay any reasonable doubt which could possibly exist in the minds of anyone.' (Laughter and interruption.) 'I need not remind this audience that, though Professor Summerlee, as the head of the Committee of Investigation, has been put up to speak to-night, still it is I who am the real prime mover in this business, and that it is mainly to me that any successful result must be ascribed. I have safely conducted these three gentlemen to the spot mentioned, and I have, as you have heard, convinced them of the accuracy of my previous account. We had hoped that we should find upon our return that no one was so dense as to dispute our joint conclusions. Warned, however, by my previous experience, I have not come without such proofs as may convince a reasonable man. As explained by Professor Summerlee, our cameras have been tampered with by the ape-men when they ransacked our camp, and most of our negatives ruined.' (Jeers, laughter, and 'Tell us another!' from the back.) 'I have mentioned the ape-men, and I cannot forbear from saying that some of the sounds which now meet my ears bring back most vividly to my recollection my experiences with those interesting creatures.' (Laughter.) 'In spite of the destruction of so many invaluable negatives, there still remains in our collection a certain number of corroborative photographs showing the conditions of life upon the plateau. Did they accuse them of having forged these photographs?' (A voice, 'Yes,' and considerable interruption which ended in several men being put out of the hall.) 'The negatives were open to the inspection of experts. But what other evidence had they? Under the conditions of their escape it was naturally impossible to bring a large amount of baggage, but they had rescued Professor Summerlee's collections of butterflies and beetles, containing many new species. Was this not evidence?' (Several voices, 'No.') 'Who said no?'

"DR. ILLINGWORTH (rising): 'Our point is that such a collection might have been made in other places than a prehistoric plateau.' (Applause.)

"PROFESSOR CHALLENGER: 'No doubt, sir, we have to bow to your scientific authority, although I must admit that the name is unfamiliar. Passing, then, both the photographs and the entomological collection, I come to the varied and accurate information which we bring with us upon points which have never before been elucidated. For example, upon the domestic habits of the pterodactyl—' (A voice: 'Bosh,' and uproar)— 'I say, that upon the domestic habits of the pterodactyl we can throw a flood of light. I can exhibit to you from my portfolio a picture of that creature taken from life which would convince you—'

"DR. ILLINGWORTH: 'No picture could convince us of anything.'

"PROFESSOR CHALLENGER: 'You would require to see the thing itself?'

"DR. ILLINGWORTH: 'Undoubtedly.'

"PROFESSOR CHALLENGER: 'And you would accept that?'

"DR. ILLINGWORTH (laughing): 'Beyond a doubt.'

"It was at this point that the sensation of the evening arose—a sensation so dramatic that it can never have been paralleled in the history of scientific gatherings. Professor Challenger raised his hand in the air as a signal, and at once our colleague, Mr. E. D. Malone, was observed to rise and to make his way to the back of the platform. An instant later he re-appeared in company of a gigantic negro, the two of them bearing between them a large square packing-case. It was evidently of great weight, and was slowly carried forward and placed in front of the Professor's chair. All sound had hushed in the audience and everyone was absorbed in the spectacle before them. Professor Challenger drew off the top of the case, which formed a sliding lid. Peering down into the box he snapped his fingers several times and was heard from the Press seat to say, 'Come, then, pretty, pretty!' in a coaxing voice. An instant later, with a scratching, rattling sound, a most horrible and loathsome creature appeared from below and perched itself upon the side of the case. Even the unexpected fall of the Duke of Durham into the orchestra, which occurred at this moment, could not distract the petrified attention of the vast audience. The face of the creature was like the wildest gargoyle that the imagination of a mad medieval builder could have conceived. It was malicious, horrible, with two small red eyes as bright as points of burning coal. Its long, savage mouth, which was held half-open, was full of a double row of shark-like teeth. Its shoulders were humped, and round them were draped what appeared to be a faded gray shawl. It was the devil of our childhood in person. There was a turmoil in the audience—someone screamed, two ladies in the front row fell senseless from their chairs, and there was a general movement upon the platform to follow their chairman into the orchestra. For a moment there was danger of a general panic. Professor Challenger threw up his hands to still the commotion, but the movement alarmed the creature beside him. Its strange shawl suddenly unfurled, spread, and fluttered as a pair of leathery wings. Its owner grabbed at its legs, but too late to hold it. It had sprung from the perch and was circling slowly round the Queen's Hall with a dry, leathery flapping of its ten-foot wings, while a putrid and insidious odor pervaded the room. The cries of the people in the galleries, who were alarmed at the near approach of those glowing eyes and that murderous beak, excited the creature to a frenzy. Faster and faster it flew, beating against walls and chandeliers in a blind frenzy of alarm. 'The window! For heaven's sake shut that window!' roared the Professor from the platform, dancing and wringing his hands in an agony of apprehension. Alas, his warning was too late! In a moment the creature, beating and bumping

along the wall like a huge moth within a gas-shade, came
upon the opening, squeezed its hideous bulk through it, and
was gone. Professor Challenger fell back into his chair with
his face buried in his hands, while the audience gave one
long, deep sigh of relief as they realized that the incident
was over.

"Then—oh! how shall one describe what took place
then—when the full exuberance of the majority and the full
reaction of the minority united to make one great wave of
enthusiasm, which rolled from the back of the hall, gathering volume as it came, swept over the orchestra, submerged
the platform, and carried the four heroes away upon its
crest?" (Good for you, Mac!) "If the audience had done less
than justice, surely it made ample amends. Every one was
on his feet. Every one was moving, shouting, gesticulating.
A dense crowd of cheering men were round the four travelers. 'Up with them! up with them!' cried a hundred voices.
In a moment four figures shot up above the crowd. In vain
they strove to break loose. They were held in their lofty
places of honor. It would have been hard to let them down
if it had been wished, so dense was the crowd around them.
'Regent Street! Regent Street!' sounded the voices. There
was a swirl in the packed multitude, and a slow current,
bearing the four upon their shoulders, made for the door.
Out in the street the scene was extraordinary. An assemblage of not less than a hundred thousand people was waiting. The close-packed throng extended from the other side
of the Langham Hotel to Oxford Circus. A roar of acclamation greeted the four adventurers as they appeared, high
above the heads of the people, under the vivid electric lamps
outside the hall. 'A procession! A procession!' was the cry.
In a dense phalanx, blocking the streets from side to side,
the crowd set forth, taking the route of Regent Street, Pall
Mall, St. James's Street, and Piccadilly. The whole central
traffic of London was held up, and many collisions were reported between the demonstrators upon the one side and
the police and taxi-cabmen upon the other. Finally, it was

not until after midnight that the four travelers were released at the entrance to Lord John Roxton's chambers in the Albany, and that the exuberant crowd, having sung 'They are Jolly Good Fellows' in chorus, concluded their program with 'God Save the King.' So ended one of the most remarkable evenings that London has seen for a considerable time."

So far my friend Macdona; and it may be taken as a fairly accurate, if florid, account of the proceedings. As to the main incident, it was a bewildering surprise to the audience, but not, I need hardly say, to us. The reader will remember how I met Lord John Roxton upon the very occasion when, in his protective crinoline, he had gone to bring the "Devil's chick" as he called it, for Professor Challenger. I have hinted also at the trouble which the Professor's baggage gave us when we left the plateau, and had I described our voyage I might have said a good deal of the worry we had to coax with putrid fish the appetite of our filthy companion. If I have not said much about it before, it was, of course, that the Professor's earnest desire was that no possible rumor of the unanswerable argument which we carried should be allowed to leak out until the moment came when his enemies were to be confuted.

One word as to the fate of the London pterodactyl. Nothing can be said to be certain upon this point. There is the evidence of two frightened women that it perched upon the roof of the Queen's Hall and remained there like a diabolical statue for some hours. The next day it came out in the evening papers that Private Miles, of the Coldstream Guards, on duty outside Marlborough House, had deserted his post without leave, and was therefore court-martialed. Private Miles' account, that he dropped his rifle and took to his heels down the Mall because on looking up he had suddenly seen the devil between him and the moon, was not accepted by the Court, and yet it may have a direct bearing upon the point at issue. The only other evidence which I can adduce is from the log of the SS. *Friesland*, a Dutch-American liner, which asserts that at nine next morning, Start Point being at the time ten miles upon their starboard quarter, they were passed by something between a flying goat and a monstrous bat, which was heading at a prodigious pace south and west. If its homing instinct led it upon the right line, there can be no doubt that somewhere out in the wastes of the Atlantic the last European pterodactyl found its end.

And Gladys—oh, my Gladys!—Gladys of the mystic lake, now to be re-named the Central, for never shall she have immortality through me. Did I not always see some hard fiber in her nature? Did I not, even at the time when I was proud to obey her behest, feel that it was surely a poor love which could drive a lover to his death or the danger of it? Did I not, in my truest thoughts, always recurring and always dismissed, see past the beauty of the face, and, peering into the soul, discern the twin shadows of selfishness and of fickleness glooming at the back of it? Did she love the heroic and the spectacular for its own noble sake, or was it for the glory which might, without effort or sacrifice, be reflected upon herself? Or are these thoughts the vain wisdom which comes after the event? It was the shock of my life. For a moment it had turned me to a cynic. But already, as I write, a week has passed, and we have had our momentous interview with Lord John Roxton and—well, perhaps things might be worse.

Let me tell it in a few words. No letter or telegram had come to me at Southampton, and I reached the little villa at Streatham about ten o'clock that night in a fever of alarm. Was she dead or alive? Where were all my nightly dreams of the open arms, the smiling face, the words of praise for her man who had risked his life to humor her whim? Already I was down from the high peaks and standing flat-footed upon earth. Yet some good reasons given might still lift me to the clouds once more. I rushed down the garden path, hammered at the door, heard the voice of Gladys within, pushed past the staring maid, and strode into the sitting-room. She was seated in a low settee under the shaded standard lamp by the piano. In three steps I was across the room and had both her hands in mine.

"Gladys!" I cried, "Gladys!"

She looked up with amazement in her face. She was altered in some subtle way. The expression of her eyes, the hard upward stare, the set of the lips, was new to me. She drew back her hands.

"What do you mean?" she said.

"Gladys!" I cried. "What is the matter? You are my Gladys, are you not—little Gladys Hungerton?"

"No," said she, "I am Gladys Potts. Let me introduce you to my husband."

How absurd life is! I found myself mechanically bowing and shaking hands with a little ginger-haired man who was coiled up in the deep arm-chair which had once been sacred to my own use. We bobbed and grinned in front of each other.

"Father lets us stay here. We are getting our house ready," said Gladys.

"Oh, yes," said I.

"You didn't get my letter at Para, then?"

"No, I got no letter."

"Oh, what a pity! It would have made all clear."

"It is quite clear," said I.

"I've told William all about you," said she. "We have no secrets. I am so sorry about it. But it couldn't have been so very deep, could it, if you could go off to the other end of the world and leave me here alone. You're not crabby, are you?"

"No, no, not at all. I think I'll go."

"Have some refreshment," said the little man, and he added, in a confidential way, "It's always like this, ain't it? And must be unless you had polygamy, only the other way round; you understand." He laughed like an idiot, while I made for the door.

I was through it, when a sudden fantastic impulse came upon me, and I went back to my successful rival, who looked nervously at the electric push.

"Will you answer a question?" I asked.

"Well, within reason," said he.

"How did you do it? Have you searched for hidden treasure, or discovered a pole, or done time on a pirate, or flown the Channel, or what? Where is the glamour of romance? How did you get it?"

He stared at me with a hopeless expression upon his vacuous, good-natured, scrubby little face.

"Don't you think all this is a little too personal?" he said.

"Well, just one question," I cried. "What are you? What is your profession?"

"I am a solicitor's clerk," said he. "Second man at Johnson and Merivale's, 41 Chancery Lane."

"Good-night!" said I, and vanished, like all disconsolate and broken-hearted heroes, into the darkness, with grief and rage and laughter all simmering within me like a boiling pot.

One more little scene, and I have done. Last night we all supped at Lord John Roxton's rooms, and sitting together afterwards we smoked in good comradeship and talked our adventures over. It was strange under these altered surroundings to see the old, well-known faces and figures. There was Challenger, with his smile of condescension, his drooping eyelids, his intolerant eyes, his aggressive beard, his huge chest, swelling and puffing as he laid down the law to Summerlee. And Summerlee, too, there he was with his short briar between his thin moustache and his gray goat's-beard, his worn face protruded in eager debate as he queried all Challenger's propositions. Finally, there was our host, with his rugged, eagle face, and his cold, blue, glacier eyes with always a shimmer of devilment and of humor down in the depths of them. Such is the last picture of them that I have carried away.

It was after supper, in his own sanctum—the room of the pink radiance and the innumerable trophies—that Lord John Roxton had something to say to us. From a cupboard he had brought an old cigar-box, and this he laid before him on the table.

"There's one thing," said he, "that maybe I should have spoken about before this, but I wanted to know a little more clearly where I was. No use to raise hopes and let them down again. But it's facts, not hopes, with us now. You may remember that day we found the pterodactyl rookery in the swamp—what? Well, somethin' in the lie of the land took my notice. Perhaps it has escaped you, so I will tell you. It was a volcanic vent full of blue clay." The Professors nodded.

"Well, now, in the whole world I've only had to do with one place that was a volcanic vent of blue clay. That was the great De Beers Diamond Mine of Kimberley—what? So you see I got diamonds into my head. I rigged up a contraption to hold off those stinking beasts, and I spent a happy day there with a spud. This is what I got."

He opened his cigar-box, and tilting it over he poured about twenty or thirty rough stones, varying from the size of beans to that of chestnuts, on the table.

"Perhaps you think I should have told you then. Well, so I should, only I know there are a lot of traps for the unwary, and that stones may be of any size and yet of little value where color and consistency are clean off. Therefore, I brought them back, and on the first day at home I took one round to Spink's, and asked him to have it roughly cut and valued."

He took a pill-box from his pocket, and spilled out of it a beautiful glittering diamond, one of the finest stones that I have ever seen.

"There's the result," said he. "He prices the lot at a minimum of two hundred thousand pounds. Of course it is fair shares between us. I won't hear of anythin' else. Well, Challenger, what will you do with your fifty thousand?"

"If you really persist in your generous view," said the Professor, "I should found a private museum, which has long been one of my dreams."

"And you, Summerlee?"

"I would retire from teaching, and so find time for my final classification of the chalk fossils."

"I'll use my own," said Lord John Roxton, "in fitting a well-formed expedition and having another look at the dear old plateau. As to you, young fellah, you, of course, will spend yours in gettin' married."

"Not just yet," said I, with a rueful smile. "I think, if you will have me, that I would rather go with you."

Lord Roxton said nothing, but a brown hand was stretched out to me across the table.

Coachwhip Publications

CoachwhipBooks.com

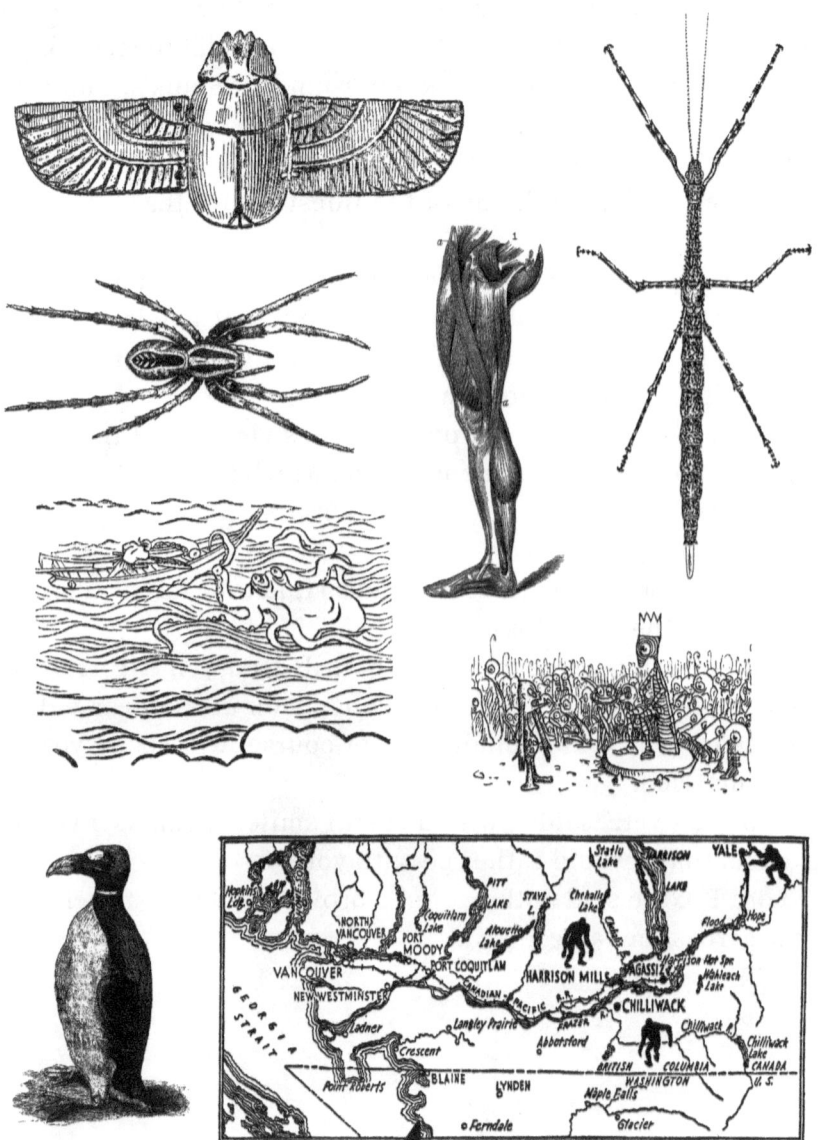

ALSO AVAILABLE

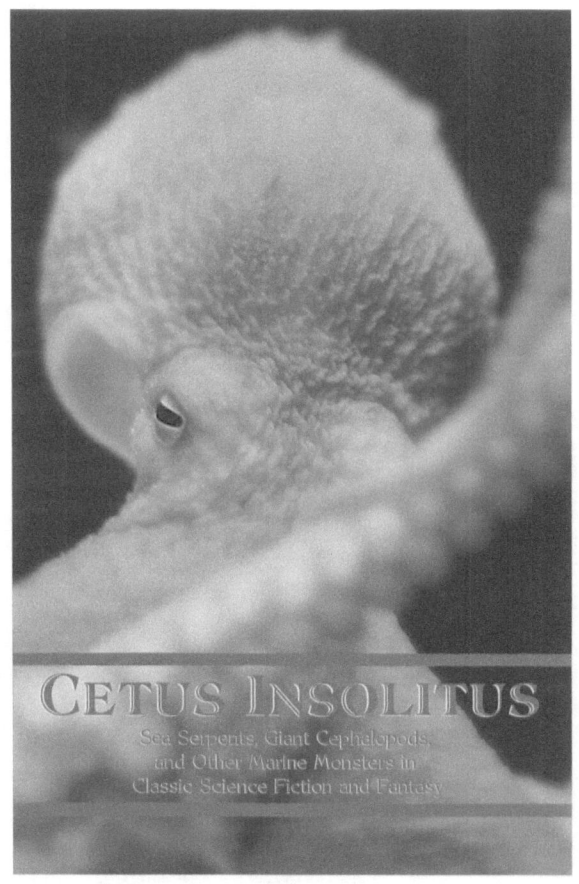

CETUS INSOLITUS:
Sea Serpents, Giant Cephalopods,
and Other Marine Monsters in
Classic Science Fiction and Fantasy

ISBN 1-930585-66-7

ALSO AVAILABLE

INVERTEBRATA ENIGMATICA:
Giant Spiders, Dangerous Insects,
and Other Strange Invertebrates in
Classic Science Fiction and Fantasy

ISBN 1-930585-65-9

ALSO AVAILABLE

FLORA CURIOSA:
Cryptobotany, Mysterious Fungi,
Sentient Trees, and Deadly Plants in
Classic Science Fiction and Fantasy

ISBN 1-930585-56-X

A Queen of Atlantis &
The Devil-Tree of El Dorado

(2 Lost Race Novels by Frank Aubrey)

ISBN 1-930585-74-8

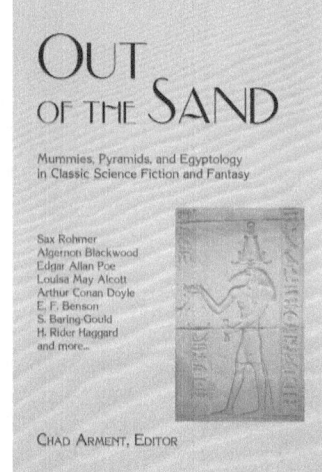

www.ingramcontent.com/pod-product-compliance
Lightning Source LLC
Chambersburg PA
CBHW020506020726
47493CB00001B/199